*You don't have to remember
a place to have it be home...*

W9-BRX-414

"A warm
and satisfying read."
Mary Jo Putney

"You're Nina Lane's daughter, aren't you?"

Tess froze. She felt her mouth grow dry. Her silence had answered Ned's question. "I don't have anything to say about her," Tess said. "I don't remember her at all, and my grandparents never talked about her. If I seem mysterious, it's simply that I am a private person."

"You are? You don't seem like you would be."

"I'm not shy, and I like other people a great deal. But neither of those is inconsistent with being private, with not needing to share everything with everyone."

Or never having had anyone to share everything with.

"I suppose not," he agreed. "But privacy's not a big concept around here. Have you ever lived in a small town?" Tess shook her head. "It's very easy to be sentimental about small towns, about how friendly and hospitable we are. And we are, but there's a cost to all that friendliness. People are so used to stifling their thoughts and their preferences that no one knows how to be direct. It hits the women especially hard, and I think a lot of them seethe way down inside."

"Until someone explodes," Tess said.

Also by Kathleen Gilles Seidel

Summer's End

KATHLEEN GILLES SEIDEL

Please Remember This

AVON BOOKS
An Imprint of HarperCollinsPublishers

This is a work of fiction. Names, characters, places, and incidents are products of the author's imagination or are used fictitiously and are not to be construed as real. Any resemblance to actual events, locales, organizations, or persons, living or dead, is entirely coincidental.

AVON BOOKS
An Imprint of HarperCollins*Publishers*
10 East 53rd Street
New York, New York 10022-5299

Copyright © 2002 by Kathleen Gilles Seidel
Excerpts from *Head Over Heels* copyright © 2002 by Susan Andersen; *Please Remember This* copyright © 2002 by Kathleen Gilles Seidel; *Love Will Find a Way* copyright © 2002 by Barbara Freethy; *Lola Carlyle Reveals All* copyright © 2002 by Rachel Gibson; *You Never Can Tell* copyright © 2001 by Kathleen Eagle; *Black Silk* copyright © 1991, 2002 by Judy Cuevas
ISBN: 0-06-101387-0
www.avonromance.com

First Avon Books paperback printing: February 2002

Avon Trademark Reg. U.S. Pat. Off. and in Other Countries, Marca Registrada, Hecho en U.S.A.
HarperCollins ® is a registered trademark of HarperCollins Publishers Inc.

Printed in the U.S.A.

10 9 8 7 6 5 4 3 2 1

When I moved into my neighborhood, she was the first person I borrowed anything from. She was the first friend whom I told that I was writing a book, and she offered to type it for me. Her daughters decorated my house when I brought my babies home. She's the one I call when I am bored in the afternoon; she was the one I turned to when I had a funeral to plan. In hopes that every woman who picks up this book has a friend like her, it is dedicated to—

Donna Vilsack

∞ *Chapter 1* ∞

It was part rock festival, part Star Trek convention, and part plain old down-home country fair without the baby pigs and homemade jams.

Nina Lane had been a writer of speculative fantasy, creating in her three books a medieval-like, magic-filled universe that had inspired cultish devotion since her death twenty-four years before. She had spent the last four years of her life living in a rented farmhouse outside Fleur-de-lis, a small river town in northeastern Kansas, and every year during the first weekend in May, more than six thousand of her fans gathered at the county fairgrounds there for the Nina Lane Annual Birthday Celebration.

If you were a Nina Lane fan, it was the place to be. Inside the livestock-judging hall, people took turns reading aloud from Nina Lane's books, and when local bands weren't playing on the outdoor stage, groups of fans acted out scenes based on her narratives. Part of being at the Celebration was knowing all there was to know about Nina Lane and, regardless of your gender, dressing like her as well. So vendors wheeled in rolling wardrobe racks full of crocheted vests and long black skirts patterned with

large flowers. For a few dollars you could find someone to do your hair like Nina's, spraying it black,
scraping it into a bun, pinning a flower over your ear.

Even if you weren't a Nina Lane fan, the day was
fun. There were pony rides for the kids, popcorn and
cotton candy, chili dogs and beignets, the square little
doughnuts from New Orleans. Many vendors displayed merchandise that had nothing to do with the
author or her books. Potters brought their earth-
toned mugs and bowls; woodworkers brought pine
birdhouses and little mirrors framed in walnut. Tess
Lanier was particularly interested in the beaded jewelry. Some Native American Indians were displaying
several pieces that she thought were marvelous. She
was going to buy herself a pair of earrings.

Back at home—Tess was from California—she had
twice set up a booth at a crafts fair to sell the vintage
linen that she collected—place mats, napkins, table
runners, and dresser scarves. In her own quiet way,
she had enjoyed it thoroughly. She liked talking to
the people who were knowledgeable collectors; she
liked chatting with those who weren't. She liked the
bright, fresh anticipation with which everyone set up
a display in the morning; she even liked the shared
weariness of knocking the displays down in the
evening.

Because she was not a Nina Lane fan, Tess was often looking more closely today at a vendor's portable
canopy or collapsing trellis than she was at the actual
merchandise. She saw no one displaying linens. One
of the larger tables was covered with a quilt. It wasn't
for sale, it was merely the table covering, but she
went over to look at it. It was a scrap quilt, made of

hundreds of little hexagons in a myriad of fabrics. It seemed to be hand-pieced and machine-quilted.

"Are you interested in the quilt?"

Tess looked up. The woman behind the table was speaking to her. She was small, and her features were delicate. She was wearing gold-rimmed glasses and her skin was beautiful, clear and soft, even though her feathery-cut hair was graying. She was not dressed like Nina Lane.

Tess, at twenty-four, had a medieval, even other-worldly air to her appearance; she was narrowly built, her honey-colored hair spilled over her shoulders in a pre-Raphaelite swirl of waves and ringlets, and she wore light, flowing garments that she usually made herself of vintage fabrics.

"Yes," Tess answered. "It's beautiful."

"Look closer, then. See the pieces that are the most worn." The woman came around the table. She moved some of her products so that she could pick up a corner of the quilt. "They were feed sacks."

The woman was standing very close to Tess. "Oh?"

"Yes. During the Depression, the sacks that live-stock feed came in were often the only uncut fabric a family had, and they sewed with it, making clothes, quilts, everything."

Tess knew this. Her grandmother had grown up here in Kansas; she had told Tess about wearing dresses made out of feed sacks.

"So the companies printed patterns on the sacks," the woman continued. "Some of the patterns were rather pretty, but the fabric wasn't a good quality. It didn't last. Here, do touch it. You really can feel the difference."

It was clear that she wanted Tess to touch the quilt, that it was important to her to have Tess touch the quilt. She was now standing even closer.

Physically, Tess had been an enchanting child, golden and delicate. Her grandparents had taught her to be wary of people who wanted to stand too close. "No, no, thank you," she answered. "I can see."

"Then perhaps you're interested in the soaps or the lotions." The woman gestured toward the line of herbal products displayed on the table. "I grow all the herbs myself. The roses are wild. Here, you must smell this one. I think you'll like it." The woman picked up a knife and, from a bread-loaf-sized cake of homemade soap, sliced off a small wedge and thrust it at Tess. A sharp scent of lavender stung her nostrils. She had to force herself not to pull back.

"I knew you would like it," the woman exclaimed, stressing the "you" as if she had privileged knowledge about Tess and her tastes. "It has such a healing aura. Do sign the guest book. I'd love to send you my catalog."

Tess shook her head. "I never buy anything by mail. It would be a waste of your money."

"I don't mind. I treasure connections of all types."

The connection of a mailing list? What was to treasure about that? Tess shrugged and leaned forward to write her name and address—her work address—in the guest book. The pages of the book were a pale gray green, and across the top of each page, "Celandine Gardens" was printed in golden-yellow. All the products on the table were wrapped in the same pale green with the golden yellow letters.

"That's a pun, isn't it?" Tess heard herself say. "Celandine Gardens . . . celadon green."

"Why, yes!" The woman clasped her hands, thrilled. "I've never known anyone to get that so quickly. It pleases me so . . . not that it matters to me if other people understand, I did it for myself. But you're right. It is a pun, a verbal-visual thing, since, as you know, the etymologies of two words have nothing to do with each other. Celandine is a plant, of course, and celadon . . ."

Why had she said anything? Why had she encouraged this person? Tess waited until the woman was finished with her thought, then smiled a polite, thin smile and moved away, careful not to look back. She didn't stop until she had rounded a building and was out of sight of the Celandine Gardens table.

What had she expected at a Nina Lane event? A polite conversation about the weather? A knowledgeable analysis of the National Hockey League? These were Nina Lane fans. They were crazy.

For about fifteen seconds during her freshman year in college, Tess had affiliated herself with a group of Nina Lane fans, and it hadn't ended particularly well. She had dreaded running into any of them today. At best, there would be awkward apologies for not keeping in touch and false promises about doing so in the future. At worst . . . well, Tess didn't really know what would happen if she saw Gordon Winsler himself, but she truly hoped not to find out.

So far, however, she had recognized no one, and no one had recognized her. Occasionally people looked at her curiously, but her airy, tea-dyed dress with its many rows of pin tucking probably looked a bit like

a costume. They just must be wondering which of
Nina Lane's characters she was impersonating.

The tables in this part of the fairgrounds were
closer together, so there was more jewelry and fewer
clothes. A baby in a stroller was wearing a little
headband with a Nina Lanesque flower perched over
her ear. The man pushing the stroller had a T-shirt
with a map of Nina Lane's kingdom on it. At least he
hadn't dyed the baby's hair black.

One table was devoted to publications. It displayed
used copies of Nina Lane's books and piles of pam-
phlets, little home-published booklets stapled inside
covers of colored copying paper. Tess picked one up.

> Nina swept past Kristin, her dark eyes flashing
> at Duke Nathan.

"What's this?"

"Which one is it?" The girl sitting behind the table
looked up. She too was dressed like Nina Lane. "Oh,
that's the scene right before Nina killed herself when
she confronted Duke. You know he left her for
Kristin."

Tess knew that. That was one of the first things a
person learned about Nina Lane—how her lover,
Duke Nathan, had left her and she had followed him
to New York and killed herself. "And this is an account of that? Who wrote it?"

"I did," the girl said proudly.

"How do you know these things?" Tess flipped
through the booklet. It was full of dialogue and detail, Nina flicking the flower in her hair, Kristin cow-

ering in a corner. "You talked to the people who were there?"

"Oh, no," the girl said confidently. "Duke Nathan won't talk about it. He never has. What could he possibly say? He left her. It was all his fault."

"So you made all this up?"

"I didn't really 'make it up.' You see, I'm *very* connected to Nina."

Tess had no idea what that was supposed to mean. "And that gives you the right to write about these people like this?" Duke and Kristin weren't characters in one of Nina Lane's book; they were real people, still living.

"What do you mean, 'the right'?" The girl frowned. She was growing suspicious of Tess.

"Aren't people entitled to some privacy, to—"

The girl snatched the booklet out of Tess's hand. "Well, you don't have to buy it if you don't want it. And I'm not the only one who does it. Everyone does."

Everyone was making up stories about Nina Lane's final hours? That only made it worse.

Tess moved on, listening to the conversations around her. Many people were discussing Nina Lane trivia. Who was the third son of Refleveil? Tess had no idea. She had read the books, but she didn't remember a Refleveil. In which direction did the river Ghyfist flow? Apparently that was a very controversial question.

The conversations that weren't about Nina Lane's three books were about her life: how she had come to Kansas from the West, how the Settlement had grown up around her. The Settlement had been an informal artists' colony, a community of artists and writers. They rented empty farmhouses and walked barefoot across the fields. They gathered sunflowers and picked wild mulberries by day and wrote their books late into the night. Tess heard an odd, urgent tone in the way that the people at the fairgrounds were talking about this long-gone community. They must all be yearning to have been a part of it, to have lived in a farmhouse down the road from Nina Lane, to have crossed a weathered front porch and knocked on the wooden frame of a screen door, to have heard Nina's voice inviting them inside.

If it hadn't been for Duke Nathan, they could have. That was what everyone seemed to believe. If it hadn't been for Duke Nathan, Nine would be alive today. If it hadn't been for Duke Nathan, Nina Lane would have finished *The Riverboat Fragment*. If it hadn't been for Duke Nathan, Nina Lane would have been here, she would have been with us today, she would have been our friend.

It was almost enough to make a person feel sorry for Duke Nathan. If people this weird hated him, surely he couldn't be all bad.

Tess tried to recapture the feeling she had had before stopping at the Celandine Gardens table. She looked up at the sky; it was bright, but the sunlight was gentler than in California. She had never been in the Midwest before, and the landscape was softer and prettier than her grandparents' descriptions of their Dust Bowl childhoods had led her to expect. It was a green and pleasant place, the contours of the earth folding softly like a rumpled bed first thing in the morning. When she had driven to the fairgrounds, she had seen violets blooming along the roadside, and the plowed fields had been rimmed with lines of broad-crowned cottonwood trees.

Tess looked for the concession stand. She wanted to get something to drink. She went to stand in line. The people in front of her were whispering, something about a Dave Samson and "the pictures." She tried not to listen, but their hushed voices were urgent and insistent. This Dave Samson had "the pictures"; the person standing on the left was sure of that. Yes, Dave had been denying it for years, but he had them.

"Why won't he share them?"

"I guess they're pretty gruesome."

Tess opened her purse and took out some money, putting it in her pocket so that she wouldn't hold up the line when she was finally served. The people were still talking about the pictures. Someone else joined them, and in a moment Tess couldn't help but understand what the chatter was about.

A bystander had taken photographs of Nina Lane's mangled body as it lay on a New York City sidewalk moments after her death.

Tess turned with a jerk, wanting to leave the line. Her shoulder bag banged against someone, and as she began to apologize, instinctively raising her hands, she knocked the man's drink out of his hand. It spilled all over the papers he was carrying.

"Oh, my God, I am *so* sorry." Tess seized a stack of napkins from the chrome dispenser on the concession counter and tried to blot the spill. The papers were still in the man's hand. They were brochures, printed on a good-quality glossy paper. The liquid was starting to bead up. "I can't believe I did that. I am so sorry."

"Don't worry about it." The man moved the brochures out of her reach. "I have a million of them." He dropped them and his cup into a nearby trash can.

"But I'm *so* sorry. I—"

"It's no big deal. I now have whatever is twenty less than a million. Please. It doesn't matter."

She believed him, but still she wanted to explain. "But I'm never clumsy. You have to understand. I don't know what came over me. I'm not like this. I'm usually—"

She stopped. He was looking amused.

What was wrong with her? Nobody liked it when you kept saying what kind of person you were. If they couldn't figure that out on their own, it was because they weren't interested.

She took a breath, hoping that some oxygen would restore her reason. "You can't possibly care what I am normally like."

"Oh"—he smiled—"I wouldn't be so sure about that."

There was nothing smarmy about his smile or anything excessively come-hither in his voice. He was, in fact, probably the most normal-looking person she had seen all day. He had a slightly rounded face with open, Midwestern features. His light brown hair was sun-streaked, and his eyebrows were darker than his hair. He was wearing rumpled khakis and a polo shirt, and he had an alert, intelligent look about him.

"You have been very gracious," she said firmly. "I appreciate it."

With that, the conversation was over. She nodded farewell, and he did likewise.

She was ready to leave. Her car was not at the fairgrounds, whose lot had been full when she had arrived. A uniformed Boy Scout had directed her to park in the Kmart south of town. A school bus was shuttling people between locations.

The bus had let passengers out at the fairgrounds' front gate, but the driver had warned everyone that after two o'clock he would be picking people up by the livestock entrance. Tess had no idea where the livestock gate was. She wasn't even sure she knew what a livestock gate was.

Whom should she ask? The people around here, while knowing every bend in the fictional Ghyfist River, would probably have no idea how to catch the real-life parking shuttle.

The information table at the main gate was surrounded by people dressed in green elfin garb. They seemed to have no intention of moving. A hand-lettered sign behind the table did say that the parking shuttle was leaving from the livestock gate. An arrow pointed heavenward. Tess did not find that helpful.

She picked her way back through the crowd, assuming that the livestock gate might be on the other side of the fairgrounds. More and more people were sitting on the ground, and it was sometimes hard to move around them. She was starting to lose her bearings when she saw the man whose drink she had spilled. He was obviously manning a table, but no one was in front of it, so he was leaning back against a tree, his hands in his pockets, looking very sane and normal.

Gratefully she went up to him. "You don't have to be afraid of me. I won't hurt you, and even if I do, I swear I won't apologize. But could you tell me where the livestock gate is? I'm supposed to meet the parking bus there."

"You can apologize all you want," he said. "But do you really need to leave? I'd be willing to bet that you haven't had any cotton candy yet . . . although you're too late if you want the pink. They're out of that. You'd have to settle for the blue."

He was urging her to stay longer. "Thank you, but I don't think even the pink would tempt me."

"Do you have a long trip home?"

"Actually, yes. I'm from California."

"Oh." He shrugged, acknowledging that there wasn't much point in getting better acquainted. "In that case, the livestock gate is easy to find. Do you know where Sierra's table is? It's right in back of her."

"That doesn't help me." Tess didn't know whether Sierra was a person, a character in one of Nina Lane's books, or a mountain range.

"Do you see the water tower? You may have to stand on your toes."

Tess looked at where he was pointing. "I see it."

"Then just go in that direction. You'll have to zig and zag around the buildings, but if you keep heading in that direction, you'll hit the livestock gate."

"I can do that." Tess thanked him. "It would probably be easier if I were a crow, but I can do it."

"Lots of things would be easier if we were crows, but we're not. Here, let me give you one of these. It's still dry."

It was his brochure. Tess supposed that he was selling something. She looked at it. In large, scrolling typeface were the words "*Western Settler*." Tess had heard of it. "That's the riverboat, the one that sank, isn't it?"

He nodded. "I'm going to dig it up."

The *Western Settler* was a pre–Civil War steamboat. In 1857, while the boat was en route from St. Louis to Nebraska Territory, an underwater log had pierced her bow, and she had sunk into the Missouri River. Everyone on board had survived, but all the cargo, the personal belongings of the passengers, the settlers' household goods, and the merchandise intended for the frontier merchants had been lost. The passengers had trudged in their sodden high-buttoned shoes to the nearest town and started life over with nothing.

Nina Lane had been fascinated by the *Western Settler*. The manuscript left unfinished at her death, while set in her fantasy universe, was based on the riverboat's story.

"You're going to *dig* the boat up?" Tess asked. "But isn't it underwater?"

"Not anymore. The river's changed course over the years. It's now under a cornfield. So as soon as the crop is in, we'll start."

"That should be interesting." At least it would be real history. He was looking for something that had actually been there, not just something that Nina Lane had imagined. Tess approved of that. She slipped the brochure into her purse, nodded farewell, and followed his advice, moving toward the water tower. A few minutes later she found herself at a chain-link fence with a gate wide enough for a tractor-trailer truck. The gate was tied open.

"Are you here for the bus?" someone asked. "We just missed it."

"That happens, doesn't it?" Tess said lightly. She didn't mind waiting.

There were benches on either side of the gate. She sat down and looked at the brochure the man had given her. The steamboat had been carrying both freight and passengers. The cargo was merchandise destined for little frontier towns, and the majority of passengers were from the French communities in Louisiana, having transferred from another steamboat in St. Louis. The brochure went on to describe the technology and funding of the new excavation project, providing considerably more detail about its dewatering system than interested Tess. She folded up the brochure. There was still no sign of the bus. So she took out her tatting shuttle and the piece of lace she was working on.

A shadow fell across her work. She looked up. Oh, no. It was that woman from the herb table.

The woman spoke. "You're making lace?"

Apparently they were about to have another "connection." Reluctantly Tess spread her work so the woman could see it. "My grandmother taught me."

"She did? It's lovely. What do you do with it? Do you wear it?"

Tess shook her head. "I'm not the type." Tess's style was too simple for much embellishment. She loved lace. She loved looking at it, owning it, making it. Its beauty restored her, bringing her serenity, but she didn't wear it.

"Do you sell it? No"—the woman anticipated Tess's headshake—"it must be so much work that you can't think about doing it for money."

That was true. Tess had to give her credit for the insight.

The woman touched the lace. "Lace—it's like a metaphor for a woman's soul, isn't it? It looks so fragile, yet it is really quite strong, although it gets its strength from tight little knots." Behind the lens of her glasses, her eyes were intent. "And the patterns are made of holes; it's beautiful because of the holes."

Tess did not consider herself, or any other woman she knew, to be "made of holes." Nor did she think her strength came from tight little knots.

"Think of herbs," the woman went on, "the way some of the least lovely ones will hold their scents the longest."

Tess supposed that was a metaphor too.

Tess was a nice person. She knew that about herself. She was an art therapist, working in a retirement home, and the residents liked her. You have to be nice for that to happen. She was also a patient person. People who were in a big rush about things did not make lace. And like most women, she wanted to be liked, she wanted to make a good impression, she didn't want unnecessary conflict.

But she also had a core of self-reliance that came from being a child raised by grandparents, a child who could never be like the other children. She knew how to be alone; she liked being alone. She looked at the woman directly. "I know this will sound offensive, but my job keeps me working with people all day long. I was hoping to be alone this afternoon."

The woman blinked. She looked hurt. "I'm sorry you feel that way, Tess. I had wanted to get to know you."

Tess didn't answer. She wasn't going to feel bad about this. A person has the right to draw lines, to tell other people where they needed to stop. She met the woman's gaze and gave her head the slightest shake. *This isn't going to happen.*

"I'm sorry," the other woman said again, and then she turned and left.

Tess let the lace drop to her lap. Why did this woman want to get to know her? Tess had walked over and looked at the quilt covering a table. That was all. Why did the woman feel there was something at stake?

Tess should have known that the day was bound to turn weird. What did she expect, being surrounded by Nina Lane's fans, by people who were "connected" to Nina Lane, by people fascinated by the grisly details of her death. The fans all seemed to feel as if they had a special relationship with Nina Lane, as if they knew Nina the most, as if they loved her work the most. Tess herself didn't feel that way about Nina Lane.

And she was probably the one who should.

Because, as much as Tess ignored the fact, as much as she asserted that it really had nothing to do with her—how could it when she had no memories?— she had been born among that little colony of artists and writers, and Nina Lane was her mother.

∾ *Chapter 2* ∾

She'd always known that her mother had been a writer. Grandma had kept copies of the trilogy on a shelf in her bedroom, and Tess used to creep in and look at them sometimes, only to become bewildered by the long paragraphs and strangely spelled names.

But she liked the idea that they had been written by her mother. She didn't brag about it. Grandma had said that good girls didn't "put themselves forward." Good girls didn't "give themselves airs." So it was her own little secret, something that no one else seemed to know about. Her grandparents had rented their house when she was a baby, and neither of them talked about her mother much, especially to the neighbors.

Her sixth-grade English class began its library-research unit with an assignment to pick a dead person and see what could be found. She chose Nina Lane, and within moments she learned that her mother had committed suicide.

The next thing she remembered, she was sitting in the nurse's office waiting for her grandmother to come.

It was her grandfather who came. He had left work to pick her up.

He put his arm around her as they walked out to the car. "We should have told you, we know that. But it's been so hard . . . it still is."

Tess didn't answer. She couldn't.

"Nina was a handful. We were always baffled. We couldn't understand her. On one hand, she seemed to hate us, but she couldn't stand to be alone. Sometimes she even slept in the hall outside our room. And she was stubborn . . . Lord, how she was stubborn. That's what we thought, that she was just stubborn and selfish. We tried so hard. Your grandmother was always having to go in and talk to her teachers, begging people to give her a second, third, even fourth chance. We did our best, we really did. Then to have tried so hard, to have done so much, and have her give up on herself when we had never given up on her . . ."

Tess hadn't minded having a mother who was dead. That was all she had ever known, but to have a mother who had *chosen* to die, had chosen to leave her, that was different.

Her grandfather was still speaking. "Now they're saying that she had some kind of sickness in her head. We had no idea, and maybe it would have been different if we had known. You can't know what it is like, Tess, this feeling that you didn't do right by your child."

Tess wasn't listening to him. Her mother had decided to kill herself. Her mother had chosen to leave her. That was hard to live with.

If I had been adopted, I wouldn't know about her.
That seemed like an answer. She would pretend

that Nina Lane didn't exist; Tess would never talk about her, never think about her. That seemed to be what her grandparents did. At the end of the school year they moved again, and none of Tess's new friends had heard about Nina Lane, and in the new house Grandma didn't have a bookcase in her bedroom.

Quiet and artistic, Tess had done well in school, and she got a scholarship at Stanford. Then it wasn't so easy to pretend that Nina Lane didn't exist. There was an organization—the Nina Lane Enthusiasts Society— and its members knew that Nina's last name had really been Lanier, they knew that she had had a baby, and they knew how old the baby would be. And it wasn't long before one of them approached Tess. *Is it possible . . . are you . . .*

It had been fun at first to be important, especially when it had been so easy to feel lost as a freshman. Everything in the Nina Lane Enthusiasts Society was now done to please Tess. Doughnuts at the meetings, or cookies? An easy decision . . . which did Tess like? Should they pay extra for colored ink? Tess was an art major; she would like colored ink.

No one expected Tess to stuff envelopes, letter posters, or keep track of the mailing list, even though she was actually very good at that sort of thing. In fact, none of them saw that she was good at behind-the-scenes work, that she could keep things organized . . . because, she eventually realized, none of them saw anything about her. They weren't looking at her, Tess Lanier; they cared only about Nina Lane's daughter.

And Gordon, the one who said he was her boyfriend, he was the worst.

Tess was almost relieved when she had to leave Stanford.

Her grandparents were ill; they needed her help. Tess transferred to a local branch of the state university, taking a very light course load so she could help her grandparents. Doctors' appointments, prescription refills; low-fat, low-salt, low-fiber diets; the loss of hair, appetite, and bladder control; the paperwork; the decisions—she had taken care of everything, waking up each morning determined to be patient and good-humored and not mind that Grandpa kept the volume on the television painfully loud and Grandma's eyes would bulge froglike as she struggled to swallow her pills. Her grandparents had raised her, providing the only home she remembered. She had owed this to them.

It was during those years that she learned to love linens and lace. She spent so much time in doctors' waiting rooms that she craved intricate, time-consuming handiwork, and lace certainly provided that. She couldn't lose herself in a novel—not with the television on so loud—so she checked out books about textiles. She wanted to give little gifts to her grandparents' health-care aides; she found that she could buy a dresser scarf or a set of napkins at a flea market. After an hour or two of getting out the stains, starching, and ironing, perhaps embroidering a butterfly in one corner or adding a new trim, she would have an elegant, even rather valuable, gift.

Grandma had died first, and one day after her death, Grandpa had motioned to Tess to turn off the television. "They do this thing in Kansas on Nina's birthday."

Tess had been reattaching a filet lace border to a linen table runner. She stopped her work. "I know."

"I always thought it might be interesting to go. Your grandmother, she didn't want to have anything to do with it, but I thought it would be interesting."

Tess knew that her grandparents' lives were full of things to regret—having to leave their farms in Kansas, never having enough money, bringing up such a difficult child. Her heart twisted at this additional regret.

"So, Tess, would you go? I'd like to think that you were going to go."

"Yes, Grandpa, of course. If you want me to, of course I will go."

He had died in March, and it wasn't possible for Tess to go to Kansas that first May. She had no money, none at all. As soon as the lease was up on her grandparents' house, she would be moving into an apartment with three young women. She was going to have to take a cash advance on a credit card in order to pay for her share of the security deposit. But since she kept her promises, she did go the following year.

In the intervening twelve months, she had been completely on her own; there was no other family, and her grandparents had not had any particularly close friends. The year hadn't been easy, but Tess had not been unhappy. Her job was as good as a person with a B.A. in art therapy could expect. Willow Place was a well-run, luxurious retirement home. The facility was immaculately clean, smelling of fresh flowers and lemon-oil furniture polish. The residents had private incomes and cooperative families. Tess's own

living arrangements were also as good as could be expected. She didn't have a lot in common with her
roommates, but there was no conflict and not much
friction.

So her life was fine for now. She did sometimes
wonder about the future. Her job was secure, the
benefits were excellent, and the salary was adequate
for her needs, since she was living with three other
women and driving her grandparents' paid-for car.
But the car would not last forever, and she didn't
want to be living with roommates year after year.
Salaries didn't rise quickly in her field, and there were
never stock options or performance-based incentives.
Tess wasn't sure she would ever be able to afford to
live alone, much less buy a little house. Yes, she had
made enough money to pay for the Kansas trip by
selling linens, but she couldn't expect to raise a down
payment by ironing place mats.

Her roommates survived on credit cards, maxing
out one account after another, paying only the
minimum each month, never worrying about how
they would retire the full debt. They all believed
that they would marry someday, and Tess supposed
that they secretly assumed that their husbands
would rescue them from their debts. Although if
that were the case, then they really needed to be dat-
ing guys different from the ones who drifted through
the apartment now. Tess wouldn't have trusted those
fellows to change a flat tire.

She didn't date much herself. The ladies at Willow
Place didn't understand that. They thought she ought
to have a boyfriend.

"I'm fine," she would say. "I don't need a boyfriend."

She had never imagined herself married. Even as a golden-haired little girl, she hadn't fantasized about being a bride. She wondered now if that was because her grandparents had always seemed more like brother and sister to her than husband and wife. They had, after all, grown up together; their families had left Kansas together. But she hadn't grown up with anyone, and given the kind of men whom her roommates went out with, it was just as well that she felt no great need to be married.

"Duke, it's me. She came to the Birthday Celebration."

Sierra Celandine was the sort of person who called you once a year and said, "It's me." But Duke Nathan had a good auditory memory. "The what? Oh, that thing they do for Nina? Who came? Who are you talking about?"

"Western Settler. The baby. Your daughter. But she goes by Tess, Tess Lanier."

"You can hardly blame her for that." What had Nina been thinking of, naming a baby after a sunken riverboat?

"I wasn't *blaming* her for anything." Sierra was instantly defensive. "I was just telling you. And, oh, Duke, we had the most wonderful conversation. She really is a beautiful young woman, inside and out. She's an ectomorph like Nina was, not all that tall but willowy, with narrow bones and long fingers. And she has this spiritual glow to her, this aura. A person doesn't have that unless she is in touch with her true essence."

Duke Nathan knew exactly what Tess Lanier looked like. He had less information about whether or not she was in touch with her true essence. "Did she tell you who she was?" As far as he knew, she had never come forward, identifying herself publicly as Nina Lane's daughter.

"No. I recognized her. I mean, these Celebrations can be so hard, even after all this time, to see all these girls dressing like Nina. I had just seen someone who must have weighed three hundred pounds, waddling around as if she looked like Nina. And then I noticed this girl and instantly thought, 'No, there's Nina.' It was clearly my powers of higher intuition, because, except for her build, she doesn't look like either one of you, and actually, I almost doubted my instinct—and you know me, I never doubt my instincts—but when she signed the guest book with *Lanier*, I felt sure. I suppose Nina's parents still use that name."

"I would think." Duke couldn't imagine Nina's parents doing anything else. Why would they have abandoned their own name in favor of their daughter's pen name? "But they're both dead now."

"Oh." Sierra didn't seem very interested in Nina's parents. "She said she was in a job working with the public. I wonder what she does."

"She's an art therapist in a retirement home," he answered.

"An art therapist?" Sierra was clearly delighted. "I knew she had to be a healer of some kind. She has that presence."

Duke Nathan closed his eyes. Sierra hadn't always

been like this. Once, she had been impassioned and knowledgeable, a young woman full of conviction. "Actually, I think that the job is more of an activities director. She doesn't do much therapy."

"Oh, I'm sure she does. I can't imagine her not truly touching other people's inner beings." Sierra paused, waiting for Duke to agree with her. He didn't. "How do you know all this about her? I thought you weren't in touch with her."

"I'm not." Duke and Nina had not been married, and at the time of her death, Kansas law would have given him few rights even if he had wanted custody of a three-month-old baby, which he had not. "But I make sure that I know people who are."

What times those had been, those years in Kansas, years that had left Duke one of the most reviled men in American popular culture.

He had met Nina in college during their freshman year at UCLA. Like so many other girls professing to be free spirits, Nina moved around campus, braless and barefoot, her long hair flowing. But Nina was different from the rest. She had talent, and everyone knew it. Duke was taking a creative writing class with her, and whatever the assignment, she turned in pages from the book she was writing. Everyone else in the class planned to write a book; Nina was doing it.

The professor didn't like the way she was ignoring his assignments, and one day he set out to get her. He took her work and read it aloud to the class, stopping every few sentences to call attention to her point-of-view violations and her awkward transitions. Technically, he was correct in his comments, but it was the worst criticism to direct to a freshman writer. It could only demoralize or paralyze. His tone was vicious. He mocked the work, he made little jokes.

Anyone else would have withered. Any other student would have gathered up his papers and stumbled out of class.

Not Nina Lanier. She seemed oblivious to the professor's tone. She listened to his criticism, shoving her black hair over her shoulder, leaning forward in her seat. Within minutes she was noticing mistakes that the professor hadn't caught. Duke was impressed. She seemed so strong and brave, rising above the professor's nasty pettiness. Duke knew that he couldn't have done it.

Of course, he knew now that strength and bravery had had nothing to do with it. She hadn't noticed the personal attack. Nina simply didn't register certain kinds of information. But he hadn't known that then.

He had hardly begun what might be called his courtship of her when she looked him straight in the eye. "I'm going to Kansas as soon as I can."

It was a warning. *Don't expect anything of me unless you are willing to go to Kansas.*

Her reasons made little sense. There was a family history, something about losing farms during the Depression. Her parents had grown up in Kansas, but as children, they had had to leave, their families tying mattresses to the roofs of cars like characters in *The Grapes of Wrath*. It sounded like an ordinary enough story to him, nothing in it to make her so determined to go there, but he didn't care whether or not she made sense. He was infatuated. If Kansas was where she was going, then that was where he was going.

She finished her book the summer after their freshman year and within six months had sold it to a small alternative press under what Duke now knew to have been a terrible contract. It labeled the book as "work for hire." Nina got money up front, but in exchange she gave up all her rights. She would receive no royalties, no additional money based on the amount of actual sales. But because the contract bought the rights not only to this book but also to two more that she hadn't yet written, the money had been enough for her to quit school and move to Kansas. Duke went with her.

The other students in the creative writing program were envious and disbelieving. They all felt they had gotten a bad deal. It was a lousy time to be a college student. Nothing important was happening. The war in Vietnam was over. Watergate was over. Woodstock was a memory, something your older brother and sisters had gone to. What was the point of being a free spirit if no one was trying to restrain you? Why be a rebel when there was nothing to rebel against? They felt cheated.

But Duke and Nina had created their own Woodstock. The two of them were going to Kansas.

They went first, then others followed; and once Nina's book was published, word traveled. *If you're in the Midwest, go to a town on the Kansas side of the Missouri River. It's called Fleur-de-lis, and there's a group of people called the Settlement.*

It wasn't a commune. There was no organization,

no clear list of who was on the bus and who wasn't. People had to fend for themselves financially, but those old rural houses were big and the farm economy was so bad that living was cheap.

It hadn't been the perfect idyll that people now portrayed it as, but there had been parts that had been very good. You could hear the meadowlarks singing through the open farmhouse windows. People did sit up late, talking about books and music, watching the fireflies flit through the dark prairie grasses. Sierra Celandine would come across the road from the little tenant shack she lived in to bake bread in Duke and Nina's kitchen. She would make four loaves at a time and leave them cooling on the windowsill. She made crabapple jelly and plum jam, their jewellike lights glowing through the thick glass of the Ball jars.

Duke's own writing went well. He wrote conventional science fiction and soon he too had a novel under contract with Nina's publisher. He was more successful than a new writer could expect to be, but his success was nothing compared with Nina's.

That was one thing they still said about him—that he resented her for having been more successful. It wasn't true. He didn't resent her success. He'd resented her talent. Who wouldn't? To be able to do what she had done—what writer wouldn't want that?

But that wasn't why he had left.

It had bothered him that her talent excused her from all other responsibilities. Sometimes there'd be a bunch of people living in the house, and Sierra would make up a duty roster. His name was certainly on them, he had chores, but Nina never did.

But that wasn't why he had left.

She would never do anything that felt hard to her. If someone had been staying in the house too long, it was Duke or Sierra who had to tell the person to find a place of his own. If Nina thought she was going to miss a deadline, it was Duke or Sierra who had to tell her publisher. If the car was making strange noises or the roof was leaking, Duke or Sierra had to take care of it. Her writing was hard enough, Nina said. She couldn't take on anything more. Sierra didn't seem to mind, but he was a writer too, and having to take care of everything meant that it took him an extra year to write his book.

But that wasn't why he had left.

Nor had Nina seemed to care very much about the rest of them. One girl had lost all her canvases when someone's car had caught on fire. It was a heartbreaking loss, two years' worth of work gone, but Nina hadn't said anything to her. Nina hadn't cared. She was selfish and self-centered.

But that wasn't why he had left.

He had left because she was manic-depressive.

He hadn't known it when she was alive. She was "creative"—that was the label that explained all her behavior. But several years later he had been reading an article about bipolar disorders, and he had recognized Nina's symptoms immediately. She had had periods of high energy during which she couldn't stop talking, couldn't stop working, followed by those times when she withdrew into her writing room, sometimes not speaking to anyone for two or three days.

She was draining, she was demanding. Whether she was manic or depressed, she sucked up all the oxygen in the room and left none for anyone else to breathe. She was mentally ill.

That was why he had left. She was so exhausting and exasperating during her manic stages that he was almost relieved when she became depressed. He hated himself for feeling that way. That was why he had left. He hated the person her mental illness had made him become.

That Nina Lane had been manic-depressive was now well accepted. A psychiatrist writing about bipolar disorders in creative people had used her as a case study. Even without as much information as Duke had, the doctor had convinced most people of his diagnosis.

Although not her most die-hard fans. They ignored it. They didn't want anything to have been wrong with Nina Lane. It was easier to blame Duke Nathan. They had wanted a simple story. Duke Nathan had left Nina, so she killed herself. It was all his fault. That was a good story.

Duke, of course, had many regrets. He wished he had been stronger, better able to live up to the challenges of a mentally ill partner. He wished he hadn't left with Kristin; that made his leaving seem more of a romantic issue than it really had been. He wished he hadn't been so surprised by Nina's suicide. He wished he could have helped her, stopped her.

Publicly he had said nothing about her. He never would. There would have been no point. Her fans wouldn't have listened, and no one else would have cared.

Being Duke Nathan hadn't been easy. It wasn't a job for sissies. A writer supporting a family—he and Kristin had married and had kids—needs to teach, edit journals, and give lectures, but even to this day some doors were closed to him because he was the bad guy in the Nina Lane story.

But what could a person do? Life had cast him in a low-rent version of a Ted Hughes-Sylvia Plath saga. He had soldiered on with as much dignity as he could muster.

Tess had bought more linens while she had been in Kansas, and she spent her evenings the first two weeks after getting home working on them, repairing damages, treating stains, starching, ironing, getting ready for a weekend antiques show. At the show, a lady with a shop offered to take some on consignment, but after she explained the financial terms, Tess declined the offer.

The next morning at work, she found in her office mailbox a personal-looking envelope. Her name was handwritten. The lettering on the envelope flap revealed only an address in New York City, but no name.

She slit open the envelope and unfolded the monarch-sized paper. Splashed across the top of the paper in bold blue letters was the name *Duke Nathan.*

Dear Tess,

I trust my name is familiar to you.

Sierra Celandine tells me that you were in Kansas during the Nina Lane Annual Birthday Celebration. Presuming that that reveals a very understandable interest in Nina, I am going to venture to introduce myself to you. I will be in Los Angeles teaching a workshop, and I will come to Willow Place in the middle of the afternoon on Wednesday, June 5.

Please don't reply to this. If you don't want to see me, simply tell whoever guards the entrance. Forgive me for sounding like Sierra, but I would like you to do whatever feels right at that moment.

With my best wishes,
Duke Nathan

Tess stared at the letter. Duke Nathan ... of course she knew who he was. He was her father.

If her grandparents hadn't said much about Nina, they had said even less about Duke Nathan. To speak of him would mean speaking of Nina's suicide, and that was never done. A child, as Tess knew from her training, readily adopts her caregivers' assumptions. Her grandparents never thought about him, so Tess hadn't either.

During her first semester at Stanford, her acquaintances in the Nina Lane Enthusiasts Society thought that she should go to New York and confront Duke Nathan. "He walked out on you," Margaret kept saying. "He *abandoned* you. You should go make him explain himself."

Tess couldn't afford to go to New York and confront anyone. "What earthly good would that do?"

"He should be accountable for what he did," Gordon insisted. "He should be made to pay."

"My grandparents would kill me if I ever took money from him."

Gordon blinked. "We weren't talking about that kind of compensation." Gordon got a huge allowance from his parents; he never gave a moment's thought to what things cost. "Money's not the issue here, not at all."

Their extravagant anger against Duke Nathan bewildered Tess. She tried to examine her own feelings about him, and all she could say for sure was that she could never be that angry at anyone. But shouldn't she be angrier than they were? Wasn't she the one with the most at stake? Somehow their flamboyance was robbing her of the emotion that was rightly hers.

So what was she going to do when he came to see her now? Would she tell the guard not to admit him? No, of course not. She was curious. Why was he coming? She was suspicious. What did he want?

On Wednesday, June 5, she crossed Willow Place's gleaming lobby and put out her hand. "I'm Tess Lanier."

"Duke Nathan." His hand closed around hers.

He was a burly, bearded man. She could see nothing of herself in him.

He apologized for being late. "I live in New York, and even so, I didn't expect the traffic to be this bad.

But I've been admiring the building. It looks like an attractive facility. Will you show me around?"

She nodded and gave him the tour just as if he were looking for a place for his aging mother. He asked her no personal questions and said little about himself.

This is my father. What does that mean?

Nothing. It meant nothing. He could have been anyone.

He was wearing a wedding ring. Did he have children? Did she have brothers and sisters? She couldn't imagine herself with brothers and sisters.

Her special ladies, the ones who took her drawing class, looked up interestedly when she opened the door to the South Activities Room. She introduced him, not as her father, but simply as "Mr. Nathan from New York." Mrs. Gettis asked him how he knew Tess; he said that he had known her grandparents when he was much younger.

He invited her to dinner, and she accepted. So far, they had talked about nothing but Willow Place.

The maître d' held out her chair and shook her napkin out for her. When he moved away, Duke Nathan spoke. "That wasn't true about my knowing your grandparents. Nina never took me home."

"Oh?" Tess opened the menu. A number of the dishes were made with cilantro. She didn't like cilantro. *Nina.* He had said the word so calmly, as if this were a normal thing to talk about.

"But she didn't hate her parents," Duke Nathan continued. "She was miserable growing up, but she didn't hate them."

"They would not have deserved it." Tess felt very

loyal to her grandparents. How could anyone have hated them?

But hadn't there been moments when she had? When Grandma wouldn't even try to swallow those pills. Yes, they were huge, and when Tess cut them, they became powdery and bitter, but still . . . And Grandpa and the television. Yes, it was wonderful that one of the local channels started to show *Gunsmoke* reruns just when he needed his favorite program the most, but he had kept the volume so loud . . .

She should think about cilantro. It was all right to hate cilantro. "That's really why I was in Kansas," she said quickly, "for my grandparents. I was trying to find their farms." Grandpa had suggested this after asking her to go to the Birthday Celebration, and she had gone looking for the properties on Sunday morning. "They were both born there. Their families—"

She broke off because he was nodding. He knew. How odd to be around someone who knew her family history. No one in her life now knew anything about her past. Her roommates kept forgetting that she had been raised by grandparents.

"It sounds like you didn't find them," he said.

"No." Tess had been disappointed at not finding them, but she had told herself that it didn't matter. She was not the type to have had a mystic experience blending with her ancestral earth. "And it wasn't a very good weekend to ask around."

"Your grandfather had the directions turned around, which isn't surprising, since he was only seven when his family had to leave. It took Nina a while to figure that out. The Lanier place is four miles north on County Route Five, and the Swensons were off Dr. Bird Road. You turn left just beyond the culvert and go about two-tenths of a mile. Nina went to both places a lot."

Tess had been on County Route Five and she had probably gone at least four miles. She would have driven by her grandfather's home without knowing it.

"I would like to write those directions down, but I don't imagine I'll ever be back."

"Why not?"

"Money. I have hardly traveled at all. I'm not going to go to the same place twice."

He looked up, surprised. "You don't have anything from Nina? I know that the trilogy was done as work for hire, but surely there had to be a different contract for *The Riverboat Fragment*. Its sales are nothing compared to the trilogy, but even in the worst case, even with a four percent contract . . . the thing's never been out of print."

"I don't know what you're talking about." The manuscript Nina had left unfinished had been published in its incomplete form after her death, but Tess knew nothing more than that.

"Don't you have her contracts? *The Riverboat Fragment* would have been the option book under the initial contract, but it would have been a different deal."

Tess still didn't know what he was talking about. "We don't have any papers of hers. I cleaned up my grandparents' house after they died, and there was nothing."

"There wasn't a contract for *The Riverboat Fragment*? It would have been between the publisher and

Nina's estate. Your grandparents would have been involved in the negotiations."

"I know nothing about it."

He had no choice but to accept her words and change the subject. He closed his menu. "So do you have questions for me? Things that you want to know?"

What kind of man leaves his suicidally depressed partner and his newborn baby? "No."

"I never talk about Nina, not to anyone, but of course you're different."

Tess had had her little episode with being different because she was Nina Lane's daughter. She wasn't going to repeat it. "No, I'm fine."

"All right." He sounded as if he didn't believe her, but surprisingly, he let the matter drop. "Sierra Celandine said that when you were in Kansas, you and she had a wonderful conversation."

"In Kansas?" Tess was puzzled. "I had a wonderful conversation with someone in Kansas? I hardly talked to anyone." Then she remembered. "You don't mean that lady who sold the herbs, do you?"

Duke nodded and smiled. "So it seemed a little different from your end?"

"She was too intense for my taste." Tess realized that she needed to be careful. He might be good friends with the woman. "But of course I had no idea that she knew who I was."

"She claims to have recognized you instantly, although I never know how much to believe. All one can know for sure is that she fervently believes herself." He paused. "You do know who she is, don't you?"

Tess shook her head.

"She came to Kansas when Nina and I were there. In fact, she was there when you were born. I mean that literally. She cut the cord, all that. She was the midwife at your birth. After that she was your nanny. She took care of you for the first three months of your life. Apparently it about killed her when you were taken back to your grandparents."

"Oh." That woman had been her midwife and her nanny? "Oh."

"You didn't know any of this?" he asked.

"No." She really hadn't liked that woman. Not at all.

"Who did you think took care of you?"

"I never gave it any thought, but I would have assumed it would be my mother."

"Nina? Take care of a newborn baby?" This was clearly an impossible thought. "I don't know what Nina would have done if Sierra hadn't been around, but that was the thing with Nina. There were always people like Sierra around to take on her responsibilities."

There was an edge of bitterness to his voice. He certainly didn't have very fond memories of Nina Lane. Tess made herself change the subject. "I was abrupt with her, with this Sierra. I wish I hadn't been. Do you have her address? I feel like I should write and apologize."

"Don't. Not unless you want to have a relationship with her. You can't write a nice note to her and be done with it. There's no halfway with Sierra. Either don't get in touch with her at all or be prepared to have a very intense relationship."

"Those can't be the only choices."

"No, trust me on this one. She's—" He broke off. "But you have no reason to trust me, do you? And my saying there are only these two options must sound self-serving, that I am trying to justify the choice I made to have no relationship with you. But that's not why I'm here. I have to live with what I did. It's my cross. I won't ask you to help carry it."

"Then why *are* you here?" she asked. "I didn't see anything in the papers about you teaching a workshop. You just made that up, didn't you? So I wouldn't feel that you had made a special trip to see me."

He nodded, acknowledging that she was right. He had flown across the country just to see her. "Your turning up at the Nina Lane Annual Birthday Celebration seemed very odd. I have two kids of my own. I'm enough of a dad that I wanted to be sure you were okay."

Two kids of his own? What was *she*? "My grandfather asked me to go to the Nina Lane thing. I went for him, not for myself."

"Your grandfather? Not your grandmother?"

"No, it was my grandfather . . . after my grandmother died."

He nodded as if her reply made sense.

Tess didn't like that nod. It was as if he knew something about her grandparents that she didn't. He could know all he wanted to about Nina Lane, but Grandma and Grandpa, pills, television, and all . . . they were her property.

"I did feel an obligation to you, Tess," he continued. "I knew that you had no other family, your grandfather had been an only child and that your grandmother's sisters had died in early adulthood. So clearly, if something would have happened to your grandparents, if you had been on your own, I would have felt responsible for you. I would have brought you to New York. It would have been a disaster. My wife and daughter have always felt we were living in the shadow of Nina Lane, that Nina was somehow the main character in our story, so I'm sure they would have resented the hell out of having Nina Lane's daughter live with us."

Tess sat back in her chair. Duke would have "felt" responsible for her. What was this "felt" business? He would have *been* responsible for her. Feelings had nothing to do with it. And his other children resenting her? Was this the Middle Ages? They could spit on her because she was legally a bastard and they weren't?

She had to speak. "This doesn't add up. You seem like a decent man. You came because you were concerned about me, but what you just said was appalling."

He blinked. He was startled. Then he thought for a moment. "Yes, it must have sounded that way."

"Why do you mean 'sounded'?' " she asked. "It *was* appalling."

He took a breath. "Tess, I have been appalling people for twenty-four years. I am used to it." He sounded weary, resigned to her thinking badly of him.

This was not the whole story. Her instincts said that he was not a bad man. He was decent, he was honorable. He was sensible and sensitive. Yes, he had done something reprehensible when he had been twenty-two, but he had paid for it. Over and over.

"Is there something I should know?" she asked.

"I'm not lying to you," he answered. "Everything I've said, everything I'll ever say to you, is the truth."

"But is it the whole truth? My grandparents never told me that Nina Lane committed suicide. I found out on my own when I was twelve. Lies of omission can hurt as much as the other kind."

His lips tightened beneath his beard. He glanced around the restaurant as if checking to see who was there, and when he spoke, his voice was low. "You aren't mine, Tess. You aren't my daughter."

"What?" She couldn't have heard him right.

"Only my wife and children know. Even Sierra thinks I am your father, but I'm not. That's why Kristin would have resented having to raise you . . . it would have been one more responsibility that Nina dumped on someone else."

"I don't understand. You aren't my father?" That was a stupid thing to say. Of course she understood. He wasn't her father.

"My name is on your birth certificate. I was with Nina when they took her to the hospital. I wasn't going to argue at a time like that, especially since none of our friends knew."

"But why . . ."

"Why? Nina lived by her own rules. You know how—" He stopped. "I don't know what you know. When she was in a manic stage, she hated being alone. She wanted someone else in the room when she wrote. She left the door open when she went to the bathroom. I see now that it was genuinely pathological, but at the time, it just felt very hard to take. Anyway, the winter before you were born, she was really over the top, and I was looking for a break. A couple of us started planning to go to Mardi Gras. When you live in Fleur-de-lis, you hear a lot about New Orleans, since that's where many of the riverboat passengers were coming from. So we decided to go. Nina, of course, didn't want to go because she was working, and she didn't want me to go. She was furious with me, calling me selfish, but I went anyway."

"And so she punished you by sleeping with someone else?" Was there anything good about Nina Lane as a person?

"That was part of it. She also truly couldn't bear to be alone. Being with someone at night was one way of not being alone. She just didn't think like the rest of us, didn't think of herself as having obligations to anything except her work. I know that makes her sound so selfish," Duke continued, "which, of course, she was. But her selfishness was so uncalculated. She didn't walk around thinking, 'I expect Sierra to make my dinner; I expect Duke to keep the car running.' She simply never thought about it. If dinner was on the table, she didn't wonder how it had gotten there."

"If she was so self-focused"—Tess could hear how tight her voice was—"why didn't she have an abortion?"

Duke paused, before saying, "I'm not sure she realized she was pregnant. Sierra was the one who finally asked her if she was. Sierra was thrilled, and Nina must have known that if she had an abortion, Sierra would have left, and we were very dependent on Sierra."

So here was another reason for Tess to be grateful to Sierra Celandine.

"Do you know who the father was?" Tess asked. "My father."

He shook his head. "No, I don't know. I didn't ask. I had one foot out the door of the relationship anyway—I wouldn't have gone to Mardi Gras otherwise. So I figured that it didn't make any difference who the fellow was. I held on, hoping that maybe the baby—you—would change her. When it didn't, I gave up. He probably was one of the painters who were there for a couple of weeks that winter, but they had left by the time Nina realized she was pregnant. He wouldn't have known about you."

"When you say 'painter' . . ."

He smiled. "I do mean artist, not house painter."

Tess had occasionally thought it odd that the offspring of two writers should have as little literary talent as she did. Whatever gifts she had were visual. She had a good sense of design and an excellent eye for color.

Now she knew why. But what difference did it make? "Why haven't you told anyone that you weren't the father?"

He shrugged. "Because I decided a long time ago that I wasn't going to try to explain or excuse myself. That was my only hope for a life with any dignity. I had told Kristin before we left Kansas, and I did feel like I needed to tell my own children. I didn't want them thinking that there was a family member we were ignoring, and I certainly didn't want my son believing it was okay to conceive a child, then walk away."

He didn't have any good answers, he said, to questions about what were one's obligations to the mentally ill. "Running away as I did isn't the answer," he said, "but Nina wouldn't let me have a life of my own. I had to live for her, and I couldn't do that. But believe me, Tess, I had no idea she was suicidal. I was stunned when she killed herself, and then when people started saying she had done it because I had left her . . . that isn't right. I just wasn't that important to her. I was useful, but she didn't love me. She didn't love anyone except your grandmother. It makes no sense that she would kill herself over me."

"She was mentally ill." Tess had studied manic-depressives in school. Suicide attempts most often occur when the depression is starting to swing back into mania. She reached into her purse and took out a small, flat, tissue-wrapped parcel. She had brought it impulsively, unsure whether or not she would give it to him. "Does your wife like lace?" she asked. "Would you give this to her for me?"

She handed the gift to him, and he gestured, asking permission to open it. She nodded and he unfolded the tissue. "My God," he exclaimed. "I know nothing about this, but it's unbelievable. And so beautiful. Is it old?"

"The linen in the center is." It was a table topper, an eighteen-inch linen circle surrounded by a three-inch crocheted border. "But I made the lace."

"You made this? You *made* this?"

Tess could feel herself flush. She liked it when people had this reaction to her work. *This is me. This is what I do. I can't write. I can't tell stories. I'm not Nina Lane. But I can take old things and make them beautiful again.* "Crocheted lace goes pretty quickly, and I like working with vintage linens." The center of this piece had come from the back of a turn-of-the-century blouse whose front had been mottled with stains.

The restaurant was dimly lit. Duke Nathan was holding the work up to the candle in the middle of the table, shaking his head as people who knew nothing about needlework always did. "I can't imagine Nina ever doing anything like this. She'd never have had the patience."

"I'm not Nina Lane." They hadn't understood that, the people she had known at Stanford; they hadn't understood that she was not Nina Lane.

"No, of course you aren't. But I suppose that was part of what Kristin dreaded about you, that we would end up raising a mini-Nina, a child as difficult and selfish as Nina had been as an adult."

"There may be a lot wrong with me, but one thing I can say for sure is that I'm not difficult or selfish."

He smiled. "That's a good thing to know about yourself. Kristin is going to have a million questions for me when I get home, so tell me everything you can bear to have me—and her—know. What kind of place do you live in? Do you like your job?"

Three days later Tess got a note from Kristin Nathan, thanking her for the linen. It was written on thick, expensive paper with a calligraphy pen. Kristin wrote that she would always think of Kansas when she looked at it, and she hoped that if Tess was ever in New York, they could have dinner together.

The week after that, Tess got a call from someone named Alexa Surcast. She said she was with the contracts department of a publishing company. It was a big company, one that Tess had heard of.

"We bought Sprawl Press a number of years ago, and we're doing a routine update of their files. We can't seem to locate our copy of *The Riverboat Fragment* contract. Could you fax us a copy of yours?"

The Riverboat Fragment, Nina Lane's incomplete manuscript, had been published twenty-three years ago. Why were they suddenly looking for the contract? And why did they need it faxed? After twenty-three years, couldn't they wait for the regular mail?

"I don't have it," Tess said. Then, because she didn't believe for one instant that this was routine, she added, "And that's strange, because my grandparents kept all legal documents. They were afraid of lawyers, so they kept everything."

"It might have been very brief, just an extension of the trilogy contract,"Ms. Surcast said. "We do have a record of a payment. This is simply routine updating, nothing to get concerned about."

Tess wasn't concerned, but she certainly was interested. What should she do? She knew only one person connected to publishing—Duke Nathan. Could she call him? Yes, she could.

Would you have felt so comfortable if he really had been your father?

No, of course not. His being her father would have complicated everything.

Duke answered his phone. She told him about the call from the publisher. "Did you start something?" she asked.

"Of course I did. Your grandparents might have signed another perfectly dreadful contract, but let's be sure."

"But if Sprawl Press did pay for *The Riverboat Fragment*, surely the legal issue is moot."

"Maybe it's moot legally, but morally . . . they have made so much money off Nina's books. If her fans found out that none of it has gone to her estate, they'd be up in arms."

"I don't want Nina Lane fans finding out anything," Tess said instantly. "I don't want to have anything to do with those people."

"I can understand that, believe me, I can, but they're your leverage."

"My leverage?" Tess wasn't sure she wanted to have any leverage. "I'm afraid I'm out of my league here."

"You could use good representation," Duke acknowledged. "I would help you if I could. I hope you know that. But if my name gets involved with this, everything will become more complex than you can ever imagine. I can give you the names of some very good people I haven't had any association with. You'll have to pay them fifteen percent of anything they get for you, but it will be worth it."

"These are agents?" How odd to think of herself as having an agent. So many people in California were always looking for agents, and now the highly unambitious Tess Lanier might be getting one.

"Of course."

Tess took a breath and called the first name. She had to leave a message—her name and that she needed to discuss a literary contract.

"Ms. Turchon's assistant will call you back in a day or so," the receptionist told her.

That didn't sound promising. For the second name on the list, Tess left a different message. "I'm Nina Lane's daughter"—she hadn't said that since Stanford—"and it seems as if there are some questions about her contracts with Sprawl Press."

Barbara Ansell herself called Tess back fifteen minutes later.

By the end of the week the agent had seen a copy of the trilogy's contract. The author and her estate were indeed entitled to nothing beyond the initial payment. "It's completely legal," Barbara said. "But it is a disgrace to the publishing industry, and this is not an industry that disgraces easily. I'm sure if Nina had lived, they would have renegotiated the contract, but without pressure from the estate, there was no reason to."

The problem for the publishing company was *The Riverboat Fragment*. The check—which Barbara had also seen a copy of—was for exactly one-third the amount of the trilogy contract, suggesting that the terms of that contract had simply been extended. But no one could find the extension.

Barbara did locate someone who used to work at Sprawl Press, and he remembered what had happened. One of the other writers living in the Settlement community had sent the press Nina's unfinished manuscript. "We started to negotiate with the parents," the ex-employee said, "but it was clear we could get away with anything as long as they didn't talk to any agents or lawyers. So we decided to pay them one-third of the total paid for her first three books and have them sign a one-page rider extending the first contract. We kept telling them that it was routine. But I'd bet anything we never sent them the rider for fear that they would show it to a lawyer. We really were a bottom-feeder press, and we were just starting to make money off Nina Lane. We were terrified that we would lose her."

The publishing conglomerate, which had purchased Sprawl Press primarily because of its rights to Nina Lane, had over the years fought several legal battles against pirated editions of the trilogy and amateurish attempts to finish *The Riverboat Fragment*. In the latter case, the company had been protecting rights that it didn't have.

"They are screwed," Barbara said cheerfully. "Totally screwed."

The first few days of the following week seemed to Tess as if they were happening to someone else. Every morning the publisher would make an offer, threatening to take it off the table if Tess didn't accept it by five that afternoon. Every afternoon at five-fifteen, her agent said no, thanks; for that kind of money they'd take their chances in court. So the next morning the publisher would offer more. After four days of this, Barbara had terms that she liked.

Tess would receive a lump-sum payment for the previous unauthorized publication of *The Riverboat Fragment*. A new contract provided for royalties on future publication of that work. Barbara Ansell had also renegotiated the trilogy contract so that royalties would be paid on the future sales of those books as well. So from now on, Tess would received 12½ percent of the cover price of every English language edition sold in North America, and various other percentages on other editions in other markets, etc., etc. The contract went on for pages, and the numbers seemed like Monopoly money to Tess.

But it wasn't Monopoly money. It was the actual stuff. Within thirty days some of it would be in her checking account, waiting for her to spend it.

She was rich.

"No, you aren't," Duke told her. "Don't think you can wing off to Paris for the weekend every time you get bored, but if you are halfway sensible, you can send your kids to private school and you won't have to worry about what their summer camps will cost."

That sounded rich to Tess.

She could do anything. She could quit her job; she could live alone; she could buy a computer, a computerized sewing machine, a computerized car. She could get a cell phone. She could buy theater tickets for full-scale, all-effects-included productions of touring Broadway shows. She could go to New York and see the shows on Broadway. She could shop for her clothes in Beverly Hills. She could stop in at Starbucks on her way to work. She could stop in again on her way home. She could stop in every hour on the hour. She could drink overpriced cappuccino drinks until her bladder burst.

She couldn't sleep. Her mind raced. *Why me?*

"This makes no sense," Tess said to Barbara Ansell. "What have I done to deserve this kind of money?"

"Don't say that," Barbara pleaded with her. "Don't say that to anyone. Of course you deserve it. Your mother would have wanted you to have it."

When the residents at Willow Place said things like that, Tess smiled and listened politely because that was what she was paid to do. But she was not being paid to listen to Barbara Ansell. In fact, she was paying Barbara Ansell to listen to her. "My mother may not ever have changed a diaper, and then she committed suicide when I was three months old. I don't think we can say that she had my interest foremost in her heart."

Barbara couldn't quarrel with that. "Okay, how about this—the law wants you to have it. How's that?"

"That's all right, I guess." Tess had always been very law-abiding.

But she still couldn't sleep.

Of course, this wasn't just a little extra income. There was some serious money here. It wasn't the money itself that worried her—although she knew nothing about investments, about the stock market or mutual funds. Okay, so the money itself was worrisome, but the real source of her anxiety was change. She was afraid of change.

Here it was, the beginning of July. Surely by Christmas, even by Thanksgiving or Labor Day, her life would have completely changed. She would be living somewhere else, doing something else, and she had no idea what or where.

There was nothing weird about being disconcerted by that.

She didn't want to not work. She knew that. It

would be too easy for her to retreat into a nunlike world of vintage linens and lacemaking. That was what she had done when her grandparents were alive, and she had felt like Cinderella watching everyone else her age get ready for the ball. She wanted to be with people. She wanted to have friends and activities. To live alone and work with people—that was what she wanted. That was a start. That was some kind of decision.

But live alone where and work at what?

Not at a retirement home. She had gotten her job at Willow Place because she had understood so much about the elderly. It was time to learn about the rest of life.

"What do you want to do with your life?" Duke Nathan asked her during one of their frequent phone conversations. He was the only person besides her agent who knew how very much money she was getting. She had merely told her roommates and the people at work that her grandparents' estate had been settled and she would be getting "some" money. "What are your dreams, your fantasies?"

"I don't think I have any."

"Everyone has dreams."

"I don't. I suppose as a child I wanted to live someplace where it snowed, all Southern California kids do, but that never became my life's ambition."

"That what has been your life's ambition?"

"I don't know. I probably just wanted to please my grandparents, to make things easy for them, and they were always so anxious about money that the best way to do that was to never want anything."

"Why couldn't my kids have picked that route?"

he sighed. "They've never wanted to make things easy for me, or if they did, I don't want to know what difficult is."

Difficult. Duke had said that his wife would have hated to take Tess into their home, fearing she would have to raise another Nina, selfish and difficult.

As she lay in bed that night, it occurred to Tess that her grandparents had probably felt exactly the same way. They, better than anyone, would have known how difficult Nina had been; they, more than anyone, would have dreaded facing that again.

Nina had tortured them with her longings and ambitions, her dreams and fantasies. So what had happened? The next child they raised hadn't been allowed to have any dreams or ambitions.

As soon as it was 9 A.M. on the East Coast, Tess called Duke again. He answered the phone.

"I wanted to be Miss Kitty of the Long Branch Saloon."

"Miss Kitty?" He was puzzled. "Oh, you mean from *Gunsmoke*?"

"It was my grandfather's favorite show." Surely Nina would have mentioned that. The show had originally aired throughout much of Nina's childhood. "Whenever he told me bedtime stories, it would be about the *Gunsmoke* characters."

"And, of course, you wanted to be Miss Kitty." He had a daughter. He understood little girls.

"Who wouldn't? She had the best clothes in town. She didn't really fit in"—Tess was too used to feeling different from everyone else to imagine herself ever truly fitting in—"but she belonged. She had put down roots. And she had a business that was at the center of everything. It was a place where people could meet, where they would feel less isolated."

"So open a bar."

"I'm not going to do *that*." Tess's roommates went to bars to meet men. Bars only made her feel more isolated. She hated the smoke; she disliked the drinking. "I could open a shop selling vintage linens, but that could be a truly isolating experience." A card table at a flea market was one thing; a whole store was quite a different matter. "I think I might be spending all day every day alone if I do that."

Duke admitted that he wasn't likely to patronize such a shop. "Do you want to know what Nina would have done with that money?"

"I don't mind knowing, but her answers aren't likely to be the same as mine."

"She would have gone back to Fleur-de-lis and bought the Lanier Building and the Prairie Bell School."

"The Lanier Building? There's a building named after my family?" Tess hadn't known that.

"It's downtown. One of your ancestors built it back in the 1880s. It was looking pretty seedy twenty-five years ago; I can't imagine what it's like now. But it was made of stone. I'm sure it's still there."

"What kind of building is it? I wish I had known when I was there. I would have liked to have seen it."

"I think it was originally a dry-goods store, whatever that is. But the economy was so bad when we were there that I don't think it was much of anything. I don't know what Nina would have done with it, but she was obsessed with her family's history, at least the Kansas part of it."

"So what did the schoolhouse have to do with family history? And why can you buy a school?"

"It isn't a school anymore, just the building. It was the one-room country school that your grandfather had gone to. Apparently going to California really tore him up, and the last thing he did before his family left was sneak back to the schoolhouse, crawl behind the bushes, and scratch his initials into the foundation."

Her grandfather had done that? Tess hadn't known.

There hadn't been money for many family photographs, but she had one of her grandfather as a boy. He looked bright-eyed and pixieish, nothing like the weary, gentle man Tess had lived with. What a gesture that had been, to scratch his name on a building. *I will be back.* Kansas had been his home, and he was determined to return.

When had he given up on that dream? Tess stared down at the pencil cup on her desk. Grandpa had asked her to go back to Kansas, but he hadn't told her about the schoolhouse. He had told Nina. Why? *Did you love her more than you loved me?*

Mr. Greenweight was Willow Place's resident Internet expert. His son had given him a computer, and his grandchildren had taught him how to use it. He overwhelmed the other residents with the information he acquired. The more alert ladies had learned never to mention the name of any medication they were on. Two hours later Mr. Greenweight would come clumping down the hall, the canvas bag attached to his walker full of postings about the medication's perilous side effects.

Tess asked him if he could find out anything about the Lanier Building or the Prairie Bell School in Fleur-de-lis, Kansas. Right after lunch he brought her a printed document full of bright graphics. The town had its own Web site, designed to attract tourists and investors.

A local historian would start digging up the riverboat in the fall—Tess remembered the brochure about that—and the town was attempting to attract new businesses. One page of the site was devoted to commercial properties for sale or rent, and although there was nothing about the school, the Lanier Building was listed with a price so low that Tess, accustomed to California real estate, had to smile. It would feel like buying a doll house.

And the building already had her name on it.

A store selling only vintage linens did not seem like a good idea. If by some extraordinary stroke of luck she did have customers who did buy things, it would be too hard for her to keep up the inventory; finding and restoring the linens was too labor-intensive. And she did not want to open a bar, at least not one that stayed open late, serving alcohol. But what about a coffee bar? A Starbucks-type place—wasn't that today's equivalent of the Long Branch Saloon? Lots of the coffee bars around her neighborhood also had little things for sale. She could sell her linens and other gift items. She could be Miss Kitty on caffeine.

Gunsmoke was set in Kansas. She had never

thought about that before. All roads kept leading to Kansas. The Lanier Building was in Kansas. Grandpa had scratched his initials on a schoolhouse in Kansas. Nina Lane had written her books in Kansas.

It was time to go back to Kansas. There was something there.

❦ *Chapter 3* ❦

D r. Matt Ravenal set his parking brake. He didn't need to. On the wooded bluffs south of town you sometimes needed a parking brake, but Sierra Celandine lived on the flat river plain to the north. You never needed a parking brake out here. But setting a parking brake took—what?—a good three, four seconds, and that was another three or four seconds of not walking up to Sierra's front door.

She'd been renting this four-room tenant house since she'd shown up in town twenty-six or -seven years ago. The big farmhouse across the road had burned down about ten years ago when the renters had left candles lighted all night. Fred Hobart, who owned both that house and Sierra's, hadn't been too cut up about the fire. He had good insurance, and in truth, it was getting to be a nuisance owning the house that Nina Lane had lived in. Strange people appeared there to pick the lilacs and chant at the moon.

But Sierra's little house looked good. It was neatly painted, with a new screened-in front porch. She had put up a greenhouse, a good-sized aluminum drying shed, and a fence around the field where she grew her herbs.

Matt got out of the car. There were a couple of high school kids out in the field—Celandine Gardens was one of the steadiest sources of minimum-wage employment in town. Matt's own kids had worked for Sierra during their high school years. Besides their three daughters, Matt and his wife Carolyn had raised his two nephews, Phil and Ned.

Matt waved at the kids. He knew them all, and they knew him. That was what happened when you were the only doctor in town. "Is Sierra around?" he called out.

"She's in the hothouse."

Matt lifted a hand, thanking them, and followed the gravel drive toward the back of the property. The hothouse had a full-view screen door; the glass inset panels were still in place. The light inside was thin and watery, and the rough plywood tables were nearly empty. It was July. The seedlings that would have been crowding the tables in April were flowering in the fields.

Sierra was seated at a long work bench. She looked up at the sound of the door.

When she had first come to town, she had worn aviator-style glasses, and she had parted her long hair down the middle. The two heavy slabs of hair had screened her face into a narrow slit. That was all you noticed about her, the hair and the glasses. But now her hair was short and her glasses were gold-rimmed and small, emphasizing how delicate her features were. And her skin . . . Matt had told his wife over and over that its beauty came from good genes as much as from any Celandine Gardens moisturizer.

Carolyn had laughed. "You're probably right. But in case you're not, I'm using anything she sells."

Sierra stood up when she saw Matt. "Matthew Ravenal, what a pleasant surprise." Over her long skirt she was wearing a canvas butcher's apron. "Can I offer you some tea?"

"That would be nice." Sierra's teas were interesting. She blended them herself, and most of the flavors Matt didn't have much use for, but every so often one would be great.

Sierra took off the apron and slipped her bare feet into a pair of clogs. She was wearing a scoop-necked T-shirt. There'd been times, especially in that first year or so after Nina Lane had died, when Matt had worried about how thin she was, but she looked healthy now.

And he was not here about her physical condition. Her health was none of his business. She had never consulted him professionally. If she had routine checkups—and Matt suspected that she didn't— she went out of town.

She told Matt to go wait for her at the Adirondack chairs over by the pear tree. "You could move one into the shade, but on a day like this, you can feel the sunlight right here." She touched the lower curves of her cheekbones. "Tilt your head back and you can feel the vitamin D flowing through your body."

The vitamin D flowing through his body? This was going to be worse than he had thought.

It was a clear day, bright and hot; a strong wind had swept away yesterday's mugginess. Matt sat in one of the Adirondack chairs, and chairs like that almost forced you to tilt your head back. The strong sunlight did feel good.

Annoying people would be a whole lot easier to take if they were wrong all the time. Sierra was right precisely the wrong amount. She was often full of such goofy earnestness that no sane person could stand to listen to her. But she was right just often enough that you needed to. This time she was right. He could have sat here all afternoon.

"This tea is new," she said as she crossed the grass a few minutes later. She was carrying a tray with a pitcher and glasses. "I think it may be too sweet."

It was. He had to struggle to keep his face straight.

"Now, Matthew"—she waved a finger at him—"you don't need to pretend with me. We've been through too much together for that. This tea tastes like artificial fruit-scented lip gloss, I know that. There's an interesting undertaste, but it takes you a while to notice it. Now, tell me what sends you out this way."

Matt put down his tea. "Phil sent me. I'm here to talk business."

"Oh, no." She pretended to shudder. "Not business. That's so dull."

He didn't believe her, not for a moment. She didn't find business dull. But the price of dealing with Sierra was at least pretending to believe these self-myths of hers.

"I know that, but things are happening in town," he said. "Changes I want to talk to you about."

"Business may be dull, but change is thrilling, isn't it?" She hunched up her shoulders as if she were giving herself a little hug, and Matt could feel the performance coming on. "I love change. There's such an energy that emanates from change. What is that law of thermodynamics, about there being a constant amount of energy in the universe? I don't believe that. Change creates its own energy, don't you think?"

Well, no, he didn't, at least not on a molecular level. However, thermodynamics was at least something he had heard of; most of the time when you started talking to Sierra, she was going on about the Eternal River of Healing, which was not something he had learned about in medical school.

She hadn't always been this way. She hadn't always been silly. When she first moved here, she cared about things that mattered. She had been completely wrong, but you could talk to her. You could engage with her, you could argue with her. She would listen. Everything was different now. She was up into the clouds, floating around, saying things that had no relevance to anything.

And why was she talking as if she liked change? She had been renting the same house for more than twenty-five years. And every time there was any kind of change in town, she hated it. The Kmart had been open for nearly a year, and as far as Matt knew, she had yet to set foot in it.

"You've been downtown, haven't you?" he asked.

Her face tightened. "What else could you have expected?"

A year ago a discount superstore, a Kmart, had opened on the highway south of town. It had a pharmacy, a grocery, and a small lunch counter with

white plastic bistro chairs. It had housewares, auto-
motive supplies, clothing, and a gardening center.
The store was bright and clean, with wide aisles, low
prices, well-stocked shelves, and convenient parking.
People used to cross the river and do their discount
shopping in St. Joe or Kansas City, both of which
were in Missouri. Now people could keep their
money in Kansas. While it was hardly a Kansas-
owned business, at least the jobs were in Kansas and
the state was collecting sales tax.

But just as its opponents had predicted, the Kmart
had killed the downtown.

Dennis Gatkin, the drugstore owner, hadn't even
tried. He closed his place and went to work as the
Kmart pharmacist. "So what if I'm not my own boss
anymore? I'll make sure people get as good service,
and you'll see, the prices will be lower."

The prices were lower on everything at Kmart.
Two other stores had closed before Christmas, and
four more since. Now you went downtown only for
the bank, the dry cleaners, and the municipal building. Red-bordered FOR SALE OR LEASE signs studded
empty store after empty store, and through the dusty
windows you could see the card racks and display
counters that the business owners had left behind,
the empty cartons that they had been too tired to
throw away.

The Town Council had gotten Kmart to pledge to
hire people full-time, giving them benefits. So Dr.
Matt was seeing new faces in the office, people who
had never had health insurance before. That was
great, but Barb Eislinger, whose husband had the
electronics store, hadn't brought her kids in for camp

physicals this spring. She couldn't afford camp or the checkup.

This was what Matt's older nephew, Phil, had taken upon himself to fix.

Phil was a lawyer, aged thirty, with a real leader-among-men personality. As a kid, he had liked organized activities: Boy Scouts, team sports, and clubs. Since Matt's wife Carolyn was the daughter and sister of Kansas governors, he had gotten interested in politics early. After law school he had gone to Washington, D.C., to work on the staff of the local congressman, but when he saw what Kmart had done to the downtown area, he had come home. He had opened a law office, but as far as Matt could tell, he was too busy to practice law. He had gotten himself appointed to the town's Economic Development Council; he spent all his time working on Fleur-de-lis's problems.

There was no solution within the local economy. That was clear. There was also little chance of attracting a new industry, and no chance of getting a new prison built. Phil's idea was to revitalize Fleur-de-lis's downtown by encouraging weekend tourism.

His brother Ned, Matt's younger nephew, was a historian. He was going to be digging up the riverboat this fall. It was a major undertaking and had already attracted more publicity than Ned had the patience for. People were going to want to come look at the project, and Phil wanted to give them something to spend their money on once they arrived in town. The primary draw would be Ned's excavation and the exhibition of any artifacts that he uncovered, but those visitors needed to come downtown and spend money.

With the congressman's help, Phil had already gotten a federal beautification grant, and Main Street's cracked concrete sidewalks were being dug up and relaid with pretty brick. The utilitarian streetlights had been replaced by scrolling black wrought-iron ones that arched elegantly over the streets. State money was providing low-interest loans to business owners to paint their storefronts and buy new awnings. Financial packages had been put together to tempt new business people.

Phil went looking for these new businesses, approaching individuals no one else would have thought to talk to. A very nice, almost elderly lady, Mrs. Ballard, Dennis Gatkin's older sister, had been the first to open one. She had been collecting teacups for years, and her kids didn't want them. Since Dennis still owned the pharmacy building, she could arrange her collection on his shelves rent-free. Charles Dussel, who was a bit of a bird nut, was going to sell bird seed and his handmade wooden birdhouses in a shop he was calling Happy Little Bluebirds. Barb and Pete Eislinger were opening an old-fashioned sweets shop in their electronics store to sell fudge, ice cream, lemonade, and popcorn. Phil had persuaded Mr. Twitchell, the shoe-repair man, to carry a line of leather gift items. He was having less success at getting Mrs. Cavender to install a cappuccino machine in her bakery. "It's so much work for just one cup," she fussed.

But even if there had been a cappuccino machine,

none of these new businesses would bring people into town. The one business that might draw people, independent of the riverboat excavation, was Celandine Gardens, Sierra's mail-order line of herbal soaps and lotions. It was clearly a successful enterprise. A number of well-heeled patrons came to the Nina Lane Birthday Celebration only for the sake of the Celandine Gardens table. A full retail outlet might bring people to Fleur-de-lis year-round. But thus far, even the very persuasive Phil hadn't been able to get Sierra to consider it. So he asked Matt to talk to her.

Phil's motives were not pure. He never concealed that. The congressman was retiring at the end of this term, and Phil wanted his job. "But people are going to say that I've had it too easy, that I've never done anything for the town. I need to come home and prove myself."

His efforts weren't universally popular. Some people hated change so much that they couldn't be realistic. They hated the Kmart, they hated the stores closing, they hated them reopening as tourist shops. They seemed to think that if the town did nothing, things would eventually go back to the way they used to be.

That wasn't going to happen. Fleur-de-lis would never again have a downtown that serviced its local residents. It was going to attract either tourists or no one at all. That was the choice.

So Matt was here talking to Sierra.

"You could really do a lot to bring about change," he said. "I know Phil's talked to you about this. It will be a lot easier to get other people to open shops if we can promise them that you'll be there. You'll bring in the traffic."

"What are you saying?" she asked. "You want *me* to open a store? Me? A store . . . that's so capitalist."

How could anyone who had been running a successful business for twenty years complain about capitalism? "You'd meet a lot of interesting people, Sierra."

"But a store is such a commitment, Matthew, such a restriction of one's freedom. Opening times, closing times. You know me, I'm a free spirit. I can't be tied down."

Matt was suddenly angry. She was a free spirit? Maybe the dead were free to be spirits, but the living had obligations and responsibilities, things that did tie you down. "Ten years ago the School Board asked if you'd come in three times a week and teach an hour of French or German—nobody cared which— and you said you didn't want to be tied down to a full-year contract. Since then, for a whole decade, every single kid at that high school has had to take Spanish because you didn't want to be tied down, and I can't see that you've gone anywhere."

"Hindsight is always twenty-twenty, Matthew." She was looking at him straight on. "And you're making it sound like I didn't have the right to say no. Am I morally obligated to come in and teach simply because the School Board refuses to fire that stupid Spanish teacher and hire someone who can teach more than one language?"

That stupid Spanish teacher was a great basketball coach, and it was true there was no way that the School Board would ever fire him. Matt sighed. He never stayed angry for long. "No, you weren't obligated to, but it would have done a lot of good."

Why did she keep calling him Matthew? No one called him Matthew. He drained his tea, suddenly noticing a clear, clean taste rising up through the sweetness. "I can't figure out what motivates you, Sierra. I know it's not money; that much I do believe about you. But if you really mean what you say about growing and changing, you'll do this. I'm not saying that you owe the town anything, but don't you owe something to yourself? You used to make sense. You were wrong, but you made sense."

"Why are you bringing that up? Are you saying I owe you?'

"I'm not saying anything like that, and anyway, it's not me. It's the town." He was not going to let her personalize this, to make it a Matt-and-Sierra kind of thing. "We'd like you to open a retail establishment and do your best to make a go of it."

"It's been almost twenty-five years. I'd be out of jail by now."

Matt shut his eyes. That had nothing to do with this.

He hadn't wanted to come out here. He knew that the conversation would end up like this. "You wouldn't have gone to jail."

"You might not have been able to stop it."

"I'm the doctor. I sign the death certificates."

It had all been so long ago.

Matt had grown up in Fleur-de-lis, but if things had gone according to plan, he wouldn't have settled there. He wouldn't have gone into a private medical practice. He had been full of ideals; he had wanted to change the world. During the final year of his residency, he had been talking both to the Peace Corps and to Doctors Without Walls, a French organization. His older brother, Phillip, would stay home and take care of the problems in Fleur-de-lis. Matt would save the rest of the world.

And there were problems in Fleur-de-lis. It was the latter part of the 1970s, and family farmers, faced with rising energy costs and nearly punitive interest rates, were losing their land at a pace not seen since the Great Depression. Big agro-businesses, based across the river in Missouri, were buying up Kansas farmland.

The Ravenal family had never been farmers. They had been doctors, lawyers, and businessmen, but there had been Ravenals in Fleur-de-lis since the riverboat had sunk. They cared about the town. So Phillip had taken the County Extension agent job, determined to help the small farmer. With the energy and enthusiam that his older son would bring to the problems of the downtown twenty-five years later, Phillip was trying to negotiate better loans and to set up energy-purchasing co-ops. Everyone liked him. He was outgoing and personable with a pretty wife and two little boys.

Then Matt had gotten a phone call. Phillip, the outgoing, personable Phillip, and Polly, his pretty wife Polly, were dead, killed in the crash of a small airplane.

Matt couldn't imagine the world without his older brother. The sun had gone behind a cloud. The whole town felt that way. No one could believe that Phillip was gone. Phillip had been the town's best hope. He was going to make everything right again.

Matt went home for the funeral, knowing that this was his future now. He was the boys' guardian. He was responsible for a five-year-old and a baby.

"We'll take care of them for as long as you need us to," his parents said immediately.

But he knew that wasn't a permanent solution. When Phillip and Polly had been making out their wills, everyone had said that children shouldn't be raised by grandparents if there were any younger relatives who could do it.

So he finished his residency and returned home to start practicing with old Doc Bailey.

He was twenty-eight. His own friends from high school, the smart kids, were long gone. One was in San Francisco, a road manager for a rock band. Another was in England, studying at the London School of Economics. The rest were in Kansas City, building lives for themselves there. That was what happened in Kansas—too many of the smart, ambitious kids left. The people Matt's age who had stayed in town were the ones who hadn't gone to college, the ones settling down to work the farms, pump gas, and repair cars. By now many were already divorced with eight-, nine-, even ten-year-old kids. They were good people, but Matt had little in common with them.

Of course, south of town were "the hippies"—at least that was what Fleur-de-lis called them. Matt knew they weren't hippies; the day of the hippie had already come and gone. But they had chosen a counterculture lifestyle; they were artists and writers. Well read, alert, and full of laughter, they were interesting people. Matt hungered to know them.

But they had come to Kansas determined not to be Matt Ravenal. Matt had obligations, responsibilities to the boys and his patients. He wore a tie and had a payroll to meet. He was the Establishment.

None of them came to him for health care, even though several of the women were pregnant. He assumed that they were going over to the free clinic in the next county. Time passed, and he saw one of them at the post office. She had a newborn with her.

He could tell that she was proud of her baby. She was gazing at the other people to see if they were looking at the child. They had been, but as soon as she tried to make eye contact, they looked away. After all, she was one of the long-haired hippie freaks.

So he spoke. "That's a sweet-looking baby. Is it a boy or a girl?" The baby's little T-shirt was tie-dyed in shades of red and purple.

"A boy. His name is Freedom."

That was going to be a real hit on the playground when the kid was in third grade. "Is he doing well? Is he an easy baby?"

"He's a dream. I'm convinced that the hospital environment is so hard on babies, all that light and those noises. It's too stressful for them."

Matt had to agree with her. Healthy babies didn't need the harsh lights and humming equipment, but the technology had to be there for the babies who weren't healthy, and you could never know ahead of time which baby was going to be healthy. So the healthy babies had to put up with it for the sake of the sick ones.

"Did you go to the birthing center in Kansas City?" That was the closest alternative facility.

"Oh, no. I had him here. Duke and Nina have set aside a room in their house."

Matt had been stroking the baby's little foot. His hand froze. "You had him at home?" He and Bailey were the only doctors in town, and there was no trained midwife. "Who delivered him?"

"Sierra, of course. Sierra Celandine. She's wonderful. She takes care of us all. She can treat anything. She has these herbs that you've never heard of, and they really do work. You don't know her? You'll have to meet her."

Matt had to force himself to keep his voice level. "I'll have to do that."

"Is this any of my business?" he asked his father when he stopped by that night. The boys were still living with his parents, but Matt visited them twice a day.

"How are you going to feel if something happens to one of the babies or if someone dies from a routine strep throat? Will you feel that you should have made it your business?"

That made it easy.

He went over to his mother's kitchen phone. Fred Hobart owned a lot of the houses these people were renting, and so he called Fred's wife. Mrs. Hobart flipped through her rental agreements. Sierra Celandine had a month-to-month lease on the little tenant house across from Fred's grandparents' place, the one that was rented to that writer Nina Lane.

Matt knew where it was. He kissed little Ned's

sweet-smelling head, gave Phil a sticky high five, and walked home to get his car.

The place was run-down. The front porch must have recently been torn off; the outer walls had pale outlines of the supports that attached it to the house. The door was weathered, and a couple of cinder blocks were serving as front steps.

A girl with long hair and big glasses came around from the back of the house.

"Hi." Her greeting was full of life. "I don't know you, do I?" She was petite and barefoot and wore a flower in her hair.

"I'm Matt Ravenal." And though he always felt like a pompous jerk when he said it, he added, "Dr. Matt Ravenal."

"What kind of doctor?' She spoke teasingly. "Are you a poet with a Ph.D.? Or a psychologist who feels inferior because you aren't a psychiatrist? No, I know. You're the high school principal and you've got one of those night-school Ed.D.'s because you wanted to get your salary up."

In another context he might have enjoyed this. "Actually, I'm an M.D. I have a practice in town."

"Oh," she said. "And you make house calls?" She wagged her finger at him. "I'm telling the A.M.A. on you. They won't like that. They'll revoke your membership."

"Are you Sierra Celandine?"

"That's not what's on my birth certificate, but yes, it's my name."

Matt wasn't sure what point she was trying to make. "I've heard that you are out here practicing medicine without a license."

"Oh, no." She shook her head. "I'm not practicing medicine. You're practicing medicine. I'm healing people."

"But you're attending at births."

"Two gorgeous baby boys." She mocked a Yiddish accent. "The cutest little shmekels you'd ever want to see."

People around here didn't affect Yiddish accents; they hardly knew what they sounded like. "That's not legal."

"What, having a shmekel? I have been completely wrong about this country. What a great place it is, to outlaw penises. What do we get to do with all the suspects?"

"You know what I mean."

"No, I don't." She was suddenly serious. "It's illegal for a woman to give birth at home? You can be *arrested* if you don't go to the hospital? What if the baby comes too fast, and you end up having it in the car on the Kansas Turnpike? Is that illegal?"

"I was referring to your role."

"My role? I'm the woman's friend. Is friendship illegal?"

In truth, Matt was not sure exactly what the law was. It never occurred to him to look it up.

But what had he been expecting? That he would show up and his "I'm Dr. Ravenal" would make her cower?

"Follow me," she ordered and pulled open the door.

The room inside was dim. There wasn't much furniture, but board-and-brick bookshelves covered one wall. She bent down and pushed a plug into a wall socket. An overhead light bulb flicked on.

She took a book off the shelf. "You read German, don't you? Here, look at this."

She thrust it at him. Matt did not read German, but clearly she did. The volume was dog-eared, and she was pointing to a passage highlighted with yellow marker. She held the book open and after a moment, when it was obvious he wasn't going to respond, she flipped it shut.

The paper cover was a table of contents and most of the authors' names had strings of initials following them. This was a medical journal. She was reading medical journals in German.

He knew that the Germans were working to establish whether or not traditional folk medicines had any efficacy that could be clinically proven. He knew almost nothing about the research, but these books of hers represented serious, respectable scholarship. This wasn't witchcraft. If she had absorbed a third of what was on her shelves, she would be very knowledgeable. "Do you have any formal medical training?"

"No. I don't want to know what they teach in American medical schools." She wasn't joking anymore. "I want to learn what they don't teach you there. I want to show people that you can be well without all those wires and testing and invasive techniques."

"And you want to do this from eastern Kansas?" He could hear the sarcasm in his voice.

"Yes, I do. You have Native Americans here, or didn't you know that? I want to study their healing methods."

Matt did know that there were Indians in Kansas. Once a month he drove for two hours to staff a clinic for the people who didn't live on the reservations, and whatever healing methods they had sure weren't doing a very good job of controlling the diabetes and hypertension in that population.

"Okay," he acknowledged, "you may know a lot about some kinds of illness and even basic first aid." He could see an array of Red Cross manuals. "But this childbirth has got to stop."

She bristled and he sensed that she was about to attack. He had already heard all the arguments— *fetal monitors cause more problems than they detect . . . childbirth is natural . . .* But her mocking smile returned. "I don't see how we can stop childbirth. I think a lot of pregnant women would really object to that, to say nothing of the American College of Obstetricians and Gynecologists. Can you imagine what that would do to their incomes?"

He wished she'd be serious. "When things go wrong at a birth, they go wrong fast, and they go wrong nasty."

"Nothing's going to go wrong."

"You don't know that, and the legal consequences for you will be enormous if they do. You aren't assisting at these births as a friend. You know you aren't. You're acting as the midwife, and if something goes wrong, you'll be held criminally liable."

"Nothing's going to go wrong."

"Do you have any idea what a local jury would do to you? You aren't going to get any sympathy."

"I don't want anyone's sympathy. What I'm doing is right. You don't need sympathy when you are right."

There was no reaching her.

There was also no getting her out of his mind. She had been so full of life. He was aging too fast; he had too many responsibilities.

When they would run into each other, she would tease him and flirt with him, and he had to admit that he liked that. If it was hot outside, she would have her hair twisted up and the outline of her breasts would be visible beneath her T-shirt.

He was like a kid with a crush. He went to unusual places at odd times, hoping she'd be there. He never asked her out in any conventional sort of way. What would be the point? They disagreed about too much.

He did keep his eyes open. None of the women in that community was pregnant. But he resolved that as soon as one was, he would speak to her directly. *Do not allow Sierra Celandine to deliver your baby.*

In August, Matt filled out all the kindergartners' school health forms, and in September, he gave the high school football team another round of physicals. He wouldn't sign off on one of the fullbacks; he didn't like the sound of the boy's heart. That wasn't making him any friends. October brought a nasty case of head lice to the second grade. The town had never seen anything like it before. Kids kept getting infected and reinfected. Their mothers were going nuts, and the Laundromat had to extend its hours. November was cold, but everyone seemed in pretty good health.

Then one night in the middle of the month, he heard a pounding on his door. He'd been asleep, but he was out of bed instantly.

The porch light was on, and through the pane in the door he could see her, Sierra. She wasn't wearing a coat. Her ankle-length dress was light-colored and splattered with dark splotches.

It was blood.

He pulled open the door.

"Oh, Matt . . ."

Her voice said it all. She was thin and cold, a wild bird, swooping through the sky, suddenly smashing into a plate-glass window that she hadn't known was there.

Except she wasn't a bird, and she hadn't shattered a window. There was a mother and child.

"Do I need my bag? Is there anything that can be done?" It might well be too late. Both mother and child might already be dead.

"No, they're both stable. Duke called an ambulance. They're on their way to the hospital."

"That's good." The hospital was in the next county. A doctor there would take the call. There was no need for Matt to go. "Come in. It's freezing out here."

She let him lead her inside and close the door. But she didn't sit down.

"What can you tell me?" he asked.

She moved restlessly. "You were right. It was clear that things weren't happening right, but I kept expecting any instant it would suddenly all turn around and be fine. Instead it all kept getting worse. It never let up. And there was no one to help me. There were plenty of people, but none of them would believe me that this was bad—no one else believed that she actually might die. Everyone was just waiting for the commercial because they were all thinking that this was like a TV show. It couldn't be really happening."

"Why didn't you call me?"

"The phone was out. Do you believe that?" She tilted back her head. "Duke and Nina had forgotten to pay the bill. Everyone can be so disorganized around there. I don't have a phone. Finally I got someone to go up the road, and of course that took forever. We heard the ambulance siren when the baby finally slid out. Then no one wanted her to go to the hospital, but I didn't want to be responsible anymore."

"You made the right decision there," he said. "The mother needs to be looked at." This was exactly what he had been trying to avoid. "I hadn't noticed any women who were pregnant. Who was it?"

"It was Nina."

"Oh." Nina Lane did seem to be the center of everything out there, but she was the one the locals never saw. She never came into town.

Sierra needed to talk. She went over and over what had happened.

Even in a hospital, Matt concluded, this birth would have been tricky. At a minimum they would have used forceps. The pain had made Nina panic. But if she had had an epidural, she could at least have listened and helped push.

Matt didn't say, "I told you so," but he also didn't pretend. If anything had gone wrong, he would have blamed Sierra.

She stayed for an hour, telling the story again and again, and then, as abruptly as she had arrived, she left. "I can't stand looking at this blood anymore. I have to change."

Three days later he came home and found her sitting on his front steps. She had three cardboard boxes stacked up next to her.

She stood up. "These are my books." She was speaking without making eye contact. "I was going to burn them. But my grandparents are Jewish. I can't make myself burn a book. So will you do something with them? Give them to the university library or something?"

"Of course I will. The K.U. Med Center will be glad to have them."

Sierra Celandine was out of the healing business.

At work the next week, Matt's nurse showed him a new chart. "Take a look at the name of this baby," she whispered.

Matt peered at the label on the chart. *Lanier, Western Settler*. It took him a moment to figure it out. Western Settler was the baby's first name. "Lanier used to be a local name, didn't it?"

"There is that building downtown. But this is Nina Lane's baby. Apparently Lanier is her real last name. She and the father aren't married."

"That's none of our business," he reminded her.

"But they named the baby after a *boat*."

"That wouldn't have been my first choice," he acknowledged. He took the chart and opened the examining room door, wondering how Nina Lane was faring as a mother.

But Sierra Celandine had brought the baby in. Matt greeted her and began the examination. The baby was a girl and perfectly healthy. She was on formula. That surprised Matt. All that talk about natural childbirth seemed consistent with breast-feeding. But he didn't comment. He talked instead about vaccinations. Sierra was opposed to two of them.

"Certainly vaccines can be refused," he said. "But you can't do it. It needs to be the parents."

"Nina doesn't know anything about the risks of inoculation."

Most new parents didn't. "And the father?"

"Duke?" She paused. "He can be surprisingly conventional sometimes."

But not conventional enough to have married the mother. That might keep him from having certain rights. Once again Matt didn't know enough law to talk to Sierra. "We don't do anything for another month, so you have time to talk to them. Or have them come in next time."

She could tell he was wondering why they weren't here now. She looked away. "Nina's still pretty rattled about how the birth went."

Matt wondered fleetingly about postpartum depression. "Well, try to get one of them in here."

That didn't happen. For the six-week checkup, Sierra once again brought Miss Western Settler.

"Things are hard for Nina right now," she explained. "Duke left."

Matt winced. "It's good that she has you to help."

The baby had gotten over her newborn-squished look. She was rosy and sweet with a few wisps of hair. Matt gave her her first DPT and polio vaccines, and the next thing he heard about any of them was that Nina Lane had committed suicide in New York City.

He went to the funeral. It was an odd affair, held in an abandoned schoolhouse north of town, presided over by a young man in a purple caftan and supervised by a blank-faced Jack Frederickson, the local mortician. He and Matt were the only men in coats and ties.

Sierra had the baby with her, but everyone in the Settlement was making it clear that the two locals weren't welcome, so Matt left without speaking to her.

A week after that, he got a call from a lawyer in California who represented Roy and Violet Lanier, the parents of Nina Lane. Was it true that she had a child? Did Matt know its whereabouts?

Nina's parents hadn't known that she had a baby, and their lawyer acknowledged that they were daunted at the prospect of raising another child. "Nina was quite a handful, but they know their duty."

They knew their duty? This baby girl was going to be raised by people who knew their duty? It was a chilling thought. At least Sierra would love her.

He could stall, but what would be the point? Duke and Nina had not been married. Even if Duke had wanted the child, every judge in this county would give the baby to the grandparents.

That night he drove back out to Sierra's. She had no curtains on her windows, and he could see her lights.

He knocked. She eased the door open, her finger on her lips. Obviously the baby was sleeping. "I'm sorry about Nina," he whispered.

She shrugged. What was there to say?

"I got a call from her parents' lawyer, asking about the baby."

Sierra's eyes flicked toward the bedroom. "Oh."

Had she been thinking that the baby was now hers? Of course she had.

"I told the people in California," he said, "that there was no rush, that the baby was being very well taken care of. But my guess is that she'll be picked up next week."

"Next week?" Sierra sounded blank.

I understand. The baby is your life. You've given up medicine; she's all you have. And you love her. You can't imagine giving her up. "I don't know the exact day, but I will let you know."

He was warning her, giving her a chance to run. *You'll need to go to Canada.* He prayed that she could hear what he could not say. *You can hook up with the draft dodgers there. They'll help.*

It turned out that the Laniers had never flown before, and the prospect of being on a plane, much less with an infant, unsettled them. They were talking about driving out.

"What would make sense is for one of us, someone from Fleur-de-lis, to take the baby there," Matt's mother said. "Then if there seems something strange about Mr. and Mrs. Lanier, we can alert the California authorities."

She would have gone herself, but, of course, she was raising her own grandchildren. So Kate Carruthers, Doc Bailey's daughter, said she would make the trip. Her kids were in high school; they could manage without her for a few days.

Matt didn't say anything. He didn't think that the trip would need to be made.

He was wrong. Two days before Kate was scheduled to leave, he found a note on his doormat.

Dear Matt,

With all my heart I believe that Western Settler would be better off with me than with Nina's parents. But what right do I have to be so sure of myself? I was sure of myself the night she was born, and I was wrong then.

So tell Mrs. Carruthers that she will be ready.

Sierra

Time passed. Matt rarely saw Sierra, and as the people from the Settlement began drifting away from town, he assumed that she would leave as well. But then every few months he would see her. She had lost too much weight and her color was bad.

He would speak to her. She was using her herbs to make soaps and lotions, she said. Was she trying to sell them? he asked. She supposed she would have to someday, she answered.

She gave him a little basket of products for his mother. Mrs. Ravenal was enchanted with their fragrant richness. One of her friends' grown daughter belonged to the Junior League in Kansas City. Samples of the products reached her circle, and Celandine Gardens was born.

Sierra began to need things from town—packing tape, boxes, the UPS truck, a construction crew to put up a hothouse, teens to work in the field. She started to look healthy again, but she sounded like a distorted version of her old self. Instead of being passionate and determined, she now was just weird.

Doc Bailey retired, and Matt took over the practice completely. He was in Topeka, talking to a Senate committee about health-care issues, when he met Carolyn Shelby, daughter of the former governor. She was a wonderful woman, compassionate and practical, so committed to Kansas that she would never have lived anywhere else.

The responsibility of Matt's two nephews didn't daunt her. Ned and Phil came to live with them as soon as they were married. They had then had the three girls of their own, and despite all the normal exasperations of family life, things had really been okay.

Carolyn was his partner, his companion, his helpmate. But Matt always had a feeling that if they had had the chance, Sierra would have been the love of his life.

∞ *Chapter 4* ∞

They were farms, nothing more, nothing less. Even before checking into Fleur-de-lis's only motel on the last Friday in July, Tess had followed Duke Nathan's directions to her grandparents' childhood homes. The Swenson place was inhabited; white bed sheets flapped on the clothesline and a brownish dog lay under a locust tree. The fields on the Lanier farm were still under cultivation, but all that remained of the homestead was the concrete slab over the well and the foundations of the house and the barn.

Tess saw them and she felt nothing. She could have been anywhere. If this was what she had come to Kansas to find, the trip hadn't been worth it.

It wouldn't have been this way for her mother. Her mother would have felt something. History wasn't a single straight line for Nina Lane. Time was like a bolt of fabric folded over and over on itself with only the thinnest space dividing the past and the present. Sometimes the two could blur, fusing together as if different moments were happening at once. The past could erupt into the present with dark violence, or it could seep through with warmth, giving the present a richness and a glow.

But that was Nina Lane. Tess was not Nina Lane. She was going to be Miss Kitty.

During the Nina Lane Annual Birthday Celebration, the Fleur-de-lis Best Western had been full, and Tess had had to stay across the river in Missouri, but at the end of July, there were plenty of rooms.

The motel clerk had never heard of the Prairie Bell school. "But if you hold on, I'll call my aunt. She might know."

The aunt did indeed know. Not surprisingly, the school was north of town, a half mile or so from the old Lanier place—after all, it was where Tess's grandfather had gone to school. Ned—whoever he was, both the desk clerk and his aunt spoke as if Tess would know—was using it for storage.

It was after five when Tess arrived at the schoolhouse. A dusty black pickup was parked under a tree, and someone was standing at the edge of the road, his arms folded. He was staring across the road at a corn crop.

It was the man she had spoken to during the Birthday Celebration, the rumpled one whose eyebrows were darker than his hair, who had given her directions to the parking gate.

She pulled her car over to the side of the road and got out.

He came over to greet her. "Can I—" He paused. "Oh, wait a minute, you were at the Birthday Celebration. What are you doing here? I thought you lived in California."

He remembered her. How nice. "I do, but I'm back again."

"That's great. I certainly didn't expect to see you again. What a nice surprise." He put out his hand. "I'm Ned Ravenal."

His grip was firm and warm. He must be the Ned who was storing stuff at the schoolhouse. Then it all made sense to Tess. He was the local historian in charge of the riverboat excavation.

"I'm Tess Lanier."

"Lanier . . . that's a local name. At least it used to be."

"My grandparents were born around here, but I grew up in California."

"So is that why you came back, to look up family history?"

"Not in any serious way, no." Tess wasn't going to talk to anyone about her plans just yet. She would hold her cards close to her chest. Surely that was what Miss Kitty would want her to do. "I just wanted to see a few places. This is the Prairie Bell school, isn't it? I think my grandfather went here for first and second grades."

"He sure might have. Do you want to come in and look around? I've got some stuff inside, but you're welcome to snoop to your heart's content."

Tess's ideas about country schools were from Laura Ingalls Wilder's *Little House* books. She envisioned them as narrow shanties with the wind whistling through the unfinished pine walls, but this gray stucco building was solid and prosperous-looking.

Inside the double doors was a foyer that had been used as a coat room. Benches were attached low to the wall and coat hooks were arrayed above. A half flight of stairs led up to the classroom. The stairs were wide, with railings on either side and a third railing running down the center. Tess could imagine children on these stairs, pushing and jostling each other. A timid child might have clung to one of the railings. She would have been such a child, afraid of the big boys and their rough noise.

The classroom itself was big and light with a fifteen-foot ceiling. The front wall was still covered with blackboards, and there were windows on the side walls. The ones on the left looked across the road and the cornfield to the trees at the river's edge. Scars on the floor showed where the desks had been bolted down. They had been the kind where the seat to one desk had been attached to the desk behind it. Tess had seen such desks in antiques shops. They had slanting lift-up tops with little pots for ink. Filling the inkwells must have been the responsibility of the most careful pupil, probably a girl, someone like herself. Tess could have filled inkwells without ruining her dress. Even if the dress had been made of calico from a feed company, she wouldn't have wanted to get ink on it.

Tess felt a funny tickle in the back of her throat. She wondered if she was allergic to something, dust or pollen, perhaps.

Suddenly the room came to life. It was full of sounds. Tess was surrounded by sounds, shoes scuffing across a wood floor and desk lids closing with muffled bangs, children whispering, a pencil being sharpened, a bell—

"Are you okay?" She heard a voice coming from far off.

It was the man—what was his name? Ned Ravenal.

"Oh, of course," she said quickly. "I'm fine." She wondered what had just happened. "I was looking out the window. I don't know how much I would have learned if my school had had a view like that." The fields were so open and green.

"The kids were all farm kids; they were used to seeing fields. In fact, some of them were probably sick to death of fields and were thrilled to be inside, sitting down, reading."

She wondered about her grandfather. He must have been one of those kids who had loved school.

The space was currently being used as an office. A sleek-looking computer sat on a battered desk. A long table held a roll of blueprints. There were empty shelves made of raw wood and a number of boxes. One was open. It was full of the brochures describing the excavation of the *Western Settler*.

Tess felt the tickle again, the tickle in the back of her throat. Her vision blurred. The room was unfurnished, crowded with people, oddly dressed in robe-like garments of muddy turquoise and muted yellow. There was guitar music and someone in purple . . .

Tess cleared her throat. This was strange. She spoke quickly. She didn't like things that were strange. "So are you spearheading this riverboat project?"

"I hope we don't get to the point of needing spears, but if we do, I guess I will be the one throwing them." He explained that he had originally planned to start as soon as the sweet corn had been harvested, but was now waiting for a groundbreaking ceremony on Labor Day. "I'll be chomping at the bit, but it's in the best interests of the town to have some whoopla." Then he grew a little hesitant, jamming his hands in his pockets and looking out the window as he spoke. "Listen, I don't want to sound unfriendly here, but the legal position is clear. All the artifacts are ours. If something can definitely be traced to a particular family and it doesn't have unique historical interest, we will consider passing it along, but I'm not making any promises."

"That makes sense," Tess said politely, then realized that she had just told a complete lie. "Actually, it doesn't, at least not to me. I have no idea what you are talking about."

He tilted his head, his dark eyebrows pulling close together. "You're not interested in your family's stuff?"

"I can't imagine that my family had much stuff. That's why they had to leave. They were broke, the Dust Bowl and all."

He waved his hand, dismissing everything she knew of her family's history. "No, not those people. I'm talking about the ones on the riverboat. We probably won't be able to identify the owners of most of the personal belongings, but the Laniers had so much more money than anyone else. If we find rich-people stuff, it was probably theirs."

"Whose? What are you talking about? There were Laniers on the riverboat?"

He drew back. "You didn't know that?"

"No." Tess had never heard anything about this. The banks taking away the farms, she knew about that. Her grandparents each having had an uncle killed in World War I, she had heard about them. But

Laniers being on the riverboat? Her family ties to Kansas were even stronger than she had realized.

"Their names were Louis and Eveline," Ned was saying. "He was the younger son of a reasonably important New Orleans family. They had a seventeen-year-old daughter named Marie with them, and Eveline was pregnant. Six months after the wreck, Herbert was born. He was the one who built the Lanier Building."

Tess wondered if Nina Lane had known this. Of course she had. Everyone said she had been obsessed by the riverboat.

So why hadn't Tess's grandparents told her? *Grandpa, you told me the story of every* Gunsmoke *episode. Why didn't you tell me our own story?*

Were you afraid that I would become obsessed too?

"Apparently they were going to spend the summer in the St. Louis area," Ned continued. "I don't know what made them decide to go West, and I doubt that we'll find out. No paper on board—no books, diaries, or correspondence—will have survived. But the Laniers certainly were luckier than everyone else. The boat sank in less than five minutes. People only had what they had on their backs, but Eveline Lanier had three hundred dollars in gold coins sewn into the hem of her petticoat."

"Three hundred dollars . . . that was a lot then, wasn't it?" Tess had never heard of any Laniers having money.

"It certainly was. It was more than enough to have gotten them back to New Orleans, but they stayed on and used the money to build a decent house and get a sawmill started. Years later she wrote an account of the wreck. I suppose you haven't read it or you'd have known about your family. But I'll make a copy of it for you."

"That would be nice." This was all so surprising. "I would like to read it."

"Don't be so sure," he said bluntly. "It's so full of high-minded, insincere, Victorian moralizing that you want to choke her, and she's an incredible snob, even though she keeps claiming that she isn't. Have you seen the Lanier Building yet?"

"That was my next stop. Will it be easy to find?"

"Yes. I'm heading into town, so will you let me show it to you? Can I give you a ride, or would you like to follow me in your car?"

"I'll take my car."

The road in front of the schoolhouse wasn't paved, and small clouds of dust rose from his rear wheels, but in a moment they were on the county blacktop and then, after another two miles, they were in town.

Main Street ran perpendicular to the river. The street was wide, with angled parking on either side. The new Beaux Arts-style wrought-iron streetlights that Tess had read about on the town's Web site gave the commercial district a slightly Parisian air.

The left signal light on the rear of Ned's pickup flicked on in the middle of the last block; he was obviously about to turn into a parking space. Tess did likewise.

"I guess I should have warned you," he said after they got out of their vehicles. "The place is a little run-down."

That was not an exaggeration. Tess looked up at the building that one of her ancestors had built and named after himself. Made of rough-hewn blocks of limestone with an entranceway recessed into the façade, it had obviously been quite grand once. It had four tall, arched windows and the entry recess was a generous five-sided niche. The floor of the niche was covered with tiny hexagonal tiles. Black tiles against a white background formed the words "Lanier Building," and the stone above the entranceway was also carved with those words.

The problem was that at some point someone had attempted to paint the building teal, but the stone was rough and porous. It hadn't taken the paint well at all.

"You have to understand. We did our time as the Haight-Ashbury of eastern Kansas, and apparently back then, someone thought that teal paint on top of limestone was a good idea."

"It wasn't," Tess said simply.

"I have to agree with you there. Do you want to go in? The Lutherans have been storing their extra tables here because of the trouble they've been having with water in their basement, and since I keep needing to borrow more and more tables for the museum, they gave me a key."

What was he talking about? What Lutherans? What basement? If Tess had been in his shoes, she would have just said, *I have a key. Do you want to go in?* "Yes, I'd like that."

He held open the door for her. It was a big space, empty and dusty, with a flimsy partition running down the middle. The Lutherans' long tables were folded and leaning up against one of the outer walls.

The partition probably wouldn't have stood up to their weight.

"It's good-sized," he said, "bigger than anyone needs now."

"But I hear you're getting a number of new businesses."

"It's pretty incredible . . . although I sure hope we haven't been selling people a bill of goods about how much attention the boat is going to draw. I know that I'd drive a couple hours to check out something like this, but then, I'm the guy who is digging it up, so I'm probably not a great reference point."

Tess noticed that she was smiling. *I like him.* The thought was clean and simple. He was a friendly, interesting person. She could see that if he ever really got started talking about the riverboat, he might never shut up—there were parts of his brochure that had been pretty boring—but he seemed to know that about himself. "You mentioned needing tables for a museum. Will that be for the things you find on the boat and are refusing to give back to their original owners?"

"Absolutely. In fact—"

A shaft of light shot across the floor, interrupting him. The door had opened. "Ned?" It was a man's voice. "Are you here? I saw your truck. Are you stealing more tables?"

"This is my brother, Phil," Ned told Tess. "Come meet him. He's the one to blame for all the development outside."

Phil Ravenal was taller than his brother. His face was narrower and his hair a richer, more golden color. He was wearing crisp gray trousers and a white business shirt. The sleeves of the shirt were rolled up, and the collar was open. The fit of his clothes appeared better than the fit of Ned's, in part, no doubt, because Phil's posture was better. Ned introduced them.

"Lanier?" Phil touched Tess's arm with his left hand as he shook her right. "You must be one of us."

One of us. Tess had never, not once, heard anyone use that phrase to describe her. She had always been the different one, the one raised by grandparents.

Phil Ravenal was handsome. There was no other word for it. His features were even, his cheekbones were strong, and his jaw was firm. It might have taken her twenty minutes to realize that she liked Ned, but with Phil . . . her reaction was immediate. He was an extremely personable man.

"So Ned has been telling me," she said. "I didn't know I had family on the riverboat. It's very exciting."

And if the family history was exciting, what about this pair of brothers? She couldn't help finding them interesting too. She glanced first at Phil's left hand, then at Ned's. Neither one of them was wearing a ring. Was it possible that both were single?

"Don't get too excited," Ned cautioned her; presumably he was talking about the riverboat. "Your people were cabin passengers—that's like first-class. They had staterooms on the upper deck, and Eveline explicitly says that all her jewelry and such were in her cabin. The boat's upper structures would have been broken up and carried away by the current. There's not a prayer that we'll find any of that."

"How can I be disappointed? I've only known about these people for thirty minutes."

"Then what does bring you to town?" Phil asked. "Do you have three hundred dollars sewn into your petticoat? Are you here to buy the Lanier Building and restore your family name to its rightful place in Fleur-de-lis?"

Tess didn't answer.

The men stiffened at the same instant. Phil took a step forward.

Tess cursed herself. She should have been paying more attention. She shouldn't have been thinking about the way the hair on Phil's forearms glinted in the sunlight slanting through the open door. Now nothing she could say would rid them of the impression that she was interested in buying the Lanier Building. Ned looked curious; Phil was intent and alert.

"Let us show you around town," Phil said. His voice was suddenly deeper. He had something to sell her. "Some interesting things are happening." He touched her arm, leading her outside.

Immediately across the street from the Lanier Building was another limestone building, the former courthouse, now the Riverboat Museum. "How about this for American optimism?" Phil joked lightly. "Ned opened the museum even before he's started to dig."

"*Ned* opened it?" Ned queried. "That's not exactly how Ned recalls it."

"What do you have in it?" Tess asked.

"An exceptionally professional display of the town's

history," Ned answered, "or at least as professional as I could make it in the two weeks *he*"—Ned jabbed his brother in the side with his elbow—"gave me to slap it together. Next week the local quilters are putting on a show. We're letting anyone use the space."

Tess would have liked to see the quilt show. She was glad to hear that there were women in town who sewed. She wondered how good the local fabric stores were.

The courthouse building itself looked very good. The yellowy-gray stone seemed fresh; the lawn was green and edged, the foundation bushes trimmed, the front walk replaced. The Lanier Building could be made to look like this.

"Once a year we get more than six thousand out-of-towners here for the Nina Lane Birthday Celebration," Phil was saying. "Since we know how to handle those crowds, we're thinking of adding a Renaissance Fair and, because of the historical connection to New Orleans, some kind of Mardi Gras festivity—although our weather and our liquor laws mean that it would be somewhat different from the real thing."

"That's a bit of an understatement," Ned added.

They were walking down Main Street. The stores were closed, but Tess could see that the new ones were geared to the tourist trade. She halted in front of one. Celandine Gardens.

"Do you know Sierra's products?" Phil asked. "She's going to open in time for Ned's groundbreaking, and she's making one special batch of soap that she'll only sell that weekend. That alone will bring people into town. Do you want to see her shop?"

Phil tried the door. It was locked. "There's probably a key around here somewhere." He reached overhead and was feeling along the top of the lintel.

"No, no," Tess protested. "I don't want to go in if she's not there."

She had to speak to Sierra Celandine. She knew that, but she had no idea what she would say. *Thank you for changing my diapers . . . I'm sorry I was abrupt with you . . . what do you want from me?* She didn't want to compound the awkwardness by trespassing.

A candy shop was already open, and a new candle-and-stationery store would also be opening at the groundbreaking. Two small antiques shops were trying to upgrade. A third of the storefronts were vacant, but Phil treated that like good news. Last January it had been half.

"We've really been pushing people," Phil said. "We need to have as many businesses as possible open by Labor Day. We need to make a great first impression. Some people think we're rushing, but if we try to build slowly, we'll miss the Christmas shopping season."

"I don't see a fabric store," Tess said. Fabric stores were important to her. "Is it in another part of town?"

"There isn't another part of town," Ned said.

"Or a fabric store," Phil added. "We don't have one."

They were at the end of Main Street. Facing one of the side streets, but visible from Main, was a big, white, beautifully restored Victorian house set in the middle of a green lawn and surrounded by a wrought-iron railing. It was a restaurant, The Cypress Princess, and its parking lot looked to be full.

"The *Cypress Princess* was the steamboat the *Western Settler*'s passengers took up from New Orleans," Phil explained. "That's why Wyatt and Gabe used that name. You're probably wondering how such a small town can support a fine-dining restaurant—"

It had never occurred to Tess to wonder about that.

"—and the answer is that we don't. But for years this was the only place in western Missouri or eastern Kansas to get authentic Cajun and Creole cooking. Wyatt is from New Orleans, and Gabe's not local either. They came to town with those people who hung out with Nina Lane. The two of them and Sierra are the only ones left."

"If you get fine-diners from out of town on Friday and Saturday nights, shouldn't the shops be open then too?" Tess asked.

"We're working on that." Phil glanced at his watch. "Tess, I have to apologize, but I must run. Ned, why don't you go see if Wyatt and Gabe can give the two of you a table for dinner? It's still early. They might have space." He looked at Tess. "You're at the Best Western? Will you be here for the rest of the weekend? I know our mother would love to have you to the house for dinner, but I need to touch base with her. Can I get back to you?"

Tess blinked. Sometimes during her childhood when people had been rude or unfriendly, Grandma's lips would tighten and Tess would know that she was thinking that things had been different in Kansas. This must be what she had meant. *One of us.* Tess was *one of us.* "I don't want anyone to go to any trouble."

"Then you shouldn't have come to this town," Ned said. He had a more direct, down-to-earth style of speech than his brother. "That's what we do here, go to trouble for other people, and you have to consider what kind of trouble Phil will be in if he *doesn't* invite you. Mom will kill him. So she either makes dinner for you or goes to prison for the rest of her natural life."

"He's not far off," Phil said and lifted a hand in farewell, promising to leave a message for Tess at the motel. Then he set off down the street. Tess glanced at Ned.

"I'm game for this if you are," he said.

His wording might not be gallant, but the good will behind his invitation was unquestionable. "Am I dressed up enough for this place?" She was still wearing the ankle-length linen skirt that she had traveled in.

'You're fine. Nobody around here dresses up anymore."

There were people waiting on the restaurant's front porch, and the host threw his hands up when he saw them. "Ned, please, I don't have a thing."

Ned seemed to have expected that. "It's August, Wyatt. What business do you have being so successful in August?"

"We can't help it," the host said. "And it won't be August for another week."

Ned laughed and directed Tess back out the door, careful not to touch her.

"We'll go pick up sandwiches at Kmart," he said,

"and eat in the park. That's not as gruesome as it sounds." He started giving her directions.

The directions weren't complicated, but she held up her hand, stopping him. "You can drive. I'll ride with you." She would be safe with him. She was *one of us*.

Twenty minutes later they were unwrapping sandwiches at a green picnic table near a nice little playground. There was no one else around. "Nobody's here in the evening," Ned said. "The high school kids go outside the city limits to drink, and it's a little early for that . . . although in August, who knows when they start?"

Why did he keep thinking that it was August? Probably because he wished it were September so he could break ground on his excavation. "I don't want to hear that," Tess said. "This is such a pretty town. I want it to be perfect. I don't want to hear that the high school kids drink."

"Well, they do. Some of them do it a lot."

She made a face at him. "I'm curious about you and your brother. You grew up around here?"

"We did. He's the older, and—" He broke off. "Why are you nodding your head? Is it that obvious?"

Tess hadn't realized that she had reacted. "He took over the minute he walked in, and you let him. He's so obviously the older that I'm surprised he didn't give you money to take me to dinner."

Ned looked chagrined. "He wouldn't do that. Neither one of us is making a dime at the moment."

Her roommates had occasionally allied themselves with men who didn't bother with gainful employment, but those men had never admitted it as immediately as Ned just had. "That's such an attractive feature in a man."

"It is, isn't it?" He had a quick, wry smile. "Fortunately, we don't have to make money. We have some from our parents. We can't do this forever, but we'll be okay for a year or two."

"So you're freeloaders? That's even more attractive."

"Actually, we're orphans. We get the pity vote."

"Orphans?" Tess frowned. "Then I'm confused. I thought your mother was going to invite me to dinner."

"It's more complicated than that."

He explained how his parents had died when he and Phil were young. They'd lived with their grandparents until their uncle had married. "And when we moved in with Dr. Matt and Carolyn, we started calling them Mom and Dad, even though technically they are our aunt and uncle. Our three younger sisters are really our cousins, but they abuse us like sisters. Anyway, when we say 'our parents,' we usually mean Phillip and Polly. But when we say 'our folks' or 'Mom and Dad,' it's Matt and Carolyn, so either you have to pay incredibly close attention or not bother at all. I would recommend the latter."

Tess noticed the parallels between his story and her own, the absent parents, the grandparents, the money. But there had been no Matt and Carolyn for her.

She folded up her sandwich wrapper and finished the last of her drink. "You've certainly rearranged your evening for me. It was nice of you. I do appreciate it."

"The pleasure was mine, believe me." He wadded

their trash into the Kmart bag. He looked at the bag, turning it around in his hand. "You're Nina Lane's daughter, aren't you?"

Tess felt her mouth grow dry. A man had asked her that once before.

But Gordon, her college boyfriend, had wanted her to be more than Nina Lane's daughter. He had wanted her to be Nina Lane.

"How did you know?"

"Your name. I knew that she was a Lanier. I also knew that she had named the baby after the boat, and 'Tess' seemed like a reasonable variation of that. You said almost nothing about yourself; that was the big tip-off."

"I didn't mean to be mysterious."

"Well, you have been. I mean, it's not every Friday in August that women who look like you show up in town. Being Nina Lane's daughter not only explains why you are here, but it also explains why you're being so mysterious about it."

"I don't have anything to say about her," Tess said. "I don't remember her at all, and my grandparents never talked about her. Maybe I am a private person, but I am not mysterious."

"You're private?" He was surprised. "You don't seem like you would be."

"I'm not shy, and I like other people a great deal. But neither of those is inconsistent with being private, with not needing to share everything with everyone." *Or never having had anyone to share everything with.*

"I suppose not," he agreed. "But privacy's not a big concept around here. Are you really thinking about moving here? Have you ever lived in a small town?"

Tess shook her head. "But it's not like I take great advantage of the cultural resources of where I do live. Traffic and parking are so bad that Kansas City is as easy a trip from here as downtown L.A. is from where I live."

"That may be true, but that's not what I meant. You talked about privacy— our lives are very public here. You need to account for everything you do. Everything needs an explanation."

"I did notice that you had to tell me about the problems the Lutherans are having with the basement of their church in order to explain why you had the Lanier Building key."

"I did?" He didn't remember. "See, it's so automatic, we don't even notice that we're doing it. And the other thing is that it's very easy to be sentimental about small towns, about how friendly and hospitable we are. And we are, but there's a cost to all that friendliness. Everyone is so afraid of conflict that we avoid any confrontation that smells of friction. We make nice all the time. People are so used to stifling their thoughts and their preferences in the name of avoiding conflict that no one knows how to be direct. It hits the women especially hard, and I think a lot of them seethe way down inside."

"Until someone explodes," Tess said, "and it's all dreadful and messy for a little while, but then just gets glossed over without being fixed."

He looked surprised.

"And the one or two people who do pride themselves on 'speaking their minds,' " she continued, "actually only speak the negative things. They manage to repress any hint that they admire or approve of something."

"I thought you said you hadn't lived in a small town."

"I work in a retirement home," she explained. "It has its own little culture."

"Then maybe you'll do all right here, and I should leave you to your fate." He stood up. "But let me warn you about my brother. He's great, and he's usually always right."

"That's a warning?"

"Sure. If he weren't great and right, he wouldn't be dangerous, would he?"

In the World-According-to-Ned-Ravenal, Tess should not have told Sierra that she wanted to be alone at the Birthday Celebration. Her remark was overly direct. It violated the principle of unceasing gregariousness and sociability. It might have Hurt Someone's Feelings—obviously the greatest of all sins.

Tess had stayed out of the conflicts and embarrassments that Willow Place's residents sometimes deliberately, sometimes inadvertently, inflicted on each other. If she moved here, she was also going to stay out of Fleur-de-lis's similar messes. Had Sierra been the complete stranger that Tess had thought her to be, she would have not regretted her remark in the least. But Sierra was not a stranger, and Tess owed her something. She didn't know what that something was, but it was there.

Shortly after ten on Saturday morning, Tess parked in front of the Celandine Gardens shop. The Kmart lot had been nearly full, but there were very few cars downtown.

The door to Sierra's place was open, held ajar by a brick. Tess rapped lightly on the doorframe to announce herself, then stepped inside.

It was going to be a pretty shop. The walls were already painted, a semigloss lacquer two or three shades darker than the celadon green Sierra packaged her products in. Three fabrics were draped across a round fiberboard table. Obviously Sierra was selecting a tablecloth. All three had a Provençal air; they were golden yellow and cobalt blue. But the large print, while the most appealing on its own, would draw a person's eye away from the products. One of the smaller prints had too much blue and not enough yellow. It had to be the third. It seemed like an easy decision to Tess.

Sierra was fitting brass-finished shelf braces into brackets that had been installed on the wall. She glanced over her shoulder at the sound of Tess's entering. "Oh," she said. She was surprised. "It's you."

Tess moved farther inside. "I'm not quite sure what to say." That wasn't being indirect or overly nice. It was the truth. "When I saw you in May, I didn't know who you were."

"I'm not like you." Sierra's words came out in a rush. "I'm not one for hiding how I feel. Some people can't handle that. But I'm not going to change. This is who I am."

Tess wasn't aware that she was asking anyone to

change. "I really do appreciate your calling Duke. He came and saw me." Sierra would think that Duke was her father. "I liked him."

"Honesty is the key to an authentic inner life. Without openness there can be no nurturing wholeness."

What did that have to do with anything Tess had said? *You're not being honest. You're hurt that I didn't like you immediately. You're talking about openness, and you aren't making eye contact. You're angry and you won't admit it.* "I want to apologize because I know I must have seemed rude."

Sierra turned away and started fitting another bracket into its slots. "I don't think people should apologize for what they have done. People need to celebrate their mistakes. You should accept your errors and integrate them into the fabric of your being. Apologies are shields that keep you from reuniting your spiritual fragments."

What? *Apologies are shields* . . . That made no sense to Tess, none at all. Maybe if she saw it written down, she could sort it out, but her best guess now was that whatever it meant, her grandmother wouldn't have agreed. Violet Lanier had believed in apologies. "All right."

"I don't know why you're here," Sierra continued. "But you need to know that I believe in living in the moment. The past is not a goddess to whom we must pay tribute."

What on earth was she talking about? Tess had occasionally helped out in Willow Place's Alzheimer's unit. Her standards for other people making sense were pretty low.

"To valorize that time"—Sierra was still speaking—

"as something magical implies that other moments are not, and we should honor all time as sacred."

Now Tess got it. Sierra didn't want to answer questions about Nina Lane. That was fine. Tess had only one question for Sierra—*What is wrong with you?* "I don't expect that kind of conversation at all."

"For your sake, I hope that's true. But only you can evaluate the clarity of your expectations." Sierra pointedly turned and started looking at her fabric samples again.

Last night Ned had warned Tess about small-town life, how hard it was to be honest. Now Sierra was saying that she was secretive, inauthentic, and fragmented. It sounded like she was going to fit right in.

Tess got in her car and drove out of town. She was glad to see that Ned's truck wasn't at the schoolhouse. She was looking forward to seeing both him and his brother again, but she didn't want an audience for what she was about to do.

She stood in front of the solid, square building. If she were a young boy wanting to brand the building with his initials, where would she do it? The parents would be back at the farm, tying mattresses to the top of the car. It would have been summer; the teacher wouldn't have been at the school, but there might have been people on the road from whom the boy would need to hide.

Jutting out from the side of the building farthest from the road was a cellar door that projected beyond the foundation and slanted down to ground level, the kind that Auntie Em had struggled to open during the tornado in the *Wizard of Oz* movie. A child crouching behind the base of the door wouldn't be seen.

Tess went around to the back side of the cellar stairs. A cluster of forsythia bushes hid the foundation. Springtime's yellow blossoms had come and gone, but the willowy branches were lush with narrow green leaves. If there had been bushes here in 1937, they would have been dried and twiggy. The earth would have cracked and shrunk away from the building.

Tess lifted the forsythia. Would the boy have knelt down or stood? She liked to think of him as remaining standing, holding up to a little bit of pride. She ran her hands over the stucco. Her fingertips rasped against the grainy material.

But it was low on the wall that she felt the pattern of lines. She blew the dust away. R.H.L. Her grandfather's initials.

I came back, Grandpa. And everything's green. You don't remember Kansas this way, but your parents must have told you how green it can be. The sunflowers are higher than the fence posts, and I'm here.

Hobbing, as Fleur-de-lis was then called, was little other than a cluster of shacks at a river landing with but two families of respectable character. Yet all rallied to provide us with shelter and garments. Although the Western character often comes with an unrefined surface, it has an open heart and generous hands.

News of our catastrophe was spread by passing boats. The Gaithers family, the St. Etiennes, and many of the deck passengers elected to continue their voyage on other west-bound steamers. One such boat was persuaded to open its cargo hold and sell us the nails, hinges, doorknobs, frying pans, water buckets, boots, and cloth required by those of us who had decided to stay where Fate had landed us. The two Mr. Ravenals negotiated these purchases for us.

Our own family party had a tolerable dwelling within a very short time, and all the *Western Settler* passengers were snugly housed by winter.

We kept to ourselves that fall, but our first Christmas in our new settlement was not unhappy. By our second winter we had renamed the town and had established a school and a literary society. By the following summer, Mr. Troyes, an acquaintance of ours from New Orleans, arrived to start a newspaper.

The war years visited most grievous afflictions on our connections in New Orleans. When travel on the Mississippi became safe again, we welcomed friends and family eager to start life over in the West. Although often destitute, many were individuals of education and taste, and Fleur-de-lis became a town of no small degree of sophistication.

Mrs. Louis Lanier (Eveline Roget),
The Wreck of the Western Settler,
privately printed, 1879

∽ *Chapter 5* ∽

When they had married, Dr. Matt and Carolyn moved into one of the old Victorian houses on the bluff overlooking the river, and that was where Ned Ravenal had done most of his growing up. He was there on Saturday evening, sitting in the dining room. The room faced west, and the light from the setting sun slanted in through the lace undercurtains Carolyn had in the windows, making pretty patterns on Tess Lanier's cheeks and arms.

Ned didn't see much resemblance between her and the picture of Nina Lane. Nina had had a modern crispness to her face, and she had always looked drawn, her eyes alert but wary. Tess had a more exotic face, her lips soft and full, her chin rather narrow. Her coloring was rose and gold. When he and Phil had run into her on Friday, her hair had been clipped back with tendrils escaping at ears and temples, hinting at an unruly wildness. When she had come to his parents' house for dinner tonight, she had brushed it out, but while loose around her shoulders, it wasn't wild. She clearly had it under control.

He suspected that she had most things under control. No wonder she and Phil were getting along so well.

Dinner was over, and Phil was talking to her about investing in Fleur-de-lis's future. He had demographic studies to show her and prenegotiated insurance packages to explain to her. As a new member of the Chamber of Commerce, she would have access to discounted advertising and would be able to use the Chamber's copier, fax, and bulk-mailing services. She would get help with "workforce development," and she would receive business-counseling services. Phil had even gotten a set of plans for the Lanier Building with a rough outline of the kind of work that would need to be done. But, he had told her quickly, if she made improvements to the building and those improvements resulted in a higher assessed value, she would be eligible for a refund on the additional taxes, thanks to the Neighborhood Revitalization Act.

This was Phil being Phil—poised, organized, likable, and prepared, magazine-ad handsome and good at cocktail-party conversation. Ned himself was none of those things, especially the cocktail-party business, but even as he sat there, watching Tess Lanier being so interested in everything Phil was saying, he would not have been Phil for the world.

Of course, he hadn't felt that way as a kid. He had seen the expression on teachers' faces too many times, and sometimes they had even said the words— *Why can't you be more like Phil?*

Phil had played team sports and had belonged to clubs. He had stayed out of trouble and had gotten perfect grades. Ned, on the other hand, had been more solitary and more adventurous, a Tom Sawyer of a kid, living for dark caves and longing for buried treasure. The earth existed to be dug up, tunneled into, and burrowed under. And if that wasn't enough, there was the river, the broad, muddy Missouri. Swollen by the spring rains, it would surge down from South Dakota and through Nebraska, leaving all kinds of grand debris clogging the riverbank—beer cans, broken chairs, dog leashes, safety-orange hunting vests, all waiting to be fished through. How could any right-thinking ten-year-old resist that?

Ned's grandfather liked old license plates and rusty fishing lures every bit as much as Ned did. "What we really need to do," Grandfather used to say after a long Sunday afternoon spent on the riverbank, "is to dig up Farmer Martin's cornfield. They say the *Western Settler*'s down there."

Grandfather had told him how they really did have buried treasure right here in Fleur-de-lis. A boat with a steam engine and paddle wheels and all kinds of other great stuff had sunk here, *right here*. Grandfather told him how everything on deck had cascaded into the water—the boxes, the barrels, the stools people had been sitting on—and how the passengers had all been screaming, clinging to the deck railings as the water rose. A little boy was the first in the water, and a very brave man jumped in to save him.

"Were you the little boy?" Ned had asked the first time he heard that part of the story.

Grandfather had laughed. "Oh, no. Even I am not that old. It was my great-grandfather who was on the boat. He and his brother were going to Nebraska to open up a store. They had boxes and barrels full of things they were going to sell to the pioneers, and all of it went down with the boat."

"Was our great-grandfather the very brave man?"

"No." Grandfather had smiled. "And he was your great-great-*great*-grandfather. No, the very brave man was a Negro slave, and that's the best story of all."

There had been two slaves on the boat, a man and his wife; they belonged to one of the New Orleans families. They did survive the wreck. People saw the man in the water, helping people to shore, and the woman was on the riverbank, quieting the children. "It might have been the first time some of those people had ever been touched by a black person."

But by nightfall, when all the passengers had gathered in the little town that was now Fleur-de-lis, the two slaves were gone. They had escaped. "They landed on the Kansas side of the river. If they had been on the Missouri side, they might not have dared to run away, but in Kansas there would have been people who would help them."

Ned knew about that. It was one thing you always learned in school, how Kansas had been settled by abolitionists from New England, people who didn't believe in slavery. You learned to be proud of it—that Kansas had always been free soil. That felt important. Kansas was a place where a very brave man could set himself free.

As an adolescent, Ned had grown as interested in odd bits of knowledge as he had once been in river debris. He had become the sort of kid who could spend hours in front of a set of encyclopedias, tracking down some breathtakingly irrelevant piece of information. But he would have taken notes on a legal pad instead of on three-by-five-inch cards as the teacher had wanted, so he would lose a full letter grade on the paper.

He could have easily turned into the sort of man who relies on a woman to keep him organized, a woman who would nag him into using the assigned three-by-five notecards. He could have ended up as the dad who disappears into the basement every night after dinner to work on his elaborate electric-train landscape.

But one person saved him from a lifetime of indirection and ineffectiveness—his uncle's wife, the woman he thought of as a mother, Carolyn Shelby Ravenal.

Carolyn had grown up in Kansas's premier political family, surrounded by men who were articulate, organized, rational, and ambitious. That was why she had been able to guide Phil so well; she had seen him many times before.

It was also why she had a very special place in her heart for Ned. She had loved that he wasn't like the Shelbys. She had encouraged every one of his messy adventures. She never told him that his science projects were too involved. When he had come back from the river full of stories about buried treasure, she had listened and listened.

"When I grow up," he would say, "I'm going to get a big shovel and dig up that boat."

"You do that," she had said, never laughing. "You do that."

"You have interests, Ned," she said throughout his high school years. "That's what makes you special. Follow them. Believe in them. Keep them in the center of your life. Don't worry if they don't make sense

to other people. If they make sense to you, that's all that matters."

When Phil had graduated from high school, he had gotten a car. When Ned graduated from high school, he had gotten a manila envelope. It had a deed in it. Matt and Carolyn had bought the cornfield from Farmer Martin and were giving it to him. Whatever was left of the riverboat, however much had survived after more than a century of water and mud, was his.

He had gone back East to college, only to discover that no one in an Ivy League history department cared about a nineteenth-century Kansas riverboat. But history wasn't the problem. He knew the history. He needed to learn how to dig. So he had transferred to the Colorado School of Mines, figuring that if anyone knew how to excavate ground with an eleven-foot water table, it would be those guys, and he had been right. He had then gone to New Orleans, where a number of the passengers, including his own ancestors, had started their journey. He earned a master's degree in history from Tulane, spending his time researching the passenger list. After that he spent six months as a volunteer with the Canadian national park system. If he found the boat, any artifacts on it would have to be preserved, and the Canadians, it turned out, knew more about freshwater preservation techniques than anyone else.

Then Carolyn and Dr. Matt made him travel, backpacking around Europe and India for a year.

Stuff happened when you traveled on a student budget. Trains that had been running every other day for ten years suddenly switched to an every-third-day schedule with no notice. A bus conductor would take both sections of your ticket, and even though the two pieces were right there in his pile, he would swear he had taken only one and would refuse to look. You got strange rashes on your feet. But nothing had happened that Ned couldn't handle, and he had learned not only to be self-reliant but to like it. He liked being able to take care of himself, and he now avoided women who wanted to do it for him. He wanted a woman who had interests of her own, who had her own three-by-five-inch cards to fill up. He didn't want anyone who was going to make him her career.

Great-uncle Bob, the family's oddball bachelor uncle, had died while Ned was traveling. "Can we hold on to his house?" Ned had written Matt and Carolyn. "I need somewhere to live. If I start out at home, it will be too easy and I'll never leave."

He was surprised to find, when he got back to the States, that Phil also had moved back to Fleur-de-lis. He was living at home; apparently he had nothing to prove on the self-reliance front. "What's the deal?" Ned asked him. "How come you're not still in Washington?"

"You're going to start digging up the boat, aren't you?" Phil returned.

"You bet." He had waited long enough.

"If I know you," Phil went on, and Ned was startled at the affection in his brother's voice, "you'll just dig the thing up and preserve all the artifacts for the state historical society."

"What else would I do?"

"Use it as a focus for redeveloping the town's economic base. Try to pull in out-of-state tourist dollars."

Ned couldn't think of anything he would like less. "I'm not going to do that."

"I know you aren't," Phil said easily. "That's where I come in. Have you been downtown yet?"

"Yeah. Mom and the girls use this sunscreen that has this funny smell. It smells like . . . I don't know, toilet disinfectant that's trying not to smell like toilet disinfectant, so I thought I'd go to the drugstore and get something normal."

But the drugstore hadn't been there. The hardware store was gone too. And the shoe store and Eislinger's Electronics. It had been pretty depressing. Those stores had been there as long as Ned could remember. And Don Pierce, who ran the town's air-conditioning/furnace business, had stopped him on the street, saying that if he was going to be digging in the winter, some of Don's guys would be really glad of the off-season work.

Ned had mumbled something. He hadn't started thinking about a crew yet.

"These men have mortgages and families, Ned," Mr. Pierce had said. "Their wives are already working for Kmart. They don't want to work there too."

This was serious. Ned wasn't a ten-year-old mucking around the riverbank anymore. He had funding, and people needed jobs. He took a breath, looked Mr. Pierce straight in the eye, and called him by his first name. "I'll hire local people, Don. I promise."

"So here's the deal," Phil was saying that first evening Ned had been home. "You dig up that boat and you make sure you find something down there in all that mud. Ideally, it will be something that women want to come see—dishes, dresses, whatever it is that rich ladies from Kansas City will come look at. You get them here, and I'll make sure there is something for them to spend money on once they are here."

So clearly Tess Lanier and her plans for an espresso bar and gift shop were exactly what Phil had had in mind.

Tess was going to do this. She was really going to do this. She was going to quit a job that had a steady paycheck and good benefits, and she was going to move to a town where there were no movie theaters or Chinese food, no flower shops, bookstores, or fabric stores. Kmart sold little travel sewing kits with cheap threads on black plastic spools.

But why not? For the first time in her life, she had enough money to take a risk. There was nothing to keep her in California. The real estate prices were awful, the traffic horrible. She didn't have to live near the ocean; the sight of its endless waves didn't speak to anything in her soul.

She wanted to put down roots, to create a place for herself. So what if the building with her name had been painted teal? She wasn't afraid of teal paint.

And so what if this was the one town where every single resident had heard of Nina Lane? She wasn't afraid of Nina Lane either.

Ned was ready. The financing was set, the equipment had been purchased or leased—two big generators to run the dewatering pumps, a bucket drill, a bulldozer, a track loader, a one-hundred-ton crane for lowering sixty-five-foot lengths of well casings, the discharge pipes, a trailer for a night watchman to sleep in, hoses with adjustable-pressure nozzles.

The sweet corn had been harvested. Little orange surveyor's flags flapped in the wind, marking the outline of the boat. He had spent two days walking the field with a proton-magnetometer. Then, for another two days, he and Pete Dermott, the guy from whom he was leasing much of the equipment, had drilled. At thirty-five feet, the drill would start to shake, indicating that they had touched wood.

Not just wood. The boat. The *Western Settler.*

They had marked each spot with an orange flag. Ned's three sisters had come out with cans of white spray paint and connected the flags, forming what, from the air, must look like a 170-foot pencil, long and narrow, pointed at one end, flat at the other.

Phil's groundbreaking ceremony was set for the Saturday of Labor Day weekend. In the morning there would be a frisbee golf tournament—Ned could not figure out the logic to that one—and the groundbreaking itself would take place at one o'clock. Phil's former boss, the congressman, was giving a speech; the high school band would play; and Carolyn's family, the Shelbys with the two former governors, was coming up from their base south of Kansas City. Carolyn herself would be the one to break ground. She had had her backhoe lesson, and with Pete, the backhoe's owner, seated next to her, she would guide the shovel to make the first cut into the earth. Grandfather Ravenal had died while Ned had been in college; otherwise he would be at the controls.

"It's a shame that Grandfather didn't live for this,"
Phil had said earlier that day.

Ned had shrugged. "It's not like we can do anything about it." *And we don't need to. He knows. He
will be here.*

But that wasn't the sort of thing you said to Phil.

> Life aboard our steamboats was merry. On the
> *Western Settler*, the ladies' salon was forward,
> thereby giving us some measure of protection
> from the noise of the engine and the paddle
> wheels. Five family parties had been together
> since the *Cypress Princess* had left New Or-
> leans. Although our different stations in life
> would have made social intercourse unlikely in
> our home city, we found them all to be worthy,
> respectable people and congenial companions,
> and that they were not as accustomed to life's
> pleasant little elegances proved to be of little
> matter. The Ravenal brothers also had a cabin.
> Both of those gentlemen sang well and often
> joined us in the ladies' salon for an evening's
> entertainment.

> The *Cypress Princess* had been manned by
> an African crew, and on the trip up the Missis-
> sippi we were amused by their boisterous an-
> tics and the lively melodies of the songs which
> they sang to lighten the tedium of their duties.
> The laws of the Territories, however, were un-
> certain in those days, and the terms under
> which the crew had been leased from their
> masters did not allow for them to go farther
> than St. Louis. So the *Western Settler* was

tended by a crew of white individuals who seemed far surlier and less content with their lot in life than our Africans.

Mrs. Louis Lanier (Eveline Roget),
The Wreck of the Western Settler,
privately printed, 1879

Tomorrow. It was happening tomorrow. Ned knew that he wouldn't be able to sleep. He stayed at the site all night.

The three-quarter moon shone on the stubbled cornfield, and the little orange flags were dark and limp. The boat was down there. Thirty-five feet down. The test drills, the proton-magnetometer readings, had left no questions. The *Western Settler* was there.

You couldn't see the river from here. It was a quarter mile away. The cottonwoods and sycamores had grown up along the water's edge. If he were a little closer, he would be able to hear the rustling leaves and the river's rushing current, but here by the boat, the night was silent.

Back in California, Tess told her roommates that she would be leaving at the end of September, but would pay her share of the rent through the end of the year. They all gasped, saying how sorry they were, how much they would miss her. Tess believed them. They were sorry and they would miss her . . . but not for very long.

It was approaching two in the afternoon when our dear boat received her mortal wound. A

female relation and I were near the railing of
the bow of the upper deck. We had come
around a sharp bend and were in mid-channel.
The river ahead looked as ever; its greenish-
gray current broke into splatters of white foam
against the hull of the boat. We were heavily
loaded and rode low in the water.

The captain had told us about snags. Full-
grown trees, felled by storms or riverbank ero-
sion, clogged the river in the early spring. As
their wood became waterlogged, they sank,
their heavy root balls becoming imbedded in
the mud. The river's current snapped off the
branches and limbs, leaving only the heavy
trunk, perhaps two feet in diameter, slanting
upwards, waiting for some unhappy craft to
impale herself on its spear.

Our snag announced itself with a grinding
shudder. My companion and I clutched at each
other as we were knocked against the railing.
The boat lurched to the starboard side, and below us, barrels and boxes splashed into the
river. Water began to wash over the guards of
the lower deck.

Our good captain had kept the bow stairs
clear to enable servants to reach their masters,
and now the deck passengers surged up those
stairs, seeking higher ground. The boat continued to list. All was chaos.

Even in the confusion a mother's cry ripped
through our hearts as her child slipped over-
board. A person of African descent flung him-

self into the river, grabbed the child, and, holding on to a barrel, floated the lad to the Kansas shore.

Others were being swept into the water, but there was much floating debris for them to cling to. Order was quickly established on the upper deck. Gentlemen pulled loose a section of railing and attempted to hold it steady in the water. Encumbered by our fear and our gowns, we ladies did not have an easy time of it, but those who did not have the resolution to enter the cold and muddy waters voluntarily soon entered involuntarily.

In ten minutes the boat reached the river bottom. Only the small hurricane deck and the two brave smokestacks remained above water.

Despite the harsh material losses, Providence had indeed smiled upon us that day. All lives were spared. The current carried some sufferers to the Missouri side of the river, where they lingered for several hours while a yawl was found to do ferry duty. The Misses Picards clung to a fallen tree with no way to reach dry ground until the captain ordered men from the crew to rescue them.

How misfortune shows us the truth of the human heart and wipes away the meaningless distinctions that society imposes upon us. Those of us in the salon called encouragement to the deck passengers struggling and splashing in the river, and their menfolk, made

> hearty by their rugged life, stayed in waist-
> deep water to assist us to shore.

>   Mrs. Louis Lanier (Eveline Roget),
>   *The Wreck of the Western Settler,*
>   privately printed, 1879

Of course people wanted Ned to start finding things
five minutes after breaking ground, but the first two
weeks had to be spent on the dewatering systems,
drilling thirty-inch diameter wells, sinking sixty-five-
foot steel well casings, and hooking up the pumps to
diesel-powered generators. Ned estimated that he
would eventually need at least twenty such wells,
able to pump twenty thousand gallons of water a
minute.

It wasn't glamorous work, but it had to be done.

Tess was learning about electronic water-level autofill
systems, boiler sizes, steam wands, and NEMA con-
figurations. She ultimately selected a commercial
espresso machine from an Italian manufacturer, primarily because they had a representative and a repair
service in Kansas City. She did not want to run an
espresso bar with a machine that was out of order
until further notice.

An architect was supervising the renovations in
Kansas. Tess visited dozens of espresso bars in California and went into countless gift shops. She designed the company logo and ordered the mugs
herself, but she paid someone to do a lighting plan
and help her with the furniture placement. She did as
much as she could while working out her notice at

Willow Place, and she was good at getting things done.

She talked to Phil Ravenal constantly. It was almost like a game—which one of them could be more efficient, which one could get more done—and part of the game was understatement, never bragging about what you had accomplished. Tess suspected that her problem-solving skills were as good or better than his, but, of course, he was the one with the local resources, so he was winning. She didn't mind.

Ned was too close to the generators to hear Pete Dermott's shout, but he saw everyone else rushing toward the trackhoe. He thrust his wrench in his tool belt and took off, half running, half sliding down to the base of the twenty-five-foot crater. Pete had raised his bucket and maneuvered the trackhoe out of the way. By the time Ned got there, the others were probing with pipes, digging with shovels, scooping with their hands, jostling one another to try to get a better look. Phil grabbed him by the shoulder and pulled him close.

There it was, shining golden in the heavy gray sand, a curving piece of oak—the larboard paddle wheel of the *Western Settler.*

Chapter 6

Tess spent her last week in California on the road, looking for linens. She drove to the Nevada border where she found an extraordinary collection of drawn-thread work. She headed north, looping up past San Francisco, stopping in all the dusty little towns. At the edge of the Sonoma Valley, she found bed sheets that were one hundred percent linen, trimmed with handmade lace and priced by the value of the trim; the owner had no idea that the sheets were linen or what that would do to their price. She picked up an unhemmed damask tablecloth so large that no one else had unfolded it all the way to discover the twenty-four matching napkins, all unhemmed, all unused. She unearthed tea cloths and tablecloths, placemats and runners, napkins and pillowcases. Each day she would follow two-lane roads; at night she would stop at a little motel. She was accountable to no one, and no one knew where she was. She loved it.

In the evening she reread *The Riverboat Fragment*. It was, after all, paying for the motel room and the boxes of linen, for the gas she put in the car and the bottled water she bought at the filling stations.

The premise of the book was that a group of people escaping on a riverboat from a disaster in their own village were stranded by the boat's sinking. They sought shelter with a community at the river's edge. One of the conflicts between the two groups was that the existing community had magical powers while the riverboat people did not. According to the introduction to the edition that Tess was reading, the tone of the two-hundred-page fragment made it clear that the riverboat people would triumph, that the completed book would have chronicled the last days of humans dwelling in a world both natural and supernatural. The people without magic were the ones who survived.

Tess found that she liked the unfinished book a great deal more than the trilogy. Lush description—green moss creeping across shadowed gray stones and that sort of thing—occasionally overpowered the trilogy, but in the fragment the description was tighter. There were fewer details, more carefully chosen. Tess also considered the characters more interesting. The personages in the trilogy were heroic myths; these were much more like ordinary people. They had irritating habits; they got on each other's nerves. The riverboat people were, of course, grateful for the hospitality they were receiving, but pretty soon they became sick of having to be so grateful. Everything about the fragmented story seemed more mature than the trilogy; the insights were more sophisticated, the writing was better controlled . . . and it ended in mid-sentence.

Following the text were several brief articles by different scholars and critics who speculated on

how the book might have ended. All seemed to
agree that it was less than a third of its intended
length, perhaps even only a quarter. One article
argued that, ultimately, the main characters would
not have been the young men in the two communities, but a mother and daughter from the riverboat
people.

*We can't be overly influenced by the patriarchal
assumptions of the trilogy,* the article stated. *Nina
Lane was being exposed to strong feminist thought
within the community in which she was living. Once
she began working with more realistic psychological
material, the women characters grew more important to her.*

Tess reread the scenes between the mother and
daughter. The daughter, nearly grown, was frail and
irritable. The mother felt obligated to protect her, to
explain her to others. The daughter got power from
her irritability; she knew that and disliked herself
for it.

But at their most fractious moments, they would
remember the boat wreck; how, when thrown into
the water, each had instantly swam toward the other.
The bond between them was more powerful than any
other relationship in the narrative, this love between
mother and daughter.

And this was written by my mother.

Tess dismissed the thought. This story had nothing
to do with her. She knew that. Yes, Nina Lane had
been pregnant through much of the writing of the
manuscript, but Nina hadn't known that she was
having a daughter, and if what Duke had said was
true, she hadn't been very interested in being a

mother. This wasn't about Nina as mother and Tess as daughter.

It's about Grandma. It's about her and Grandma, about the two of them as mother and daughter.

Tess was donating her old car, her grandparents' car, to the National Kidney Foundation. It was, she was surprised to realize, the one thing she felt sentimental about. Her grandparents had had it for so long; they had driven it on so many careful little errands. Tess herself had driven it to their doctors, to their hospitals, to their funerals. Its last trip, the last thing Tess was going to do before leaving California, on the very morning of her flight to Kansas, was to visit their graves.

Every Memorial Day her grandmother had brought flowers to the family graves. She had had a routine. She would go first to her husband's parents, the Laniers, and then to her own parents, the Swensons, then to her two sisters, who had died while growing up. The graves were close to one another, all within the sight of the same tree.

Grandma had always let Tess lay the flowers on the graves. But then she would touch Tess's shoulder, motioning her to stand with Grandpa. Grandma would go alone to the tree and place her last bouquet at its roots, even though no grave was there. She would stand there for a moment, staring at the flowers. Her face would change, her lips growing narrow and her eyes blinking. Tess had wondered if she was going to cry.

"What's she doing?" Tess had asked Grandpa. "Who are those flowers for?"

"They're for all the people who aren't here."

"The people back in Kansas?" Even as a little girl, Tess knew that they were from Kansas.

"Yes, them, and people elsewhere too. Both Grandma and I had uncles who fought in World War One. They're still in France."

And Grandma would always be very quiet on the drive home, and sometimes she'd go straight into her bedroom and close the door.

On this final visit, Tess followed her grandmother's routine. The Laniers, the Swensons, the sisters, then her grandparents themselves, and simply because this was what her grandmother had always done and that made it important, Tess laid some flowers at the foot of the tree.

Grandma had brought flowers from the yard; Tess had had to buy her flowers. She had chosen lilies, nine sprays of white lilies, each surrounded by a halo of baby's breath and tied with a white ribbon. The first eight rested on green grass, but the ninth one, the one for the soldiers in France, shone against the rough bark of the tree. The streamers on the ribbon followed the curve of the trunk as it rooted into the earth.

These flowers weren't for the soldiers in France. Tess suddenly realized that the story her grandfather had told her wasn't complete. Those young men had died before either of her grandparents had been born. Grandma would have respected their memory, but she wouldn't have gone into her bedroom and cried for them.

The flowers at the tree had been for Nina, Grandma's daughter. Nina was the person who wasn't here. Nina was the person whose memory had made Grandma cry. Grandma had brought the flowers for her.

But where was she? Where was Nina Lane buried? Tess had no idea.

How could she not know? Her grandparents would have. They were the legal next of kin; there must have been forms they had to sign, documentation that would have been sent to them.

But when Tess had closed up their house, there had been nothing about Nina Lane, not even a death certificate.

There was an accident on the freeway. The traffic was bad, and Tess barely made it to the airport in time to turn the car over to the Kidney Foundation, check her baggage, and get on the plane.

She had had no time to call Duke. She would have liked to ask him where Nina Lane was buried, but she would have to wait until she got to Kansas.

Or she could call from the plane. That was what rich people did. If they needed to make a call, they used the telephones on the airplanes.

Of course, really rich people probably also flew first-class. Tess had not done that.

Tentatively, she eased the phone from its housing in the seat back in front of her. Duke answered, and Tess, feeling rather pleased with herself, got straight to the point. "Where is Nina Lane buried?"

"In Kansas. In Fleur-de-lis. Didn't you know that?"

"No. How did it happen? Why didn't Grandma and Grandpa bury her in California?"

Duke sighed. "That was my doing, I'm afraid. Everything that happened was such a shock. I know that people keep imagining a final scene among the three of us, but there wasn't one. Kristin and I had no idea that Nina was even in New York. I was on the phone, and Kristin was out in the hall, taking the trash down to the chute. She had paused to talk to a neighbor, and later she thought she might have heard the elevator open, but she couldn't be sure. We had no idea of anything until we heard all the commotion in the street, and I went down just out of curiosity, not even knowing there had been a suicide, much less that it was—" He cleared his throat. "Anyway, because I knew her, the police kept turning to me. She was just another dropout, runaway street person to them. I had no money, but a couple of people in Kansas had enough to pay for everything involved in bringing her body back. We had the funeral there. It was a bizarre ritual, I'm sure. The only qualification of the guy who officiated was that he owned a purple robe."

"Did my grandparents come?"

"No. And that's where I was wrong. We were so young then . . . and we were so determined to be independent and everyone was pretending that a person's background and family didn't matter. We didn't decide not to call Nina's parents. It just never occurred to us. As a parent now, I'm appalled at that. If something happened to Jemima or Jeffrey . . . Anyway, it was the cemetery people back in Kansas who asked if her family had been notified, and then the funeral, such as it was, was the next day."

Tess couldn't imagine her grandmother receiving

the phone call saying that her daughter had committed suicide the week before.

You loved her, didn't you? You loved her with a fire and intensity that I can't imagine, because those qualities left you when she died. She took them with her.

And not to be able to go to the funeral . . .

You must have said your own prayers. After all those years of talking to Nina's teachers, begging them to give your flippant, defiant daughter another chance, after she gave up and ended her own life, was your final talk with God, begging Him to give her another chance?

Everything went smoothly in Kansas City. All of her baggage arrived safely, and a young man from a car dealership was there to take her to her new car. The car was ready, and it was precisely what she had expected it to be. The road north of Kansas City ran level and open through the Missouri River Valley. Tess crossed into Kansas at the Fleur-de-lis bridge.

Phil had sent her the most detailed map the town had ever made of itself. Tess scanned it for cemeteries. There were some in the churchyards, but she didn't suppose that Nina Lane's friends had bought a site in a churchyard. The only other cemetery was west of town.

It was set on a gentle rise, surrounded by a black iron fence that rose into a little arch over the entrance. The parking area was gravel and empty. Tess stopped her new car near the arch. Attached to one of its supports was a small sign. THIS IS A PLACE OF REST AND REPOSE. PLEASE TREAT IT WITH RESPECT. NINA LANE'S GRAVE IS DESIGNATED BELOW. There was a small

map with one grave marked in red. A trash barrel
lined in black plastic sat beneath the sign.

The cemetery wasn't large, perhaps an acre or so,
and the one distinct path headed toward Nina Lane's
grave. Tess turned away from the path, away from
Nina Lane's grave.

There were a number of French names—descen-
dants of the riverboat people, and, as Tess could see
from the dates, some of the riverboat people themselves. Suddenly there was her name. LANIER. Louis
and Eveline shared a headstone. They were Tess's
great-great-great-grandparents. Ned Ravenal had
told her that when he had sent her Eveline's account
of the wreck. Louis and Eveline were buried next to
their daughter Marie, who had died in 1858, less
than a year after the sinking. Their son Herbert, born
in 1857, had built the Lanier Building. His "beloved
wife" Antonia had been fifteen years younger than
he; their children were born in the 1890s. Their son,
Cecil, 1892–1914, had a commemorative plaque, not
a headstone. He must have been Grandpa's uncle, the
World War I soldier whose body was in France. Eva
Louise had a single day after her name. She had lived
for less than a day.

This was Tess's family; this was her history.

Why wasn't Nina buried here with the other
Laniers?

Because no one in the Settlement had thought of
her as a Lanier.

It must, however, have been terribly important to
Nina herself. It was why she had come to Kansas,
why she had written *The Riverboat Fragment*.

Tess moved slowly toward Nina Lane's grave.

It had an impressive marker, unlike anything else in the graveyard, an irregular boulder, rounded and rough, its surface dark gray and pebbly. One slab had been sliced off and the remaining flat surface was polished to a mirrorlike black. NINA LANE.

The afternoon sun shone against the tombstone. Tess could see a dark reflection of herself. Her mother's name was carved starkly across the blurred image of her face.

That was what it had been like at Stanford. Her friends, even her boyfriend had been able to see only Nina Lane's name across her face.

But I am nothing like her.

Nina was disorganized, her life chaos. Tess was systematic and fastidious.

The other graves were among the trees; their headstones were shaded. Not Nina Lane's. The sun turned her headstone into a mirror.

She's not my mirror. I'm not like her. I will not be defined by her.

Nina was intrusive, Tess solitary. Nina was rebellious, Tess compliant. Nina used people, Tess was everything helpful. They could not have been more different.

But wasn't being different a kind of definition?

Grandma and Grandpa had indeed been terrified at the thought of having another Nina to raise. They must have been desperately relieved, desperately grateful, whenever Tess did something that marked her as different from Nina. That would have been the behavior they would have praised and encouraged.

So Tess had become someone who was not Nina Lane. That was the most important thing about her—that she was not Nina Lane.

Is that who I am? Simply not Nina Lane?

She turned away from the grave, no longer wanting to see her face blurred behind Nina Lane's name. She heard a car door slam. Someone else had come to the cemetery.

She forced herself to turn back to the grave. *I am still me. It doesn't matter why I am this way. I am me.*

And she could be herself even here in Fleur-de-lis, even in the one place Nina Lane had loved.

Perhaps that was the reason she had come to Kansas; she had to prove that she could be herself in the place where Nina Lane's shadow would be the longest and the darkest.

She heard footsteps. She looked over her shoulder. A uniformed law enforcement officer was approaching her. "Just checking to see if everything was okay, ma'am."

"I was about to leave."

"No, no rush. Take your time." He moved closer. "Have you been here before?"

"No," Tess answered. "This is my first time." She felt that she ought to say more. "This headstone doesn't look twenty-some years old."

"It's not. It's only been there for a few years. But we kept losing the others. People would chip off little bits as souvenirs, and then the whole thing would disappear."

"People stole the headstone?"

"Pretty ghoulish, huh? But no one's touched this one. It looks more like something you shouldn't touch. The fan clubs paid for it." The officer paused. "Are you one of her fans?"

Tess took a breath. She wasn't running away from this. "No, I'm her daughter."

∞ *Chapter 7* ∞

Phil Ravenal had arranged for Tess to rent a house on Olive Street. It was small, he had warned, but would be fine for one person. It didn't have central air, but there was an attic fan and a window unit in the bedroom. He had offered to meet the moving van and arrange for the phone and utilities. He would leave the key under the flowerpot to the left of the door.

Fleur-de-lis was laid out on a grid with the numbered streets running north-south and the named streets in alphabetical order going east-west. Six-thirty-five Olive Street was exactly where Tess expected it to be, two blocks south of Main and six blocks west of the river. The house looked exactly like the pictures Phil had sent, a gray stucco bunga-low with a deep front porch. The key was exactly where he said it would be.

Someone had planted scarlet geraniums in the flowerpot and in the window boxes. The front porch had been swept, and there was a welcome mat. Inside the house, Tess's one carpet had been unrolled and her furniture carefully positioned on top of it. The new bookcases that she had ordered from a catalog had been placed exactly where she would have put them—although that was hardly surprising, since there was only one possible spot for them.

The kitchen was narrow and dated, but immaculate. A note was propped up on the counter.

Dear Tess,

Welcome to Fleur-de-lis!

We found a box labeled "sheets," so we made up your bed for you in case you get in late. Didn't see anything that looked like kitchen stuff, so Mom had us bring over some paper products and an extra tea kettle. Brenda Jackson sent the cake that's in the icebox; the casserole is from us. It's turkey. There's also some fruit.

Call us if you need anything—645-2293.

Love and welcome,
Emma and Brittany

P.S. Dad said you'd probably need a utility knife for opening the boxes.

Tess had no idea who Emma and Brittany were. But right next to the note was a utility knife with extra blades. Paper cups and plates were stored in the cabinet; a forest-green tea kettle sat on the back burner of the stove. Inside the refrigerator was a foil-covered casserole dish, a few apples, a three-inch slice of watermelon, and a chocolate Bundt cake. Tess couldn't imagine what she was going to do with a whole Bundt cake. In the bedroom, the bed was made, the towels had been hung in the bathroom, and a roll of toilet paper installed.

This could have been so hard. She could have been standing in the middle of an empty house that was dreary and smelled of mildew. It was late on Saturday afternoon. She could have had no water, no electricity, no phone, and no idea where the movers were. But instead, all her belongings were inside this freshly painted little playhouse. Everything was going right. She wasn't used to that.

Things hadn't gone right for Tess's grandparents. Houses had been dreary and mildewed. Automobile tires had gone flat on rainy nights. Medical tests had come back with "not quite the results we were hoping for." Their daughter had been manic-depressive.

But it's her money that's making things work for me. Your raising her wasn't for nothing. Knowing that would have been a comfort, wouldn't it?

But they hadn't known.

The air-conditioning unit in the bedroom was running, so Tess closed that door and went around the rest of the house opening the windows. She had started looking for the switch to the attic fan when she heard a knock on the door.

On the porch were two young women, probably college-aged. Clearly sisters, both had sandy blond hair and freckles.

"Mrs. Parkinson across the street called and said you were here. We're so glad you made it today." One girl started speaking the instant the door opened. "We're just in town for the weekend— classes are in session—and we were afraid we'd miss you."

"I'm Emma," said the other girl, the smaller one. "And this is Brittany."

So these were her magic elves. "Come in, please come in. And thank you. You did so much. It was wonderful."

"Dad said that maybe you wouldn't have liked us opening the bedroom box, since you aren't from the Midwest and all," Brittany reported. "He said it might seem like we were snooping, but by then it was too late, because we'd already done it."

"It hadn't even occurred to us not to, which shows you that we most definitely are 'from the Midwest and all,'" said Emma, as lively as her sister. "But at least we didn't unpack your clothes, even though we had heard all about how great they were. We *knew* we'd be snooping there. I do hope your kitchen stuff didn't get lost. We couldn't find anything."

Tess wondered what being or not being from the Midwest had to do with being grateful for a roll of toilet paper. "I didn't bring any kitchen things. I didn't have much and so I left it all for my roommates. I'm going to buy everything new."

"Oh, that will be fun," Emma exclaimed. "Especially now that we have the Kmart. They have everything. Otherwise you'd have been in trouble. They're open late on Saturdays, so if you need anything tonight you can run out and get it."

"Or we can go for you," Brittany offered. "It's no problem."

"Thank you." Tess could not continue in ignorance anymore. "Forgive me, this is awkward when I am so grateful—but who are you?"

Emma and Brittany stared for a moment. Emma clapped her hand over her mouth, and Brittany laughed. "What idiots we are," Brittany said. "We're so used to every one knowing everything about us. We're the Ravenal girls, at least two of the three. Caitlin's in dental school and she can never get away. Dr. Matt is our father, and Phil is our older brother. He gave us the key and asked us to do what we could to make you feel welcome."

"You certainly succeeded at that." When she had had dinner with Dr. Matt, Carolyn, Phil, and Ned, the daughters had been away at the university, and as far as Tess could remember, everyone spoke about them as "the girls," never using their first names. "Come in and tell me what's happening with Ned and the riverboat. The last I heard, he had found one of the paddle wheels."

"That was almost two weeks ago. He's now uncovered the engines and the boilers and is moving back toward the other paddle wheel. He's very happy, but unless you're wildly interested in steam engines, it's a little boring."

Tess was not wildly interested in steam engines. "Has he found any artifacts yet?"

"No; the river current washed everything off the deck. Anything interesting will be down in the cargo hold, but he's not going to get to that for a while. He's being Mr. Systematic about everything. But why are we standing around like this? Put us to work. We can always talk while we work."

Tess had a feeling that refusing their help would violate all that the town stood for. "Let's start in the bedroom. You can snoop through my clothes if you'd like."

The movers had roped Tess's chest of drawers shut, and all her folded clothes were still in place. She had paid for wardrobe boxes, so that her other garments had remained on hangers and now only had to be transferred to the closet. But Brittany and Emma took their time about it, looking at everything. Both of them knew how to sew, and they marveled at the detail Tess had put into her clothes: the godets, the cannon pleats, the drawn work.

"How did you pull off this inset?" Brittany wondered. "I couldn't get those corners so nice in a hundred million years. Mother's going to love this. I can't wait to show it to her. They ought to be here soon, shouldn't they, Em?"

"Dad just had to finish his calls. Mother secretly wanted to come over with us," Emma explained to Tess, "but she thought it was more grown up to wait for Dad. Oh, wait, that's them now, isn't it?"

The doorbell was ringing and indeed, it was Carolyn and Matt Ravenal. Carolyn had a big bouquet of sunflowers with her. "Welcome to Kansas," she said. "I'd hug you, but I've got too much vegetation."

"Well, I'll hug you," the doctor said and he gave Tess a quick, warm embrace. "But don't touch Ned. He's filthy."

Sitting on the front steps behind his parents and the sunflowers was indeed Ned, or at least his back. He was bent over, untying his shoes. He looked back over his shoulder. "I showed up just as they were leaving." He tugged off one of his heavy work boots.

He was wearing gray rag socks. "They wouldn't give me a chance to change."

"Do you care where I put these flowers?" Carolyn called from inside the house.

"No, no, anywhere you can find," Tess replied.

Ned stood up and looked down at himself. Sometime during the course of the day, he must have picked up something very dirty. Its weight had scrunched up his shirt, pleating the fabric into little folds that had remained clean, forming light streaks running horizontally across his chest. "Are you sure you want me to come in? Since I'm usually down in the pit and covered with mud, my standards have gotten really low. If I'm not actively oozing, I feel clean."

Tess hated being dirty. "Don't be silly. Come in. Your sisters said that you uncovered the engines."

He was being careful not to brush against the freshly painted walls. "It's great. For a while there, we were just sinking wells, and no one was interested except the seven-year-old boys. They seem to like anything that resembles mass destruction."

His mother looked up from the sunflowers she was positioning on Tess's coffee table. "What do you think you were like at seven?"

"I wasn't criticizing them," Ned protested. "They're great, and some of them can already subtract two-digit numbers, which is"—he was now speaking to Tess again—"apparently something to be quite proud of."

"I worked in a retirement home," she reminded him. "We never underappreciated the capacity to subtract two-digit numbers."

"Wait until you work retail," Brittany put in. "At the end of a busy Saturday, you won't be able to—"

She was interrupted by the doorbell ringing again. Tess went to answer it. This was fun. She couldn't remember when she had last had this much company.

It was Phil Ravenal.

He was better-looking than she had remembered.

You didn't come here for him. You came to start a business, to find a place where you belong. You've never needed a man before. Don't start now.

If something happened, that was fine. But she wasn't going to expect it. She wasn't going to need it.

His greeting was warm. Had the car been right? Was she finding everything she needed? Were the girls being a nuisance?

Yes, yes, everything had been perfect, things couldn't have gone better. Had she been to the Lanier Building yet? Had she seen how well it looked?

No, she had come straight here.

They were inside the house now. He nodded to his family but continued to speak to her. "I heard that you stopped at the cemetery first."

"Well, yes, I did."

"I ran into Junior Hobart, who saw you there, and he said that you said that you are Nina Lane's daughter." His tone was carefully neutral. "Is that true?"

"You're what?" Emma sat up. Brittany had been perched on the arm of her chair and she had to grab hold of Emma's shoulder to keep her balance.

"My mother was Nina Lane," Tess acknowledged. "Lane was her pen name."

"That is so cool," Brittany gasped. "Why didn't

we know? Why didn't—" She broke off. "Oh, my God, wasn't the baby named . . ."

"That's right," Tess said. "I was named after Ned's boat. Until I turned sixteen and my grandparents changed it, my legal name was Western Settler Lanier."

"Oh, gross."

Tess had to agree with that. She turned back to Phil. Could she make this sound simple? "I didn't mean to be hiding anything from you, but I don't go out of my way to tell people about it. It creates too much of a fuss."

"Of course," Carolyn said quickly. "We understand."

Phil looked across the room. "I do notice that neither my father nor my brother seems wildly surprised. Did you know?" he asked them.

"I guessed," Dr. Matt admitted.

"Why didn't you say something?"

"I didn't know for sure, but if she was, then she was my patient when she was a baby, and I don't tell patients' secrets. You know that."

"You were my doctor?" Tess liked the sound of that. She had been born here. She kept forgetting that.

"Yes, ma'am, and you were one sweet baby. Bald but sweet."

Phil was waiting patiently for this exchange to be over. "And you?" he asked Ned. "Why didn't you say anything?"

Ned shrugged. "If you'd needed to know, I would have said something, but she was already doing everything you wanted her to be doing."

The two brothers looked at each other for a moment. Tess wondered if something complicated was passing between them, but she didn't know them well enough to be sure.

"I have a cake," she exclaimed, suddenly remembering. "It's from someone named Brenda Jackson. Would you all like some?"

The six Ravenals were immediately alert. "Is that her Tunnel of Death fudge cake?" Dr. Matt asked.

"It looks to be chocolate."

"Are you going to cut small pieces?"

"I can."

"Then you'll need to give me three."

"Oh, Matt!" His wife swatted him on the arm. "You have to understand," she explained to Tess. "Brenda's husband Howard had a heart attack last year, and the doctors at the Med Center put him on a restricted diet. Brenda's doing a great job, she really is, but she's always been the best baker in town, and when she bakes for someone else, it's loaded with all the fat that Howard can't eat."

As they were serving the cake, Carolyn asked Tess over for dinner on Sunday. "I was going to ask you for dinner this evening, but I can't imagine anyone's going to feel like eating much after this cake."

It *was* rich. "Tomorrow would be lovely. I do need some time to get settled."

"Take all the time you need," Ned put in. "You don't have to socialize every minute of the day."

"Tomorrow will be fine."

Emma and Brittany gathered up the paper plates and wiped up the cake crumbs with paper towels. Phil glanced at his watch and excused himself. Dr.

Matt's pager went off; he unclipped it from his belt, looked at the screen, and made a face. "I guess I should go too."

Ned followed his parents to the door. Tess touched his arm. "When I say yes, I mean yes," she told him softly. "You don't have to protect me."

"Am I doing that?"

"Yes. It seems that you don't believe I'm going to like it here."

"No, I don't," he protested, then paused. "Yes, I guess I do. I know everyone romanticizes about small towns, but there are some very real drawbacks."

"Whatever they are, I don't need you to say no for me. I can do that on my own."

His lips tightened. He was apologizing. "So many women around here can't."

Emma and Brittany stayed for another hour, helping Tess unpack. Except for her linen collection, Tess had not brought much with her. Her grandparents had left little that had been worth saving. Her grandmother was not a sentimental woman, and the only keepsake that Tess had found among her belongings was a little packet of drawings of violets, some of them rough, some rather detailed. Tess had no idea where they had come from, but as they were the one thing Grandma had saved, Tess had saved them too.

After Emma and Brittany left, Tess went into the bathroom to take a shower. She undressed, tested the water temperature with her hand, stepped in, and realized that she had no shower curtain. She had to reduce the water to such a trickle that she couldn't wash her hair, and even then water splashed all over the floor.

The Kmart was open until nine on Saturday night. Tess took out the list she had been working on, added "shower curtain," and got back into her new car. It still smelled new.

At home, in California, back in her real life—all those phrases still fit—she hated going into large discount stores. The parking lots were crowded, the aisles were crowded, the shelves were crowded, the checkout lines were interminable. She hated being surrounded by things she couldn't afford, by people who were buying things *they* couldn't afford. She could hear the talk in the checkout lines, the weary bravado with which people were trying to justify their spending to themselves. *Don't buy it*, she would want to shriek. *It's simple. If you can't afford it, don't buy it.*

Of course, at least for her, this time was different. She did have an enormous amount to buy—pots, plates, silverware, cleaning supplies, measuring cups, and toothpaste—but this time she could afford it.

Tess wanted to get pale, soft neutrals, a sandstone gray or a biscuit color, but that wasn't what Kmart wanted her to buy. The store was showing cheerful primary colors this year. So Tess decided to get as much as she could in white and red. Her dishes were white, but everything plastic was scarlet—her dish drainer, trash can, the handle of her broom, her mop bucket, her measuring spoons. She bought red pot holders and red kitchen towels. She filled one cart, then a second.

She had never shopped like this before. This was a
Kmart. The merchandise was practical and mass-pro-
duced. There was nothing in the store she couldn't
buy. Nothing. The nicest of the juice pitchers was
made on a mold; Tess could buy one. The best wine-
glasses were six to a box; Tess could buy them.
Shower curtains could be hung with thin metal clips
or with fat, rounded hooks in the same color as the
towels. The metal ones were cheaper, but Tess didn't
even have to think; she bought the colored ones.

*It's all right if I buy a red plastic colander and get
sick of it after a year. It's all right if I make a mistake.*
Tess had never thought that way in her whole life.
*There's all this money protecting me. There's a net
underneath me. I'm safe.*

Was this how people with money felt, that they
were safe, that they could make mistakes?

Maybe, but maybe it was also how people who
were loved felt.

Chapter 8

Tess intended to go to the church her grandparents had attended as children. She was entirely capable of doing this on Sunday morning even though she had been in town for fewer than twenty-four hours. She knew where her panty hose were; she knew where her good shoes were, and if her dress needed to be ironed, she knew where her iron was.

But she didn't want to go to church. She wanted to finish dealing with all the shrink-wrap and other packaging that her Kmart trip had produced. She wanted to go to the Lanier Building and see what had been done there. The only reason for going to church would be to show everyone in town what a wonderful human being she was.

Oh, that Tess Lanier, she's so nice, she's so perfect. Let's go buy overpriced coffee from her.

But maybe it would make more sense to let them all think that she was a godless, mammonistic heathen, and then they would be pleasantly surprised to discover her good qualities. That sounded a lot easier.

So she dealt with the shrink-wrap and the boxes, then picked up the keys and the thick manila envelope Phil had left for her, and set out for her new business.

She walked. Two blocks north and then a block west. Three blocks, six minutes. This would be her commute. The worst possible traffic would add a ten- to fifteen-second pause at the crosswalk. So what if she found that she didn't like serving people over-priced coffee? She could do anything that was three blocks and six minutes from home.

The Lanier Building had been transformed. The teal paint was gone, and the limestone blocks were as fresh and buttery-looking as those in the Old Court-house building. The four tall, arched windows looked dignified and prosperous. Tess was going to paint the name of her business in gold on the windows.

Things inside were just as good. The crumbling partition had been removed and a long service counter had been installed along one wall. The pine floors had been freshly sanded; new Sheetrock had been hung over the crumbling plaster, its tape still visible beneath a coat of primer paint. The two new bathrooms with their wide wheelchair-size doors were not finished yet, but Tess had not expected them to be. The office and storage space were nearly com-pleted and, as far as she could tell, were exactly ac-cording to the architect's drawings.

But there was plenty more to do. The contractor had left tile boards and countertop samples. There was a note about the bathroom faucets. The ones she had picked were on back order; she needed to select another style. Another note said that the coat hooks had arrived in chrome instead of brass. Did she mind?

Yes, she did.

An hour later she was back in the office, opening a box of the furniture catalogs and fabric samples. She heard someone rap at the door.

It was Phil Ravenal. He was wearing a sport coat and a tie; he, superior human being to herself, must have gone to church. "I thought you might be here," he said. "Are you finding everything all right?"

"It's perfect. You know that. You're the one who made sure of it."

He shrugged. "It was nothing. My office is right over there." He pointed toward the Old Courthouse. "We've had great weather. This gave me an excuse for coming outside and crossing the street a couple times a day."

He had done a great deal more than that. "I feel as if I should offer to show you around, but I assume you've already seen it all."

He acknowledged the truth of that. "Then let me show you around. Have you been out to see the boat yet?"

She hadn't. So she got her purse, locked the door to the Lanier Building, and followed him outside. He was driving a different car from the one he had driven when she had come out in the summer. This one was a dark green Jeep.

"The girls usually drive this," he explained, "but there's so much mud out at the site that I traded cars with them for the fall . . . and I don't know what is worse for a car, being stuck in a field of mud or being driven by my sisters. It's a close call."

Although there was some mud around the wheels and on the rear quarter panel, the interior of the Jeep was immaculate. Tess wondered if his orderliness ever made relationships difficult. Was he able to be tolerant of a less tidy woman? Well, she wouldn't find out. Her car was every bit as neat as his.

The riverboat site was north of town, out County Route Five, near the Prairie Bell School. The river, redirected by various Army Corps of Engineers projects, made a jag to the northeast, so it was now over a quarter mile away from where the boat had sunk. A line of trees marked the river's current path. There was a little wind, and the narrow, darkish leaves of the willows were fluttering, their white undersides shimmering as the breeze flipped the edges of the leaves.

Bordered on the east side by the irregular riverbank and on the west side by the straight line of the country road, the former cornfield was bounded to the north and south by windbreaks of fast-growing, stout-branched cottonwood trees. Towering over the trees, dwarfing everything, was a construction crane, its cable dangling like a plumb line. Next to it was a white construction trailer and a yellow bulldozer-type thing—Tess knew little about heavy equipment—but instead of a bulldozer's blade, it had a long, arching arm with a backward-facing claw mounted to it.

Phil bumped the Jeep across a rough track that cut through the stubbled cornfield. The track continued in a rough oval around the actual excavation site, which seemed about the size of a football field. Cables were looped onto wooden posts marked with DANGER HIGH VOLTAGE signs.

Phil parked at the edge of the oval track, next to Ned's black pickup. The cables led to two big generators, perched high on mounds of excavated earth at either end of the pit. The generators were chugging steadily. A massive cylindrical fuel tank, its white paint nearly worn away, sat on another little man-made hill.

The pit itself was perhaps thirty-five feet deep. Tall, columnlike pipes rose out of the wet, sandy ground. At the former ground level they elbowed, and the pipes, now horizontal, burrowed into the pile of excavated dirt. They were, Phil told Tess, part of the dewatering system. Twenty thousand gallons of water were being pumped every minute out of the water table into a drainage ditch that Ned had built and lined with plastic.

An actual bulldozer was working down in the pit, pushing and scooping, widening the far edge. The base of the pit seemed littered. There were pools of standing water, coils of fire hoses, a green picnic umbrella, buckets, and shovels. Two sets of broken timbers poked up out of the mud, and beyond them was an iron structure, three cylindrical tanks welded together. The tanks were about three feet in diameter and twenty or twenty-five feet long, and pipes of varying sizes jutted out of them and crossed over them.

Phil touched her arm. "If you stand here, it's easier to figure things out. The stern of the boat is toward us."

The *Western Settler* had had two paddle wheels, mounted on either side about two-thirds of the way back to the stern of the boat. Tess could now see that the broken timbers were arranged in spoke patterns; they had been the supports for the giant wheels. The larboard wheel—the one to Tess's left—sat higher than the starboard wheel. The boat had sunk toward its starboard side. The big iron thing was the boat's steam boilers, positioned toward the bow of the boat. "There was still half-burned coal and wood inside the firebox," Phil said.

The paddle wheels, the boilers, and other parts of the engine were the only pieces of the boat above the main deck that had not been carried away by the current. All the upper decks, the fancy white gingerbread railings, and the cabins and lounges whose social life Eveline Lanier had described were long gone. "Basically, we will just have the hull and what you see now," Phil continued. "I think a lot of people were secretly expecting a full-scale Disneyland creation with fresh white paint and gold trim, but let me see if I can flag Ned down. He can explain this in a lot more detail than I can."

Ned was apparently the person in the bulldozer. Because it was still Sunday morning, he was working alone. "No, no, don't interrupt him." Tess was willing to admit to herself that she would have been a lot more interested in the full-scale Disneyland creation. What was exposed now was guy stuff.

But the scale of the project was staggering. Phil could only be hinting at the difficulties Ned was confronting every day. Tess looked back at the bulldozer. It moved on the kind of rolling tracks that Sherman tanks had had in World War Two documentaries. It was being driven confidently, without jerks or false starts. Ned often had a distracted, even apologetic air about him, the perpetual younger brother, but he had organized all of this. Every decision that she had been making about insurance, water, and electricity, he had been making with tenfold complexity.

"What kind of help did Ned have getting this started?" she asked.

"Not much. He did contract with a well-digging outfit because leasing a bucket drill on his own was going to be surprisingly expensive and those guys were efficient and safe, but he probably could have managed without them. He knows what he's doing. His undergraduate degree is from the Colorado School of Mines, so if you ever need a coal shaft ventilated, he can do it for you."

"Does this come naturally to him?"

"This is what he always dreamed of doing," Phil said. "Ever since he was a little kid, he always wanted to dig up the boat. He's just been putting one foot in front of the other, and here he is."

Tess suddenly wished that her grandparents could have known Ned. Nina's dreams, her urgent, inchoate longings, had tormented them. But dreams didn't have to be bad. Look at Ned Ravenal. He had had a dream that had dominated his life, but he wasn't miserable and self-absorbed. He wasn't manic-depressive. He was a nice guy with an important goal. You could do that.

All week Tess worked at the Lanier Building. She had already ordered four love seats and six large easy chairs, all of them upholstered in brown-toned leather—tobacco, camel, café, and cocoa. She wanted the walls glazed with varying shades of apricot, a friendly, unusual color, feminine without being girlish, blending well with the warm stone outside. The walls would feature reproductions of oversize

French Beaux Arts posters. She would buy round oak tables and pine harvest tables. Some of her chairs would be ladder-back; some would be pattern-backed. She didn't want anything to match; the twenty-foot ceiling would soften and unify the unusual combinations. And whenever she wondered if it was all becoming too unusual, she reminded herself that she didn't need to be afraid of Nina Lane.

Her mugs arrived. They were straight-sided, and at first glance they looked like the speckled tin cups that the forty-niners, the California gold-rush miners, had used. But Tess's were earthenware—tin would get too hot—and instead of the traditional blue, they were jade in color.

Each mug had her logo emblazoned in white. A double-lined border enclosed scrolling letters: "The Lanier Building Coffee Company." The *T* in "The" and the *y* in "Company" broke through the lines of the border. Tess couldn't remember the last time she had colored outside the lines.

Midway through her first week, Wyatt Cooper and Gabe Eldore, the two men who owned The Cypress Princess restaurant, stopped by and introduced themselves, first apologizing that they had so few memories of Nina Lane to share with her. "We came to the Settlement quite late," Wyatt said. He spoke with a slight Southern accent. "We only met Nina two or three times."

"That's fine," Tess assured them. "I'm not here for her."

They were full of good advice. Call the high school guidance counselor, Mrs. Fornelli, about which high school kids to hire for weekend and evening help.

"She knows who works hard and who needs the money." Don't post your bad checks on the wall. "People think it's really mean-spirited." Deal with Pam at the bank. "She's the smartest one there." Once Tess had a floor plan drawn up, she should show it to the chief of police. "He'll spot problems you won't have thought of—where you might lose things to shoplifters." Don't ever gossip. "You'll overhear stuff. You'll see people fighting. You'll see people crying. Just forget it all."

"I will."

"And above all, remember we are only four and a half blocks away. If ever you are caught short, whether your staff is sick or you're out of milk or napkins, please call us."

"That's extremely generous of you."

Many people were very friendly, bringing her food, inviting her over for supper. On Saturday, Phil took her to The Cypress Princess for dinner. The following week she went to Kansas City and St. Joseph, visiting the antiques warehouses that specialized in farmhouse oak. She had already ordered reproduction tables—she needed smaller sizes than had traditionally been built—but she found plenty of chairs as well as pie safes and china cupboards for displaying her merchandise.

At Phil's suggestion, she had covered her windows with butcher paper on Friday afternoon so that the weekend visitors would know she would not be open. "You don't want them looking in and being disappointed." But during the week she took the paper down. People in town were interested in what was being delivered and what was being installed.

On the next Saturday—it was now early October—
she heard a sharp rap on the glass of the Lanier
Building door. She lifted aside the edge of the white
butcher paper and peeked out.

It was Phil.

"Come on," she heard him say as she was unlock-
ing the door. "Ned's found a bedroll."

The Jeep was at the curb, the engine still running.
Tess tucked the building keys in her pocket, not bothering to go back inside for her purse. "So tell me,"
she said, climbing into the passenger side of the Jeep,
"what's the story?"

Some of the merchants in town, she knew, were
growing impatient with Ned. They wanted him to
speed up the pace of the excavation. Yes, he had now
also uncovered the pumps, the coal box, and the
steam "doctor"—whatever that was—but those
things were more guy stuff. The people coming to see
them weren't the kind to buy one of Mrs. Ballard's
teacups. Fleur-de-lis needed him to find the human-
interest artifacts, something pretty, like dishes, buttons, and silk gowns. So why couldn't he forget
about the engines and go straight into the cargo
hold? People wanted Disneyland.

"I don't know much," Phil replied. "I was on the
phone and so just got a voice mail from him. But apparently the bedroll was caught in the housing of the
starboard paddle wheel. It must have been stowed
somewhere on the deck and the current carried it
back until it got caught."

Ned's plan—"which he will stick to," Phil said;
"he's kind of obsessive that way"—was to remove
any artifacts from the boat in as intact a way as pos-

sible and bring them to the schoolhouse, where they could be examined in an orderly fashion. So Phil continued past the site to the school. Word of the find had spread, and eight or nine cars were already there, parked close to the ditches along the side of the road. Phil pulled up behind them.

"This is so good for the town," he said. "We needed this."

People were gathered around a long outdoor table. Tess moved in next to Carolyn Ravenal.

"Ned must be beside himself," Tess whispered to her as a greeting.

"He's over the moon. He won't be able to sleep for a week."

Spread out across the table was a mass of something dark. Two people from the crowd were holding green garden hoses, directing sprays of water onto it as Ned unrolled the length of textile. He was wearing rubber gloves, and the front of his shirt was soaked, clinging to his chest.

The table itself was made of a screen door propped up on a pair of sawhorses. Some one-by-sixes provided extra support for the screen. Underneath the table, a couple inches of dirt had been dug up and replaced with gravel to absorb the water that would be used for washing.

"There's two layers of wool here," Ned was saying. "But the threads that held them together must have been cotton. They've disintegrated. The animal proteins—wool, silk, beaver hair, leather—may survive because the mud has sealed them in an oxygen-free environment. All the plant-based fibers like cotton and linen will be long gone."

The wool was soggy and heavy. He had to stop and move to the other end of the table, refolding the loose end of the bedroll. The water that streamed out from below the table was dark and sour-smelling.

"Here we go." Ned eased the last of the fabric open, revealing some mud-covered lumps. He lifted one and held it under one of the hoses. A stream of water pushed aside the mud. A curved handle glittered. It was a tin cup. Ned cradled it in his hands for a moment before lifting it up.

"Deck passengers," Ned explained to the small crowd, "just paid for transportation. They had to supply their own food and sleep in whatever spot they could find among the cargo."

Phil was gesturing to him. *Pass the cup around. Pass it around.*

Ned handed the cup to the person nearest to him and continued speaking as he lifted the next artifact. "You didn't want to be a deck passenger. If someone was going to drown, it was one of them. If someone was going to be burned when the boiler exploded, it was one of them. Sometimes they even had to go ashore and help gather wood."

Carolyn handed Tess the cup. It had a little dent in it and the handle had been mended once.

It wasn't pretty. It wasn't Disneyland, it wasn't Hollywood, but it was real. It had been used. An actual person—someone who had sweated under his arms and coughed if he breathed in some woodsmoke, someone who had decided to board the *Western Settler* and had a reason for being there, a plan—had used this cup.

People were asking Ned a lot of questions, and he answered as he turned objects under the stream of water. A plate, an iron skillet, a small knife, and a clay pipe emerged. "This was probably what the passenger was using every day on the boat, but it also might have been everything he owned in the world. We know about life aboard the *Western Settler* from Mrs. Lanier, one of the cabin passengers, and it's not likely that she would have ever spoken to this man until after the wreck. Her life had a kind of *Gone With the Wind* gracious-living elegance, which his wouldn't have had at all."

The reference to *Gone With the Wind* captured the attention of several women in the crowd. Here was some prettiness. Who was Mrs. Lanier? What was her life like?

"Compared to a stagecoach, a cabin on a steamboat was a very comfortable way to travel." Ned told them about the dining parlor and the ladies' salon. "It seems that the Laniers were intending to stop in St. Louis and spend the summer there, but apparently enjoyed the trip up the Mississippi enough that they elected to keep traveling. They clearly thought of themselves as travelers or tourists, not settlers. They were planning on going back home."

Ned had finished with the artifacts, but he continued to hold the hose over the bedroll. It would have to be completely rinsed before it could be refolded and frozen for future preservation. While waiting for the water to run clear, he spoke some more about the Laniers.

"We don't really know why they didn't return to

New Orleans. I have to wonder if they weren't embarrassed to have to admit to their families that they had taken slaves in Kansas Territory."

Slaves? Tess was instantly alert. She plucked at Phil's sleeve. "The two slaves, the ones who escaped after the wreck"—she had read about them in one of Phil's many press releases—"they didn't belong to the Laniers, did they?"

He looked down at her. "Of course. Two healthy adult slaves, and the woman an experienced midwife—that's a significant investment. No one else on board had that kind of money."

"But . . ." Tess was almost speechless. Why hadn't she known this? "But that little book she wrote . . . she didn't say anything about owning slaves."

"She was writing twenty years later. Having owned slaves was nothing to brag about in 1879."

Or ever.

Tess suddenly raised her hand as if she were in third grade. "Can you tell me more about the two slaves who ran away when the boat sank?" This time she spoke loud enough for everyone to hear. "Does anyone know what happened to them?"

"No, not for sure. But six months later a supposedly free black couple showed up in Lawrence, which was a center for antislavery activity. Oral tradition there says that the pair had escaped from a boat. Furthermore, she was reputed to be an excellent midwife, which suggests that she was Octavia, although she was going by a different name. There is documentation supporting this, a few letters and such, in which women urge each other to send for Harriet when 'their time comes.' "

"Did the owners try to get them back?" someone else in the crowd asked. "Didn't the Dred Scott decision say that you could bring your slaves into free soil?"

"That's what the Supreme Court said, but the people in Lawrence had guns—Beecher Bibles they were called because the New England abolitionists would send them in boxes marked as carrying Bibles. It's hard to imagine Fleur-de-lis—it was still known as Hobbing then and was as apolitical as it was possible to be in those years—mustering the kind of force needed to have taken on Lawrence, which is what would have been involved. Plus, I like to think that Eveline realized she was a stronger and better person for not having a slave to rely on, but that may be too contemporary a thought."

My grandmother Picard, who survived the wreck of the *Western Settler*, used to tell this story. A wagon had come out from town to bring the ladies and children back to shelter. Mrs. Lanier's Negro girl, Octavia, helped her mistress into the wagon, tucking her damp skirts around her. Mrs. Lanier asked if the girl was fit to walk into town and she said that she was and would be along with the men.

There were two families of respectable character, and their womenfolk were offering such aid as they could. Mrs. Lanier volunteered that Octavia would be along shortly to lend a hand. Many of the men had stayed on the river, hoping to retrieve some of the cargo, and it was assumed that Rex and Octavia were with them, as both were extremely strong and hardworking.

Mrs. Lanier showed no signs of worrying about Octavia, and only upon her husband's return did she say that she had great need of the girl.

"They are with you," Mr. Lanier said.

They both were very quiet and, Grandmother said, simply looked at each other, not speaking. They had thought that their Negroes were devoted to them, never thinking that the pair might want to escape, and at first they didn't believe it. Mr. Lanier spoke to the captain about mounting a mission to capture the runaways, but the captain was discouraging. Few locals would support such an enterprise, and not many of the passengers would have either. None of them had come from slave-owning families.

Grandmother Picard said that on the lengthy trip up from New Orleans the passengers had come to think highly of the two Negroes. Both were respectful and willing to help other passengers. Rex, of course, won everyone's gratitude by jumping into the river to save Mrs. Delon's young son.

Grandmother used to ask Grandfather if he would have gone out to help capture the pair. "If the captain had asked, I would have gone," Grandfather always answered. "But not much further than the nearest tree."

Mrs. Lanier was not used to doing for herself, but she settled down and learned. Her daughter was sickly most of the summer and so wasn't seen much. When they had been on the boat, Mrs. Lanier had told the other ladies that Octavia was a skilled midwife, and Mrs. Lanier did have occasion to miss her greatly later that autumn.

Undated note, handwritten on
lined paper, found folded in
the Picard family copy of
The Wreck of The Western Settler

As a girl, Tess had wanted to live somewhere that it snowed, but the Kansas autumn took her breath away. The hickory tree on the Old Courthouse lawn turned a vivid yellow. The oak in Tess's yard was softening into russet, and as she walked home each evening, leaves rustled at her feet and acorns crunched against the sidewalk. The air was clear and cool, faintly scented with the smoke from wood fires. Hawks flew low, and the geese swirled in wheel patterns that seemed to cover the whole sky.

All week Ned found more artifacts caught in the paddle wheel: a coffee grinder, broken dishes, a shoe. Phil sent out daily press releases, and the discoveries on the deck of the *Western Settler* were reported not just in Kansas City, St. Joe, Lawrence, and Wichita, but in St. Louis, Davenport, and Omaha. Many more people came to town the following weekend. On Saturday the Eislingers—the family who had opened a candy store/ice-cream parlor after their electronics store had gone bankrupt—had sold out of fudge at one-fifteen. By three they were out of peanut brittle and chocolate-chip cookie-dough ice cream. Tess heard that Barb Eislinger went home that night, put supper on the table, and started to cry. For the first time, Barb could imagine that this might work; the family might be able to save their house; the kids might be able to go to camp again.

The painters were finished at the Lanier Building, and the casement pieces had been delivered. Tess began to display her merchandise. She had tablecloths and dinner napkins, place mats and lunch napkins, finger towels, hand towels, ladies' hankerchiefs, antimacassars, doilies. She had pillowcases and sheets trimmed in handmade lace; she had factory-made blouses which she trimmed in handmade lace. She had filet lace, Battenberg lace, knit lace, drawn work, appliques. She also had gift items, most of them with some degree of handiwork—soft wool hats with silk roses, earrings made from antique buttons, crystal necklaces. Many of her linens were on hangers in the armoires, but others were displayed, draped across the drop leaf of a desk with a velvet-flower brooch and a twisting silver chain. She bought board games—backgammon, chess, Trivial Pursuits, Scrabble, even Candyland—and put them invitingly on a bookshelf, encouraging people to use them while drinking their coffee. On each table she put one of those little blank books and a mug full of pencils. It was very satisfying to arrange everything so beautifully. She could do it forever.

But the town needed her to open up.

With the help of Mrs. Fornelli, the high school guidance counselor, she found some high school students to work afternoons and weekends. A beautiful, although quiet, American Indian woman named

Sasha would work weekdays. At Carolyn Ravenal's suggestion, the famous local baker Brenda Jackson was going to be providing baked goods to supplement what Tess was ordering from Mrs. Cavender's bakery.

The first Sunday in November, Ned found a barrel full of building materials, hinges, bolts, door handles, locks, and keyhole covers, and at 6:30 A.M. on Monday, the Lanier Building Coffee Company opened for business.

At 6:25 A.M. Tess heard a car door close outside her front windows. She knew that Phil Ravenal would be her first customer. He had already made a habit of stopping by early every morning and letting her practice making espresso, but this morning he had also brought his parents and his brother.

Her door was already unlocked. "We're early," Phil said, "but we're willing to stack cups and sweep floors until opening time."

"I'm ready."

The others followed him in. Tess started on Phil's usual café Americano with half water while the others looked at the chalkboard menu over her head. "Are these to go or for in here?" she asked.

"In here," Phil answered. "They'll love your mugs."

"Tess, this place is unbelievable." Carolyn was looking in every direction. "I love it. I want to move in."

Tess smiled. "You're supposed to feel that way."

"We've never had anything like this in town," Dr. Matt said. He squinted at the chalkboard again. "Oh, Lord, I never know what to order in places like this. Just give me what Phil had."

"No," Phil said. "He has a major sweet tooth. Give him something with a flavoring."

Tess complied.

"And if that's Brenda Jackson's Tunnel of Death cake, give me a piece."

"Oh, Matt," Carolyn protested. "You aren't having that for breakfast, are you?"

"I wasn't going to call it breakfast."

Carolyn rolled her eyes and spoke to Tess. "Anything wrong with this town should be directly attributed to the atrocious eating habits of the local doctor."

As soon as their coffee was ready, Phil started showing Matt and Carolyn around. Ned had not said a word until he stepped forward to order a plain espresso. He looked tired.

"What are these little books for?" Dr. Matt asked.

"For people to write in. They're probably mostly for the tourists, but I thought people would enjoying reading what other people said."

"They'll love it. And I will go first." He took a book and started to write. Phil scooted his chair over, obviously planning on reading over his dad's shoulder. "Go away," Dr. Matt ordered. "Get your own book. This one is mine."

Carolyn was at the pie safe. "I am buying both these drawn-work tablecloths, and I want them out of here before anyone sees what I am spending."

Her husband looked up interestedly.

"Including you," she told him. "I'm keeping one, I'm giving one to my sister for Christmas, and I don't want to hear one word about it."

"Okay," he said cheerfully. "I'll just write about it in this little book."

She made a face at him and brought the tablecloths over to Tess.

Ned was moving silently around the big space, glancing at the books and magazines Tess had set out for people to read. Was he just tired or did he not like the place? When she had finished wrapping the tablecloths, she went over to him. He was in front of a display of crystal necklaces. She couldn't believe that he was looking at them.

He glanced at her. "Mom was serious about not wanting people to know what she spent. You know that, don't you?"

"I hadn't given it any thought. But it's not other people's business, is it?"

"That doesn't stop anyone around here. And do you really think that people are going to sit down and play Scrabble?"

"Not necessarily, but it's supposed to make you feel like you could. Whether or not it actually happens is beside the point. The important thing is the mood, the atmosphere, how people feel about themselves when they walk in."

"I'm not sure I get it." He looked embarrassed. "I'm sorry. I must be sounding like Mr. Doom and Gloom. I was up until three drying hinges." He tried to make up for it. "You really have done a great job. This looks like something from a magazine."

"But you aren't comfortable." Tess was surprised at how little his disapproval bothered her. She'd rather have a place that some people loved and some people hated than one that no one minded. Obviously the notion of relaxing in a public place would be new to many people. "The decor's too precious."

" 'La-di-da' is the word we use around here, not precious. The tourists are going to love it, but what about the locals? I paused before coming in." Then he laughed. "But don't listen to me. I'm not getting enough sleep. I am pausing before everything."

"*What* did you say to her?" As soon as the big glass door to the Lanier Building swung shut, Carolyn Ravenal turned on Ned. "She's been open five minutes, and you are in there criticizing. You were not brought up to behave like that, and you know it."

Ned grimaced. He guessed he had been too critical. Tess was so . . . he didn't know exactly what, but he did always seem to be looking for something wrong with her. "You do have to admit that those little blank books are a terrible idea."

"He has a point there," Dr. Matt said. "I behaved myself when I wrote, but once the high school kids get their hands on them and start writing about each other, blood will flow in the streets."

"I loved the place," Carolyn insisted. "I thought it was beautiful."

"It is," Ned agreed. "I guess that's my problem. It seemed a little too fussed over. I felt like I was supposed to behave myself."

"Of course you were supposed to behave yourself," his mother told him. "I would expect that regardless of where you were."

She was looking at him, expecting an answer. Ned

didn't think he had one. He felt as if he were five years old.

Phil rescued him. "Did you see other problems, Ned? I may be too close to what she's done in there."

"What do I know about businesses?" Ned wanted this conversation over. There had been so much stuff in that barrel yesterday. The nails had to be pried apart one by one, washed, and dried. The wood items had to be rinsed and then reimmersed in water until he could prepare them to be freeze-dried. "I made a mistake. I was rude to Tess. I see that, and I'll apologize."

Phil wasn't going to let him get away with that, and so Ned ended up telling him everything. "It doesn't seem real. It's like a movie set. The tourists will love it, but do you really want this to be just a tourist hangout? What's going to make us ordinary-Joe townfolk comfortable there? Even Dad didn't know what to order."

"Good point." Phil pulled out the little leather note holder in which he kept his innumerable lists. "She had talked about giving lacemaking classes. She probably ought to start right away. She should get the high school kids in—"

"After she gets rid of the blank books," Dr. Matt interjected.

"—because once they come, it will be real enough for anyone." Phil was making notes to himself. "If the people in the municipal building would . . ."

Ned moved toward his truck. Did anyone else ever get sick of Phil? All this endless problem solving? Why couldn't he just sit around and whine sometimes? Everyone else did. Why couldn't he?

∞ *Chapter 9* ∞

Could Grandfather Ravenal have ever imagined how hard this was going to be?

Rather than trying to dig or scoop away the mud and sand that surrounded the paddle wheels and engines, Ned and his crew were using adjustable-pressure hoses to wash the muck away. These heavy fire hoses had a strong back-kick, and you had to lean forward to compensate for the pressure. By the end of the day your back was aching, your arms were stiff from the weight of the hose, and your hands were cramped from gripping the nozzle. Even with rubberized gloves and fisherman's waders, you got soaked.

The guys in the crew were used to lifting and hauling, but at the end of the day even they were stripping off their gloves and clenching and unclenching their fists and walking with a hand pressed to the small of their backs. This was hard work.

And sometimes it was easy to forget that this was what he had always wanted to do, that this was his dream, the dream his grandfather had given him. But then he would touch something, a hinge that had never been used, a broken cup, and it would all be worth it.

Finally the deck was clear. A week after Tess opened her business, Ned forced a crowbar into the mud-sealed crack around the rear cargo hatch and leaned hard. The cargo hold was where the "human-interest" artifacts should be, and there should be a good number of them. The boat should have been heavily loaded, and the oak hull should have been constructed well enough to protect the cargo in the stern, whatever the damage to the bow.

But people weren't going to come to a museum to see "should haves." They weren't going to come to town and buy ice-cream cones and herbal hand lotion because of a "should have."

The wood squeaked and then groaned. Ned leaned hard against the crowbar, feeling the muscles along the back of his shoulders strain. Suddenly the hatch popped off, sending him backward into a cushion of cold mud. He struggled to his feet and looked down into the cargo hold.

It was a stew of black, foul-smelling mud. The tightly built hull of the boat had kept the sand and gravel from washing into the hold, so this mud was from the river silt filtering down through the pine decking. It would be denser, more difficult to deal with. Someone behind Ned reached around him with a hose, shooting a high-intensity stream of water onto the blackness, and the mud stirred sluggishly, reluctantly revealing the tops of barrels and wooden boxes—the *Western Settler*'s cargo.

The suction from the underground water table would be holding everything fast in the mud. Each container would have to be dug out.

They could never do it without better access than

the hatch. Ned and Dylan Pierce removed a small section of the pine deck. Dylan was the son of the owner of the air-conditioning/furnace business whose workers Ned had hired. Dylan was becoming as interested in the boat as Ned.

If they left the wood exposed to the air, it would shrivel and crack as it dried. Each board had to be labeled and carried away for storage in a water-filled, plastic-lined trench. Once they had a good-size opening, Ned lowered himself into the cargo hold, trying to find sure footing in the mud. Dylan followed. The two of them grabbed hold of a barrel and rocked it gently. It hardly moved. Someone still on the boat's deck shot a blast of water from the high-pressure hose at the barrel. Mud splattered across Ned's face.

The thick black goop lightened into a gray ooze. Ned and Dylan could twist and rock the barrel, but they couldn't lift it.

"We're going to have to unpack it here," Ned said. So much for the plan to unpack all the artifacts at the schoolhouse.

The lid was nailed on. Dylan passed Ned a fifteen-inch pry bar, and he inserted the beveled edge close to one of the nails and eased the lid off.

A heavy, fibrous-looking thing was on top. Dylan helped Ned lift it out. It was a woolen quilt, heavy with mud.

Underneath the quilt were one family's household possessions. There was a set of white ironstone dishes—six plates, six saucers, five cups. Then came two butcher knives and horn-handled cutlery, followed by a flour scoop and clothespins, a brass lamp and a coffee grinder, a tin bucket, a set of three flatirons. Dylan adjusted the pressure on a hose and rinsed enough mud off the artifacts so that Ned could look at them. Almost everything showed signs of use. These were the things the family was taking to start their new life in the West.

The woman who had packed these dishes and folded this quilt—did she ever again have white teacups and matching cutlery or did she have to make do with the kind of battered tin that had been in the bedroll of the deck passenger? Did the family prosper? Was the wreck of the *Western Settler* a minor setback in their lives or the ruin of all their hopes? There was no way to know.

Once the family barrel was emptied, he and Dylan were able to dislodge it from the mud. The barrel next to it was full of shoes, brand-new leather shoes clearly intended for a store. No family would ever travel with so many shoes. Ned passed them up to Dylan, who was perched close enough to the deck that he could hand them up to Steve Denmark. Steve piled the shoes into red plastic laundry baskets, and Phil, who had come out when he heard that Ned was in the hold, climbed in and out of the pit, loading the filled baskets into the pickup. They had to be careful. The shoes had been stitched with a cotton thread that had dissolved. They weren't in pairs; they had been constructed on a single last, not one for the right foot and one for the left.

The interior pump, designed to take away the wash water, was becoming clogged with mud, and Ned and Dylan were standing in ankle-deep muck. Their gloves were growing slippery.

Once the shoe barrel was empty, they eased it free

of the mud and turned it on its side so they could roll
it up onto the deck. Someone turned on a hose to
rinse off the barrel. As the water washed the curving
wood clean, lettering appeared. An "A" and a "V" in
sturdy blockface letters, obviously painted on the
wood through a stencil.

Ned used his gloved hand to push away the mud.

RAVENAL BROS.
ST. PIERRE
NEBRASKA TERRITORY

"Get Phil," he shouted and pulled himself out onto
the deck, the mud making sucking noises as he
dragged his feet free. "Where's my brother?"

A moment later Phil came slipping and sliding
sideward through the excavation mud down to the
deck of the boat.

"This is the stuff for the Ravenal brothers' store,"
Ned called out, looking up at his brother. How great
that Phil was here today. They might drive each other
crazy sometimes, but they were the Ravenal brothers,
just like Dr. Matt and their father, just like the two
guys on the boat. "This is us."

Over the next week, container after container came
up marked with the Ravenal name. There was hardware, door hinges, doorknobs, cases of nails. There
were tools, hammers, levels, axe heads, and chisels.
There were even windowpanes so carefully packed in
straw that they were still unbroken. The straw was
dank and sour, clinging to Ned's arms like something
from the Jaycees' Halloween Haunted House.

Little bottles held medicine that was still liquid. Blue-tinted glass jars held tightly packed pickles. The pickles were still green, and Dr. Matt later said that they would probably be okay, but no one was adventurous enough to try. There was a barrel full of red wool riverman's shirts and black wool men's overcoats, the fabric intact, the threads dissolved.

Dylan had rigged up a winch and pulleys so that the crew didn't have to unload the barrels while standing in the mud. Volunteers from town came out to the schoolhouse and rinsed, wiped, dried, counted, and folded the contents of the barrels and boxes.

Ned was doing very little permanent preservation of the artifacts so far. His current goal was simply to try to keep them stable until after the dig was completed. Early in the summer he had leased space in an old limestone cave on the south side of town. There had been some small-scale mining inside the cave, leaving a level-floored cavern that was cool and dark. Phil drove to every farm-supply store in three counties, buying stock tanks, the thousand-gallon galvanized containers used for watering horses and cows. Ned filled the tanks with water and immersed all the wood artifacts. Anything made of wood had to be kept wet until it could be soaked in a chemical and then freeze-dried.

The leather and rubber items would have to be temporarily frozen in blocks of ice until they could be treated. Whatever textiles survived would have to be rinsed, drained, individually wrapped, and then frozen. Wyatt and Gabe at The Cypress Princess had changed their menu and cleared out their big walk-in freezer so that the leather and textiles could be stored there.

Metals would have to be cleaned and coated with archival lacquer. Any preserved food items, such as pickles or brandied fruits, would have to be resealed with fresh wax. Dishes and glasses could be washed and put on display immediately. Night after night, Ned was up until midnight dealing with the artifacts, and then he was back at the site by five-thirty the next morning.

When the gods want to punish us, they answer our prayers—who said that? Aesop? Shakespeare? Oscar Wilde? Ned was far too tired to know. He had never worked so hard in his life.

Time blurred. He never knew what day it was. He would stumble home at night, shower, and fall into bed. When he would dream, it would be about shoes, mountains of shoes, and nails, kegs of mud-encrusted nails.

> For two days following the disaster, the smokestacks of the boat remained visible, and people took wagons out hoping to locate any salvage among the riverbank debris, but little was found.
>
> The two Mr. Ravenals set a marvelous example for all. Nearly a third of the boat's cargo had been theirs; their losses were far greater than anyone's, but their hearts were brave and their optimism unflagging.
>
> Mrs. Louis Lanier (Eveline Roget),
> *The Wreck of the Western Settler*,
> privately printed, 1879

* * *

Living alone was all that Tess had dreamed it would be. Everything in the house was always exactly where she left it. She didn't come home from work to find that the kitchen counters were littered with her roommates' Diet Coke cans or her grandparents' prescription bottles. No one borrowed her postage stamps or put uncovered leftovers in the refrigerator. She didn't have to listen to anyone else's phone calls. No one turned on the TV too loud.

She wasn't the least bit lonely. It was fun to be Tess-of-the-Lanier-Building. People liked her. She was pretty enough to be welcoming, not so glossy as to be intimidating, wearing unusual clothes that other women could talk to her about because the garments' interest came from her own work, not from how much money she had spent.

She had done only an adequate job at Willow Place. She saw that now. She hadn't had the experience to distinguish between clinical depression and understandable, transient sadness. But serving coffee—she was very good at serving coffee. Her therapist training helped. She knew how to be warm and engaged but without issues of her own, how to let the moment be about the other person. And this manner didn't feel false, or as if she were denying herself. She was interested in other people; she wanted to hear them talk about themselves.

Sierra, on the other hand, was having difficulties. Her business seemed to be doing well, but Tess overheard people who came into the Lanier Building car-

rying green Celandine Gardens shopping bags. They
rolled their eyes and mockingly repeated the things
Sierra had said. Tess could imagine what was happening. Sierra, too, wanted to be Miss Kitty. She
craved acknowledgment; she needed other people to
tell her she was unique and special. That was too
much of a burden to put on people who just wanted
to buy facial scrub.

Both Sierra and Tess were keeping their businesses
open until ten on Friday and Saturday nights. Although California-born Tess thought that the evenings
were prohibitively cold, the restaurant patrons, encouraged by Wyatt and Gabe, put on their puffy down
coats and strolled along Main Street. Those women
were interested in Tess's larger tablecloths and the
more intricate laces, items that only a handful of Fleur-
de-lis residents could consider buying.

During the day on Saturday and on Sunday afternoon, a more casually dressed crowd came in, buying
the lower-priced items—the hats, the earrings, and
the bracelets—and incredible amounts of hot chocolate for their children, which, Tess quickly discovered, the children didn't like. They wanted a sweeter,
milkier drink, something more like the packaged
product they were used to. So she lowered the price
and bought a cheap mix. It took the counter help far
less time to prepare, and the little customers were
happier.

During the week, mornings were her busiest time.
It had taken the high school students two days to discover the Lanier Building Coffee Company, and between 6:30 A.M. and the opening bell at 7:25, the
Lanier Building was full of sleepy adolescents with

heavy backpacks, ordering extra large cappuccinos with triple shots and double flavoring.

A few of them were Nina Lane fans. "Biologically, I am her daughter," Tess would say, always keeping her voice pleasant. "But I might as well have been adopted. I know nothing about her."

After the high school kids left, Phil Ravenal was invariably her next customer. Sometimes he would lean against the counter and talk to her, but often he would go to a table and work, reading a document and making quick notes in the margin. He would get out his cell phone and listen to his voice mail. He would check his daily list. He kept the list on three-by-five cards that fit into a little leather folder, and he rarely left one place for another without checking that list.

In part because they knew they might find Phil there, the owners of the new businesses on Main Street would stop by before going to their own shops. Around nine-thirty, various groups of young mothers might come in after dropping their kids off at the Methodist church preschool. None of these people ordered as extravagantly as the high school kids did, but with the exception of some of the Saturday night restaurant patrons, no one ordered the way the high school kids did.

She was not seeing a full cross section of the town. She knew that. The people who had moved there to work at Kmart couldn't afford to visit the Lanier Building, and the people who disliked change, who wanted everything to be as it was before Kmart and the tourists, gathered at Mrs. Cavender's bakery. But the people who accepted, even liked, the changes, who would have voted for Phil Ravenal even if his own revered father had come back to life to run against him—that crowd came to the Lanier Building.

All was not perfectly smooth, of course. She lost some earrings to shoplifters. Someone wrote something in one of the little blank books that made one of the high school girls gasp and stumble out to her car, struggling with tears. Children pulled the Scrabble game off the shelf and emptied all the tiles onto the floor. Espresso drinks were time-consuming to prepare. If several groups came in at once, a line developed.

The early-morning line was getting to be a problem. High school students were sauntering into school late, with Lanier Building Coffee Company carryout cups in hand.

The high school guidance counselor called Tess, first saying what good things she had heard about how the Lanier Building looked and that she really hoped to stop by someday soon. "Unfortunately, you're making the kids late to class in the morning."

"*I* am?" Tess would have thought that the kids were making themselves late.

"So we were hoping," Mrs. Fornelli continued, "that at seven-ten or so, you could make an announcement and stop serving the kids. You could serve adults, of course, but not the students."

Tess wondered if this was legal. "But isn't being on time their responsibility?"

"Of course." The answer was smooth. "But it's the community's obligation to provide children with the structure they need. It takes a village to raise a child."

Tess didn't recall that she had ever been raised by a village. "It does take a long time to make espresso drinks, especially the elaborate ones the kids order."

"Good, then," the counselor said. "I'm glad you see it our way."

Tess stared at the phone. What had she said to make the woman think that? How quick people were to hear what they wanted to. It had obviously never occurred to Mrs. Fornelli that Tess would not do exactly as asked.

This was what Ned had been talking about last summer—the pressure on people in a small town to conform. You either went along or were like Sierra, determinedly resisting and rebelling at everything.

Growing up, Tess had never been able to conform. She couldn't dress like the other girls—her grandmother couldn't bear to spend money on store-bought clothes. She hadn't been allowed to stay out as late as the other kids or hang out at the mall all day. But she wasn't interested in being a rebel either; her mother had been a rebel. She simply wanted to be herself and do what she thought was right.

And that did not include enforcing the school's rules.

"I do suppose we have an overprotective mentality," Phil acknowledged when she told him about it later in the day.

"Maybe that's why there are so many divorces." Tess had expected small-town Kansas to be the home of old-fashioned values, but marriages failed here just as they did anywhere else. "People aren't allowed to make little mistakes, just big ones."

"You aren't going to find many people who agree with you," Phil said mildly.

Tess didn't need to have people agree with her, but, unlike Sierra, she also didn't need to be difficult. So she hired more counter help, and on one of the pine sideboards she set out pour-it-yourself drip coffee, to be paid for on the honor system. There was one size of cup, one price, and a little locked Lucite box with a slot. This allowed the kids who didn't mind getting to school on time to do so. The kids who wanted to be late were going to be late regardless of anything Tess did.

Phil and everyone in the crew kept reminding Ned that this coming Thursday was Thanksgiving. No one in the crew was working, and he shouldn't either.

"Okay, okay," he mumbled.

He woke up as early as ever that morning, and as long as he was up, he went out and checked on a few things at the site, but he was back well before noon to shower before going over to Matt and Carolyn's. When he got out of the shower, he couldn't find a clean towel, or any towel at all. He was pretty sure there were some in the dryer, and it probably would have been a really great idea to have checked before he had gotten in the shower, but he hadn't. So he lay down on the bed to air-dry which was stupid, since the next thing he knew, the phone was ringing. It was Caitlin, the oldest of his sisters, telling him that it was four o'clock, and Mom was planning on serving dinner at five.

"Ten minutes," he said. "I'll be there in ten minutes."

Phil and the girls had parked their cars in the driveway at Matt and Carolyn's, so Ned parked on the street and entered the old Victorian house through the rarely used front door. The door was original to the house and had a three-quarter-length oval glass window. Carolyn had never covered the window before; there was never anyone hanging around in the front hall doing anything that required privacy, but now a lightly shirred linen panel with little diamond-shaped lace insets had been carefully fitted into the oval. It was pretty. Carolyn had probably gotten it from Tess.

Ned closed the door behind him. Dr. Matt was coming down the dark-wainscoted hall from the back of the house. He would have been in the library watching football with Phil and Doug McCall. Doug was a medical student and Caitlin's boyfriend.

"I'm late," Ned said, probably unnecessarily. "I shouldn't be living in Great-uncle Bob's house. I'm going to turn into as odd a recluse as he was."

"Caitlin said you fell asleep."

As a little girl, Caitlin had been a bit of a tattletale. Ned had thought she'd outgrown it. Apparently not. "I didn't mean to."

"No, of course not. But I'm glad you're here. I need to talk to you." Dr. Matt gestured for him to go into the front room. It had been a playroom for a long time, but once Emma and Brittany were in junior high, Carolyn had packed up the electric trains and the Barbies and furnished it according to the period of the house. Now it boasted rich velvets, marble-topped tables, and stylized carvings on the arms of the chairs and the doors of the cabinets. Ned sank down into one of the wing chairs.

"When did you last have a decent night's sleep?" Dr. Matt asked.

"I have no idea."

"Then it wasn't recently enough." Dr. Matt was sitting on the other wing chair. He had his elbows on the chair arms and was tenting his fingers together, making a little bouncing motion with his thumbs. This was what he did when he had something medical to say. "Listen here, Ned, you've got heavy equipment. You've got generators, power lines, and water everywhere. And you aren't getting enough sleep. That's nuts. Someone's going to get electrocuted or crushed or something."

"We'll be okay, Dad. Really we will. We're being very careful."

"Maybe everyone else is, but you're too tired to be careful, and you're in charge. You take better care of yourself, or I'll find some loophole in the public health laws or OSHA regulations to shut you down."

"Dad!" Ned stared at him. "You aren't serious, are you?"

"You bet I am."

"But with the cargo exposed to oxygen—"

"I know all that," Dr. Matt interrupted. "And I know what your fuel costs are running, and guess what? I don't care. You have to get more sleep."

"I have my whole life to sleep." But this . . . the digging up of the boat, it would probably be the high point of his professional life. How could he sleep?

"I wouldn't count on anything if I were you," Dr. Matt countered. "Look at your parents. You know why they died, don't you?"

His parents? Why bring them up? What did their

death have to do with anything? "Wasn't there a problem with the plane? Something on the instrument panel?" Ned was sure that he knew the details, but he couldn't seem to remember.

"Yes, but an alert pilot could have handled it. Phillip—your dad—hadn't had enough sleep. He was all caught up in trying to set up that farm co-op, he was as excited as you are about the boat, and he was running himself into the ground. His reaction times were off."

"You mean it was his fault?" Everyone had always talked about Phillip as if he had been perfect. How could his death have been his own fault?

"We never made a big deal of it to you boys, but we also didn't sue the plane manufacturer either. Everyone talks about your dad as if he were Apollo, the sun god driving his flaming chariot across the sky, but part of him was Icarus, the kid who flew too close to the sun and crashed when his wings melted."

"But Phil's the one trying to be like him, not me."

"You're the one putting your life on the line. I lost my brother and I don't care to have Phil and the girls go through that. As bad as losing you would be for them, it would be worse for Carolyn, and you owe her way too much to do that to her."

Dr. Matt never talked like that; he never tried to make Phil and him feel guilty about Carolyn's raising them.

"I'm not asking you to quit," the doctor continued. "All I am asking you to do is get more sleep."

How could Ned say no to that? "All right, Dad."

"Do I have your word on it?"

"You do."

"Good." Dr. Matt stood up. "Now go out to the kitchen and say hello to your mother and the girls, and then come watch the rest of the game with Phil and Doug and me. Or rather, with Phil and me. Doug keeps drifting off. He's not getting any more sleep than you are."

Ned crossed the hall into the dining room. The table was already set with the Haviland china from the Shelbys and the heavy silver flatware with the scrolling *R* monogram. Ravenal men tended to do pretty well for themselves in the marriage department. Grandmother Ravenal had come from Kansas City meat-packing money; Carolyn was a Shelby, and Ned's own mother, Polly, had inherited a share in a couple of cement factories near Abilene. In fact, it was the cement checks that Ned and Phil were living on now.

As he approached the kitchen, the swinging door eased open, and through it came Tess, carrying a platter of cinnamon apples. The platter was large, and she had pushed the door with her elbow and was trying to keep it open with her hip. Ned hurried across the dining room to hold the door for her. She thanked him and set the platter on the table. She was wearing a dark, longish sort of dress with pretty silver buttons.

He was surprised to see her. "I didn't know you were going to be here."

"You did too," Carolyn called out from the kitchen. "I told you at least twice."

Ned thought he would have remembered something about Tess. Maybe he did need more sleep. He stepped into the kitchen and waved to his sisters.

Caitlin was at the stove, whisking the gravy and trying to step out of the way while Carolyn checked the turkey. Emma was at the sink, and Brittany was at the table, arranging a relish tray.

"I'd offer to help," he said, "but Dad is worried that I'd get hurt."

Carolyn smiled at him. "We're in fine shape, and you need to talk to Tess. She has something to show you."

Ned let the kitchen door swing back shut. The scent from the cinnamon apples was sharp and sweet. Tess had placed the platter at an angle on the dining room table. She stepped back and looked at it, then adjusted its position a bit before she was satisfied. She did pay attention to details.

"Mom says you have something to show me."

"I do." She picked up a manila envelope off the sideboard. "Apparently you don't return phone calls."

That was true. "Phil does it for me, and he's so much better at it than I am. A reporter calls with a few quick questions, and it doesn't matter how quick the questions are, my answers are always long-winded and boring. Phil has this sound-bite thing down cold. But I would have returned your calls . . . if I had known about them."

"It wasn't me calling. If I had needed you, I would have gone out to the site and grabbed you by the ear."

"That would have worked." Ned followed her into the front room. "At least I hope so." She sat down on the sofa. He scooped up a couple of the throw pillows, dropped them over the back of the sofa, and sat down next to her. She started to open the envelope. He spoke quickly; he wanted to talk about her, not the manila envelope.

"Phil says your business is going great." He paused, trying to remember exactly what Phil had said. "Your weekend trade is in the mid- to upper range of the projections, but your support from the local community is far beyond expectations."

"You sound like you memorized that for a final exam."

"No. If I had been trying to memorize it, I would have done a better job." He had always been a crackerjack test-taker. Now he was remembering more. "And you're making all the high school kids late to class."

"*I'm* not making them late." Her voice was pleasant but firm. She had said this before. "They are making themselves late."

"It takes a village to raise a child, Tess," he said, hoping to sound like the voice of Fleur-de-lis's protectionistic, paternalistic culture.

"That doesn't mean—" She stopped. "You're teasing me."

" 'Teasing' is a strong word, Tess. If you tease another kid on the playground these days, you're called a bully."

"Okay, whatever." She lifted her curly mass of hair back off her shoulder. She looked rueful, not because she minded being teased, but she minded not getting his joke. "I need you to be serious." She switched on the lamp that sat next to the sofa. The light glinted off the silver buttons of her dress as she slid some papers out of the envelope. "The author of this is going out on a limb and wants some confirmation from you that she isn't totally wacky."

"Someone wants *me* to confirm that she isn't totally wacky? That's like putting the inmates in charge of the nuthouse."

"Would you be serious?"

He would try. "Lay it on me, babe."

She made a face at the "babe"—as he had intended her to—but opened the envelope and explained. This had to do with Nina Lane's *Riverboat Fragment*. When her publishing company had been looking through their files for a copy of a contract, they had discovered the original manuscript for *The Riverboat Fragment*. It was a typescript, covered with handwritten corrections. So the company was publishing a facsimile edition of the manuscript. "Which is fabulous," Tess said cheerfully, "because I'm going to get all kinds of money."

"That's nice. Are you going to be interested in buying some used water pumps this time next year?"

"No. Apparently Nina Lane used a fountain pen and she liked to use lots of different-colored ink. Look here." She pulled out a sheet from the manuscript. "This is just a colored Xerox, not what they will be producing the facsimile from, but you can see all the colors. Obviously there was no system to it—"

"She has never sounded like a very systematic person."

"That's certainly true. When the ink in one cartridge ran out, she would grab another, screw it in, and keep going."

"Okay."

"The result of this is that they can tell in what order she did her corrections. Because there'd be this phase when the old ink in the pen would blend with the new, so you can tell that when the peacock blue shades into the midnight violet, she did the peacock blue first. Apparently she skipped around in the manuscript. She would get an idea for one kind of change and make it throughout. Then she'd get another idea and follow it through. So they scanned the whole thing into a computer this summer, and thus were able to print up a list of her revisions in the order she made them." Tess patted another stack of paper. "They send me every little thing, hoping to keep me happy."

"And what is all this revealing?" Ned had a historian's basic respect for evidence. But you needed someone to interpret it. Otherwise it was just pointless data.

"A lot of stuff that isn't very interesting." Tess found a page much earlier in the manuscript and looked at a passage in the editor's introduction. "She was turning her dependent clauses into nominative absolutes. Do you know what a nominative absolute is?"

"Sort of. But only because I took Latin," he apologized, "and know about ablative absolutes . . . or at least I used to. Is this what my wacky-meter is supposed to be operating on? Grammar?"

"No. The editor has this idea about the mother-and-daughter characters." She handed Ned another piece of paper. It was a clean typescript, probably from the editor's introduction.

On page 13, we see the violet ink shading into emerald green. This initiates a set of changes all focusing on Bracine and Rentha, the mother and daughter among the riverboat people. Nina Lane is adding physical details and developing an edgy concern to Bracine's dealings with her daughter. Rentha is not eating and is repeatedly noted as being weary.

Previous critics—all of them male—have suggested that the daughter is ill. I would argue instead that during these "green revisions" Nina Lane decided to make Rentha pregnant. All of the green revisions to the setting involve increasing the fertility of the landscape and tying Rentha to it.

This is, of course, highly speculative, but one thing that previous critics have ignored is that Nina Lane was herself pregnant while doing these revisions. She may have been recording her own symptoms.

"This is interesting," Ned acknowledged. "But what does it have to do with me?"

"The editor wants definite confirmation that Eveline Lanier was indeed pregnant when the *Western Settler* sank."

"Herbert was born six months afterwards. There's no doubt about that. A priest came from Leavenworth to baptize him, and all the records about his birth are consistent. But Eveline was the mother, the Bracine figure," Ned pointed out. "So I guess that's what's fun about writing fiction. You can do whatever you want."

It was time for dinner. As always, the family sang the doxology, and then Carolyn directed them all where to sit. Doug was next to Caitlin, of course, and Tess next to Phil. Ned was conscious of being sorry for a moment. He had enjoyed talking to her.

But what was he expecting? He had been too busy to be paying any attention to people's social lives, but clearly Matt and Carolyn hadn't invited Tess just because she was the new kid in town, needing a place to go for a holiday. She was Phil's girlfriend.

To the extent that Ned had ever thought about it, he would have guessed that Phil would fall in love with someone who was the exact opposite of himself, someone who was flaky and spiritual, sort of a younger version of Sierra. She would fascinate him and frustrate him, and then he would make them both miserable by trying to change her.

But what had Phil ever done to make Ned think he would do something so stupid? He would choose a mate with the same good sense and caution that he applied to everything.

And it was hard to find fault with Tess although admittedly Ned sometimes found himself trying. She was organized, she was efficient, she was reliable. She was not going to drive Phil nuts. Moreover, she seemed to be self-reliant. Ned thought Phil was the greatest, he really did, but Phil was not a touchy-feely sort of guy. He was best at things that could be crossed off lists. A clingy woman, one who was emotionally dependent, would be forever unsatisfied by Phil, but Tess Lanier didn't seem to be needy at all. She wouldn't be forever whining at him to stay home and pay attention to her. She had her own business and her own interests. She wouldn't need something that Phil couldn't provide.

It looked promising. Maybe another Ravenal man would marry well.

∽ *Chapter 10* ∽

Remembering his promise to Dr. Matt, Ned set his alarm for seven on Friday morning. It made no difference. He woke up at five anyway and couldn't go back to sleep. He had to return to the site. Who knew what he'd find in the next barrel?

More merchandise for the Ravenal brothers' store; that was the answer to that question. A balance scale and a spring scale. Twelve crosscut saws and eighteen keyhole saws. One hundred and thirty-six drill bits. A couple thousand cigars. Two hundred and ninety-seven wooden spools that must have held thread. A little case of china doll heads. They were Friday's strangest find.

Ned was at one of the rinsing tables outside the schoolhouse, repacking the doll heads to take them into town. They looked a little creepy, these rows of sweet-faced, pink-cheeked, disembodied heads smiling up at him from a black rubber mat. Maybe he could get someone to make one into a doll. Was that something Tess could do?

As he was labeling the dolls' box, he heard the sound of a vehicle approaching from the excavation site. It was his own truck, heavily splattered with mud. Phil was behind the wheel, obviously having driven over from the excavation site. He usually stopped by in the late afternoon to see what had been found that day.

"We've got some more passenger belongings." Phil unrolled the window of the truck as he pulled up to the rinsing table. "A couple of really nice trunks."

So far, everything had been packed in wooden barrels and boxes, but the three trunks Phil had in the back of the pickup were leather with brass fittings. Ned carried the largest over to the table and turned the hose on it. It was very well made. With brass strips covering all the seams in the leather, it might be the most watertight thing they had found. The water cleared the mud off the darkened leather. Rounded brass nailheads formed a monogram. LHL. Louis Henry Lanier.

This was unbelievable. Ned had never expected that they would know who had owned any of the artifacts. But this was clearly Louis Lanier's.

"Call Tess," he shouted to Phil. "This is her family's stuff."

"It is?" Phil was unloading the last trunk from the truck. "How do you know?"

"A monogram. Call her. Use the phone in the truck. She'll want to be here."

"She won't have her car downtown. It will be faster if I go get her. And today is the start of the Christmas shopping season. She'll probably think she shouldn't leave."

"Make her come." Tess always had plenty of counter help. "She shouldn't miss this." Ned picked up the hose again. He would have time to get the worst of the muck off before Tess arrived.

The trunks were locked. But the Canadians who had taught him about freshwater preservation had advised him to learn the basics of lock picking. He went back into the schoolhouse to get his set of lockpicks.

He had the first two trunks unlocked when Phil drove into the school yard.

Tess was flushed, pushing her hair back off her face. "I thought you said that all their belongings were in the cabins."

"I was wrong." Ned handed her a pair of rubber gloves and a jacket that was warmer and more waterproof than what she was wearing. As she put them on, he raised the lid on Louis's trunk. "These must have been things they didn't need on the journey."

There was less mud inside than they had seen before. The superb construction of the trunk had kept it out. The pieces of the first garment lifted out easily, a black wool topcoat with silk facings. It was the first time they had found any silk. None of the other passengers had packed silk. Only the Laniers had been able to afford it.

There were pants to go with the coat, and beneath them was a layer of small white buttons, suggesting that Louis—or Rex, on his behalf—had packed several cotton or linen shirts. Louis had also been traveling with a sterling-silver shaving set complete with a toothbrush holder, a little covered soap dish with a removable drainer, and a pair of small candlesticks. Across the bottom of his trunk was a layer of books. The pages were muddy pulp, but the gilt writing on the leather covers could still be read. There was a

Bible, and a novel titled *Redburn*. Ned had never heard of it, and neither had Phil or Tess, but it was by Herman Melville, the author of *Moby Dick*. There was also a collection of Longfellow's poems and two Victor Hugo novels, apparently in the original French.

"He must have left his copy of *Uncle Tom's Cabin* at home," Phil said dryly.

Tess made a face at him.

The three of them worked together to rinse Louis Lanier's belongings. The pieces of each garment were folded flat, stacked on large, gridded plastic trays used to deliver bread, and loaded back into the truck to be taken to The Cypress Princess freezer. The leather book covers received the same treatment. Phil usually couldn't endure the tedium of such work, but he was, Ned noticed, doing fine now. It probably had something to do with Tess being here.

Daughter Marie's trunk was next. She had been seventeen when the boat had sunk in May of 1857. Ironically, she had died the following January, drowning in the river.

The first thing in her trunk was a length of textile, edged by a fringe. Ned lifted it out and laid it on the rinsing table's screen inset. Phil turned a gentle stream of water on it, and a pale circle the size of a dime appeared. The circle gradually widened, revealing an ivory fabric with a paisley design in shades of coral and blue-green. It was a wool shawl, large enough to be swirled over a woman wearing a hoop skirt. Beneath the shawl, a layer of white buttons and some pieces of white silk ribbon might have come from cotton undergarments or nightwear. Beneath that were three silk dresses, two pair of shoes, and several lengths of uncut silk. Unlike every other garment they had uncovered, Marie's dresses had been sewn with silk thread. They were intact.

"Look at these colors," Tess said. "This is so strange. These are the colors I wear. Look at this." Rather than lift the heavy, sodden fabric, she knelt down and craned her head so that her face was next to a corner of a pale green gown. Ned had always thought her eyes were blue, but the fabric made them shimmer with a green light that he hadn't noticed. She stood up and started pointing to the fabrics. "There's no pure white, just ivory. There's no brown, just this apricot. Everything is light but clear. This could be my closet."

"She wasn't married," Ned pointed out, "and she moved in fancy society. She wouldn't have worn dark colors."

"It's more than light and dark. There is not a hint of gray in any of these colors. She had the same coloring as I do."

"She was your something-something great-aunt. It's not a big coincidence."

"You don't have a picture of her, do you?"

"No. The Yankee occupation of New Orleans wiped out those Laniers socially, economically, everything. The only family records left down there are the ones in the churches. And Marie died long before Fleur-de-lis got a photographer."

At the bottom of Marie's trunk were again some books—this was obviously an educated family—mostly in French, but there was one collection of the English Romantic poets. In the corner of the trunk, as if they had been wedged in as an afterthought, were a few baby things: a little silver mug and an ivory teething ring. Neither was monogrammed or appeared to have been used. They must have been for the baby whom Eveline was carrying.

"Why are they in Marie's trunk?" Phil asked and then answered himself. "Because they packed like every other family in the world. At the last minute you start sticking in stuff wherever it fits."

"That's for sure," Ned agreed. "I was always finding the girls' swimming suits in my suitcase."

Tess was still looking at the silks. "It does make them seem real," she reflected. "Rushing around at the last minute, cramming more things into their trunks. That's what anyone would do."

"They were real," Ned answered. "They were real people."

It took some time before Marie's possessions were rinsed and stored on the bread trays. Tess pushed back the cuff of her rubber glove to check her watch. "Can I use a phone? I should be sure everything is okay in town."

"Use the one in Ned's truck," Phil said.

Tess opened the driver's door and took out the phone. As careful as she had been, the front of her jacket had gotten wet, and its thin insulation clung to her. She was narrow through her torso and hips, but her breasts were surprisingly full. Of course, Nina Lane had had a bust line that was out of proportion to the rest of her frame. That was why, Ned had learned from one of his sisters, she had worn all those crocheted vests.

Eveline Lanier had packed fewer clothes than her

daughter, and they were in richer colors, a brown-orange that Tess called russet, a bottle green, a deep red.

"Are these your colors?" Ned asked her.

"Hardly." Apparently he should have known that.

At the bottom of Eveline's trunk was a wooden box and a tin one. Ned eased open the hinged lid of the wooden one. It was filled with small glass bottles with wax-sealed stoppers. Several had broken—they must have been packed in paper—but there were at least a dozen intact. Ned took one out and held it up to the light. Any label had long since dissolved.

"We'll need to get it analyzed, but I'm guessing that this is laudanum."

Tess looked at him inquiringly.

"It's an opium derivative, used as a sedative."

"Opium?" Phil asked. "That must have been addictive. Do you think Granny Lanier was a doper?"

"She owned slaves and she was chemically dependent?" Tess said. "What an admirable individual."

Ned shook his head. He didn't believe that Eveline Lanier had been addicted to anything. "She certainly recovered well enough," he pointed out. "She lived to be eighty-one. And she was the one who really turned the town into a place where you would want to live." Eveline had organized the first school and had started the public library with books she had persuaded people in New Orleans to donate. "We also don't know that the stuff was hers. You remember, Phil, when we would go on vacation, Mom would always take charge of all the medication—Emma's inhaler and everyone's acne pills. This could have been Eveline's husband's, her daughter's, or for a friend. We aren't going to know."

He labeled the box and put it in one of the buckets for underwater storage. The bottles he wiped, labeled, and wrapped carefully in newspaper. Phil was still rinsing the remainder of Eveline's dresses.

"You can go ahead and open that last box," Ned told Tess.

It too had been inside Eveline's trunk. It was tin, and the lid fit tightly. Tess had to take off her rubber gloves.

Ned heard her gasp.

"What is it?" He and Phil bumped into each other as they crowded close.

It was Eveline's work basket, her sewing things. Protected first by the well-made trunk and then by the tightly fitting metal box, the contents were far cleaner than anything they had yet seen. Everything was damp, of course, but the contents were merely grayish.

Ned motioned for Phil to get their most finely meshed tray, and he handed Tess a plastic watering can with a thin, arching spout, the kind used to water houseplants. Tess started to pour a gentle stream into the box. Bits of white thread rose and drifted in the water.

Tess stopped pouring. "Those are French knots, and this looks like a line of satin stitching. Eveline was working on something that was in this embroidery hoop."

The base fabric must have been linen or cotton, and it had disintegrated. All that remained were the silk threads and the metal hoop.

"There are hundreds of these knots." Tess looked up at Ned. "What do we do?"

There was no way of reconstructing the stitchery design. Ned handed Tess a pair of tweezers and had her collect a sample of the knotted and cut threads. The rest they let wash away.

Tess was still working bare-handed. "Look at these scissors. They are exquisite."

In her palm lay a small pair of gold-plated scissors. A scrolling design was etched along the blade and down around the handles. "I would miss these if they had been mine."

Ned took them from her. There were faint scratches in the gold plate. These scissors had been used.

"Pins . . ." Tess was still taking things out of the box. "Needles. She certainly did bring a lot of needles. But there's nothing worse than running out of needles."

The pins were loose. They must have been folded in paper or cotton. But the needles had been pierced through a small square of dark wool.

Ned started picking up the pins.

"Knitting needles . . . this must be silk embroidery thread." Tess lifted the watering can and began to pour water until the threads straightened into neat skeins. "Look at these colors . . . aren't they beautiful?"

Ned used another tray to line up the skeins as Tess passed them to him.

"Look. These needles are still threaded."

Tess was holding another piece of the dark wool. Six needles had been laced into the fabric with a single stitch, and looping around each needle in a figure eight was grayish thread. A moment later the water turned it white.

"It's the same thread as before. These were the needles she had already threaded to finish that project. You do that. You thread a lot of needles at once, and then you don't have to—"

Tess broke off. She was suddenly pale, looking as if she might faint. Ned was across the table from her. He dropped his hose and leaned forward, grabbing her shoulders in case she fell. The water from the hose splashed across his legs.

Phil had been loading bread trays into the truck. He hadn't noticed. "Are you all right?" Ned asked softly.

"It's so real . . . she threaded those needles. She was going to use them."

"I know," he murmured, his head close to hers. This had not been a utility sewing box. There had been no extra buttons, no darning egg. This was needlework done for the love of needlework.

Tess loved needlework.

"What's going on?" Phil's voice seemed to boom. "Is something the matter?"

Tess straightened and stepped back from Ned's grasp. His gloves had left two damp spots on the sleeves of her upper arms. "I was just thinking about how much everyone on the boat had lost, and I know these are just needles, but sometimes it's the little things that you miss the most."

"Sometimes those are the only things you can let yourself miss," Ned said softly.

She nodded. "After my grandfather died and I had cleared out the house, if I couldn't find something, I would picture where it was in the old house and I'd think I'd run over and get it, the new people wouldn't mind . . . not that it was there, of course."

"Did you find what you were looking for?" Phil asked.

Ned tried not to shake his head. Phil had completely missed Tess's point.

It was after eight when they were finished with the contents of the three trunks. Tess needed a ride back to town, but Ned still had to close up the schoolhouse and check at the site, so of course Phil was the one who drove her back.

Of course.

Phil had taken the truck so that he could drop off the leather and textiles at the restaurant. But Ned had kept one tray behind, the one with Eveline Lanier's sewing supplies.

He had said that he would do no preservation while the ground was open. It was just too time-consuming. Stabilize the artifacts now; preserve them for exhibition later.

The empty wooden spools, which must have once held cotton thread, he would have to put in underwater storage. You couldn't preserve wood overnight. But the silk could be washed, and the pins and needles could be dried and counted. It was exactly the sort of thing he had sworn to Dr. Matt that he wouldn't do—stay up all night to do something that could be done next year. But this was different.

This was for Tess.

* * *

Professionally, Ned accepted a conventional view of time. Time was a simple line, always moving forward. The past was over, the future hadn't yet happened. That was it.

But outside his profession, Ned was willing to accept—even if it had never happened to him—that for some people, there were moments when time's simple line doubled back on itself, twisting and knotting.

He suspected that something like that had happened to Tess by the rinsing table outside the schoolhouse. She hadn't imagined Eveline's regret. She had actually experienced it right along with Eveline. He didn't understand how such things happened or why, but he believed that they could.

Not that he was going to talk to her about it. She wouldn't have been any more receptive to the idea than Phil would have been. Her softly curling hair and rose-gold coloring might give her an unearthly glow, but she was as relentless an empiricist as Phil. She lived in the here and now. She believed in the material world, she adored it, she treasured its beauties.

She couldn't have been more different from Nina Lane, who, for all her ability to describe the physical world, viewed it as a gateway to something richer.

By 3 A.M. the wash water gushing through the brilliantly colored silk threads was running clear, and all the metal objects were dried and arranged on a velvet-lined jewelry tray. The silk threads were still too wet to be moved, but the pins, the needles, the scissors, and the hoop, he was giving them to Tess.

He went home, showered, did some research, and waited for morning. It was Saturday and Tess didn't open until eight, but he figured she would be there long before that. So he went over to the Old Courthouse to work, occasionally checking out the window for lights at the Lanier Building. When they went on, he crossed the street. Through the tall, arched windows he could see Tess moving around the main part of the room, pushing in chairs and straightening the doilies she kept on the tables. She was wearing another one of those long dresses, only this was a jumper. Underneath it she had on a white blouse with a high collar. Except for her glorious spill of hair, she looked like an Edwardian schoolteacher.

He rapped lightly on the glass. She saw him and hurried over. As he waited for her to unlock the door, he noticed that the little blank books weren't on the tables anymore.

"I'm so happy to see you," she said as soon as the door was open. "I wanted to thank you for yesterday . . . for having Phil call me. I wouldn't have missed that for the world."

"I'm glad you could be there."

"I only wished I'd looked at the clothes more carefully, how they were put together. I don't suppose you remember if the ruched trim on the periwinkle dress was piped or not?"

"I wouldn't know how to answer that even if I was looking right at it. But here"—he held out the jewelry tray—"I brought Eveline's needles and such."

She leaned forward to examine them more closely. Her hair brushed against his arm. "They look so new! What a good job you did. Are you going to put them in the museum?"

He had certainly made a hash of this presentation. "No. They're for you."

She still didn't understand. "The museum isn't ready for them? Do you want me to display them in here until then?"

Ned had sent some of the best dishes for Wyatt and Gabe to put on display at the restaurant. Eventually they would be returned to the collection, but in the meantime, it was a way of thanking the two men for the use of their freezer.

That was temporary. This was not. "You can do whatever you want with them. I kept those already threaded needles—they'll be good for the museum—but the rest is for you. It belonged to your something-great-grandmother. Now it's yours."

She was surprised. "Why? I thought—"

He knew what she thought. Every piece of publicity had said that the collection would be preserved intact. Nothing would be given away or sold. He shrugged. "You shouldn't believe everything you read."

"But, Ned—" She wasn't going to accept them.

"Didn't your moth—your grandmother raise you to accept gifts graciously?"

"Actually not." Her smile was in her eyes. "My grandparents were so tense about material things that it was hard for them to be gracious. But I guess I don't have their excuse, so I'll try to do better. Thank you."

How could he have ever thought her eyes were

simply blue? A green halo shimmered around the iris. "You're welcome."

He wished he could do more for her, he liked her, he wanted her life to be perfect, but he couldn't think of anything that she needed.

She took the tray over to one of the glass-fronted cabinets. She rearranged a few things, set the tray inside, and then, after closing the door, locked the cabinet and took the key out. "Can I get you some coffee?"

"Sure. Anything."

"Caffeine or not?"

"Definitely caffeine." He followed her to the counter and watched her work. "Did you find it odd that all the yard goods were in Marie's trunk and, if you're right about the colors, that the fabrics were clearly to have clothes made for her, not Eveline?"

This was the other reason he had come, the other thing he had for her. It wasn't a needle or an artifact; it was a story, an explanation.

She handed him one of her jade-green mugs. It was filled with something frothy and caramel-colored. "I am right about the colors, and what's the surprise about the daughter being more interested in new clothes than the mother?"

Ned had three younger sisters. No one had to tell him anything about a teenage girl's desire for new clothes. "Yes, but the mother was pregnant."

He didn't remember Carolyn being pregnant with Caitlin, but he did have memories of the time before Emma's and Brittany's births. They had been born at different times of the year, and he could remember

Carolyn borrowing maternity clothes from her friends.

But from whom on board the *Western Settler* could the mother of Herbert Lanier have borrowed clothes? She couldn't have counted on finding a Lady Madonna maternity-wear specialty shop in Nebraska Territory.

"So," he added, "Eveline would have needed new garments. The clothes in her trunk weren't maternity gowns. But all the uncut fabric was for Marie."

"Oh." That made Tess pause. "There might be more trunks."

"Of course there might be. There's no question about that. But I can't help wondering if it really was Eveline who was pregnant."

Her eyebrows went up. "You're thinking it might have been Marie?"

He had had all night to work this out. "Why would a thirty-six-year-old pregnant woman set out on a steamboat trip up the Mississippi, much less on a tour of the frontier? It doesn't matter how skilled a midwife you've got traveling with you, it's still a dumb thing to do. But if you're hiding an unmarried daughter's pregnancy, and you're going to go home and pass the baby off as yours, what better? We know they planned to spend the summer in St. Louis, but they may have gotten off there and realized that they knew too many people, so they moved on. The Picard family document talks about how Marie was 'sickly' all fall and no one saw much of her."

Tess nodded. She could see that that made sense. "It would explain why the baby things were in her trunk. Then it's more like what the new edition of *The Riverboat Fragment* is suggesting. That the daughter, not the mother, was pregnant."

Ned nodded. "In fact, I don't think I would have put all these pieces together if Nina Lane hadn't done it first."

Tess frowned. "But she was just making it up, wasn't she? She couldn't have known, could she? She didn't know anything about Eveline's dresses or the fabric or what trunk the baby things were in."

"Define 'know.' We don't *know* anything either, but her intuition was probably extraordinarily powerful."

"Or it was a lucky guess." Tess went back to straightening up the room.

"True." Or Nina could have flat-out, absolutely known in the only way a person could have. Marie had told her.

But that wasn't the sort of thing you said to Tess Lanier.

"Have you ever wondered," he asked instead, "why these people—the Laniers, the Ravenals, the Picards—why they stopped practicing Catholicism?"

"They were Catholic?" Tess was surprised. Then she shook her head. "Oh, goodness, of course they were. They were French; they were from New Orleans. I guess it would have been odd if they weren't Catholic."

"And they were—enough church records in New Orleans survived to make that clear. But the cemetery outside town where Marie is buried, that's not church-consecrated ground."

"Maybe there weren't any priests around."

Ned shook his head. He had looked all this up.

"There was a bishop in Leavenworth—he baptized Herbert—and a couple of priests were doing missionary work with the Pottawatomie Indians along the Kaw. Marie died in January. It was cold. There would have been time to get her to Leavenworth."

"What's your point? What do you think this means?"

He took a breath. "I think Marie Lanier committed suicide and enough people in town knew it, so there was no way of getting a Catholic priest to bury her in consecrated ground."

Tess had been wiping the service counter. She stopped. "She committed suicide? So you think she might have been depressed. Or manic. Do you think Eveline's laudanum was likely for Marie?"

"It's very speculative." By which he, of course, meant yes.

"She had enough of a pattern of erratic behavior that her mother traveled with sedatives, she had a baby out of wedlock whom someone else cared for, and then three months later, probably in a state of postpartum depression, she killed herself. You know whose story that is, don't you?"

He did. Of course he did. It was Nina Lane's.

∞ *Chapter 11* ∞

There was a strong genetic component of bipolar illness, Tess knew that. And she also knew that it was no accident that she had gotten her college degree in something as close to psychiatry as her artistic talents would allow. She had needed to diagnose herself. She had needed to be sure that she wasn't manic-depressive, that she wasn't her mother.

And she wasn't. She knew that with all her being.

But if Nina Lane had come to Kansas looking for the source of her madness, she might have found it in Marie Lanier.

Had Marie given Nina a map? Had she made suicide seem possible?

The Gaithers family had begun their journey in Cincinnati and thus had not been with us on the *Cypress Princess*. They had relatives in Nebraska Territory, and the family was to join that household until they could afford an establishment of their own.

Mrs. Gaithers's manner was more proud and boastful than her station in life seemed to warrant. Among her household possessions en-

218

trusted to the hold of the *Western Settler* was a set of blue-and-white dishes. She spoke of these dishes often and several times wished that they could be brought up from the hold so that we other ladies could admire them. They would be, she told us repeatedly, the finest set of dishes in Nebraska Territory. Her pride in this china was tedious, and her wailings over their eventual loss seemed, at the time, undignified.

Following the wreck, the family boarded another westbound steamboat after only a single night ashore, and my female relation and I did not regret their departure.

One's own experience of frontier life, however, makes one more forgiving. Mrs. Gaithers may have been a reluctant pilgrim, dreading the hardships of the frontier. On board the *Western Settler*, we talked about the settlers' future, using the words "household" and "establishment" as if they signified the spacious dwellings and ample household staff that make familial hospitality a gracious pleasure. At the time, we knew that such language exaggerated, but our ignorance left us innocent of the exaggeration's extent. Mrs. Gaithers was likely to be moving into a tent next to her sister-in-law's one-room sod cabin. The blue-and-white dishes would, one now understands, elevate her from the dreary grimness of the frontier's daily routine.

One does now occasionally wonder about the fate of this unhappy woman. No longer the owner of the finest set of dishes in Nebraska

Territory, she arrived at her new home without
any household or personal belongings at all.

> Mrs. Louis Lanier (Eveline Roget),
> *The Wreck of the Western Settler*,
> privately printed, 1879

Tess reread the little booklet that Eveline Lanier
had written. She never mentioned Marie by name;
she never even specified that the "female relation"
she was traveling with was her daughter. How cold-
natured that made her sound. But perhaps the opposite was true. If Marie had committed suicide,
perhaps Eveline could not speak or write about her
even twenty years later. The memories were too
painful. Tess's own grandmother had almost never
talked about Nina, her suicidal daughter.

Eveline and Marie Lanier had been by far the
wealthiest, best-educated women on board. They
must have seemed smug and snobbish to the other
passengers. But Eveline might well have been on a
desperate journey to save her daughter from social
disgrace. And if Marie had been anything like Nina
Lane, this would not have been the first time she had
tormented her mother with her incomprehensible
behavior.

Had Eveline been hopeful? Had she persuaded herself that this would be the last time her daughter
would bewilder and enrage her? Did she believe that
they could return to New Orleans once the baby was
born and that all would be well? Or did she suspect
the truth? That this turmoil would only end in death.

Sewing money into the hem of a petticoat, as Eveline had done, was not the act of a confident, affluent person. Confident, affluent people trust that whatever happens can be fixed. Perhaps hiding the money had been the slave Octavia's idea; it was an act characteristic of someone who felt powerless. Perhaps it was Eveline's own idea, suggesting that she was not nearly as assured about her good fortune as she appeared to be.

Eveline Lanier had lost her daughter, her maid, and her religion. The loss of a tin box full of sewing supplies should have been insignificant, but as Tess slipped her fingers in the gold scissors' two small ring handles, she knew that these needles and pins, these strands of silk, had been missed.

At the Lanier Building, Tess had a set of eight ivory linen napkins for sale, the fabric beautifully woven, but without any adornment. So she took them home with her, traced with a water-soluble marker an *R* on the corner of each, and since she couldn't imagine what Ned would do with a set of eight monogrammed ivory linen napkins—or rather, she could imagine what he would do with them, which was to use them to dry metal artifacts from the boat—she added a smaller *C* and *S* on either side of the *R*. Carolyn Shelby Ravenal.

She selected an ivory floss from her own collection and cut lengths, using Eveline Lanier's gold-plated scissors. She threaded six of Eveline's needles, carefully stowing the needles in a piece of scrap cloth and wrapping the thread around the needles in a neat figure eight, just as Eveline had done. She fitted one of the napkins into Eveline's metal embroidery hoop.

She would cover the letters with a satin stitch, and then, because there had also been French knots on the piece Eveline had been working on, she would accent the curves of the letters with a floral-like spray of French knots.

This project did not make sense. It was the first week of December, the start of the Christmas season. She was now staying open late on weeknights, but her high school employees were busy with exams and couldn't work many extra hours. If she was going to take any time for needlework, she should be making clothes for herself. There was nothing at Kmart she wanted to wear, she couldn't see when she would get into Kansas City to shop, and she was freezing. Her California wardrobe was inadequate for a Kansas winter.

But she wanted to work with Eveline's needles.

Tess finished the first napkin and unclamped it from the hoop, brushing off a few stray threads. She would iron it in the morning. She picked up the second napkin and began to fit it in the hoop.

This was such a simple project for her. She was surprised at how much she was enjoying it. Would it have made Eveline happy to know that her needles and scissors had been found and were being used?

Tess brought the threaded needle up through the fabric, making the first stitch. For a moment it felt as if she and Eveline were working together; the needle was sliding in and out of the fabric so easily and the thread was lying so smoothly because there were two women at work.

Why do you cut your threads short? You are having to change needles so often.

The thread gets less twisted, Tess started to explain. *The—*

Wait a second. What kind of crazy thought was that? Tess jabbed the needle into the linen and set the hoop aside. She had been working too long. She supposed there were people who believed in ghosts and that the unseen could intervene in daily life. But even they didn't think that the dead showed up to help you with your satin stitch. Or to complain about how you threaded your needle.

Another few evenings' work and the first two napkins were finished. Tess took them to the Lanier Building, cleared off a shelf in one of the glass-fronted cases, and displayed the napkins with a small notice: "Embroidery worked on a hoop and with needles salvaged from the *Western Settler*." Without saying a word to Carolyn, she then added, "Napkins property of Carolyn Shelby Ravenal."

Barely two hours later Carolyn shoved open the door of the Lanier Building. "What is all this about napkins, Tess?"

"I actually thought you would be here sooner."

"I would have, but I was in the middle of getting a permanent, and if I had left earlier, my hair would have all fried off. Now stop talking and show me what you have gone and done."

Tess showed her the napkins. "I thought you would like them."

"I adore them, but, Tess, really, this is out of the question. I can't have you doing this for me."

"It was only incidentally for you," Tess said honestly. "I wanted to work with the needles and the hoop, and I would have made something for Ned, but he just didn't seem like a hand-embroidered-monogram sort of guy."

"You're right on that count. He is your basic-black laundry-marker type. Of course, you could have made them for Phil, you know."

"For Phil?" That had never occurred to her. Why would she have made something for Phil?

Carolyn was looking at her questioningly.

Oh, God. Phil. Carolyn was surprised that she hadn't thought to make something for Phil.

One of the first things Tess had noticed when she came back to Kansas last summer was how handsome Phil Ravenal was. She had given the matter virtually no thought since.

But what would their relationship look like to other people? Tess saw him two or three times a day; he was always in and out of the Lanier Building. When people invited her over to their homes on Sunday evenings, they usually included him, and he would offer to pick her up. Sometimes she accepted a ride from him, sometimes she didn't. It depended on what part of town they were going to.

But unless other people arranged it, they rarely saw each other outside the Lanier Building. Only once had they been out on what could have been called a date—when he took her to The Cypress Princess for dinner during her first full week in town.

They weren't close. She had never asked him about his childhood or his years with the congressman in Washington, D.C. She had never told him about taking care of her grandparents; she had never told him what it had been like to suddenly get so much money; she had never told him about Gordon Winsler needing to turn the lights off when he had made love to her.

Throughout the rest of the day, Tess was suddenly aware of the number of people who would stop by and expect her to know Phil's whereabouts.

"I see Phil's car is not at the courthouse. Do you know where he is?"

She wished she didn't. She wished she could stare blankly. *Why would you think that I would know?* But, in fact, she did know. "He had meetings in Kansas City for most of the day. But leave a message at the courthouse if you need to talk to him. You know he'll check his machine whenever he can."

Did that make her his girlfriend? Wasn't it simply one local businessperson helping out another? Tess had a feeling that in this town, "girlfriend" was the answer.

But this wasn't a question for the town to answer. This was her business. Did she want to be Phil Lanier's girlfriend?

She wasn't sure.

She had put up a Christmas tree in the Lanier Building, which necessitated rearranging the furniture. One of the leather-covered love seats now sat under a front window, and late in the afternoon on the day that Carolyn had come in to see the napkins, Tess was sitting there, working on the third napkin, taking advantage of the last of the daylight. Sasha and her cousin, needing Christmas money, were both working the counter. Tess was going to go home as soon as she finished this spray of French knots. Of course, she had said that after the last four sprays.

Needlework was like that. You could never put it down.

She was starting on the sixth spray—just this one, just this one more—when the big glass door opened and Phil walked in, followed by Ned.

"What's all this about the napkins you're making for Mom?" Phil unbuttoned his gray wool overcoat as he spoke. "She's thrilled."

"And it was a good joke," Ned added, "not telling her. People are enjoying that as much as the napkins."

"I'm glad I can add to the local entertainment scene." Tess watched the brothers cross the room to join her.

There was no question that Phil was the more conventionally handsome. He was taller; his features were more even; his clothes fit him better, he carried himself with more confidence.

But physically he did nothing for Tess. She wasn't sure why, she had never thought about it—which was pretty revealing—but she couldn't imagine him in bed. He was so careful and controlled. Did he ever lose himself in something, even sex?

Ned, on the other hand, although he often seemed distracted in conversation, was completely absorbed when he was doing something. Tess had seen him drive a bulldozer; she had seen him count a bucketful of nineteenth-century hinges. He had no trouble losing himself in an activity. Ned's problem was finding himself again when it was time to stop.

Which certainly made Ned sound like a better bet in bed . . . not that she had been thinking about him in that way either.

She got the two finished napkins out of the glass-fronted case. Both men tried to be appreciative, but a healthy masculine ignorance underlay their praise.

"Neither one of you has a clue what you're talking about," she said, laughing.

"You may be right about that," Phil admitted smoothly. "But we aren't such idiots that we don't know when someone is doing something nice for our mother."

"I wanted to make them for Ned—"

"For me?" Ned was startled. "For *me?*"

"—but I was afraid he would put them in a drawer and they'd never see the light of day again, or he would have used them for dish towels."

"I wouldn't have done *that*," he protested. "But the drawer thing would be a good bet. I'm not giving a whole lot of dinner parties these days." He passed the napkin back to her. "But the idea that you did it for Mom . . . I don't know . . . I like that a lot."

She felt the brush of his hand against hers when he handed her the napkin. "That's what I was hoping."

"What was it like using nineteenth-century needles?" he asked. "Could you tell any difference?"

"Not physically, no. It was a little strange to be using something another woman had loved and lost, but I'm sure I was just projecting my own love of needlework."

"I wouldn't be too hasty. Objects can carry a great deal of emotional resonance."

"You'd think one hundred and fifty years of mud would take care of that."

But had it? She thought about hearing herself explain why she cut her thread short. She turned away from the brothers, carefully replacing the napkins in the display case. She spoke to Ned. "You said you that you'd be keeping the needles that Eveline had threaded. Did you measure the thread length?"

"Actually, I did. And now you are going to ask me how long the thread was, aren't you?" Ned squinted, trying to remember. "I think they were all around two feet, between twenty-two and twenty-eight inches, but don't quote me on that. I would need to look it up. Why do you ask?"

Tess cut her thread at eighteen inches. "I don't know."

He didn't believe her. She could tell that.

She locked the display case and avoided making eye contact with him. She couldn't help feeling as if he *knew* . . . although she couldn't say what it was that he supposedly knew. But whatever it was made her uncomfortable.

Glamorous, ambitious Phil was safer than Ned. He didn't have Ned's insight. He didn't have Ned's interest in peering into dark places. Phil would never stand here, looking as if he didn't believe her. Phil would believe her.

But she didn't love Phil.

She had to talk to him. If people were thinking of them as a couple, then he must know it. So why was he letting the impression stand?

What should she say? *I really like you as a friend* . . . That wasn't right. You told a man you liked him as a friend only when you hated him. And she did like Phil. She liked him a lot.

But how hard it was to bring things up with him. She had never realized that before. There were never any silent spaces in a conversation, times during which you could clear your throat and say, "You know, I've been thinking." He wasn't a monologist, he didn't go on and on; it was nothing like that. He was simply very good at small talk.

But sometimes talk needed to stop being small.

She tried to talk to Phil for four days, and she was wondering how she was going to make herself do it when Ned came into the Lanier Building.

That was a surprise. As far as she could remember, the only time he had come by himself was when he had brought over Eveline's needles. But late one afternoon, when Sasha and her cousin were again working the counter and business was at its quietest, she noticed him in the corner of the big main room, hanging up his parka on one of the brass wall hooks. His back was toward her. His hair, streaked by the sun during the summer, was darkening. When he turned, the contrast between his hair and his eyebrows was less striking.

He lifted a hand in greeting. "I've been promising Dr. Matt that I'd slow down," he said, "so I thought I'd come in and say hi."

He didn't need to explain why he had come in. This was an espresso bar, a place of business. She needed people to come in. "It's good to see you."

Carolyn and Dr. Matt had childhood pictures on display in their home. Phil had been an angelic-looking boy with fair hair and flawless peach-hued skin, the kind of youth you expected to see in the Vienna Boys' Choir. He looked at the camera with a steady, clear gaze, his expression the same in every picture.

Ned, almost five years younger, had looked scruffy

and uncombed next to Phil. Sometimes he would look up at Phil adoringly. Sometimes he would look sullen: *I didn't want to be in this picture.* Other times he would be grinning with mischief. He invariably had at least one bruise or Band-Aid; he had obviously been a "snips, snails, and puppy-dog tails" kind of boy.

There was something so forthright about him; she could talk to him. She waited while Sasha filled his order and then, picking up her embroidery, followed him over to the love seat under one of the windows.

She asked what was happening at the site, and after he had reported on the latest finds, she changed the subject. "I have a question. It's personal. Is it clear to everyone in town that Phil and I are a done deal?"

He stared at her over the rim of his mug. He then set the mug down without having taken a drink. "Until four seconds ago I would have said, 'Sure.' Are you saying it isn't clear to you?"

"I'm not saying anything."

"That's certainly your right," he acknowledged, "but if what you're not saying is what it sounds like, then it looks like you are out to make a monkey of my brother . . . although if you were able to follow that sentence, then you are one bright cookie."

"I followed every word of it, and I have no intention in the world of making a monkey out of anyone." That was what she was trying to avoid. Surely he knew that.

"Then what's going on?" He sat back, propping one foot up against the low table in front of him, turning toward her, ready to listen.

"Nothing. We never do anything by ourselves. We've never been on anything that could be called a date."

"You're always here on Friday and Saturday night," Ned answered. "And he doesn't have a lot of time either."

"We never talk about anything personal."

"He never does."

It seemed as if Ned was trying to talk her into something. "He has never touched me differently than he would one of your sisters."

"Oh." That made Ned pause. He didn't have an answer for that one. "I can't say that's how I would have gone about a courtship, but Phil has more restraint than your average guy."

"But this isn't a courtship. That's my point. And if everyone else is thinking it is, that could be embarrassing for him. He's done so much for me. I'd hate to humiliate him."

"Haven't you talked to him about it?"

She sighed. "I know I should have."

Ned was sitting forward now, his feet on the ground. "Then why not give him a chance? Why not see if it can turn into a real courtship? He's a great guy, he really is. He does so much for everyone else. He really does deserve to be happy."

"I'm not disputing that," Tess answered. "But I'm not the one who can make him happy."

"I don't know how you can say that. The two of you seem perfect for each other. You're both organized and efficient. You're both honorable and trustworthy. You both have these phenomenally even tempers. And you, Tess, the singular you, aren't needy or demanding. You're self-contained. You aren't going to expect things of him that he can't do."

All of that was true. Tess was a little surprised that Ned had given the matter so much thought. "What you're saying is that we are alike. That's not the same as being right for each other."

Ned had been reaching for his coffee cup. He stopped. He was not a stupid man. He knew when someone else was right.

He sat back and sighed. "There are a million differences between my brother and me. I mean, he's Phil Ravenal and I'm not. Everyone always thinks I got the short end of the stick. But it isn't so. I'm much luckier than he is. I think I was as unaffected by the loss of our parents as it's possible to be. My first memories are of Carolyn, and before she came along, I had my grandparents, who had been seeing me every day anyway. But it was so different for Phil. One day he was at home, having a mother walk him to kindergarten, and then next day she's gone, and he's living in another house. Then two years later Dr. Matt married, and he's living in yet another place. It's not that he's an emotional zero, but there is some kind of big black box inside him that he doesn't know how to open."

Tess nodded. She could believe this. That was one key difference between Phil and her; she was much more reflective and self-aware.

"I think that's why he works so hard," Ned continued. "I mean, I know I work like a madman, but that's because I'm so interested in all this stuff. I love it, I always have. But for him, it's as if he doesn't exist unless he has those crazy lists of his, unless he has accomplishments he can point to. Otherwise he doesn't know who he is."

"It sounds like he needs a therapist, not a girlfriend."

"He's not going to go to a therapist," Ned said flatly.

Tess also believed that. "What about this from my point of view? Forget about whether or not I am right for him. Maybe he is not right for me. Maybe I don't want to be so self-contained and eventempered. Maybe I want to change."

Ned had clearly never considered that. "Why would you want to change? You seem perfect."

"That's not necessarily good, is it? *Seeming* perfect."

Once again he was open-minded enough to know she had a good point. "It sure as hell makes you pleasant to be around."

"I think it makes me smug and self-satisfied."

He shook his head. He wasn't that open-minded. "No, Tess. Not you."

If not Phil Ravenal, then what did Tess want in a man?

She acknowledged that her life was nunlike, but a nun's chastity was supposed to be a sacrifice. Tess's wasn't. It seemed like the natural order of things.

Her only lover had been Gordon Winsler, a man who couldn't watch her when making love to her because she didn't look enough like Nina Lane. That had been devastating, but she wasn't going to blame everything on him.

By the time they were raising her, her grandparents'

devotion to each other had been nearly passionless. Perhaps it had always been. They had been raised virtually as brother and sister, their two families clinging to one another, sharing their exile. If there had ever been passion, it had been leached away by the capricious fury of their disturbed daughter.

They had loved Tess, she knew that. But they had been exhausted, worn down by raising a difficult daughter. Their love for Tess had been gentle and weary.

Tess had loved them in return, but they were aging. They were fading. Her love for them had been about letting go, about giving them rest. Love soothed, giving warmth and shelter, comfort and peace.

But love should be a life force, vibrant and green, rousing and rushing. Love should awaken, stimulate, enrich. Yet in Tess's own history such energy and vibrancy had been gathered in Nina, and Nina had not been a life force. She had killed herself.

There was nothing to do except try to speak to Phil as clearly and simply as she had spoken to Ned. When he came in the next morning, she made coffee for herself and joined him at his table. If people in town stuck to their routine, she and Phil would have ten minutes alone.

She didn't give him a chance to speak. "People around town are making assumptions about you and me that are far ahead of the reality."

"I'm aware of that." His voice was even, but for a moment Tess thought that he was going to look away, and she was sure that he wanted to, that some instinct in him longed to break eye contact. But he didn't. "Ned came over last night and told me that I may have been 'a courtin' too slow.' "

Tess shifted uneasily. Ned had reported their conversation to him? She didn't like that.

But she had no business minding. She had not asked him for secrecy. He hadn't betrayed her. His loyalty was to his brother, not to her.

"Fast or slow isn't the issue, Phil."

"I know a political life is difficult, Tess, but—"

She shook her head, stopping him. He hadn't heard her. His profession wasn't the problem. "Our scars match, Phil. We're too much alike. We—"

She realized there was no point in explaining. He would accept the conclusion quickly enough. That's what politicians do. They are realists. And as for the reasons behind the conclusion, he wouldn't understand, he couldn't.

If she had come to Kansas looking for a brother, then she had found him. But she was not going to marry a brother.

Her grandmother already had.

∾ *Chapter 12* ∾

Every weekend in December, and many Thursday evenings as well, there were activities to draw people to town—house tours, visits from a Father Christmas-style Santa, horse-drawn hayrides, caroling around bonfires. Each event took hours and hours to plan, hours and hours to set up. Ticket tables had to be borrowed and returned; hot chocolate had to be made and sold. Signs had to be made; extension cords had to be found. Doors and windows had to be decorated, bonfires had to be built, and manure had to be scooped up. Everyone, not just the merchants, was working—the Scout troops, the Jaycees, the high school band, the church youth groups, and the PTAs were all using the events as fund-raisers. Everyone, not just the merchants, was exhausted.

People were complaining that they had no time to enjoy their own Christmas. No one was entertaining this year because no one had the time.

The complainers usually managed to do their whining in front of Phil, and Tess marveled at his patience. He listened and listened.

"Did people entertain all that much last year?" Tess had to ask.

He glanced over his shoulder to be sure that no one could hear. "No. They couldn't afford to. Now they've got some extra money, but no time."

"Doesn't that drive you crazy, the inconsistency?"

"No. You have to be realistic. People are people."

Tess's relationship with him was exactly the same as before they had "broken up." He came to the Lanier Building as often; his manner was as relentlessly even as ever; their conversations were as friendly as before, as lacking in intimacy as before. In fact, Tess wondered if anyone except her, Phil, and presumably Ned even knew that this candle's little flame had gone out. Ned himself might not even know.

If people had been entertaining, she might have been able to assess the town's information about her love life from the invitations she was receiving, but everyone was far too tired for festivities. Suzanne Dragiuse of the antiques store was so weary that when she ran into Tess at the bank, she said that she and her husband would get Tess and Ned out to the house as soon as all this holiday craziness died down.

"Sounds great," Tess said. If there was a tactful way to say, "I think you mean his brother Phil, but don't bother, because he and I have gone our separate ways," Tess was too tired to think of it.

People were, of course, going to celebrate Christmas itself, and Carolyn Ravenal's invitation for Tess to spend Christmas Day with her family was as warm as her invitation for Thanksgiving had been.

This time Tess refused. "It's so sweet of you to ask,

but I am exhausted. Some days I'm here for fifteen hours. I just want to spend the day at home."

Carolyn didn't looked convinced, and indeed, the next morning Phil showed up with instructions to try again. "You could come only for dinner. You wouldn't have to spend the whole day with us."

"Thank you, thank her, but truly, I prefer to be alone. I need to be alone."

Phil shook his head. "I've done some fast talking in my day, Tess, but do you really think I can go home and persuade my mother and sisters of that?"

Tess had to smile. "If anyone can do it, you can."

Apparently he couldn't. Two days later Carolyn sent in her next wave of assault troops—Ned.

He looked terrible. He was coughing, the skin around his eyes was shrunken and gray, and his nose was red. Tess had a sudden urge to take care of him, to tuck a blanket around him, rub his shoulders, pour cough syrup into a spoon, make him hot tea with lemon.

He gestured with his hand, dismissing the concern that he must have read on her face. "I have a cold. It's nothing. I'm here to—" He broke off and looked at her blankly. "Shoot, why am I here?"

"To try to get me to come to your mother's for Christmas?"

"That's right. How did you know?" He shook his head, marveling at her wisdom. "The trouble is I'm supposed to be tactful, and I think I'm too tired to be tactful."

Tess could sympathize with that. "Then just say it, and I'll edit out everything that your mother wouldn't have wanted me to hear."

"That sounds good. I can do that." He coughed and pounded on his chest with a fist, trying to clear his lungs. "Okay, here it is. Mom and Dad know you've given Phil the old heave-ho, but they want you to come anyway. They like you for you. And so do the girls. Phil still likes you, and I do too, for that matter. And I'm sure if we asked him, Doug would say that he liked you, but in truth he probably hasn't spent a whole lot of time thinking about you because he is even more tired than I am."

Doug was Caitlin's boyfriend; he was in the first year of his medical internship. "And I like all of you too." At least she assumed that she would like Doug. She had met him at Thanksgiving, but he had barely managed to stay awake through dinner. That had made him a little hard to get to know. "But I want to be alone. I'm here fifteen hours a day talking to people, making coffee, and answering questions. I want some quiet. I don't want to hear a single sound unless I make it myself."

Ned coughed and blew his nose. "Mom would say that holidays are family time."

"I'll agree with that. But I am my own family. It may only be a family of one, but that's where I am right now, and I'm not feeling sorry for myself. I don't feel like Cinderella."

Ned's nose was still red, the skin under his eyes was still gray, his lungs sounded like the Missouri River was detouring through them, but the eyes themselves were suddenly alert, even a little soft. He got it. He understood. "Then I wish you the best."

* * *

It was certainly true that with her grandparents dead and her biological father unknown, she was her own family. But the Ravenals were not the only people unable to imagine a family of one. Duke Nathan called, asking her to join his family in New York. Wyatt and Gabe, who apparently felt a familial connection because of their days in the Settlement, also called, offering to hold a table for her on Christmas Eve, Christmas Day, or both.

"Let me get back to you on that," she said. It did occur to her that the one person from whom she had not received an invitation was the one with whom she had actually lived. For three months, Sierra must have thought that the two of them were a family, and Tess, in her self-absorbed, ignorant little baby mind, had probably agreed.

The Lanier Building was often quiet around two in the afternoon. Tess told Sasha that she was going out for a few minutes. She put on her coat—which wasn't adequate for the December winds—but she simply couldn't bear to buy one of those puffy down-filled things that everyone else wore; as soon as she had a minute she would make herself a black wool, *French Lieutenant's Woman* cape, which probably wouldn't be adequate either, but at least she would be willing to put it on her body.

A lady was leaving the Celandine Gardens shop when Tess arrived there. She was carrying two well-filled shopping bags, but she was hurrying, avoiding eye contact, her shoulders hunched forward underneath her fur-trimmed coat. *Get me out of here.*

Another person with no interest in Sierra's view of life, in Sierra's desire for "connection." Tess stepped back, allowing the shopper to escape more quickly.

There was no one else in the shop. Sierra was behind the counter. She had a little bin recessed into the counter that had been cut to the size of her Celandine Gardens tissue paper. She kept the bin full of flat sheets of the paper, and that made it easy for her to wrap people's purchases. Tess had admired it. At the moment, Sierra seemed to be straightening the tissue in the bin. Except that she couldn't be. The tissue fit the bin perfectly. There was nothing to straighten.

She knows. She knows that this isn't working, that people can't stand her.

Tess hated the thought. It was one thing to think of Sierra as weird and difficult, disliked by everyone. It was another to think of her knowing that. Tess spoke quickly. "I was wondering, after we close up on Christmas Eve, if you would like to join me for dinner at The Cypress Princess." Tess could then still be alone on Christmas Day. "Wyatt and Gabe will hold a table for us near the fireplace."

Sierra looked at her. "No."

Tess blinked. She had been prepared for a refusal—hadn't she herself been refusing invitations right and left?—but this refusal was so flat. "Well, maybe some other time," she murmured.

Why was she being a hypocrite? There wasn't going to be another time.

"Not Christmas," Sierra said. "Christmas is not a holiday I celebrate."

"Okay." What else was there to say?

"I'm Jewish . . . or at least my family is."

"Oh." Tess wondered if she should have known that. She didn't think that Celandine was a Jewish name, but it probably wasn't the one Sierra had been born with. "I'm sorry. I didn't realize that."

"I haven't set foot in a synagogue or lit a Shabbat candle in more than twenty-five years, but I do abstain from Christmas."

Tess prepared herself to hear a discourse on the emptiness of institutionalized religious rituals and the need for each individual to create his or her own sanctity. She would listen to every word of it. She would make herself do that.

But Sierra surprised her. She said nothing.

So Tess picked up some hand lotion and soap for the ladies' room at the Lanier Building. Sierra wrote the items up and wrapped them without speaking. Tess was halfway to the door when Sierra's voice stopped her.

"You know, when you were born, I gave you a Hebrew name."

"A Hebrew name?" Tess knew that her grandparents had had her baptized, having assumed that no one in the Settlement had bothered. "I don't understand the significance of that."

"It doesn't make you Jewish. Even if there had been a rabbi there—which there wasn't—a baby naming isn't the same as a conversion. I did it to make you seem more like mine."

"Do you remember what the name was?"

Of course she remembered. "Shira—it means song."

"How pretty. What a nice name." It didn't fit. Tess was not at all musical, but still, the name had a lovely sound.

Tess hated this, she really did. What kind of relationship were she and Sierra supposed to have? She was a disappointment to Sierra, she knew that. She had been disappointing her since the Nina Lane Birthday Celebration last May, but what was Tess supposed to do? She wasn't deliberately withholding the intensity that Sierra craved; she simply wasn't capable of it. She wasn't that kind of person.

Maybe I should be. Maybe this is something I should want to change about myself.

But she had no idea where to begin.

Ned had a feeling that he was going to spend most of Christmas trying to explain Tess to the rest of the world. "She's exhausted," he said to his family Christmas morning. "She wants to be alone."

Hadn't he warned her? Back in late July, when they were eating sandwiches in the park, hadn't he said that there was no place in this town for a person who wanted to be alone? Why hadn't she just painted her body blue and run naked through the subfreezing night, or engaged in some other behavior that people would have a chance of understanding? Wanting to be alone was close to severe psychosis around here.

"But on Christmas?" his mother called out from the kitchen. It was still early; they hadn't started opening the presents under the tree. "How can you want to be alone on Christmas?"

"Who wants to be alone on Christmas?" Brittany said. Still in her bathrobe, she was coming down the staircase.

"Tess." Ned was sitting in the blue velvet wing chair that had been wedged in an odd corner to make room for the tree. "She says that the secular aspects

of Christmas—Santa and the presents and the tree—
don't mean very much to her. Apparently her grandparents were always so stressed about spending
money during the holiday that it was hard to enjoy
things. She likes the lights and the music and the pag-
eant at church. And we did see her at the church last
night. She was there."

"But you can value the religious aspect of the holiday without needing to be alone." Caitlin came into
the living room carrying a tray of Christmas cookies.
The dental student, she was the clearest thinker of
the three Ravenal sisters. "Christmas is for families."

"You aren't going to say that when you see what
lousy gifts I got you guys." Ned had warned everyone that his holiday shopping had been limited to
spending one hour on-line buying books and CDs
and then throwing himself on Sierra's mercy for his
share of the stocking stuffers. "And anyway, we
aren't Tess's family."

"Well, not technically," Caitlin conceded. "But she
feels like some kind of cousin, having people on the
boat and all."

"Does snow count as secular or religious?" Dr.
Matt entered with another tray of Christmas cookies.
The fact that it was not yet 8 A.M. did not impact this
family's cookie-eating habit. "I may be an old guy,
but I still want it to snow at Christmas."

"Snow is definitely religious." Phil followed Dr.
Matt into the room. "As are Nana's candy-cane
cookies." He reached across Ned to take a cookie.
"Candy canes themselves are secular, but Grandma's
cookies are a spiritual experience."

"It's how we remember the departed," Dr. Matt

agreed, also reaching across Ned for a cookie. "Through their recipes. Your grandmother was a wonderful woman, kids."

All these carbohydrates passing under his nose were making a convert of Ned. He wasn't sure exactly what he was converting to or from, but he took a cookie anyway. Ropes of white and red dough had been twisted into a candy-cane shape and then rolled in crushed candy before baking. Not anything to run out and brag to your nutritionist about, but Ned's personal definition of nourishing food was pretty elastic, especially now that that stupid cold was gone and he could taste again.

"You know," Caitlin said suddenly, "you've gotten sort of hunky, Ned."

"Me?" He had a mouthful of cookie. "Chunky? I'm not chunky. Look at this." He swallowed the cookie and pulled at his trousers. They were loose. "These are not the pants of a chunky man."

"I said hunky, not chunky. Your shoulders have gotten broader and your butt is sleeker."

"My butt has always been sleek," he protested, although he had never given the matter a moment's thought. But Caitlin was right about his shoulders, upper back, and arms. He was doing hard physical labor day after day; his shirts and sweaters were getting tighter, and his pants looser.

He certainly did deserve another cookie. Maybe even two. He could smell bacon frying in the kitchen. Bacon and homemade Christmas cookies—you couldn't beat that for breakfast.

He sat back in the wing chair. This was exactly what he wanted Christmas to be. The only thing that would make it better would be when Caitlin and Doug got their act together and had babies. Worrying about little ones eating the ribbons off the presents and pulling the tree down on top of themselves—that was all they needed to make their family Christmas perfect.

That and a little snow.

Tess had a glorious Christmas. She had planned for the day. Thanks to being able to order on-line, she had new music to listen to and a new book to read. She had ordered a new dress, which she put on even though no one would see it but herself.

She wasn't being like Sierra, she wasn't avoiding Christmas. She went to church on Christmas Eve. On Christmas Day she listened to Christmas music and read to herself from the Book of Luke. She bought the tiniest container of whipping cream, separated a single egg, and made herself eggnog. She was celebrating the holiday. She was just doing it alone.

Duke Nathan and his family sent her a box of the most wonderful writing paper. The paper was creamy and handmade, flecked with little threads of blue rag. The ink from the walnut-barreled fountain pen they had enclosed soaked into the rich paper, and the lines of Tess's pretty handwriting thickened into stateliness. She spent Christmas night writing a long letter to everyone at Willow Place.

She couldn't imagine anything better.

∞ *Chapter 13* ∞

Weekend crowds remained surprisingly good through January. People weren't spending as much money as they had in December, but they were coming to town, still buying T-shirts, still eating fudge.

The riverboat was the attraction. Every day Ned was finding something new, and people who lived as far as a hundred miles away brought their kids every Sunday to see what had happened during the week. The high school art teacher was giving students extra credit for photographs of the excavation, so, while there weren't many artifacts in the museum yet, there were plenty of pictures.

And how could you go to the museum and look at those pictures without then moving on to the Lanier Building for some coffee and cake? Tess was now recognizing a number of these weekend regulars.

She had stayed open late on weekday evenings during December, intending to return to a 6 P.M. closing in January. But the high school kids persuaded her otherwise. Several groups of students had started meeting at the Lanier Building to study, and they wanted to continue. Of course they bought no gifts, but they ordered flavorings and extra shots so profligately that Tess knew she would at least cover her costs.

Then two weeks into the new year, it snowed.

The snowfall had been predicted for two days. Tess kept stepping outside to feel the air grow heavy and cold. At first a few white specks floated lazily outside the upper panes of the Lanier Building's four front windows. Tess refolded a pile of scarves. When she looked up again, the snow was falling more steadily, the flakes melting as they landed on the street and the brick sidewalk, but catching hold on the grass and the tree limbs. When people came in, their hair was glistening with snowflakes and the shoulders of their coats were dusted with white. The snow piled in little ridges along the bare branches of the hickory tree on the lawn of the Old Courthouse, and by evening the whole town looked magical.

Tess borrowed a pair of boots from Brenda Jackson's daughter-in-law and spent an hour walking through the neighborhoods, looking at the way the snow would cling to one side of the pickets on a fence. She loved the serenity, the beauty. Since her first moments in town, when she had been standing in the cemetery, looking at her reflection in her mother's headstone, she had never questioned her decision to come to Kansas. But the snow confirmed her certainty. How could something this beautiful not be right?

"Does the snow make things harder for Ned?" Tess asked Phil the next morning.

"No, not really. It's not all that cold yet, and no amount of precipitation is going to make things any muddier."

The residents of Willow Place had been, thanks to Mr. Greenweight, following the process of the excavation through Fleur-de-lis's Web site. In response to Tess's Christmas letter, Mrs. Johanisberg, a former English teacher, sent her a wonderful quote from *The Adventures of Tom Sawyer* about buried treasure. Tess got out gold paint and carefully traced the words onto one of her windows.

Time disappeared down in the cargo hold of the *Western Settler*. Every box, every barrel, was its own little challenge—where to tug, what to wash away, how to get it out. The wriggling and rocking, the gratifying sigh the mud gave when it released its suction, would have been satisfying even if the boxes and barrels had been empty. But they weren't empty. Each was filled with things people were carrying to the West. One family had packed their children's toys: a doll, a tiny wheelbarrow, five lead soldiers. A store in Omaha had ordered astonishing luxuries: bottled cherries, French brandy, and ladies' perfume.

Could anything ever be better than this? Ned woke up every morning at four or four-thirty, wide awake, urgent to be at the site. At night he had to force himself to quit.

He did sometimes feel as if the whole world were conspiring to keep him out of the excavation pit. Dr. Matt had started it at Thanksgiving with this business of sleeping at least six hours a night, and now lots of other people were joining in. On weekends it was the out-of-towners who drove out to the site, full of questions. Phil did his best to help out. He was at the site or the schoolhouse all day Saturday and Sunday, talking to people, but Ned would overhear the questions, and some of them really were so interesting that he couldn't help himself and he'd start talking, and suddenly the day would be gone. During the week it was the journalists and photographers who were never satisfied with talking to Phil, even though Phil was much better at this interview stuff than Ned would ever be. And now there were school field trips. It was too muddy and cold for the kids to get very close to the site, so Ned had to bring things up to the schoolhouse and talk to the kids there, which took a big chunk out of a morning, but how could he say no? His grandfather had given him such a gift, making him care about the past; how he could say that he didn't have time to talk to kids who might not have grandfathers like that?

A couple days after the first snowfall, Phil was helping him load up the artifacts that needed to be taken to the limestone mine for underwater storage. As they were finishing, Phil did what he always did: pulled out the little leather case that held his list, checking to be sure he hadn't forgotten anything. "Good thing I wrote this down. You didn't get over to Tess's today, did you?"

Ned shoved one of the washtubs farther back into the truck and raised the tailgate. It clicked into place. "I haven't seen her since before Christmas."

"You need to get over there. There's something in her window you need to see."

"In her window? What is it?"

"I'm not going to tell you," Phil said. "Go see for yourself."

Phil didn't usually play little teasing games. "Tell me what it is. I don't have time for stuff like this."

"You don't know what it is, so how can you know that you don't have time for it?"

That was a little hard to answer. "Okay, then"—Ned tossed Phil the keys to the truck—"you go take this to the cave."

The old limestone mine was only five miles away, but once you were there, you had to get out of the truck to unlock the gate across the drive and drag it open, then get out again at the mouth of the cave and unlock yet another gate and drag that one open. Then you have to drive into the underground quarry and, working in bad light, take the artifacts, one at a time, out of the water-filled washtubs in the back of the truck and put them in the water-filled stock tanks. It was a wet and tedious chore, and Ned did it almost every day.

Phil caught the truck keys and gave Ned the keys to the Jeep. Ned went home, showered, and drove downtown. It was nearly eight o'clock, but the lights in the Lanier Building were still on. The tall, arched windows cast bright rectangles on the brick sidewalk and glittered against the circles of snow around the black iron lampposts. As Ned grew closer, he could see new gold lettering twinkling on one of the windows.

There comes a time in every rightly-constructed boy's life when he has a raging desire to go somewhere and dig for hidden treasure.

—Mark Twain, *The Adventures of Tom Sawyer*

Ned put his hands in the pockets of his coat. This was about him. Tess had put a quote referring to him on the window of her business. He hoped that she was inside. She shouldn't be. She should be at home, doing whatever she did at home, but he hoped she would be here.

He went in. Toward the back of the room a couple of tables had been pushed together, and a group of high school kids was studying together. The backpacks were on the floor next to their chairs, books were piled at their elbows, and Tess's jade green mugs were balanced on their open binders. Tess herself was seated at a front table, doing something with a piece of lace. She looked up and smiled.

"Is that how you think of me?" he asked. "As a boy?"

"A 'rightly-constructed' one."

He wondered if there was any way she might mean that sexually. Not likely. "It's a good quote. I don't remember it, but I haven't read the book in ages."

"I didn't find it. One of the ladies at the retirement home I used to work at sent it to me. Now, what can I get you?" She started to fold up her work.

"Nothing. Don't move. Show me what you're doing."

He sat down and she started to explain.

Ned was a bright guy. He knew that about himself. So he supposed that if he tried, he would have been able to follow what Tess was saying, but in truth, it was nice to just sit here, listen to the music she was playing, and watch the shadows made by the curls in her hair. She was wearing it loose, and its honey color looked as if it had stored up enough summer sunlight to carry everyone through the winter ahead.

Why had he ever thought anything was wrong with this place? It was pretty, it was restful. Tess was here.

"Did you understand a word of what I've been saying?" she asked suddenly.

"I didn't try."

She laughed. "I love you, Ned. You are sweet."

Sweet? That was just what every fellow wanted to hear. "You're lucky that only the high school kids were around to hear you say that. Otherwise the whole town would have written *Romeo and Juliet* by tomorrow."

She reached for her little scissors to snip a thread. "But they already have."

"What?" He was confused. "What are you talking about?"

"It's not actually *Romeo and Juliet*. I think they're hoping for something more positive. Apparently the only thing that convinced people I wasn't passionately in love with Phil was the idea that I was passionately in love with you."

"With me?" Ned couldn't have heard her right. "With *me*?"

She nodded. "At first I thought people were making a mistake, simply using the wrong name, when they said they wanted to invite the two of us over, but now it's clear. I'm like Katharine of Aragon or Queen Mary when she was Princess of Teck." Her voice was even; she was almost smiling. "When Son Number One proves to be a nonstarter, you're bumped down to Son Number Two."

"Wait a minute . . ." He couldn't believe what he was hearing. "Where did people get this idea?"

"Where does anyone get any idea? I don't know." She looked at him curiously. "This bothers you, doesn't it?"

"Of course it does."

"What do you mean 'of course'? Last month you told me not to worry about what people were saying about Phil and me, and now you're standing on your ear because they're talking about you and me."

"But this is different," he protested.

"I don't see how."

"For one, you're taking it differently. The idea of being with me seems like a big joke to you."

Why had he said that? It made him sound like a whining little boy.

"Oh, Ned, that's not fair. It's got nothing to do with you. Or Phil. That's why it seems like a joke. There're so few single men in town. Clearly, I'm destined to be paired off with every one of them. I am not going to get upset about it. It's part of being an unmarried woman in a town like this." She stood up. "But it's not worth talking about. What did you find at the site today?"

"Hinges, nails, wood screws. Same thing I found yesterday." He was sounding less than gracious. "I'm sorry. I guess I'm frustrated by how behind schedule we are."

"I know. But Phil has said that you're really cooperating with the media and trying hard to do what is right for the town."

Phil, Phil, Phil. Was Phil the only person she ever

talked to? He stood up so abruptly that his chair almost fell. "I think I'd better leave."

What was wrong with him? Why was he acting like this?

He stood on the sidewalk for a good thirty seconds looking for his truck. Phil's Jeep was here, but—oh, right, he had been driving Phil's car. Phil had taken a load of artifacts out to the cave.

He supposed that Phil would expect to meet him at Matt and Carolyn's to trade vehicles, but Ned didn't dare go near his mother, even though there was a whole lot better chance of getting actual food there. Carolyn would take one look at him and want to know what was wrong. And he didn't know what was wrong. Or if he did, he didn't want to talk about it.

So he went back to Great-uncle Bob's little house, leaving Phil's Jeep parked out in front.

Whatever Tess had said about Katharine of Aragon and Queen Mary, it was nice to see that she knew her history; he'd hate to think that a place as attractive as the Lanier Building was owned by someone who couldn't keep her Tudors and Stuarts straight. But a romance with him was not an idea that would have occurred to the town on its own. Someone had started it. And he knew who.

He paced through the house, opening and closing the refrigerator, not really looking for something to eat, waiting for the sound of his truck. When he heard it, he jerked open the front door.

Phil was crossing the dark yard. "I thought you'd be at—"

"What have you been saying about Tess and me?"

Phil paused. "Not much."

That was the wrong answer. That was completely the wrong answer. "Nothing" was the right answer. "Not much" was way too much.

"When people talked about having her and me over," Phil continued, "I simply said that perhaps they should include you too."

Simply said. Why not put up a billboard, paint graffiti on the side of the municipal building, post it on the town's Web site? "Why the hell did you do that?"

"What's the problem with it?"

"I don't want you interfering in my life."

"But, Ned—"

Ned was mad. He was mad at Phil. This was new. He had resented Phil, he had envied Phil, but he had never been flat-out mad at him before. "Didn't she just ditch you?"

The porch light was on. Ned could see Phil's lips tighten. "According to her, there was nothing to ditch from."

"You didn't like it, did you?"

"A person needs to move on. You accept defeat, figure out what lessons there are to be learned, and then you move on. That's the name of the game."

That was so Phil. Did he always sound exactly like himself? "It's not a game, Phil. And maybe sometimes you don't move on so super-duper fast. Maybe sometimes you just sit on a stump and feel crappy."

"All right." Phil was speaking slowly and carefully. He wasn't mad. He was puzzled. "But you and I don't come from an emotionally self-indulgent culture. We are expected to accomplish things."

"But that doesn't mean we can't take a breath now and then. That doesn't mean we have to be doing something all the time. We don't always have to be making everything better. Why can't we sometimes wallow in it being worse?"

"I'm not completely following you here, Ned."

Ned wasn't sure that he was following himself. It just bugged him how Phil could never do nothing. It was like he didn't exist if he wasn't trying to fix something.

But what was new about that? This was Phil. This was how he had always been. "Do you want a drink?" Ned asked suddenly.

Phil blinked. Neither of them drank during the week. "Sure."

That was probably a lie, but Ned didn't care. He went inside. He remembered having seen the tops of liquor bottles in the back of one of the kitchen cabinets. He opened the cabinets and starting groping through Great-uncle Bob's various jars and bottles, the garlic salt and white vinegar. He found some vanilla extract. That had alcohol in it. Then he pulled out an after-dinner liqueur with a picture of a pineapple on it. He passed the bottle to Phil, who had followed him inside.

"You aren't expecting us to drink this, are you?" Phil asked.

"God, no. Put it in the recycling."

Phil unscrewed the top and poured the bottle's contents down the drain. A cloyingly sweet smell fumigated the kitchen.

Ned found some Scotch. He had never heard of

the brand. "Do you want ice? It might help kill the flavor."

Phil looked at the bottle. "Ice, definitely ice."

Of course, Ned's ice had its own little dead-freezer odor, but it didn't smell as bad as the Scotch. Phil swirled the drinks for a moment, but even so, Ned could feel himself grimace at the first swallow. They should have tried the vanilla extract. "Do you remember Nana and Grandfather telling you about our parents dying?"

Phil had not expected that question. He looked at his glass. "Yes and no."

"What does that mean?"

"It's one of those memories where you don't remember the actual event. The memories kick in a couple seconds later."

Ned leaned back against the counter. "And?"

"I was on the swings in back of the house on Grace Street. They must have picked me up at school and taken me home. I really liked the swing set, so they must have taken me out there. I don't remember hearing what they said; I just remember starting to pump really hard. I guess I thought that if I could swing high enough and fast enough, our parents would come back."

This was probably the most personal thing Phil had ever said in his life. Ned took another drink. "Are you still trying to do that? Trying to swing high enough and fast enough?"

Phil shrugged. "I don't think that way. Keeping busy suits me."

So that was what Phil had been doing, "keeping

busy." Rather than let himself mind about Tess spurning him, Phil had immediately begun promoting a relationship between her and Ned.

As long as they were having this brotherly chat, Ned figured he'd go all the way. "You know, don't you, that our father didn't have a prayer of saving the little farms."

Phil was again watching the ice cubes move around in his glass. "If anyone could have done it, he could have."

That was certainly the town mythology. "But no one could. There were powerful economic forces at work."

Phil shrugged again, acting as if he couldn't be sure. But that was crazy. He had to know. He had to understand economic forces far better than Ned did. He just didn't want to admit the truth. He didn't want to admit that their father would have failed. " 'What if' doesn't get us anywhere." Phil had his head tilted back. He was looking at the overhead light fixture. "It sounds like I acted too hastily in regard to you and Tess. I'm sorry."

Ned believed him. "It probably doesn't matter one way or the other. She thinks it's a marvelous joke."

"Is it?"

"Probably. We are completely wrong for each other."

"You are?" Phil sounded surprised.

"Yeah. Trust me on this one. We are."

Ned was not so completely lacking in self-esteem as to view his nonromance with Tess as a Beauty and the Beast tale. But even if it were, didn't anyone ever stop and look at things from the Beast's point of view? Why was everyone so sure that Beauty was going to make him happy? Yes, at the end of the story, he shed his fur and horns, but for what? Powder-blue satin pants. That was a happy ending?

Tess Lanier was light and air. She was the sunshine that bleached old stains out of vintage linens. She made things orderly and quiet. She brought peace and beauty.

And none of that was important to Ned. He got his energy from earth and muck, from mystery and dampness. He didn't need things to be peaceful, he needed them to mean something, and he would, he knew, eventually find life with her to be empty and unsatisfying.

That was why she was right for Phil. It was true that she adored beauty in a way that Phil didn't, but ultimately she was as utilitarian as he was, as able to master systems, as concerned with getting things to work. Her love for beauty was about surfaces, about what you could see.

But Ned found beauty in what lurked underneath the surfaces of things. Eyes weren't enough for him. They were enough for Tess.

So why wasn't he laughing this off? Why wasn't he enjoying the joke?

Because he knew that she didn't have to be this way. He knew, as surely as he knew anything, that there was a bed of fiery coals shut behind an air-tight furnace door. There was an underground river surging through her soul, its dark current searching for the fissure that would allow it to geyser forth.

How did he know this about her? He had no proof, no evidence. There wasn't a cornfield he could walk with a magnetometer. There was nowhere to plant orange surveyor's flags. There was no reason to believe this about her.

Except for one thing. She was Nina Lane's daughter.

∽ *Chapter 14* ∽

In February it turned cold. The Kansas wind was wet and heavy, burrowing its way through coats and gloves. Ned and his guys were miserable. Dressed in long underwear and insulated coveralls, heavy wool socks and chest-high fisherman's waders, hooded water-resistant parkas and eye goggles, they slogged through the frozen mud, covered with icy slime. At the end of each day they had to disassemble the wash-water pumps and drain the hundreds of feet of four-inch wash hoses. Otherwise the water in the pumps and hoses would freeze, and the equipment would burst. Then each morning they had to re-assemble the pumps and unroll the hoses.

They were in the bow of the boat now. The cargo was different here. Much of it was still intended for merchants along the river, but unlike the Ravenal brothers, who were opening a new store, these merchants were restocking. So a single barrel would have a far greater variety of supplies: two dozen pewter spoons, six brass powder flasks, two steel-toothed beaver traps, and a couple of tin candle molds, all of which represented a merchant's entire order.

Ned found more of the settlers' belongings, boxes

packed with frying pans, shovels, and ironstone plates. He found a wooden box that almost certainly belonged to the Lanier family. A silver backgammon set, an ivory chessboard, at least twenty books—many of them in French—and a cut-crystal inkwell that nestled into a footed silver tray were arranged among some silk and wool shawls. But he couldn't be sure because the box had been near where the walnut log had pierced the hull. The water that had rushed in and sunk the boat had worn away any paint that might have identified it.

He found Mrs. Gaithers's beloved blue-and-white china, the dishes that would have rescued her from appearing to be a "poor relation" when she moved in with her husband's family in Nebraska Territory.

She had packed the dishes so carefully that even after one hundred fifty years of being underground, not one was even chipped. At first Ned thought that there was something wrong with them because the pattern was blurred, but the blurring was underneath the glaze. He called Mrs. Ballard, who owned the antique teacup shop in town, and as soon as he used the word "blurry," she ordered him not to move. "Don't even breathe on them. I'll be right out."

"It's below zero. I—" But she had already hung up.

Mrs. Gaithers's dishes were, Mrs. Ballard said, mid-Victorian flow blue, currently a very popular collectible. "This is a complete set that's never been used," she said. "You have no idea how valuable these are."

"Then tell me." Ned wasn't planning on selling the dishes, but he certainly liked the sound of "valuable."

"I don't know," Mrs. Ballard admitted. "Things like this don't come on the market. They just don't. And with the history . . . that we know how important they were to the original owner and her sense of herself as a lady . . . that adds even more to the value. You'd have to put them up for auction to get a price. There's no telling how high some people might go. Some flow blue collectors are truly obsessed."

Poor Mrs. Gaithers. Apparently she really would have had the finest dishes in Nebraska Territory. Ned had tried to trace what had happened to her, but had learned nothing. Eveline Lanier's paragraphs were all they would ever know about her.

But flow blue china had its own collectors' society. Phil called the organization, suggesting that its members take a block of rooms at the Best Western for a weekend in March. They could come to the courthouse and examine the dishes as carefully as they wanted. Oh, no, said the president of the organization, the board couldn't publicize this to its membership unless someone had authenticated the find. Would the dishes be available this weekend?

"The guy I was talking to couldn't wait until March," Phil reported. "He and his wife are flying out this weekend."

Ned shrugged and went back to work.

The strong river current had twisted the bow of the boat slightly, and the boxes wedged into its vee had splintered open. One box seemed intact, but when Ned and Dylan Pierce attempted to raise it, its bottom split, a goulash of pebbly mud oozing outward.

The pebbles were buttons. However they had once been stored, whether on cards or in small cotton bags, they were now loose, floating in the murky pools of wash water. Ned called for the wash hoses to be turned off, and using sieves, he and Dylan scooped up the buttons, dumping them into five-gallon buckets and then emptying those into the washtubs. There were thousands of buttons, still coated in gray mud. They would have to be taken up to the schoolhouse and rinsed so that the wood and rubber ones could be sorted out and put into stable storage. What a chore that was going to be. Ned would store the buckets and washtubs in the school-house overnight and worry about what to do with them in the morning.

Except he couldn't resist looking at a few of the buttons. He switched on the schoolhouse's outside lights and dumped one bucket out onto a mesh tray positioned in the center of a rinsing table. Hundreds of buttons cascaded out. Ned directed a stream of water on them.

As the mud washed away, an amazing variety emerged. There were brass buttons with raised patterns of stars or eagles, and china buttons with patterns, designed to adorn calico dresses. Some of the china buttons were dark: burgundy with an ivory honeycomb, navy with a green leaf, maroon with a pink sprig. Others had a white or ivory background with a colored design—wavy red lines, pale green starbursts, a tan scallop design, a periwinkle-blue dot, a green cloverlike cluster, a brown gingham check, a mustard-dotted stripe, a rose squiggle. Ned picked out the wood and rubber ones, set the mesh tray aside, and picked up another bucket, another mesh tray.

Once again he lost track of time. Only the sound of his brother's Jeep made him look up.

Phil had heard about the buttons from someone in the crew. He lifted up one of the trays, looking at it in the light. "We need to get this into the museum for the weekend."

It was Thursday. Eight-thirty on Thursday evening. "You'll have to do it. I'm too tired."

"Okay." Phil started scooping the metal and china buttons into a big Ziploc bag. "But stop with this bucket. It's too cold to be working with water, and this is the sort of thing that the weekend people will love to do."

That was certainly true. Midwesterners weren't the type who just wanted to stand around and watch. They wanted to get right in there and help. And one of the joys of visiting the *Western Settler* excavation was that if you didn't mind getting muddy, if you didn't mind taking orders, you got involved.

Phil drove off. Ned closed up things around the schoolhouse, draining the hose there, and then checked back at the site to be sure that those hoses were all drained too. He went home to shower, but instead of going to bed, he drove over to the Old Courthouse to see what kind of display Phil had created with the buttons.

None. A display case had been cleared out, a few computer-generated descriptive labels were neatly stacked on one of the glass shelves, but there was no sign of the buttons. On Phil's desk was a press release which Ned read with interest. On the Sunday of the long Presidents' Day weekend, The Western Settler Salvage Corporation, which was another name for

Ned, was hosting "The Great American Button Sort." The text was lighthearted and informative. People from all over the Midwest were being invited to Fleur-de-lis to sort buttons salvaged from the boat.

You had to hand it to Phil. He did know what he was doing.

On Ned's desk was another copy of the press release and a note. "Check this. If you can live with the idea, I'll send it out tomorrow. Tess has the buttons."

Why did Tess have the buttons? Ned went around into the front stairwell and looked out one of the windows that faced Main Street. Although it was nearly eleven, the lights of the Lanier Building were still on.

Halfway across the street, he wished he hadn't left his coat at the courthouse, but when he knocked, Tess unlocked the door quickly.

"I have been thinking for the past two hours that I was a complete idiot," she said. She was laughing, pushing her hair off her face with the air of someone who had been doing something. "But at least I would have put my coat on if I were going outdoors. You must be freezing. Did you come for the buttons? I'm not done with them."

"What are you doing with them? Did Phil ask you to figure out how to display them?"

"Yes, and to try to come up with a good system for sorting them when you have a whole bunch of untrained people working. And once I got started, I couldn't stop." She shook her head, laughing at herself. Ned couldn't recall when he had heard her talk like this. "Here I think of myself as the queen of self-restraint and deferred gratification, but get me started on something like this, and I am as obsessed as you. But come look. I have found fifty-seven different patterns."

She had pushed together two of the long tables, and their surfaces were covered with her small glass cake plates. Many of the plates had a single button on them; some, as many as thirty. "Phil didn't ask me to do the actual sorting," she assured Ned. "I don't think it occurred to him that I would."

No, it wouldn't have occurred to him. Phil was certainly capable of working long hours if a job needed to be completed, but it was the goal that kept him going, not the process. He didn't know what it was like to be mesmerized. He didn't know what it was like to love doing something so much that you couldn't make yourself stop.

But Tess clearly did. Ned had to wonder why he had ever thought that she was like Phil. There was an undercurrent of fervor and intensity in her soul. It probably didn't surface very often, but when it did, it left her as she was now, a little puzzled with herself, but feeling alive and full of energy.

"I probably shouldn't have started," she continued, "but as long as I have, I need to finish so we can put them away." She scooped up a button, glanced at it, and, without even needing to look at the glass plates, put it on the correct one.

"Then let me help."

Of course Ned wasn't familiar with any of the patterns, so he had to search the table for each match. Then he would finally find the right cake plate, and his arm would bump into Tess's. He did two buttons in the time she did fifteen. And if he hadn't been there, she probably could have done eighteen.

"You aren't much help," she pointed out. "So unless you've having as much fun as I am, maybe you should quit."

He dropped the button he was trying to match. "It did occur to me that I was just getting in your way."

"You could sit over there and pick out the metal and the metal-rimmed buttons. That's going to be the volunteers' first step."

He could do that, but he wasn't going to. He was going to sit by her and watch Tess. She really was good at this. She never hesitated. She seemed to remember what was on each of the fifty-seven glass cake plates and exactly where that plate was.

"Do you have a photographic memory?" he asked.

"It's probably something like that," she answered, picking up another button, glancing at it, putting it on the right plate with a single gesture. "My grandparents weren't the type to make a big deal over your abilities, and for the longest time I assumed everyone remembered things the way I did. But that's why I know so much about lace. I remember almost every piece I've ever seen."

He supposed it made sense that her memory was so visual. Sight clearly mattered more to her than sound, taste, or smell.

It was also no surprise that she did have at least one truly exceptional ability. Look at who her parents were.

And it was also no surprise that she didn't make

much of her exceptional ability. Look at what her mother had done.

She must have been taught to hate the unusual, the exceptional, the passionate, the obsessive. Thank God he had had Carolyn always telling him to be falling-to-his-knees grateful that he was the sort of person who had such strong interests and dreams. *It's a gift,* Carolyn had said.

"You like these buttons, don't you?" he said.

"Yes. I've certainly seen more beautiful ones, more interesting ones, but these are special."

"But it's different from how you reacted when we unpacked Eveline Lanier's sewing things?"

"I suppose." She kept on working. "That was personal. Those things belonged to someone who must have missed them."

"But your reaction to her sewing box was very strong, wasn't it? I thought you were going to faint."

"I don't remember that," she protested. "In fact—" Then she stopped talking. Even if she didn't remember her initial reaction, she was remembering something, something she was uncomfortable with. "What are you getting at, Ned? What's your point?

He wondered why he was doing this. "Hear me out on this one. I have to wonder if, when you were holding the sewing things, that wasn't you reacting, but Eveline."

She clenched the button in her hand. "I beg your pardon?"

A sensible man would stop right now. Stop, apologize, cough politely, blow his nose loudly, anything. "Just listen to me. Would you be willing to consider that in that moment Eveline might have been reaching out to you? That those were her feelings you were experiencing?"

"Reaching out to *me*? What are you talking about? She's dead. She's been dead more than a hundred years. Have you lost your mind?"

"No. I can't say that I believe it for sure. But I'm not willing to rule it out. People have intuitions. It's another way of knowing things. All I'm saying is that we don't necessarily know what is the source for that kind of knowledge."

"Ned." She was horrified. "You're saying that intuitions come from the dead? This isn't why you are digging up the boat, is it? In hopes of having a séance?"

"No. This isn't going to happen to me. I know that. I don't know why I know it, but I do. Perhaps it happened to my grandfather, but it won't happen to me."

"Well, it's certainly not going to happen to me either. I have to be the last person on earth whom something like that would happen to."

"I don't think that's necessarily true. I think it may have already happened."

"You think Eveline Lanier is talking to me? Do you hear how crazy that sounds?"

" 'Talking' probably isn't quite the right verb."

She wasn't in the mood for a grammar lesson. "Why would this be happening to me? Why not to you? Why isn't someone trying to contact you? You're a nice guy. If I were a dead person, I'd be happy to talk to you."

"I can't explain any of this." She probably wouldn't want to hear that he believed Marie had had some communication with Nina Lane. "We can't even be sure that it happens. But I do have to wonder if our mother or father hasn't tried to say something to Phil."

"To *Phil*?" Tess was shaking her head. She obviously thought that he had lost his mind. "Phil's going to be really receptive to communiqués from the other world."

"I know. That's what could be the tragedy. That they have reached out in some way, and he can't hear."

Why had he gotten started on this? Did he really think that a few yammerings from him were going to change the messages she had heard her whole life?

"I mean, really, Ned—" Her expression changed. It eased, it lightened. "How much sleep did you get last night?"

Sleep? Was that what she thought this was about? All his beliefs about a richness beyond the linear restrictions of time and behind the solidity of objects and atoms . . . were they to be labeled delusions caused by the lack of sleep?

Yes. This was the Midwest, this was Fleur-de-lis. And in the Midwest, in places like Fleur-de-lis, you got along with one another. That was the most important thing, everyone getting along, everyone agreeing, everyone being nice. So he shrugged and admitted that he had no idea how much he had slept last night—which was true—and he ate a piece of Mrs. Jackson's carrot cake while Tess finished sorting the buttons. Together they then emptied each cake plate into its own little Ziploc bag, both of them pretending that everything was all right, that they were getting along, that they were agreeing.

☯ *Chapter 15* ☯

The buttons got publicity, the blue dishes got publicity. In fact, Phil's publicity was so good that it was getting its own publicity. *Dynamic young attorney brings national attention to small Kansas town . . .*

As a result, Ned started hearing from some people he hadn't heard from in a long time, including a group that he had met while backpacking last year. Ryan Vandersee, Amanda Dean, Brigitta Muller, and three other guys had read about the excavation, and as they were all in the United States, they decided to come to Kansas for a week or so. The "or so" was very typical of the backpackers Ned had met. They generally didn't plan beyond lunch.

As he struggled with the long, mud-slickened planks taken up from another section of the *Western Settler's* deck, Ned tried to remember this particular group. Ryan's personality he remembered, but nothing about his life. Was he American or Canadian? Ned couldn't recall. He remembered Amanda talking about her stodgy middle-class upbringing in the middle of England, but that was it. And Brigitta . . . well, certainly his memories of Brigitta were the most detailed.

You had relationships on the road. You would link up with people, and during long waits at train stations, when you were leaning against your backpack, you'd end up talking about yourself. Some people would share things that they would not have told people back home. It was a false intimacy, one without accountability or responsibility. People who were backpacking didn't want accountability or responsibility. They didn't want to do anything that would keep them from being somewhere else in a week.

His relationship with Brigitta had been physically intimate as well. He had met her in Nepal and then traveled with her to India. They'd talked about meeting up again in Hong Kong, but she hadn't appeared, and a month or so later he got word that people had been scared off by the prices in Hong Kong, for which he couldn't blame them.

He let his mother and brother know that his friends were coming. "It's no big deal," he said to Phil. "They'll have sleeping bags, and they can sleep at my place. They're very self-reliant. They'll expect to make their own meals."

"Did you tell Mom that part about them making their own meals?"

"Oh, gosh, maybe I didn't." Ned tried to look disingenuous. "Why don't you?"

"What a coward you are."

"Absolutely," Ned agreed.

The travelers arrived during the day. Phil brought them out to the site, but since none of them had heavy enough coats or boots to be outside for long, they waved, looked around a little, and returned to town.

They were already at his parents' house for dinner by the time Ned got home to shower and change. He greeted them all with equal enthusiasm, hugging Amanda and Brigitta with the same warmth.

Although rooted in Kansas themselves, Matt and Carolyn loved talking to people who traveled, and the conversations were lively. Halfway through dinner the phone rang. Dr. Matt groaned and excused himself, but the call was for Ned. Nick Rewey, the site's night watchman, was on the line. One of the generators had stopped. They had to get it going. If they didn't, not only would the water table start rising again, but the water in the dewatering pumps would freeze and the pumps would burst.

"Do you want us to come?" Ryan asked.

"It's too cold. I'll meet you back at the house. Don't wait up for me."

Ned returned to his house after eleven. As he expected, the lights were off. His friends had been tired from traveling.

He opened the door quietly. Enough light from the porch fixture filtered through Great-uncle Bob's fraying curtains that Ned could pick his way among the bodies lined up on the living room floor. In his bedroom, one of the bedside lamps had been left on.

There was a glow of blond hair on the pillow. It was Brigitta.

Ned sat down on the straight chair Great-uncle Bob had kept in the corner.

If Brigitta had unrolled her sleeping bag on top of the bed, that would have meant that she simply wanted to be comfortable. Bed or floor? Why not take the bed? But her sleeping bag was still neatly rolled and attached to the base of her backpack. She was underneath the blanket and the sheet.

And no one else was in the room. No one else had stretched out a sleeping bag in the warm spot between the radiator and the bed.

This hadn't been a choice between the bed or the floor, it had been a choice between Ned or not Ned.

She didn't want anything that he couldn't provide. She didn't want a commitment; she didn't want to settle in Kansas or have him leave with her. She would want to be someplace else next week. She simply wanted to sleep with him, to have sex with him.

Sex . . . He ran a hand across his face. He had been so cold . . . and it had been so long. He hardly remembered—no, he was remembering too well. An army of little fishhooks clawed inside his groin.

Wasn't this exactly what he needed? Sex without strings, intimacy without commitment, relief without responsibility . . . everything that seemed impossible in Fleur-de-lis. In Fleur-de-lis, you were accountable for everything you did. Everything had consequences.

Brigitta's hair shone in the lamplight. Her hair was lighter than Tess's.

But didn't he want a life with responsibility and accountability? He should never have come back to town if he didn't.

He had to get out of here. He couldn't sleep here. His resolve wasn't that strong. Where should he go? The heat wasn't on in the schoolhouse. It would be too cold there. He could go to Matt and Carolyn's. Carolyn kept all the rooms made up.

He put his coat back on and checked his pockets for his gloves. He would walk. The wind was so sharp that it made the fillings in your teeth hurt. He needed that.

What fun Ned's friends seemed to be. Tess had met them when Phil had brought them by the Lanier Building for tea. They were bright and laughing, telling stories about how hot it was in Calcutta, about finding cyber-cafés in Nepal. They were so adventuresome. Tess couldn't imagine being like that. She felt overly prim, overly cautious.

They would obviously be going to Matt and Carolyn's for dinner. They would have fun. Dinner would be good too.

And if you want to go, all you have to do is ask Carolyn if you can come. She will be delighted. There's no reason to feel like Cinderella, sitting in the ashes.

But Tess didn't call Carolyn. Hadn't she declared at Christmas that she was her own family? That she didn't need to be included in every Ravenal family event? So she sorted through her inventory of place mats. She rearranged several of the displays. Even if it was the same merchandise, people looked at it differently if it was moved around. When the kids working the evening shift came on at six, she went home. She had prepared a small eggplant casserole last night, setting the oven to time-bake. It was important during the winter, when you were living alone, that you planned your dinner ahead of time so you could have something filling and warm.

And aren't you just perfect? Don't you do everything right?

She had been so pleased with herself at Christmas.

She had gotten the business of living alone exactly right. It had been a completely satisfying day. But she had done it once. That was enough. Any more and she'd start getting proud of herself for being so good at living alone. And then she would want everyone to know how good she was at it. She would want them to admire her for it. She would become Sierra.

So to show herself that she wasn't so perfect after all, she completely wasted the evening. She set up the ironing board but didn't iron anything. She examined the stains on a table topper she had just purchased, but she didn't do anything about them. She looked through four catalogs, folded down the corners of some pages, but didn't make up her mind about anything. She changed into her nightgown, but she wasn't tired, so she put on a robe and spent twenty minutes clicking through all the television channels even though she knew from the newspaper that there was nothing she wanted to watch.

Then, surprisingly, someone knocked at her door. She glanced at her watch. It was after eleven. This was very strange. She lifted the batiste panel covering the window in the door and peered out.

It was Ned.

"I saw your lights," he said as she opened the door.

Tess waited for the explanation. *I saw your lights and wanted to be sure that everything was okay . . . I needed to use the phone . . . tell you that you left your headlights on . . . your basement door open . . . the cat out . . .*

She didn't have a cat, and for once, there was no explanation. She was keeping him on the doorstep in this freezing weather, waiting for something that wasn't coming. He wasn't going to explain why he was here. He simply *was*.

"Come in, come in," she said quickly. "It's so cold out. Do come in."

She took his coat and as she hung it on a hook on the oak wall stand, she saw in its mirror that he was plucking at his sweater, tugging at the shoulders. He was doing that more and more these days. His body was changing, and his clothes didn't fit him anymore.

She gestured for him to sit down. He hooked his elbows over the back of the sofa as if stretching out the muscles of his upper back. He was doing a lot of that too, stretching out his back and shoulders. She hadn't realized that she had noticed, but apparently she had. Half embarrassed by her thoughts, she spoke quickly. "Your friends came into the Lanier Building this afternoon. They seemed to be a lot of fun."

"They are."

The way he was sitting and how closely his sweater fit made her aware of the rise and fall of his chest.

He was breathing. What was so remarkable about that? "They did make me feel a little old, as if I hadn't done anything exciting."

"I guess I can understand that," he agreed. "But they're standing on quicksand. The one thing they need from life is to keep moving."

"That life probably wouldn't suit me." She still felt like a stick in the mud.

"Nor me."

It was odd to be so aware of him physically. But wasn't that good, a sign that she wasn't completely gone over to convent life? "I suppose they also have a more casual attitude about sex than do most people around here."

Now that was really odd. She was not the type to introduce sex into a conversation.

Ned indeed looked surprised, but he answered evenly. "As a matter of fact, yes."

Then suddenly things made sense to her. He was out roaming the streets because one of the women had made herself available to him, and he, for whatever reason, wasn't accepting. And that was why Tess herself was reacting to him as she was. On a simple biochemical level, he was emitting pheromones, or whatever they were called, stirred up by someone else. She wondered who the stirrer was, the blond one or the brunette with an English accent. What were their names? Brigitta and Amanda?

He moved suddenly, standing up, obviously aware of her silence. "I need to get moving here. I want to see if Carolyn's got the Luke Skywalker sheets on my old bed."

She was the precise opposite of Brigitta-Amanda. That sexual encounter might not have enough commitment for Ned, but staying here with her—if he even wanted to do that—would involve extreme complications. People in town would make assumptions, they would speculate, they would gossip.

But I'm aware of you. You are making me feel alive.

Well, she'd just have to figure out some other way to feel alive. She got his coat off the hall stand, and rather than handing it to him, she held it out by the shoulders, raising it. He turned his back and, catching the cuffs of his sweater in his hands, slipped his arms into the sleeves.

He turned to face her, to say good night, but the light in her living room was strong. It wasn't soft and romantic like the lighting she had paid so much for at the Lanier Building. She did needlework here in the evenings, and she needed good light.

So he must have been able to see well enough to read her expression.

He stepped back. Tess could tell that he was surprised. He had not expected this. He must have been thinking about Brigitta-Amanda. He must have been thinking about whether he really would go off to the Luke Skywalker sheets or if he would go back to his own house. "Tess . . ."

He might have been surprised, but he wasn't offended. The idea didn't disgust him. She was glad of that. A dull flush rose up his throat.

What would she do if this were okay with him? It wouldn't be—of course it wouldn't. He understood the town. He knew what it would be like. He knew it all better than she did.

But, just pretending, what if he thought that none of that mattered? What would she do then? Because, after all, he did know the town better than she did, and if it made sense to him, then perhaps . . .

But he was shaking his head. It was the softest, smallest movement, but it was still *no*.

She nodded, showing him that she agreed and that it was, of course, better not to say anything because it would be easier that way. They understood each other. That was all that mattered. *Don't say any-*

thing. We understand each other. Leave without speaking.

He spoke. "We are all wrong for each other." And with that he left.

Tess stared at the blank slab of her front door. All wrong for each other? That wasn't the reason they weren't spending the night together. It was the town, not them. What was he talking about?

She had been written off by men before. She didn't drink enough, she didn't have money to lend, she was too much of a long shot sexually, but the guys thinking that had all been jerks and creeps. They hadn't been Ned Ravenal. They hadn't been men she liked and admired and was attracted to. So why did he, a man she did like, admire, and was attracted to, think she was so wrong for him?

For a while he had thought that she was perfect for his brother, because she was as much of an emotional zero as his brother. But surely he understood she wasn't really like that. She had been raised to be the opposite of Nina Lane, and if anything would superficially resemble Phil Ravenal, it would be anything which was the opposite of Nina Lane. But what did that have to do with her being all wrong for Ned?

Over the course of the next week, Tess started to wonder if Ned was avoiding her. It was a little hard to tell, especially since she was, in fact, seeing him more than ever. With his friends in town, he came to the Lanier Building every morning, but he didn't say anything to her that couldn't be said in front of everyone. Then, after his friends left, he didn't show up unless he was with Phil . . . which, of course, was exactly what it had been like before, but she still felt like he was avoiding her.

Yet wasn't he the one person in this town whom she could be completely honest with? The one person she could say anything to? She would go talk to him. It wouldn't be like trying to talk to Phil. You could talk to Ned. Within fifteen minutes of deciding to talk to him, she got the opportunity. It was late in the afternoon. Phil had come in, and while waiting for his coffee, he pulled out his little leather card holder and was, as always, looking at his list. Tess saw him wince.

"Did you forget something?" she asked.

"Yes, because I didn't write it down." He didn't sound happy with himself. "You'd think that a person wouldn't forget a washtub full of rolling pins sloshing around in the back of his car, but I did." He pushed back the sleeve of his coat to look at his watch. He grimaced, the look of a man who needed to be in two places at once.

"Does the washtub go out to the limestone cave?" Tess asked. "If you've got time to bring it to my house and put it in my car, I can take it. I was just getting ready to leave for the day."

"That would be great." Phil could accept a favor without making a fuss about it. "But if you don't mind, let's just trade cars. I have the Jeep. It's had water sloshed on it before. Ned'll unload for you. He'll be out at the cave for another hour or so."

That was what she had been hoping for.

Tess had not been out to the cave before, and Phil warned her that the turnoff was unmarked, but she found it easily. The dirt road was obviously heavily traveled; the mud had frozen into tire-tracked ruts. A newish-looking electrical line swooped between widely spaced poles. About a quarter mile down this road, a chain-link gate was propped open. A short distance beyond that was a low limestone bluff, topped by now leafless trees. Chiseled into the bluff was a rectangular entry about ten feet high. Its gate was also open.

Tess stopped the Jeep, rather pleased with herself for having negotiated it over the bumpy lane. She opened the door and stepped out, calling Ned's name.

A moment later he emerged from the darkness. He had on heavy rubberized gloves that reached over his forearms, but despite the cold, he wasn't wearing a coat. The front of his flannel shirt was damp. "Tess!" He was surprised to see her.

"I have your rolling pins." She explained about Phil's forgetfulness.

"I was wondering where he was. If you pop the latch on the rear door, I'll unload."

"Do you want me to drive in?" Apparently that was what he had done with his truck.

"No, it's only this one thing." The washtub must have been heavy, but Ned lifted it easily and started carrying it into the cave. Tess followed him.

A narrow tunnel opened into an arching underground canyon, its walls chiseled slabs where the limestone blocks had been cut during mining operations. A single electric wire was held in place by little black brackets drilled into the limestone, and bare electric bulbs provided irregular splotches of light. Ned's truck was pulled in as far as it could go. The rest of the space was taken up by a dozen thousand-gallon galvanized livestock watering tanks, each with a clipboard hooked to the edge. A portable electric pump was making a whooshing noise as it churned water through a black hose and into one of the tanks.

It was surprisingly warm in the cave. Tess unbuttoned her coat. Ned made a note on one of the clipboards and then began to unload the artifacts from the tub into the tank, easing them one at a time into the water.

"Do you want some help?" Tess offered.

"No. No sense in us both getting wet."

She walked between two of the tanks. She could see a break in the wall, a rough unlit passage. "How far back does this go?"

"Quite a ways. My grandfather and I used to climb it. We never got to the end. It starts to slant downward too sharply. Even Grandfather said we shouldn't go down, and he'd go anywhere. I haven't been back there in years. There are plenty of other interesting caves around."

Tess couldn't help shuddering. "You like crawling through places like that?"

"It's great," he said simply. "At least it was when I was a kid. But it's not your cup of tea, is it?"

Tess was suddenly suspicious. Was this why she was all wrong for him? Because she didn't like caves? She wanted to protest that she had never had the opportunity to crawl through a dark, spider-filled, rock-lined underground passage, but that would not have been the whole truth. She was delighted that she had never had such an opportunity. "I am more comfortable aboveground."

"I would have guessed that."

Was that a criticism? His voice was very even; it didn't sound like he was criticizing her. And why on earth should she mind being criticized for this? Her sense of self-worth was not rooted in her spelunking abilities.

Ned had finished unloading the rolling pins. He dumped the rest of the water into the tank, slapping the bottom of the washtub. It rang with a hollow echo.

She had waited long enough. "When you were at my house the other day, why did you say that we were all wrong for each other?"

The light was behind him. His face was shadowed, and she couldn't read his expression. But she could hear him exhale. "I believe in mud. I don't think you do."

Tess didn't understand. "What do you mean, believe in mud? What's there to believe in? I believe it exists. I believe this water tank exists." She was starting to feel annoyed by his answer. "I am a big believer in the reality of the physical world. In fact, I probably believe in the physical world more than you do." She wasn't the one running around hearing dead people's voices.

"I'm not talking epistemology. I know you're an empiricist," he said. Clearly, he understood himself. "That's a whole different problem. What I mean is that I believe that mud is good metaphorically. I believe that exciting things happen unpredictably, that creativity comes out of mess and disorder. I'm suspicious of anything that is perfect."

Nina Lane had been the messiest of children. That

was one thing Tess's grandparents had told her about her mother. "I am fastidious," Tess acknowledged. "But you're no slob. Look at this." She gestured at one of his clipboards; his recordkeeping was immaculate.

"I'm not talking about physical order. I'm talking about the sources of creativity, about—"

Creativity? Did he find her insufficiently creative? Was that what was wrong with her? Well, if so, then good riddance. If he wanted Nina Lane, he would have to go somewhere else. "I'm not an exceptionally creative person," she said, almost with a snap. "I have a good eye, I have a good sense of design, but I'm not her, and no amount of primal ooze is going to make me as creative as her."

"Her?" He was puzzled. "Who are—" He broke off, understanding. "Tess, I didn't mean it that way." His tone was apologetic. "I wasn't thinking about your being Nina Lane's daughter. Please believe me, that's not a part of it."

"Apparently you would like me better if I were." She must be sounding like a whining child. She must be sounding hurt.

Well, she *was* hurt. It might make no sense for her to feel hurt at his rejection, but she was.

He ran a hand over his face. "Liking you is not the issue here. My feelings aren't what's at question. It's that I would make us both miserable. I would try to change you. I know I would. It's stupid and unfair, but I have this notion of you that I would try to force on you, and we'd both be miserable."

"Notion of me?" Tess really didn't know what he was talking about. Perhaps it was this business of being underground. She couldn't think down here. "I don't understand." Her voice sounded thin and cross.

"I don't understand either." He tossed his gloves into the washtub and picked the tub up by one of its handles. "Most of the time I think you are about the most extraordinary person I have ever met. Why would anyone want anything about you to be different? And then I can't help myself—I start feeling like something's missing."

"Something's *missing?* In me?"

Tess knew that she must have sounded offended, because right away he started to apologize. But she wasn't offended. She was horrified.

The flat glare from one of the bare bulbs shone on him. His jeans were worn pale at the knees and pulled taut by his newly muscled thighs. The winter sun, glittering off the snow, had given him color in his face. "I didn't mean it that way," he rushed to say. "It's just a way of saying that we aren't right for each other, that we experience life differently, that we hear different cues, that we—"

She shook her head; she wasn't listening. Whatever he thought he was talking about, she knew what he meant. Or at least should have meant. "You're talking about love, being able to love."

"No, I'm not," he protested instantly. Now he was horrified. He'd never intended for them to be talking about love. "I guess I do need to talk about epistemology and—" He stopped. "I don't know. Maybe love's part of it. Maybe being able to hear what I'm talking about is connected to love. I don't know about you, truly I don't, and believe me, I'm not talking about you now, but Phil. He is very, very loyal, but he may not know how to love. And maybe if you can't love, you can't hear."

Hear what? Tess wanted to grab him by the front of his damp shirt and shake him until he explained it to her. But that would do no good. She knew—and he did too—that he could explain and explain until even he was sick of explaining, and she wasn't going to understand. That was the problem. That was why she was all wrong for him . . . because of something she didn't understand.

There was nothing to say. He walked her back out to the Jeep, opening the door, telling her the best spot to turn around. He was gentle, and his voice was quiet.

She understood gentle, she understood quiet. But that wasn't enough.

∽ *Chapter 16* ∽

The cold weather lasted through February. The wind remained strong into the beginning of March, but the temperatures eased. Ned was at last nearing the end of the excavation. He found a long, narrow box with two dozen flintlock guns packed in straw. A merchant might have planned to trade them to Indians for beaver skins. Ned also found another box of a settler's belongings. The clothes must have been made of linsey-woolsey; all that was left were nests of woolen fibers, the linen ones having rotted. The final box contained mostly glass beads, also designed to be used in trading with the Indians. Ned had raised nearly two hundred tons of artifacts. Now all that remained for him to do was to hoist up the engines, and then that would be everything. He would shut off the pumps and within two days his big hole in the ground, the one he had dreamed of digging since boyhood, would be full of water.

Phil, of course, wanted to make a big whoopla out of shutting off the pumps—another town festival with more ceremony and speeches, another excuse to get people to come to Fleur-de-lis and buy cornhusk dolls and antique cups.

But Ned refused. "Some things need to be private."

He had learned that from Tess. She liked being alone.

It was strange, thinking about the excavation being over. It had been the most exhilarating thing he had ever done, or that he would ever do. Finding a barrel, wriggling it loose, hoisting it free, prying off the lid, not knowing what might be inside—how would anything ever compare to that? He wanted it to go on forever.

It had also been the most exhausting, grueling, tedious thing he had ever done. He was bruised and aching; the skin on his hands was split; his lips were so chapped that they bled. He didn't see how he could keep going another minute.

One evening, not making a big deal of it to anyone, just lifting his hand in farewell to the guys as they were leaving, saying that he would see them tomorrow, which he would because they still had a lot of cleanup to do, he climbed up the mounded levees, first to one generator, then to the other, and cut off the power to the pumps.

How silent the night suddenly was. He had been hearing those generators every day since the first of December. Their diesel fuel had had a high-pitched acrid smell, and the generators had burned their way through hundreds of dollars' worth of it each day.

The flooding would be fast. The pumps had been taking twenty thousand gallons of water out of the ground every minute. By morning the boat itself would be completely covered, and then by the end of the following day the pit would be full, a little lake in the middle of a cornfield. Ned sat down in the shovel of the bulldozer. The steel was cold.

He was leaving the boat's hull in the ground. Raising it and preserving it would be too expensive. The boat would be safer underwater than up in the light and air. Flooding the site was like pulling a blanket over a sleeping child. That was how he needed to think of this; he was watching a child fall asleep. But it didn't feel like that. It felt worse, much worse.

He heard a car door slam. Probably Phil's.

He didn't want to see Phil. He loved his brother, he admired him, and, God knew the logistics of this project would have been a nightmare without him. *We need more stock tanks, Phil . . . more freezer space . . . these calls need to be returned . . .* Phil always took care of it.

But right now he wasn't up to being with Phil. Phil couldn't sit here quietly. Phil wouldn't let him mourn the end of the excavation. Phil would want to start planning the first major museum exhibition.

There were challenges ahead. He knew that. Preserving the artifacts, setting up a museum, educating the public. It would be a satisfying professional life with independence and influence, one that most historians could only dream of, but tonight he couldn't think about that. He wanted to sit and watch the water creep in over his boat.

So several moments passed before he looked around the shovel of the bulldozer to greet his brother. But it wasn't Phil who had driven to the site. A woman was picking her way through the mud. It wasn't his mother. It wasn't Tess. He had to wait for her to come closer.

It was Sierra, wearing a canvas coat and calf-high rubber boots. A heavy blanket was draped over her arm. Ned stood up from the bulldozer.

"I heard the quiet from my place," she said. "And I guessed you must have turned your pumps off."

"About a half hour ago," he answered.

"Are you sitting shiva for the boat?"

Sitting shiva was a Jewish mourning custom, not something people around here knew much about. "I suppose. Do you want to join me?" He gestured toward the broad shovel. "Be careful of the teeth."

He helped her spread out the blanket. A sweet, musty scent clung to her.

"Rituals like that can be important," she said. "Even if you don't believe in what they stand for, they give you a way of grieving and saying good-bye."

He wondered just how muddled his head was because what she'd said seemed to make sense. "So it's not completely idiotic to be sitting here in the shovel of a bulldozer?"

"No," she said simply.

During high school Ned, like many kids in town, had worked at Celandine Gardens. He had enjoyed the physicalness of the labor, the bending and the lifting, the warm dirt crumbling through his fingers. Most of the other kids had made fun of Sierra, mocking her efforts to share her philosophy with them. Ned had never joined in the teasing—he hadn't considered her as weird as the others had—yet he hadn't gone out of his way to talk to her.

But he was glad that she was here now.

The night was cloudy. The willows lining the riverbank were dark masses, and there were no stars. Ned couldn't see down into the base of the pit, but he could feel the water rising.

"You aren't too cold?"

"No," Sierra replied. "I'm fine."

He remembered Dr. Matt once telling Carolyn that Sierra was the sort of person who was happiest when she was needed, that everyone in the Settlement had relied on her. Nina Lane's talent might have been what had brought people to the Settlement, but the earthy magic, the homemade bread and the sunflowers gathered in galvanized milking pails, had come from Sierra.

But who needed her now? She was the weird lady on the outskirts of town.

"Did you grieve, did you sit shiva when the Settlement broke up?"

For a moment he didn't think she was going to answer, but then she said, "No, not really. It happened gradually. There wasn't one day that you said, oh, it's over . . . and giving up the baby, that was what was hard. She was what mattered to me. After that, nothing else seemed important."

"The baby . . . you mean Tess."

"I didn't call her that."

"When you see her now, do you connect her with the baby you took care of?" Ned wanted to talk about Tess.

"She's so different from what I thought she would be. I used to think that she would be a poet. I would look into her eyes and I was sure I was looking into the soul of a poet."

"Are you disappointed in her?"

"Doesn't she seem very flat and conventional to you?"

"Tess?" He shook his head. "She's certainly very even-tempered, but that's not the same as being flat. And if she seems conventional, you've got to remember that's what her grandparents wanted."

Sierra didn't say anything for a moment. "That's not what I would have wanted. She would have been different if they had allowed her to stay with me."

The truth of that was undeniable. "Yes, she would have been."

The wind rose, and they moved farther back into the shelter of the shovel. The charcoal-colored clouds stirred against the night sky, and every so often a few stars would appear for a moment or two and then hide again. Ned listened to the sounds of the night, the faint rush of the river, the rise and fall of a distant car.

It was over, the excavation was over; he had to accept that.

> Loyal to their birthplace, the two Mr. Ravenals returned to New Orleans in 1861. The older one was lost at Vicksburg, but after the war the younger returned to Fleur-de-lis, bringing with him two orphaned cousins. He said little about what had happened to our beautiful, occupied city, leaving us to cherish our memories. What we had loved was no more.
>
> Gone were the gentle cypresses, the soft Spanish moss, and the gleaming magnolias. Around us now were a blazing stand of sunflowers, thunderstorms rolling in from the

western plains, and a white-tailed deer pausing
at the edge of a thicket, its head turned, its
ears perked, and its eyes alert. This was our
home now.

 Ad astra per aspera. To the stars through
difficulties. This is the motto of our adopted
home state.

Mrs. Louis Lanier (Eveline Roget),
The Wreck of the Western Settler,
privately printed, 1879

Tess wondered if spring would ever come. She had
grown up hearing immigrants to California ache for
the changing seasons, for the first days of spring, for
the light, lilting feeling of a world flowering back to
life. They had praised the glories of a fresh snowfall in
the winter; they had delighted in the warm spring sun.

What they hadn't talked about were the dreary
days before the season changed, the tedium of
March. Leftover snow, dingy and crusted with gray
ice, lingered under bushes and at the edges of the
driveways. The mornings were cold enough that you
needed your heavy coat, but the afternoon's pale sunshine made its weight feel stupid and cumbersome.
No one felt like doing anything.

And Ned was the worst of all. In the three weeks
since he had flooded the boat, he had done nothing.
At first everyone understood. He was exhausted. He
had done so much. What was facing him would
daunt anyone—one hundred and fifty sharpening
stones, five thousand hairpins, one hundred and
thirty socks, two thousand feet of rope, four thou-

sand shoes, two thousand one hundred candles, maybe as many as a million nails. The contents of the *Western Settler* were stored in meat lockers, water tanks, and padlocked storage sheds, stable but in no condition to be displayed or, in many cases, even exposed to oxygen.

But the artifacts had to be displayed. The town was counting on it. The first weekend after the generators had been turned off, a number of the regular weekend people returned to see the flooded site, and that was also the weekend when the flow blue china collectors were in town. But the following weekend shocked everyone. Main Street was quieter than it had been since August. A few people came to shop, but not many, not enough. The next weekend was even quieter.

"We need the museum to open." There were mutterings among the merchants. "We need Ned to get the museum open."

Technically, the museum was open, but it held only the hastily arranged displays of whatever artifacts hadn't required time-consuming preservation. When there had been something new each week, people had enjoyed making repeated visits, but now there was no reason to see the exhibits more than once.

"I know that Ned's tired," people kept saying. "I know that he's done a lot, but . . ."

But their businesses weren't doing well.

Phil was reminding everyone that the town's marketing effort was multifaceted. There was still the Renaissance Fair planned for the fall, and the Nina Lane Annual Birthday Celebration in May. And as soon as the weather got better, more people would

show up to shop. "We knew that all the business after Christmas was a result of the excavation, that we
couldn't count on that again."

But people *had* been counting on it, and they
couldn't help blaming Ned. Why wasn't he working
harder to get a proper museum opened up?

This anxiousness was, Tess acknowledged, quite
different from fuss and gossip about other people's
love lives. People had a genuine stake in the outcome
of this. Their businesses were their livelihoods. They
had nothing else, no savings, no insurance.

Ned stopped coming into the Lanier Building. He
didn't want to see anyone. Tess noticed his car
parked at the side of the Old Courthouse, but she
never saw him.

Phil insisted that there was no reason to worry
about Ned. "Oh, he'll come around. He'll be fine. He
just needs a breather."

This was one thing Tess was not going to trust Phil
on. She crossed the street, intending to search Ned
out. She hoped he might be in the exhibit space, but
instead he was in his basement office, seated at his
desk, his back to the open door. Over his shoulder
Tess could see the green light of his computer screen.
He was playing solitaire. It was a game called
Minesweeper, played on a grid. The player tried to
avoid the mines concealed on the grid. Mr. Greenweight back at Willow Place had been addicted to it.

She rapped lightly on the doorframe. Ned clicked
the wrong space on the grid, and the game exploded
on him. He swiveled his chair and looked up.

A sudden, fierce joy flashed across his face. His

eyebrows rose, his chin lifted, his face seemed to open up. Tess was taken aback by the intensity of his expression. But just as quickly as the joy had come, it retreated.

"So are you here to lecture me too?" he asked. There was no energy in his voice, and the winter tan had faded from his face.

"You know me better than that."

He shrugged. Yes, he did. "I don't know how this happened. I never set myself up to save the town. I just wanted to dig up my boat and then help the state historical society figure out what to do with the artifacts. Now all of a sudden it's my fault that the tourists aren't coming to town anymore."

He should have gone away. He should have taken a month and gone to Hawaii or the Caribbean or someplace where no one would have expected anything of him. "Are you feeling trapped?" she asked.

"You bet."

"Well, you aren't," Tess said unsympathetically. At least her voice was unsympathetic; her heart was sinking at his lifelessness. "Sell the flow blue china, and hire a curator to set up the museum for you."

"I'm not letting anyone else do this," he muttered. Then his voice grew more firm. "And I'd sell my share of the cement plant before I'd sell the flow blue."

"Just remember that you do have options. This does need to be done, but not necessarily by you. If you only want to do the excavation and not the preservation, then tell Phil to figure out some way to get the museum underway and go find yourself another boat."

She let him go back to his computer game and she went upstairs. He needed time to decide if he was going to do this himself. She wanted to give him that time.

She had cooperated with every one of Phil's plans, but she had never taken any initiative, she had never planned any promotions herself. She had felt too new in town, too concerned with her own business. But this wouldn't be for the town; this was for Ned.

Phil's offices were in the courthouse's upper story, and, not surprisingly, he wasn't there. The one thing—surely the only thing—that Phil Ravenal had in common with Nina Lane was that he couldn't stand to be alone. Tess sat down in the outer office to write a note.

If we can make it clear that this is not going to be about Nina Lane, then I'll be happy to talk to the Kansas City papers about my linen.

So far, Tess had resisted any publicity that had focused primarily on the Lanier Building Coffee Company and its collection of antique linens and laces. Other businesses had needed the promotion more.

Then I can be available a couple of Saturdays to evaluate and appraise people's family linens. Perhaps we can get a quilt expert in. We would have to pay her, of course, but the appraisals would be free to the visitors.

Suddenly April became Needlework Month in Fleur-de-lis.

Tess would have thought that these things would take months to plan, but Fleur-de-lis could get things done because the organizations were in place—the Scouts, the churches, the service clubs, the PTAs, the parents of the high school marching band—and because everyone knew who could do what or, more important, who wouldn't do what.

The newspaper article about Tess appeared in the Sunday Kansas City paper. It featured her linen collection and included photographs of the napkins she had made for Carolyn Ravenal, using her three-times-great-grandmother Eveline's needles. A sidebar detailed the April activities in Fleur-de-lis. People could bring in their linens and quilts for appraisals. On Sunday afternoons in the church basements, there would be old-fashioned quilting bees so people could make crib quilts for needy babies. One Saturday would be devoted to a "Stash Meet." Apparently a number of women had bought many lengths of fabric that they ended up never using. They were invited to bring these to Fleur-de-lis to sell or exchange. On another Saturday, the high school was opening its computer lab for people to try out quilting and pattern-drafting software.

How Phil had come up with these ideas, Tess did not know. Any messages he was getting from the dead had P. T. Barnum at the telegraph key.

The worst of the weather was over. The stiff, narrow tips of daffodil and jonquil foliage were appearing in the flower beds. Outside town, the winter wheat was sprouting, glazing the plowed fields with light green. The heads of the wild grass were tight but thick, needing a little sunshine before flowering.

The needleworkers coming to town didn't buy any T-shirts or very much fudge and were certainly capable of making their own pot holders and cornhusk dolls, but at least they were there, and that made everyone feel better. The townsfolk were fussing less about the museum.

They also had the Nina Lane Birthday Celebration to think about. Scheduled as always for the first weekend in May, it was going to be bigger than ever. In previous years, all of the activities had been confined to the fairgrounds, and many of the attendees never came down to Main Street. But Phil had been working with the organizers to get vendors to set up booths in the park across the street from the municipal building. The Lanier Building and the Old Courthouse—the first commercial locations on the west side of town—were only a block away.

Tess had seen the list of the new vendors. They would be selling railroad memorabilia, Adirondack outdoor furniture, homemade doggy beds. "What do these have to do with Nina Lane?" she asked.

"Not a blessed thing," Phil replied evenly. He didn't care about Nina Lane. "Does that bother you?"

"No. Quite the contrary. I'm sure if I had a dog, I would want it to have its own homemade bed." Which was more than she could say of anything the Nina Lane vendors were selling.

"The two main organizers are coming to town next week. I think most everyone understands that you don't want any fuss made about your being Nina Lane's daughter."

"I'm not trying to hide from that fact. I simply

don't want the fans pawing all over me. Do people find that strange?"

"Lord, no. Considering how strange we all find the Nina Lane fans, people would find it odder if you did want to be a part of it." Phil never wanted to have long conversations about people's feelings. "Did I tell you that Charles Dussell is definitely going to close?"

Charles Dussell owned Happy Little Bluebirds. "I guess that's no surprise." He had run the business very badly. Everyone knew that. But still it would be depressing to see a GOING OUT OF BUSINESS sign on Main Street.

Phil went on to tell her that a retired Kansas City dentist and his wife were negotiating to buy the Victorian mansion across from the restaurant, hoping to open a bed-and-breakfast, but the house was in such bad shape that Phil didn't think the deal would go through. At the other end of town, Mrs. Kleinhardt was buying too much inventory for her antique shop. It was so crowded that people couldn't stand to go in it. A lady from St. Joe was coming into town this afternoon to look at space for a yarn shop. No one in Fleur-de-lis thought that a shop selling nothing but yarn was a very good idea. Quilt fabrics would broaden the store's appeal, but the lady wasn't a quilter. She wasn't interested in quilts. She liked yarn. She was determined to open a shop for knitters. The quilters could just learn how to knit.

The following week, two strangers entered the Lanier Building, arriving just as the high school students were leaving. They had to step back to keep from getting bumped by the kids' heavy backpacks. Both wore jeans, T-shirts, and desert boots although the man coming through the door first was in his fifties. He was of medium frame, with high cheekbones and graying hair worn in a ponytail. The other man was younger and bigger. He was—

He was Gordon Winsler, Tess's one and only lover, the one who needed to keep the lights off so that he could pretend she was Nina Lane.

He hadn't seen her yet. He was looking around the Lanier Building, surprised, as newcomers often were, by the bold use of color and the artistically displayed merchandise. He had gained weight since college, making him appear a little burly.

Tess could not believe this. Gordon Winsler, walking into the Lanier Building—things like this didn't happen. It was too much of a coincidence.

"This place is new, isn't it?" the older man said as he approached the counter. "It's nice."

Gordon was now gazing up at the overhead chalkboard, still not seeing Tess—not that he had "seen" her even when they were lovers.

She kept her voice even and pleasant. "Hello, Gordon."

His eyes jerked down. He stopped dead, stunned. "Tess?"

She nodded.

"You two know each other?" the other man asked, his look of curiosity so acute that it felt intrusive. "That's funny. I thought this business was new."

She nodded. "It is. Gordon and I knew each other during our freshman year in college."

Gordon still looked as if he had been hit in the

stomach by a hardball. "Where did you go? You just disappeared."

"I had to go take care of my grandparents. There wasn't anything mysterious about it. Everyone in my dorm knew." But he wouldn't have asked. Their parting had been bitter. He had done something that Tess could not forgive, and she had said something that he could not forgive. "Now, what can I get you to drink?"

Tess supposed that she had reason to be grateful to Gordon Winsler. He had shown her how she didn't want to live, that she didn't want to stake her identity on being a Dead Celebrity's Daughter. Nonetheless, she hoped he and his friend would take their coffee to a table. She didn't want to talk to them, but they lingered at the counter. Gordon introduced the other man as Brian Something-or-other. Tess heard his name, but an instant later found that she couldn't remember it.

They talked about the improvements in town. The place did look dramatically different than it had last year. Tess mentioned the various state and federal projects that had helped fund the improvements. Neither of them seemed very interested. Brian drifted off to examine Tess's merchandise. Gordon remained at the counter, obviously not sure of what to say. Tess felt obliged to ask him what he had been doing since college.

His answer was a little hard to figure out. He was apparently helping individuals with computer and Internet issues. He did some Web page design. But most of his efforts went to "this." He mentioned "this" several times. Finally Tess lifted her hand in a gesture of ignorance.

He looked surprised, obviously having assumed that she knew why he was in town. He and Brian were the main organizers of the Nina Lane Annual Birthday Celebration. They weren't traditional promoters; they had no financial interest in the event. They did it out of love for the books. Brian had been involved in the event for nearly ten years; Gordon's level of responsibility was more recent.

Phil had indeed warned Tess that the organizers were coming to town, and she now realized that when the older man had first walked into the Lanier Building, she had assumed he was such a person. The surprise over seeing Gordon had sent the thought out of her mind.

So it was not such an astonishing coincidence, his appearance at the Lanier Building. He was a Nina Lane fan with leadership skills and organizational abilities, definitely someone whom a festival like this would need.

"So"—he leaned toward her confidentially—"what can you tell me about this Phil Ravenal fellow?"

"He's a local attorney and chairman of the town's Economic Development Council. He's been the primary force behind the revitalization of Main Street."

"He did get the parking organized last year with the shuttle and all. That was good."

These might have been words of praise, but it was clear from Gordon's tone that he didn't trust Phil. That was not fair. Phil was exceedingly trustworthy, in part because he was always open about why he was doing what. If Gordon wanted to trust Phil, all he needed to do was understand that Phil cared almost nothing about the Birthday Celebration as an entity in itself. He cared about the local economy.

Phil and Gordon had different goals. As long as their journeys toward their respective goals kept them on parallel paths, they would probably be an effective team. But when they came to a fork in the road, and Phil wanted to go one way, and Gordon another . . . Tess didn't want to be around to witness it.

She had a feeling that she would be.

The two men finished their coffee, leaving, Tess noticed, a used paper napkin crumpled on the floor. Gordon hadn't said anything about Tess's being Nina Lane's daughter.

But that wouldn't last. Gordon was going to want her to give a talk during the Celebration or make an appearance at whatever was his equivalent of a VIP cocktail reception. And she would say no. It would be simple. She would say no.

At two that afternoon, Brian and Gordon were back at the Lanier Building.

Brian was fizzing with excitement. "Gordon just told me. This is so incredibly cool. I can't believe it. Are you really Nina Lane's daughter? Really and truly?"

The man was at least fifty. Why was he still using an expression like "really and truly"? "I am."

"It's amazing," he continued to gush. "Why haven't you ever surfaced before? People must be so interested in you."

"We talked about this," Gordon said heavily, sounding as if he were far older than Brian instead of nearly twenty-five years younger. "The most loyal readers like to think of themselves as having a monogamous relationship with the books. They secretly feel that the books were written for them and that no one loves the trilogy as much as they do. Tess's presence is a barrier to that, someone who would have meant more to Nina Lane than they do. It's confusing the author with her work, but people do that."

People certainly did, most notably Gordon Winsler himself. "It is not clear that I meant all that much to Nina Lane," Tess pointed out. "She committed suicide when I was three months old." Neither man winced at the word "suicide." "But if you are here to ask me to keep a low profile during the Celebration, I'm happy to do that." This might be easier than she had ever imagined.

"That's what we would like this year," Gordon said.

"*This* year?" Tess didn't like the sound of that.

"You must feel like we do," Brian said, his words coming out in a rush. "The Celebration's gotten too big. It's nothing like it used to be. Not at all. You remember what it was like at first, when it was really about Nina and the books. You must miss that."

"Actually, I've only been to one. Last year."

That caught him by surprise. "Oh, right. I guess Gordon would have known if you'd been coming all along. Anyway, this guy Ravenal is only going to make things worse. I'll admit his idea last year about the parking shuttle to the Kmart lot was a good one, but now he also wants people parking at the high school, and he wants to have vendors and exhibits in the park."

"I know that," Tess said evenly. "It will be good for the downtown store owners."

Brian acted as if she hadn't spoken. He cared nothing about the downtown store owners. "I don't understand where he gets off being involved in the first place. He's not the mayor or anything. And as far as we can tell, he knows almost nothing about the books. He might not even have read them."

Tess could have reassured them on that matter. Of course Phil had read Nina Lane's books. Not to have done so would have made him unprepared, and Phil was never unprepared. But she couldn't imagine that he had liked them.

"Too many of the new people are like that," Brian continued. "They don't care about Nina. They know nothing about her."

"And I don't know much more," Tess pointed out.

"When Brian says 'Nina,'" Gordon interjected, "he means the books, not the author as a person."

"Does he?" Tess asked dryly. *You didn't.*

His eyes shifted away. "Many people posing as fans," he said slowly, "just think of Nina as the Goddess of the Weird, that she just stands for anything Gothic. But she was much more than that. She was an intellectual. She read everything. You can see that in the books. The books got me to read Jung and to look at Art Nouveau, the things that she loved. I got an education from her." He shook his head. "But the new people . . . a lot of them are pseudointellectuals, people who pretend to know this stuff and then they don't. Sure, it's fun to draw maps of the books—we all can do that—but what's important are her ideas, and everyone's losing track of that now."

If he had been anyone else, Tess might have felt some sympathy. If she didn't like the weird pedants and countercultural freaks among Nina Lane's fans, how more wounded must be the readers who genuinely loved the trilogy. But this was Gordon Winsler, whom she had accused of necrophilia. "What does this have to do with you wanting me to keep a low profile *this* year?"

"We're thinking of splitting off," Brian said, "and starting a new festival in California. The core group of fans, the ones who really care about Nina, are generally from the West. It's the people from Colorado, Texas, and the Midwest, the ones close by, who show up just to party and make money. We want to get back to something authentic and meaningful, where it's more important to understand the thought behind the books than to spray your hair black."

"I'll keep a low profile at that one too," Tess volunteered. "I have no problem doing that."

"That's not what we had in mind," Gordon said. "It's not going to be easy, starting something new. This place has a lot of momentum going for it. We would need a draw, something that clearly marks us as the authentic event, the one for serious fans to go to."

"But serious fans of the books would have no interest in me. Didn't you just say that?"

"We'd pay all your expenses . . . if you don't mind flying coach. It wouldn't take a lot of preparation on your part. Some opening remarks, of course, and then maybe one seminar about your memories of Nina, but mostly it would be—"

"I have no memories of her. You know that."

"I realize that you don't remember her and that your grandparents never talked about her. But you remember *them*. No one's ever had a good sense of what Nina's relationship with them was like. You could at least tell us about them. And growing up in the shadow of someone famous who wasn't talked about . . . that's interesting. There's still a legacy there."

Tess did not answer. Was he serious? Did he honestly believe that she would ever talk about that?

"Or you don't have to give a speech." Brian spoke in a hurry to fill the uneasy silence. "It will be enough that you are there. You could sit on the podium and be introduced. That would be enough."

She would be like a trained pony. A zoo exhibit. A professional daughter. A professional daughter of a suicide. Oh, yes, she would be the center of attention, the most important person in the room, but not because of anything she had done. "No, I will not do it."

"Then can we at least count on you not to make an appearance here?" Gordon asked.

"I will not ever appear in public as Nina Lane's daughter, not here, not anywhere." She turned her back and started to tidy the back counter. The teas were supposed to be in alphabetical order, but they weren't. Behind her, she could hear the door open and close. They had left.

She dropped into a chair. Why did they want this? What was all that talk about the readers' monogamous relationship with the books? Who was she to interfere with that, whatever it was? She was no homewrecker.

And why did they think that she could add authenticity to their festival? Surely she would be the least authentic exhibit there. The only thing about her that had anything to do with Nina Lane was her mitochondrial DNA, and she gave her blood to the Red Cross, not to the Nina Lane Birthday Celebration.

But it seemed that she had escaped. Gordon did not want her to appear at the Birthday Celebration in Fleur-de-lis, and there was no way on earth she was going back to California to attend an event next year. That would be easy. It would be there. She would be here.

Nonetheless, she was restless and nervous all afternoon, and since she was usually the least jittery of people, the high school kids who came in for their after-school shift were looking at her strangely. "Are you all right?" one of the girls asked, her voice both gentle and timid. "Did something happen?"

Tess was not about to bewilder them with the complexities of her life history, but she found herself untying the strings of her jade green Lanier Building Coffee Company butcher's apron. "Do you mind if I go out for a minute?"

"No, of course not. You know we don't."

A moment later Tess was crossing the street to the Old Courthouse. Both Phil and Ned had offices there, but it never occurred to her to climb up the stairs. She went into the basement.

Ned was again at work on his computer. This time the screen was covered with dense, single-spaced prose. The diagrams and drawings on his desk suggested that his work had more to do with engineering than with history or tourism, but that was better than playing Minesweeper.

"We've got strangers in town," she said.

He leaned back in his chair. "Phil made me have lunch with them. God knows why. You can't imagine any two people less interested in the *Western Settler*. Nina Lane was. They should be."

For all that Ned claimed to accept that the boat was his own personal obsession and that no one else was obliged to be interested in it, in truth, he was always startled when people weren't. Tess found that innocence quite endearing. She waited for him to say more. He didn't . . . which meant that Gordon had said nothing about knowing that she was Nina Lane's daughter.

She spoke. "You remember that night when your friends were here and you stopped by my house? If you had stayed, would you have wanted the lights on or off?"

"The lights?" He stared at her, startled at her change of subject. "The lights? I suppose if I had to choose, I would have voted to keep them on, but trust me, that would have been way down on the list of things I'd care about."

Tess patted him on the arm. He had given the right answer.

He was still eyeing her suspiciously, utterly puzzled. "I don't suppose there's a chance in hell that you're going to tell me why you asked that question."

He was right. She wasn't going to tell him. No, wait a minute, she was. This was Ned, engaging, forthright, surprisingly sexy Ned. "You've met Gor-

don Winsler. He was the younger of those two men.
Believe it or not, he was my boyfriend for a while in
college, and he insisted that the lights—"

"Whoa." Ned held up his hands, trying to stop her.
"I don't think I need to hear this."

"That the lights be off so he could pretend I was
Nina Lane."

Ned's hands fell to his sides. "That bites."

"Yes, it does."

He gave her a twisted grin of sympathy. "And here
I thought you were just being high-minded about not
wanting to get a book contract for a memoir about
having no memories. You've already been burned.
Did it really hurt?"

"It did," she admitted. She had never discussed
this with anyone before. "I felt unclean, unimpor-
tant, unwanted . . . you name it, I felt it."

"I can imagine," he said warmly. "Well, no, I
probably can't imagine how bad it was. People are
always saying they can imagine something precisely
when they can't."

"You're getting off the subject."

He grinned again. "I usually do. So the organizers
of the Celebration know who you are?"

She nodded. "But it's okay. It's complicated, but
okay." She explained, as best she could, the theory of
a monogamous relationship between reader and
writer or writer's books. Ned seemed to understand,
which was amazing in light of how bad her explanation was. "So they don't want me to do anything. But
then they completely contradicted themselves by
wanting me to appear at something next year." She

explained that, and even though this explanation was a lot better, Ned was starting to frown.

"Have you told Phil about this?"

She started to say no when Phil himself interrupted from behind their backs. "Tell me what?" He was at the office door. "I just got in and heard Tess laughing."

"Actually, I'm not sure how funny it is," Ned said. "Go ahead, Tess, tell him."

Tess assumed that she was to tell Phil about Gordon and Brian's future plans, not about her own sexual humiliations. She complied.

"They want to start a rival festival." Phil was frowning too. "They certainly haven't said anything to me about that. I wondered why they weren't objecting to people selling railroad memorabilia. But this explains it."

"It does?" Tess was bewildered.

"They are committed to this year, and they need to protect their reputations as organizers so all the logistics will be fine, but from their point of view, the less the event has to do with Nina Lane, the better. The serious fans will be disappointed and more inclined to go somewhere else next year. Brian and Gordon are laying the groundwork now." He grimaced. "And I played right into their hands."

It wasn't often that someone outfoxed Phil Ravenal. "So what are we going to do?"

"We're stuck with the vendors . . . and activities in the park will be good for Main Street. So we need to be sure that the program is good and that it is about Nina Lane. Last year those guys were saying it was harder and harder to find someone with something new and different to say. I bet they didn't even try this year. The speakers will probably be people everyone has heard a million times before." Phil pulled out his list. "So if we want to keep this the primary Nina Lane event, we need to make sure this year's program is strong."

He looked up, and Tess recognized the expression. "Oh, no," she said firmly. "I'm not going to make an appearance, Phil. You know I'm not."

Ned's chair creaked. "He didn't ask you. And"— Ned's voice was very firm—"he's not going to."

"I'm not?" This was from Phil.

"No, you're not."

The two brothers were looking at each other, their gazes steady and focused. It was Phil who looked away first. "I'll start with Sierra. I'm sure she'll say no, but maybe Wyatt and Gabe will come through for us." He pulled out his little notecase and started writing. "They say that they saw her all of four times, but that's four times more than anyone else in the crowd. And Sprawl Press. They make enough money off Nina Lane that at least they could pay for printing a program and maybe even the parking shuttle."

So Phil got to work, but over the next week Tess was surprised at the tension she sensed in him. He was consulting his list more frquently and seemed distracted, less able to hide when he was thinking about something else.

"You're worried about the Birthday Celebration, aren't you?" Tess finally said one morning when they were alone.

"Not for this year. But in future, it could be a problem. All of our calculations and projects took the Celebration for granted. It's been a big source of revenue and publicity. There is no way we can replace it."

"Replace it? Surely it won't come to that."

"Oh, there would continue to be something here for a couple of years, but the weaker the link with Nina Lane, the more it will look like every other town's Pioneer Days craft show. We're now getting vendors and visitors from both coasts. Name me one other town this size that gets that."

That was true. The Nina Lane Birthday Celebration was the only time during the year that the Best Western imposed a two-night minimum stay. It was the only day when all the cashier lines at the grocery store were staffed from six in the morning until ten at night. The beauty parlor closed so that the stylists could help at the other retail establishments. After the Celebration there was more money in local pockets and better dinners on local tables. But that would change if the Celebration became merely a regional event.

"But Sprawl Press is doing something. Won't that help?"

"This year it will. This year is going to be great. It's next year that I'm worried about. And the year after that. Sprawl Press has no loyalty to Fleur-de-lis. They're going to follow the fan base."

Tess couldn't remember when she had heard Phil admit to being worried. He had always been challenged by problems.

Could she make a difference? Probably. All she had to do was promote the festival. Phil would tell her

what to say—how this was an honor to her dear
mother's blessed memory . . .

Would she do it if it would save a child from being
flattened by an oncoming train?

Yes, of course.

Well, what if it were an adult? Would she do it for
an adult?

Ned and any of his family, yes. And she probably
ought to add Sierra to that list; she owed her. That
would be one way of repaying her, and really, when
you thought about it, was it right to only save people
that you love?

But exactly how would her giving a speech to a
collection of crazy people stop an oncoming train?

Her stomach, her mind, and her heart were twisted
into dreary, little knots. She wasn't sleeping. She
would stupidly doze off early, at nine, even eight-
thirty, and then she would wake at three A.M., exhausted but unable to go back to sleep. She would
sometimes walk to the Lanier Building in the gray
predawn light, hearing the slow chug of the newspaper truck and the rhythmic slap of the papers landing
on the driveways.

So she tried staying late at work, hoping that perhaps working would keep her awake and get her
back on a reasonable schedule. She was simplifying
her displays in preparation for the Nina Lane crowd.
No longer did a silk-trimmed hat rest on an artfully
draped dresser scarf with a necklace flowing over the
crown of the hat. The hats were all together, the
necklaces were all together, the linens were hung in
stiff rows on padded hangers.

She worked with dim lights so that no one would

think that the building was open, but one evening around ten she heard a rap on the locked glass door.

It was Ned. "I stopped by your house, and since your car was there and you weren't, I thought I'd try here."

She stepped back, letting him in. She hadn't seen him in several days. He seemed well rested and confident. His eyes were clear, his shoulders straight. "You look good."

He blinked. He was always surprised when someone noticed his physical presence, because he never thought about it himself. "I guess I feel pretty good. But I shouldn't. My brother screwed up, and I'm—"

Tess interrupted. "Phil made a mistake?"

"He does have some blind spots. People who are very emotional or needy . . . he sometimes reads them wrong."

Maybe he was too afraid of becoming like them. "Was it Sierra?" She was certainly emotional and needy.

Ned nodded. "He put way too much pressure on her to appear on the program, and now he says that she's suddenly started talking about closing Celandine Gardens. I thought I'd go out and see if I can tell what's on her mind. Would you come?"

Close Celandine Gardens? That would be as bad for the town as losing the Birthday Celebration. "Let me get my purse."

The sun had set and the light was fading. The big patch of wild orange daylilies that grew around the city-limits sign had closed, but the Queen Anne's lace shone white in the dusk.

Ned drove easily, one hand on top of the steering

wheel. "Phil's not coming down too hard on you, is he?"

She shook her head. "He hasn't said a word—not that it matters. I'm being much harder on myself than he would ever be."

"I wondered." Ned slowed as he prepared to turn off County Route Five. "And maybe I can bail you out. You bought me time with that needlework stuff last month—don't look so surprised. Phil told me it was your idea, and it didn't take much of a brain to figure out why you'd done it. So it looks like it's my turn now, and while I may not be the most obvious candidate to talk about Nina Lane, I'll do something—"

"Wait a minute, *you* will talk about Nina Lane?" He was doing this so she would not have to. "What would you *say?*"

"I have no idea," he replied cheerfully. "But don't worry, I'll come up with something. I'm good at this sort of thing. I'll reread the trilogy, and—"

"You'll reread the trilogy?" That seemed far beyond the obligations of friendship.

"Sure. I may have said that Phil didn't know how to love. I didn't say that about me. I am a little squeezed for time, since I figured I'd stop trying to plan the museum as a whole and just put up an exhibit of more of the Lanier family stuff, really pushing the Nina Lane connection. That's why I haven't been at the courthouse for a couple of days. I went over to St. Joe and got Marie's clothes out of the meat locker. I've been at the schoolhouse working on them."

So he was working on the artifacts. No wonder he seemed to be feeling so well.

His giving a talk at the Celebration and putting up more exhibits would not save the event for Fleur-de-lis, but they would help. They might give the town another year. And these activities were giving him a mission again; the work had brought him back to life. By helping her, he had helped himself.

Tess let her head rest against the seat back. She felt taken care of, watched over, protected. She liked the feeling. She couldn't remember when she had last felt this way, probably when she was little and her grandparents were still young enough that she wasn't worrying about them. She'd felt a hint of it the first night she had been in Fleur-de-lis and had gone shopping at Kmart. She had felt as if it was all right to make mistakes because she had enough money to make mistakes. She had wondered if that was how people who were loved felt.

I may have said that Phil didn't know how to love. I didn't say that about me.

It had been an aside, a nothing of a remark, said so casually that Tess had missed its implications. But two minutes after Ned had said it, she heard it, and it could mean only one thing.

He loved her.

∽ *Chapter 17* ∽

There was no time to think about that, no time to say anything. Ned was turning into Sierra's driveway. The Celandine Gardens van was parked by the glass hothouses and her porch light was on. One of the windows etched a sharp white rectangle in the shadowy mass of the small house.

Ned knocked on the door. "Sierra, it's Ned and Tess."

"Come in."

The door was unlocked. It opened directly into a small living room, lit by candles. A lavender scent with a pinelike tang drifted up from the wavering flames.

Sierra herself was seated. She had been reading. A slender goosenecked halogen light shot an intense white beam onto the page of her book. The light was sharply focused, hardly touching the rest of the room. Sierra switched off the lamp, and the room faded into a candlelight haze. Her face was in the shadows.

"I suppose Phil sent you," she said.

"No," Ned answered quickly. "We came to apologize if he's been a bully. We don't want you to feel bad about this. I'll give a talk. Wyatt and Gabe will. It's not great, but it's something."

"I don't feel bad about it," Sierra replied, her voice crisp. "I don't owe anyone anything."

Her tone was so defiant that Tess didn't believe her. Sierra felt as guilty as Tess herself did. "I don't want to be defined as a Dead Celebrity's Daughter. I'm sure you don't want to be defined as a Dead Celebrity's Friend."

"I wasn't Nina's friend. She had no friends. She wasn't capable of friendship."

Tess winced at the bitterness in Sierra's voice. She exchanged glances with Ned. "But we've gone on living. I refuse to act as if she is the most important thing in my life."

Sierra paid no attention. "I wasn't creative like the others. I wasn't artistic, but I knew more, and not just about herbal medicines. I could get things done. I could cook, I could organize people. They needed me."

"Dr. Matt says that you were even a midwife," Ned said.

"Just three times." Sierra tilted her head back, remembering. "The first two times, everything went beautifully. Hope and Allegra . . . they were prepared. They had done their exercises, they had practiced their breathing, and they had read and read, so that they knew as much as a person could. We were all calm, we were all confident. It wasn't easy, but it was beautiful."

"And Nina?" Tess asked. "Did she prepare like that?"

"Hardly." Sierra's tone changed. "And she lied to

me about it. She said she was doing everything. With anyone else I would have checked on her, tested her, but this was Nina. We always let Nina do things in her own way."

"Why did she have that kind of power?" Tess asked.

Sierra shrugged. "Because she insisted on it. Whether she was manic or depressed, she needed to be the center of everything."

"So what happened when Tess was born?" Ned inquired.

Nina had panicked at the first hard pains. "It was awful. She was screaming and screaming. She was hysterical. She kept ordering me to do something, to make the pain stop. With Hope and Allegra, we had been a team, everyone working together, but Nina seemed to think we were all against her, that we were causing this. Then she tore and everything was so bloody and for a moment, the most awful moment, the baby was stuck. By then someone had gone to call the ambulance, but I knew that if the baby really wasn't getting oxygen, the ambulance would never get there in time."

Tess had been that baby. She had been the one so close to brain damage or death. She couldn't imagine it.

"Weren't you angry with Nina?" Ned asked evenly. "Dr. Matt says that was the last time you did anything medical."

Sierra shrugged again. "I should have known better. I shouldn't have trusted her."

"That's what I don't understand." Tess knew that she was repeating herself. "Why was she always the exception to everything?"

"Because she had this talent. Because she was charismatic. We idolized her. We never held her responsible for anything. She was our goddess, our reason for being in the Settlement. Maybe it says more about us than her, that we needed a leader, but we were so uncomfortable with authority that we chose someone who couldn't possibly lead."

"Weren't you really the leader?" Ned said.

"I suppose," Sierra replied, "at least until the baby was born. Then she was all I cared about. That's when I started to realize that there really might be something wrong with Nina, when she was so completely uninterested in the baby. Duke knew it too. That's why he left. He didn't care about Kristin. He just wanted to get away from Nina. He couldn't take it anymore. I blame him for leaving the baby, but I can't blame him for leaving Nina."

Sierra got up and, as if she didn't know what she was doing, started to pace restlessly around the room. She was wearing an ankle-length jumper. The dark fabric was stiff, almost canvaslike; its skirt did not move with her body.

She was at the end of the long, narrow room. She reached out her hand and flicked a wall switch. The overhead fixture came on. Its bulb was incandescent, providing an ordinary light, the kind everyone had.

But even in this light, her skin was beautiful, finely grained and delicately colored.

"Nina left me a note. Before she went to New York, she left me a note. Did you know that? No, you couldn't. I never told anyone."

"Was it a suicide note?" Ned spoke carefully.

"Yes. I didn't realize it at the time. I mean, it never

occurred to me that that's what she was talking about. I was very offended by it even when I didn't know it was a suicide note, and then when I realized . . ." She shook her head. Some feelings couldn't be put into words.

"What exactly did it say?" Tess wanted to know. "Do you remember?"

"Do you still have it?" Ned asked.

"I'm not sure . . . only if it's where I put it, but who would have moved it? I'm the only one who is ever here."

Sierra went over to her bookcases, a series of boards and bricks that lined an entire wall. Tess knew that was how people used to make bookshelves. No one did it now. Ready-made shelves were cheap.

"I put the note in the back of my copy of Dr. Spock. That's what I was reading at the time. That's what I had out on the end table. Can you imagine? Me, Ms. Countercultural-Alternative-to-Everything, reading Dr. Spock? But it really helped with a newborn. So when I was packing up Settler's things, I noticed the note again, and that's when I realized it had been a suicide note. I couldn't bear to touch it. I felt as if it would burn me. So I stuck the book on the shelf without opening it. And it sat there for a long time, until I shoved another book in front of it so I wouldn't have to look at it. I suppose it's still here. Why wouldn't it be? I dust the tops of the books every so often, but I've never taken them all down to dust the shelves. My grandmother used to do that, but I don't."

She pointed to a spot on the lowest shelf. Ned went over, knelt down, and reached in behind the books, fumbling for a moment. He retrieved a paperback volume. He pulled out his shirttail to dust it off.

The cover was a faded yellow with a picture of a baby on the front. Because it was mass-market-sized, a folded sheet of conventionally sized typing paper stuck out above and to the side of the blue-tinted page edges.

Ned eased the paper out. Tess had seen him work with countless artifacts before. He worked slowly but deliberately, keeping his motions steady.

He read:

I'm going to see Duke. You need to get Settler ready to go to California. Whatever babies need to travel. I don't know.

                                                            N. L.

Sierra's lips were tight. "Do you hear that? I was the baby's primary caregiver. I was her true mother, not Nina. I was the one who loved her. She was my life. And I was to get her ready to go to California. That was it."

"People who commit suicide . . ." Tess wanted to apologize for her mother's callousness. "If they were invested in other people, they wouldn't—"

Sierra held up her hand, stopping Tess from speaking. She didn't want to listen to the platitudes of someone with a B.A. in art therapy. And Tess didn't blame her.

It wasn't—

Tess glanced up. Neither Sierra nor Ned had spoken.

"What's this drawing at the bottom of the note?" Ned asked.

—like that.

"What drawing?" Sierra took the note, which Ned had extended to her. "I don't know. It's some kind of flower, isn't it? I didn't remember it. It must not have meant anything to me."

"It's a violet," Tess said suddenly. "A violet."

"How do you know?" Ned was looking at her, his head tilted, his eyes alert. He had taken the note out of the book. Now Sierra had it. Tess had not seen it.

"My grandmother's name was Violet."

It was the only keepsake her grandmother had saved—that little packet of line drawings of violets. Some had been crude, some intricately detailed, so different from one another that Tess had thought they might have been done by several people. But they had all been done by Nina, at different times in her life, at different stages of her bipolar illness.

Tess reached for the note. Yes, this flower was nearly identical to one in her grandmother's collection.

These drawings must have been the only way Nina had of expressing her love for her mother. Until she had begun to write the riverboat book, this had been her sole vocabulary.

"They loved each other, my mother and my grandmother. Despite all the damage and disappointment, they loved each other. Grandmother may have been the only person Nina ever loved."

Was that why there was so little left for Tess? Why her grandmother's love for her had been so weary? Because she simply couldn't love like that again?

"I loved you." Sierra's voice was low and intense. She wasn't looking at Tess, but she was talking to her. "I loved you with such passion. I remember holding you, thinking that if anything happened to you, if you died, I would want to die too so that I could go on taking care of you."

Tess looked up from her mother's note, the handwriting familiar from the revisions done on *The Riverboat Fragment*'s typescript.

How much of Sierra's isolation and determined oddness had come from the loss of the baby? If Tess had stayed with her, she would have had to talk to teachers and arrange for play dates. She would have baked cupcakes for birthday parties. Raising a child would have given her life a shape and a meaning that producing hand lotion did not.

And what would being raised by Sierra have given Tess?

She might not be as independent as she was now. She might not be as observant or as serene. She might not have been allowed to develop her own style and her own voice.

But she might have had the capacity to love Ned Ravenal as he deserved. And that would have been good.

"We might have done all right together," Tess heard herself say to Sierra. "We might have done all right."

Sierra's lips tightened. "I guess I'm glad to hear you say that."

Tess took Sierra's hand and held it tight. Sierra bent her arm, pressing their clasped hands to her heart.

After a moment Tess went on. "Phil said that you were talking about closing Celandine Gardens."

Sierra pulled her hand free. "Don't blame him. I need to do what I should have done twenty-five years ago. Go somewhere else and start over. I should have never stayed here. I'm not sure where I'll go or what I'll do, but I need to make a change."

Tess remembered feeling that way early last summer. She had followed the instinct. She had left California; she had started over. It had been the right thing to do. "But that doesn't mean you have to shut down your business. You could hire someone else to run it, or you could sell it."

"I don't care enough. I want to lock the door and walk away. That's what people did in the Settlement. They would just leave. 'Hold on to my stuff until I know where I'll be, and then you can ship it to me.' It wouldn't be packed, it wouldn't be in boxes, and then most of the time we'd never hear from them. The attic of Nina's house was full of things people had left behind. Fred Hobart, who owned the place, used to be furious about it, always blaming me even though none of it was mine. It was a relief when it burned down, although we lost all of Nina's papers."

Tess listened uneasily. How could she tell Sierra to do what was good for the town when she herself wouldn't do what the town needed?

"But I'm not like that," Sierra continued. "I know I could be, I know it's my turn, but I'll do the right thing. I clean up after myself. If that means selling the business so that someone else can run it, that's what I'll do. But only if I don't have to talk to Phil. I can't stand him."

"I'll talk to him," Tess said quickly. "Or we'll leave him out of it altogether. We'll find the sort of person who specializes in selling businesses, and you'll only have to deal with that person."

"It had better be a woman."

"It will be," Tess promised. There had to be such a woman in Kansas City. If not, they would get someone in St. Louis or Chicago. She would make this work for Sierra. She would help her clean up. She owed her that.

∞ *Chapter 18* ∞

Sprawl Press had never been involved in the Nina Lane Birthday Celebration before, citing the number of used books sold there. Tess now knew that publishers—and authors' daughters—made no money from the sale of used books.

But the facsimile edition of *The Riverboat Fragment* was going to be published the week of the Celebration, and with a little urging from Tess and a lot from Phil, the publisher agreed to sell the books at the fairgrounds, underwrite the parking shuttle, and pay for printing a program that would include a schedule and a map of the vendors.

The press also wanted to host a party at The Cypress Princess on Friday night with Tess as the featured guest. She refused.

Would she come to New York and meet with key members of the sales force?

No.

Would she come to the Sprawl Press table during the Celebration and, once every hour, draw names out of a fishbowl, awarding canvas tote bags silkscreened with the cover of the facsimile edition?

No.

"They're worse than Phil would ever have been," she grumbled to Ned.

He nodded sympathetically. "So it sounds like you're going to refuse to promote the museum by having your picture taken in one of Marie's dresses?"

Tess drew back, unsure of what to say. She wasn't willing to make a public appearance as Nina Lane's daughter. What about as Marie Lanier's great-great-great-niece? Or her great-great-great-granddaughter, depending on whose story you were believing.

"You're really a mess," he continued pleasantly, "if you can't tell when someone is making a joke."

"Oh." Tess felt herself flush. People rarely teased her. But why shouldn't they? She did get too intense sometimes.

"That's okay," he said. "You're too fat to wear the dress anyway."

This was certainly a joke. He had three sisters. He knew you didn't go around telling women that they were too fat.

But it turned out he was serious. She wouldn't have fit into Marie's dresses. "It's the corsets business. Marie would have worn killer underwear. No healthy modern woman could get herself into those dresses. And if I let anyone near one of them," he went on, "I will never have a moment's peace as long as my sisters live. Caitlin is hankering after that uncut white satin for her wedding gown."

Marie's satin was not white. It was a very pale blush, but it would still make a beautiful wedding dress. "Are you going to give it to her?"

"I hope not. But you never know. I like the three of them more than is good for me."

"If you do, tell her that I will make the dress for her."

"I will not tell her any such thing, and if *you* tell her, I will clog up the wands on your espresso machine."

The publication of the new edition of *The Riverboat Fragment* would inevitably bring Duke Nathan some publicity. His publisher was releasing his latest title during the first week of June to take advantage of that attention.

"I want my books to sell," Duke told Tess on the phone, "and I'm too old a snake to care why."

He had sent her an advance copy of the book, warning her that if she didn't like science fiction, she probably wouldn't like this.

Tess didn't like science fiction, yet she was so fond of Duke that she couldn't imagine not liking his book. But she didn't, not in the least. She finished it only by assigning herself a certain number of pages to read each day.

"That's okay," Duke laughed after he had ferreted her response out of her in another phone conversation. "So many people can't abide me—or at least the idea of me—but in spite of that, they grudgingly like my work. I can live with one person who likes me."

There was a thunderstorm on the Thursday before the Celebration, drenching some of the early-arriving campers, but by Saturday morning the ground was mostly dry, with only an occasional puddle in the shaded parts of the park and fairgrounds. The day itself was sparkling and warm. The winter wheat was yellowing, ripening out of its spring green, and the richly fragrant honeysuckle was growing in such dense tangles of woody vines that they weighed down the wire fences. The sunflowers had begun to sprout, and the milkweed was blossoming with purplish-pink clusters at the tips of their downy stems. The wind was strong, but it was out of the south and was warm.

Tess was not going to be anywhere near the Lanier Building during the Celebration. Word was bound to reach at least a few fans that she was there, and she would likely get trapped. So she spent the morning in the park, where the exhibits and vendors had nothing to do with Nina Lane. How different this was from last year. Last year she had moved around the tables hesitantly, knowing that she would buy little. This year she was aggressive in examining the merchandise, hoping to place wholesale orders to stock her shop. She ran into Emma and Brittany Ravenal and had lunch with them. Ned saw them and came over. Being unwilling to stand in the long line for himself, he started taking bites out of his sisters' sandwiches. Finally Emma shoved hers at him. "I'd rather starve," she said cheerfully.

"Fine by me," he answered.

Tess pinched off part of her sandwich and passed it to Emma.

She would have thought that it would be awkward being around a man who had so casually revealed that he loved her, but it wasn't, not at all. He was Ned. Nothing would change that.

"I'm coming to hear your talk," she told him. "What did you finally decide to say?"

"The best part is about the currents in the Ghyfist River."

Tess was not going to be caught this time. This was a joke, and she knew it. "I'm sure it's riveting."

"Actually, it is," he said mildly. "It took forever to put the evidence together, but once I realized that you have to ignore the first book of the trilogy, it all fell into place."

Oh, goodness, he wasn't joking. Was this what happened when someone started to love you? You lost your sense of humor?

The four of them then took the shuttle out to the fairgrounds. Sprawl Press had covered two of the Lutherans' long banquet tables with crimson plastic-coated disposable tablecloths printed with its logo. A banner announcing the new edition of *The Riverboat Fragment* hung in a swag overhead. Piles of the books sat on the tables and young, New Yorkish-looking people, dressed in close-fitting black garments, were selling books and canvas tote bags.

The book was selling well. The piles on the tables were irregular in height and a number of people were carrying the thin crimson plastic bags the publisher was putting them in. There were also several of the bags littering the ground. Some fans had already started reading the book, a few of them sitting on the ground right in front of the table.

Ned was speaking in the livestock-judging arena, a roofed, open-sided building. In addition to the bleachers running around the perimeter, the central floor of the arena was filled with rows of backless benches facing a small permanent stage. By the time Tess got there, all of the seats were taken, and there were people standing. She saw the Ravenal family. They had arrived earlier to get seats and it looked like they were saving her one. But she didn't want to sit so close to the podium. That felt too visible. She went and stood near one of the arena's supporting pillars.

Ned probably knew as much about Nina Lane's ancestors as anyone, but he also knew his audience. They were not interested in the struggle to admit Kansas to the Union as a free state. They didn't want to hear about Eveline Lanier's civic accomplishments, Herbert Lanier's mercantile activities, or the heroism of the World War I doughboy. They didn't care how the increased production during the first World War had left Midwestern farmers vulnerable to the drought of the thirties. They wanted to hear about Nina Lane.

Dressed in an open-collared shirt and khakis, with a flip chart at his side, he began with material that Tess was familiar with. He discussed the extent to which Nina had used the riverboat's history as source material. He then addressed the notion of daughter Rentha's pregnancy, an idea now made public by the introduction to the facsimile edition. He detailed the admittedly sketchy historical evidence that he had uncovered for Marie Lanier's pregnancy. He also suggested that Marie might have had a mental instability similar to Nina's and that the absence of a Catholic burial might indicate that she too could have committed suicide.

And then he started talking about currents in the Ghyfist River. He argued that the difficulties in trying to map the river were caused by the information in the first book of the trilogy. In that book the flow of the Ghyfist was confusing and inconsistent. Nina Lane, still a California college student when she wrote it, knew little about rivers. But the books written in Kansas evinced knowledge and interest.

"I grew up playing on the banks of the Missouri River," Ned said, "and the further I got in the books, the more familiar the river felt."

People had tried before to compare the Ghyfist to the Missouri, but they were misled, Ned asserted, by the bad information in the first book and by the fact that they were using the wrong map of the Missouri.

Apologizing that there was no way to show slides, Ned lifted back the cover of his flip chart. When Nina Lane wrote *The Riverboat Fragment,* she was indeed using a map of the Missouri River, but it was an 1857 map.

There was a gasp and a rustle in the crowd. People leaned forward to get a better view of Ned's map. Those in the rear stood up. This was fascinating.

It wasn't to Tess. She couldn't possibly make herself care which map Nina Lane had used.

After his talk, Ned took questions. Some were silly. Some were thoughtful. One question made Tess draw a sharp breath. It had nothing to do with the Ghyfist River.

"You talked about Nina's ancestors. What about her child? Do you know anything about her? Wouldn't she be in her mid-twenties by now?"

The crowd stirred again.

"She would be," Ned answered smoothly. "She was raised in California by Nina's parents. There is no great mystery associated with her, but she is a person who values her privacy."

"Do you know—" The questioner tried to ask a follow-up, but Ned had already pointed to another person, whose question was again about the river's current.

"No, no," Ned said. "You have to stop thinking about the first book. She screwed up in the first book. She blew it. She got it wrong. Accept that."

Some people clearly didn't like that idea—how could *Nina Lane* have been less than perfect? But others were willing to consider it.

Tess followed the crowd out of the arena and began looking at the fairground vendors. Here was the Nina Lane merchandise, the used books, the black, flowered skirts, the crocheted vests. Once again she saw people who had dyed their hair black and fastened it back with a flower.

Their conversations bothered Tess less this year than they had last year. So what if people talked as if the Ghyfist were part of an actual waterway system? It was only talk. They weren't delusional. If pressed, they all knew the river was fictional. They were just having fun. This pseudo-history was their hobby. Why was repairing antique linens morally superior? These people didn't live like this all the time. They had normal lives with normal preoccupations. Nina Lane's books made them feel intellectually alive. They were thinking. They were having fun.

What was wrong with that?

Tess was at the edge of the fairgrounds, near one of the fences. Everyone seemed full of life and energy.

That was what she was seeing this year, not the weirdness but the vibrancy. The sun was still high in the sky, and the smell of the honeysuckle was drenching and intoxicating. People were laughing and calling out to each other. Everything was glowing with life.

How could you have turned your back on this?

It was the first time Tess ever recalled addressing a thought to her mother.

Of course, perhaps it should have been a question she asked herself. Hadn't she almost turned her back on this without ever knowing it? Willow Place had been lovely with its carefully edged lawns and curving flower beds. The long corridors were immaculate, the reflection of the overhead lights gleaming off the polished floors. It was a civilized, cultivated place for people to age with dignity. But before going there, its residents had lived. Tess had not. Hadn't the life she had been living in California been its own little version of suicide?

Tess plucked one of the little trumpet-shaped honeysuckle flowers. It was sulfur-yellow. She pinched the base of the corolla, pulling the pale green stamen out of the blossom. She touched it to her tongue, tasting the sweet nectar.

I didn't mean to.

Tess went still. That was not her thought. Those were not her words. She looked around. There was no one nearby.

I was confused. I was dizzy.

This was Nina Lane. Nina was talking to her.

I had come to see Duke, but when the elevator

door opened, I saw Kristin. I didn't expect to see her.

Tess had no sense of a physical presence, of someone being with her. There was only a voice.

I needed him to come to California with me. But I hadn't expected to see her. So I stayed in the elevator. It went to the top floor, and I saw an open door. There were stairs to the roof. I climbed up and I kept stepping on the hem of my cape. It had come undone. It had been bothering me all day.

Nina had had a long red cape that one of the women in the Settlement had made. It was her only winter coat, and there were several pictures of her wearing it in Kansas.

And I went outside, to the edge of the roof, and then . . . and then . . . I don't remember anything else . . .

Nina Lane had not committed suicide. She had fallen, her heel having caught on the torn hem of her scarlet cape. Going so close to the edge of the roof was not the action of a rational, clear-thinking person, but it had not been suicide.

If Nina Lane had wanted to kill herself, she would have done as Marie had; she would have drowned herself in the Missouri River.

Tess groped for the fence, wanting something to hold on to, but the honeysuckle was too thick. Her hands kept closing around the blossoms, crushing them.

Suicide had been her family inheritance. It had deadened her grandmother and left Tess in a fog-shrouded world. But it hadn't happened. Nina hadn't gone to New York to commit suicide. Her note to

Sierra hadn't been a suicide note. She was going to take the baby to California herself. She wanted her mother to meet her baby. That was why she had drawn a violet at the bottom of the note. She had gone to New York to ask Duke to come back to California with her. Her parents would not have liked her returning without the baby's father.

Why are you telling me this? Tess didn't know if she would get an answer. *I have been the least dutiful of daughters. I have denied you. I have hated you. I have had no compassion for your torment.*

The answer was immediate. *Because you are the only one who can reach her.*

The day's events were entering their climax, the most elaborate of the trilogy's reenactments. People were streaming toward the arena. The entry points were blocked, so the arena must already be full. There was no way for Tess to get in. She circled around to the stage end of the building, the only one with a solid exterior wall. Next to an unmarked door, a young man in a yellow T-shirt marked "Security" sat on a folding chair.

"I need to go inside," Tess said.

Apparently a lot of people "needed" to go inside. "Sorry," the man said, not meaning it. "You have to be on the program to use this entrance."

The door opened, and two people in elaborate costumes stepped outside. Over their heads she could see Gordon. "Gordon knows me. Ask him if I can go in."

The guard caught Gordon's attention. Gordon gave Tess a long look. Why should he let her in? He didn't want anything interesting happening here, not this year. But he shrugged and lifted his hand, giving permission. He owed her that much.

The narrow corridor was crowded with costumed people waiting to take the stage, but Gordon thrust out his arm, clearing the way for Tess. As she approached the stairs that led up to the stage, she saw Ned on the other side, talking to people, still with the papers from his talk under his arm. He started forward at the sight of her. She lifted her hand reassuringly. *I'm all right. I know what I'm doing.*

The crowd quieted as she stepped onto the stage. They were expecting someone to be introducing the dramatization. The canvas storm curtains had been let down, and the arena was lit with artificial light.

Tess had never addressed a crowd, and she paused, startled at how many people there were in front of her. The microphone was cold in her hand. Suddenly the interior lights went out, and a bright spotlight focused on her. She blinked. This was what she had always tried to avoid, the white-hot glare of a spotlight.

But she was not going to quit. She was Nina Lane's daughter. The spotlight would be a part of her life.

She gripped the microphone and spoke. "I was born with the name Western Settler Lanier. Nina Lane was my mother."

∞ *Chapter 19* ∞

Surprise surged through the crowd. Tess could hear people stirring; they were shuffling and murmuring. She gestured at the spotlight operator, and when he realized that she was not part of the reenactment, he turned the arena lights back on. It felt better to her that way. She would never like spotlights.

"I've never spoken before because I've never had anything to say. I have no memories at all of Nina Lane. I was three months old when she died, and it appears that even during those three months I was cared for primarily by another member of the Settlement community, Sierra Celandine."

Would knowing that Nina hadn't committed suicide make a difference to Sierra? Tess hoped so.

"The first thing I have to say is that people need to stop idolizing the person Nina Lane. She was a marvelous writer, but as a person, she was difficult. She was isolated and selfish. Her mental illness left her without the strength to be anything else. To think of her as someone who would have been your dearest friend will lead to a backlash, people determinedly trying to villify her, which won't be that difficult."

Tess wished she had planned out what she was going to say. She did know that she would not mention anything about Duke not being her father. That was his secret to tell, not hers. "Nina Lane used people, she lied to them, she was heedless of them. You can't let admiration of her work blind you to that."

The people in the front row—the ones Tess could see best—were exchanging confused looks. Her words were harsh, but her tone was without anger. She tried to explain. "I am saying all this because I don't want anyone to think that I idolize her, that I am blind to her faults. I'm probably more critical of her than anyone. But despite that, I do believe one thing, even though I have almost no evidence for it, just a line drawing of a violet at the bottom of a note, but I believe it with all my heart. Nina Lane did not commit suicide."

Another wave of surprise swept through the audience. Some people rose in their seats. Others gasped and grabbed at their neighbors' arms. Tess's gaze sought out Ned. He was looking as surprised as everyone else, but then, as he made eye contact with her, he understood. He understood what had happened; he understood why Tess believed this. She had heard.

Tess turned back to the mike. "Nina Lane was no Juliet. She was not so passionate about love that she would rather die than live without Duke Nathan. The only thing she cared that much about was her work. She did love one person, her mother, and I'm sure you can see that in the intense emotion of *The Riverboat Fragment*."

The people in the front rows were nodding. Tess looked only at them. That made it seem as if there were fewer people in the crowd.

"The new introduction argues that being pregnant changed what Nina was writing about, and I would go on to say that writing about a mother-daughter bond made her more aware of how strongly she felt about her own mother. So I believe that she had decided to take her baby—me—home to see her parents." Tess recited the note that Nina had left Sierra and explained what she thought the drawing meant. "There are a number of reasons she would have gone to Duke first. She probably didn't feel able to travel on her own with a baby. She knew that her parents were conventional people. They would have preferred to have her come with someone they could at least tell the neighbors was her husband."

Then, without saying anything about the voice she had heard, she told the alternative version of Nina's being on the roof, trying to emphasize how speculative it was—that perhaps she had stumbled, perhaps the hem of her cape had caught.

"It was ripped." A man in the audience suddenly stood up. He was standing toward the front and he turned to face the crowd. He was tall, and his voice was loud; it carried well. "I'm Dave Samson, and I know there have been rumors for years that I have photos taken by a bystander in New York that night. I've always denied it, but it's true. I do have them. I got them illegally, and I don't show them around because they aren't the sort of thing that should be seen. But I can tell you that when she was being lifted . . . well, let's just say that on one photo it shows very clearly that one section of the hem of her cape was sagging." He turned back to Tess. "I always wondered if it was significant. It might have torn when she landed, but she might have stumbled on it, she really might have."

He sat down and, holding his hands up, was already warding people off, having stepped into the mess that he, like Tess, had obviously been trying to avoid for years.

"This isn't simple," Tess said. "Nina Lane was manic-depressive. There can be no question about that. She wasn't stable. That's why everyone has been willing to believe that her death was a suicide. If she hadn't been disturbed, more questions would have been asked. But you heard Ned this morning. Nina might have been identifying with Marie Lanier. Surely if she had wanted to die, she would have drowned herself as Marie Lanier did."

Tess could see the front rows nodding again.

She was done. This wasn't much of a finish, but she couldn't help it. She had said all she had to say. She slipped the microphone back into the circular bracket at the top of the stand. Ned was waiting for her at the bottom of the stage's stairs. She couldn't imagine how he had gotten through the crowd. The re-enactors were pressing close to the stairs, but as she descended, he put out his arm, blocking the crowd. He pulled open a door nestled beneath the stage.

They were in a little room with benches built into the walls. It was being used by the organizers for temporary storage. A big orange water jug sat on a bench next to a fistful of broad-tipped markers held together by a rubber band. The flip chart Ned had used for his talk was against the wall.

"That was something," he said. "I didn't expect that."

"*You* didn't expect that? What about me? I didn't exactly wake up this morning planning on speaking to a big crowd, telling them some far-fetched story I had heard from a dead person. That wasn't in my day's plans."

She felt euphoric. She had done it. She had told the world that she was Nina Lane's daughter.

She was going to be besieged. She was going to be annoyed. People would be intrusive and tedious. But she could live with that. Anything was better than the legacy of suicide that she had been living with.

"So you think you made some kind of connection with her?" Ned asked.

"I did feel that way at the time. It felt very real. Of course, knowing me"—she shrugged, laughing at herself—"I might wake up tomorrow morning and try to talk myself out of it."

"You won't do that."

"You're probably right. I'm almost starting to like the idea."

Ned nodded. "I know. A couple of times during the dig, we would avoid a huge problem by inches or seconds, and I'd wonder if my grandfather wasn't upstairs pulling a few strings for me."

"I didn't feel that way at all. The presence I felt was not a nurturing one. I had no sense that she, it, whatever it was, cared at all about what was happening to me." Tess felt fine about that. "Let's not be sentimental here. Why should dying suddenly turn Nina Lane into a nurturing, caring individual?"

Ned acknowledged the truth of that. "So where do you go from here? You've outed yourself. There's going to be no end to the publicity."

"I know. I still have a lot of stuff to figure out."

"That doesn't sound like you."

"I know," she said again. "I've always felt very complete. Even the year or so after my grandparents died, I felt complete. Empty but complete—this was who I was, I wasn't changing. But maybe people aren't supposed to feel complete. Maybe that's too close to death."

There was a knock on the door, instantly followed by Phil's entry. "You know, Tess," he said, shaking his head, "you could have warned us—at least let us prepare a press release. We could have gotten a lot of mileage out of it." He turned to Ned. "Did you know she was going to do that?"

"I was as surprised as you were."

"Wait until next year," Tess said. "Then I'll tell everyone that Duke Nathan's not my father."

"That will cause a flurry," Phil said easily. "In fact—"

"Wait a minute," Ned interrupted. "Is that true?" Phil had clearly taken it as a joke. "Is Duke really *not* your father?"

"Not biologically. He let Nina put his name on my birth certificate even though she slept with someone while he was at Mardi Gras. He's nowhere near the cad people make him out to be."

"This is interesting." Phil had straightened. "Are you going to say anything?"

"No, and you aren't either. It's up to him. Now I'm ready to get out of here. Is there a big crowd outside?"

"Yes, and Brian and Gordon are sufficiently pissed off that I think we can count on the security staff disappearing."

"Oh." Tess had been thinking only about the personal impact of what she had done. "I suppose this looks like I'm supporting keeping the Celebration here."

"To put it mildly," Phil said. He was pleased.

"That's not why I did it."

"Motives don't matter."

Phil was another one of the complete ones. Would life's mess ever penetrate his neat little world? Would he ever be able to hear his father's voice if it spoke to him?

Probably not, but in the meantime he would make plans just as he was doing now. "Once we get out the door," he said, "keep your head down and don't make eye contact with anyone. Just keep walking." Phil lifted his arm, about to put it around her. Then he stopped. "This is your job, isn't it?" he said to his brother.

"It will take both of us," Ned answered. But he stepped forward, and put his arm around Tess.

Phil thrust out his arm and Ned used his shoulder as a battering ram, and together the three of them made it through the crowd. Caitlin, the oldest of the three sisters, had the green Jeep waiting at the livestock gate.

"Good girl," Phil praised her. He got in the front seat, letting Ned and Tess sit together in the back.

"My truck's at the schoolhouse," Ned said. "Take us there. We'll wait a couple of hours before going into town."

Caitlin swung to the north and took a back road to the schoolhouse, where Ned and Tess got out. Phil remained in the car, which undoubtedly told

Caitlin—and by extension the rest of the town—all she needed to know.

There were a few people walking around the little lake that had once been the riverboat site, but the corn was already sprouting in the field. Tess took Ned around behind the cellar door and showed him her grandfather's initials.

Her hair caught in a forsythia branch, and Ned grasped her shoulder in order to pick the narrow leaves out of her loose curls. He was standing close, and she could feel the warmth of his breath brushing against her face. "Why are you cleaning me up?" she asked. "I thought you wanted me all muddy."

"Sometimes I think I'm the biggest idiot who ever lived. I've been asking myself why I was making such a big deal about believing in ghosts. So what if you were too clean? So what if you were going to make me miserably unhappy the rest of my life? You'd be worth it."

"Do you really think I'll make you miserably unhappy?"

"Not anymore . . . but I am concerned that all of a sudden you can't tell when I'm joking."

"I will work on that," Tess promised. "I will listen to dead people when they try to talk to me while I'm in line at Kmart, and I will try harder to get your jokes. Is that good enough?"

"I also need you to do the whole white-satin deal—or whatever color it is that you wear. My life won't be worth living if my mother thinks I won't marry you. You can have Marie's fabric if you want it."

"I don't need it. I have you."

She had never thought she would marry. A year ago the best thing she could imagine for herself was being able to afford to live alone. But what had given her the courage to leave her safe job in California, her safe apartment, her safe life? Had it been someone from another place speaking to her, telling her to start over? Had it been Eveline? Eveline's daughter's disgrace had made her flee her home and start over again. Or had it been Tess's grandfather, trying to get her to return to Kansas and trace the initials he had left in the foundation of his school?

She could never answer that question, and the answer didn't matter. She had learned to listen, and that listening had brought her Ned.

> At long last, federal troops withdrew from New Orleans two years ago. But we shall not return. We have become Kansans. There are graves here that we cannot leave, and there is a future we cannot turn our backs on.
>
> Mrs. Louis Lanier (Eveline Roget),
> *The Wreck of the Western Settler,*
> privately printed, 1879

They stayed at Ned's that night. In bed they were different. Ned was spontaneous and physical. Tess was graceful and elegant. He was experienced, she was honest. They had much to learn from each other.

Tess woke early the next morning. She slipped out of bed and found a pad of paper and a pen next to the phone in the kitchen. Wrapping herself up in a quilt that was folded over the arm of the sofa, she sat on the back porch and wrote a long letter to Sierra, explaining all she had learned about Nina's death. As she wrote, Tess once again smelled the powerful, rich fragrance of honeysuckle. She ran her hand over the quilt. A few of the pieces were fraying; they had been feed sacks.

I didn't mean to, Mother. Please believe me, I didn't mean to.

It was Nina again, but she wasn't talking to Tess. Tess understood that. When alive, Nina had felt nothing for Tess. It was only her own mother whom she had cared about. Had she tried to reach Violet during Violet's life? And had Violet, like Phil, been unable to hear?

Please, Mother, please believe me.

Tess had no answer for her. She was merely the vessel.

Suddenly there was another voice, deeply familiar, dearly loved. *I didn't know that you were sick. I thought you were willful and belligerent. If I had known, it might have been different. I am sorry.*

Oh, and I am sorry too. I am so so sorry too.

The regrets and the sadness swirled in Tess's ears, an aching that mixed with the scent of the honeysuckle. But coloring the regret, infusing it with a warm golden glow, was love. These two women had loved each other, this mother and daughter. It was a love and a passion that Tess herself had never known, but she would, God willing, know it now.

The sun was rising, a thin line of shell pink appearing at the sky's edge. Soon, day would come.

Tess knew that she would never hear these voices again. The dead had made peace with each other; they no longer needed to speak.

It was time to live.

∞ *Acknowledgments* ∞

As I hope some of you realized, my inspiration for this book came from the 1988 excavation of the steamboat *Arabia* in Wyandotte County, Kansas. I have relied heavily on two books about the excavation. David Hawley's *The Treasures of the Steamboat Arabia* provided glorious pictures, and his brother Greg Hawley's *Treasure in a Cornfield: The Discovery and Excavation of the Steamboat Arabia* (Kansas City, Missouri, Paddle Wheel Publishing, 1998) gives a thoughtful, sensitive account of the daily joys and miseries of this adventure. I have used their equipment lists, their dewatering system, their artifact inventory, just about everything except their time line. There is no way that you can make fictional characters work as hard as these real people did.

The characters I put on board my boat are fictional, as are the elegant belongings of the Lanier family, but the actual artifacts from the *Arabia*—the shoes, the pickles, the doorknobs, the tools, the buttons, and the nails—are on display at the Arabia Steamboat Museum, 400 Grand Boulevard, Kansas City, Missouri (*www.1856.com*). Do go. It's an extraordinary display.

I would like to thank fellow writers Mary Kilchenstein and Susan Elizabeth Phillips for their insightful responses to the manuscript. I have a special thanks for Beth Tanner and Tracie Baker. I only know them on-line from the Pattern Master Chatter list, but they answered many questions about discount shopping in the midwest.

Your mother always told you to marry a doctor...

If we all listened to our mothers we'd have married doctors, lawyers, or perhaps nice accountants. Men with steady jobs, good salaries...no muss, no fuss—no danger!

But sometimes even Mom is wrong...

Especially for the heroines of the Avon Romance Superleaders! No regular-job guy for any of them. These women want someone special...and they all manage to get him...

Join Susan Andersen, Kathleen Gilles Seidel, Barbara Freethy, Rachel Gibson, Kathleen Eagle, and Judith Ivory on the search for the perfect man...one even Mom will love!

*We know not all mothers are like this—this is just for fun!

WHAT MOM SAYS:
"The restaurant business is unreliable. And for goodness sakes never date a bartender!"

In ***HEAD OVER HEELS***
BY Susan Andersen
Available January 2002
Veronica Davis learns differently . . .

Veronica walks through the doors of the Tonk—the local watering hole—searching for answers about her sister's murder. What—or who—she manages to find is Cooper Blackstock. He works as a bartender, but there's much more to him than meets the eye. Could he have the answer she's been looking for?

He looked up as she stepped forward and gave her a comprehensive once-over. "You're new around here," he said in a low voice. "I'd remember that skin if I'd seen it before." His gaze seemed to track every inch of it before his eyes rose to meet hers. "What can I get you?"

Veronica blinked. *Wow.* She was surprised the men of Fossil didn't keep their women under lock and key around this guy, for even she could feel the sexuality that poured off of him in waves, and he wasn't at all her type. "Are you Mr. Blackstock?"

"Yeah, but call me Coop," he invited and flashed

her a smile that was surprisingly charming for someone with such watchful eyes. "I'm always tempted to look around for my dad whenever I hear anyone call me mister, and he's been gone a long, long time." Then he became all business. "Since you know my name," he said, "I assume you're here for the waitress job."

"No!" She stepped back, her hands flying up as if they could push the very idea away. *Oh, no, no, no—* She'd sworn when she graduated from college that she would never serve another drink as long as she lived. It was a vow she'd kept, too, and she intended to keep on keeping it right up until the day they planted her body in the cold, hard ground.

Seeing those dark brows of his lift toward his blond hairline, she forced her shoulders to lose their defensive hunch and her hands to drop back to her sides. *Oh, smooth, Davis. You might wanna try keeping the idiot quotient to a bare minimum here.* "I'm sorry, I should have introduced myself." Head held high, giving her fine wool blazer a surreptitious tug to remind herself she'd come a long way from the Tonk, she stepped back up to the bar. "I'm Veronica Davis. I just stopped by to see how the place is doing."

"You want to know how it's doing?" Coop demanded coolly. "Well, I'll tell you, lady, right this minute not so hot. But things are looking up now that I've got you in my sights. Here." He tossed her something and reflexively she reached up to snatch it out of the air before it hit her in the face. "Put that on," he instructed, "and get to work. We're short-handed."

She looked down at the white chef's apron in her

fist, then dropped it as if it were a cockroach, her head snapping up to stare at him in horror. "I'm not serving drinks!"

"Listen, Princess, I've got one waitress who called in sick and another who just quit. You want the Tonk to close down and lose a night's receipts, that's up to you. But don't expect me to knock myself out if you're too high-toned to sully those lily-white hands schlepping a few drinks."

Who *was* this guy, with his farmer's body and his warrior's eyes, to tell her what to do? What gave him the right to threaten her with the bar's closure? She was the owner here, and that made her his boss. If anybody should be giving orders, it was she.

But she was just too worn out and emotional to get into it, particularly with someone who looked the type to relish a good fight, the more down and dirty, the better. Not to mention he might simply quit like Rosetta—and wouldn't *that* just be the icing on her cake.

Still, it didn't keep her from resenting his attitude. He didn't have the first idea how hard she'd worked to get away from this place, so how dare he look at her as if she were too snooty to do an honest day's work?

If she was smart, she'd just walk away right now, the way she should have done earlier.

Except . . . the Tonk was her niece Lizzy's inheritance, and now that Crystal was gone, she had to protect it.

In *PLEASE REMEMBER THIS*
BY Kathleen Gilles Seidel
Available February 2002
Tess learns all about love in a small town

Tess comes to Kansas searching for the truth about her famous mother. What she discovers is unexpected love in the arms of Ned Ravenal. Ned's a dreamer, and Tess has always seen herself as a woman with her feet firmly planted on the ground. But sometimes love is just a dream away . . .

Ned tilted his head, his dark eyebrows pulling close together. "You're not interested in your family's stuff?"

"I can't imagine that my family had much stuff. That's why they had to leave. They were broke, the Dust Bowl and all."

He waved his hand, dismissing everything that she knew of her family's history. "No, not those people. I'm talking about the ones on the riverboat. We probably won't be able to identify the owners of most of the personal belongings, but the Laniers had so much more money than anyone else. If we find rich-people stuff, it was probably theirs."

"Whose? What are you talking about? There were Laniers on the riverboat?"

He drew back. "You didn't know that?"

"No." Tess had never heard anything about this. The banks taking away the farms, she knew about that. Her grandparents each having an uncle killed in World War I, she had heard about them. But Laniers being on the riverboat? Her family ties to Kansas were even stronger than she had realized.

"Their names were Louis and Eveline," Ned was saying. "He was the younger son of a reasonably important New Orleans family. They had an adult daughter named Marie with them, and Eveline was pregnant. Six months after the wreck Herbert was born. He was the one who built the Lanier Building."

Tess wondered if Nina Lane had known this. Of course she had. Everyone said she had been obsessed by the riverboat.

So why hadn't Tess's grandparents told her?

Were they afraid that I would become obsessed too?

"Apparently they were going to spend the summer in the St. Louis area," Ned continued, "and I don't know what made them decide to continue west, and I doubt that we'll find out. No paper onboard—no books, diaries, or correspondence—is going to have survived. But the Laniers certainly were luckier than everyone else. The boat sank in less than five minutes. People only salvaged what they had on their backs, but Eveline Lanier had three hundred dollars in gold coins sewn into the hem of her petticoat."

"Three hundred dollars . . . that was a lot then, wasn't it?" Tess had never heard of any Laniers having money.

"It certainly was. It was more than enough to have gotten them back to New Orleans, but they stayed on and used the money to build a decent house and get a sawmill started. Years later she wrote an account of the wreck. I suppose you haven't read it or you'd have known about your family. But I'll make a copy of it for you."

"That would be nice." This was all so surprising. "I would like to read it."

"Don't be so sure," he said bluntly.

WHAT MOM SAYS:

"If you break up with somebody—or even if he breaks up with you—you should never date his best friend!"

In *LOVE WILL FIND A WAY*
BY Barbara Freethy
Available March 2002
Rachel Tanner discovers that this is one rule worth breaking!

Years ago, Rachel Tanner handed her husband an apple. But not just any apple—this one came from a tree in her family's orchard. Legend had it that if a woman handed a man a piece of that succulent fruit he would marry her. Rachel always believed her late husband had taken a bite—but she didn't know the truth . . .

There were moments in time when Rachel forgot the sadness. But then she'd feel guilty that she'd forgotten her pain, if only for a second. Some things, some people, should never be forgotten, and Gary was one of them.

Dylan was too, unfortunately.

The two men were as different as night and day: Gary with his golden blonde looks, Dylan with his midnight black eyes; Gary with his sunny disposition, Dylan with his dark moods. *Dylan.* Today her faded memories had suddenly been washed in bright, beautiful color, and the shadowy figure in her mind was now vibrant and real and distinctly unsettling.

As she got into her car she told herself it was the circumstances that bothered her, not the man. And there was too much at stake to allow a momentary indiscretion from a long time ago to get in the way of what she needed to do. Dylan had probably forgotten all about it by now. Chalked it off as no big deal. He probably didn't even realize she'd been avoiding him all these years. After all, it had been easy not to see each other. She lived more than an hour away, and when Gary was home on the weekends he was with her family, her friends. Dylan had rarely invaded that space, just three times that she could remember: Wesley's christening, Gary's thirtieth birthday, and Gary's funeral. Never had Dylan stayed more than an hour.

Gary had always told her that Dylan felt more comfortable in the city, and she'd accepted that explanation. Whether or not it was true didn't matter. And whether or not Dylan Prescott made her uncomfortable didn't matter. What did matter was that Dylan had been Gary's best friend for more than twenty years. If anyone could help her figure out what had been going on in Gary's mind the last day of his life it was Dylan . . .

WHAT MOM SAYS:
"Whatever you do, don't date a cop—or a secret agent—or anyone else who runs around getting shot at!"

In *LOLA CARLYLE REVEALS ALL*
BY Rachel Gibson
Available April 2002
Lola finds that with guys like Max Zamora dangerous is awfully appealing . . .

> Max "borrows" a yacht, which happens to be the one Lola's staying on. Together they outrun drug dealers, but Lola can't outrun her past—and they can't outrun the passion they feel for each other. But what happens when Max discovers the whole truth about Lola Carlyle?

"Who are you?" she asked.

"I'm one of the good guys."

"Good guys don't steal boats and kidnap women."

She had a point, but she was just plain wrong. Sometimes the line between the good guys and the bad guys was as hazy as his sight. "I didn't steal this vessel, I'm commandeering it. And I'm not kidnapping you. I am not going to hurt you. I just need to put some distance between me and Nassau. I'm Lieutenant Commander Max Zamora," he revealed, but he didn't give her the whole truth. He left out that he was retired from the military and that he currently worked for a part of the government that didn't exist on paper.

"Let go of me," she demanded, and for the first time Max looked down at the blurred image of his hands wrapped around her wrists. "Are you going to take another swing at me?" he asked.

"No."

He released her and she flew out of his grasp as if her clothes were on fire. Through the dark shadows of the cabin, he watched her take a few steps backward before he turned to the controls once again.

"Come here, Baby."

He looked over his shoulder at her, sure he hadn't heard her right. "What?"

She scooped up her dog. "Did he hurt you, Baby Doll?"

"Jeesuz," he groaned as if he'd stepped in something foul. She'd named her dog Baby Doll. No wonder it was such a nasty little pain in the butt.

"If you're really a lieutenant, then show me your identification."

Even if every piece of identification hadn't been taken from him when he'd been captured, it wouldn't have told her anything anyway. "Take a seat, lady. This will all be over before you know it," he said, because there was nothing more he could tell her. Nothing she would believe anyway.

"Where are we going?"

"West," he answered, figuring that was all the information she needed.

"Exactly where in the West?"

He didn't need to see her to know by the tone of her voice that she was the kind of woman who expected to be in charge.

"Exactly where I decide."

"I deserve to know where I'm being taken."

Normally, he didn't enjoy intimidating women, but just because he didn't enjoy it didn't mean it bothered him either.

"Listen real close," he began, towering over her and placing his hands on his hips. "I can make things easy for you, or I can make them real hard. You can sit back and enjoy the ride, or you can fight me. If you choose to fight me, I guarantee you won't win. Now what's it gonna be?"

She didn't say a word, but her dog propelled itself from her arms and sank its teeth into his shoulder like a rabidinous bat.

In ***YOU NEVER CAN TELL***
BY Kathleen Eagle
Available May 2002
Heather Reardon learns that sometimes
a man who's been alone for a while has
more than conversation on his mind!

Kole Kills Crow is the man of every woman's fantasies—sensual and mysterious . . . a man who walked away from the limelight at the height of his fame. Now reporter Heather Reardon has sought him out. But you never can tell when a man's right for you!

"Your cat looks pretty well fed," she said, stroking affectionately.

"She's an excellent hunter."

"So am I." Heather looked up from her ardent stroking to find Kole leaning over the back of his chair, his face closer to hers than she'd anticipated. "I found you, didn't I?" She hadn't meant to whisper, but that was how it came out.

"Let the feeding frenzy begin," he whispered back

as he braced his left elbow on the back of the chair and cupped her face in his right hand.

His eyes were hard, hungry, resolute. She saw his kiss coming, but those eyes mesmerized her. She didn't close hers until his lips covered her mouth, stealing her breath along with her senses. Good Lord, he was as demanding and as deft and as delicious as she'd imagined when she was a green girl watching him make news. His tongue tasted of beer and bread, but better, bolder, spiced with the zest of his masculinity. She sampled it with wonder, even as she stanched the urge to reach for him and take more than a sample. She kept her hands on the cat.

Kole came up smiling. "Your lyin' lips taste very sweet."

"I haven't lied to you," she said in a voice that was remarkably steady, considering she didn't know where her next breath would be coming from.

"You said you weren't hungry."

"You're misquoting me." She met his amused gaze. "Something I promise never to do to you."

"Promises don't faze me, honey. I inherited a pretty good immunity to promises."

"And I'm allergic to 'honey.' "

He drew back with a laugh. "Reporters always did bring out the smart-ass in me."

"Not always," she recalled. "But that was the role you generally played, wasn't it? You were the tough guy."

"How'd you come up with that?"

"Short of checking in men's drawers, I really *do* do my homework."

"Good girl. If I had a red pencil, I'd give you an

A." He pushed himself off the chair and turned to clean up the bread and cheese. "But you won't be taking your report card home for a while."

"I've been looking for you for a long time. Why would I want to go home now?" She reached for a slice of cheese, again politely shaking off his added offer of bread. "I wouldn't mind going back to the lodge, though. I don't see an extra bed here."

"What you see is exactly what I've got. Do you prefer one side over the other?"

"I prefer, um . . ." She shared her cheese with the cat as she glanced from the bed to the recliner to the door.

"Exactly what I've got."

She assessed him with a frank look. "If I decide to leave, you're not going to stop me."

"Who says?"

WHAT MOM SAYS:

"Never talk to a man you have not been properly introduced to. . .after all, you don't know if his intentions are honorable."

In ***BLACK SILK***
BY Judith Ivory
Available June 2002
Submit Channing-Downes
breaks that rule . . .

Submit was young and proper—a woman who lived strictly within the guidelines of English society—when suddenly, because of a legacy in a will, she's thrust into the embrace of a man she has just met. Aristocratic Graham Wessit is roguish, dangerous, and tempts Submit into sensuous surrender. Soon, she's engaged in a tumultuous battle of wills with a man who is a most improper stranger.

"Is a small enough thing to ask."

Tate sighed.

Clouds rumbled distantly. The weather dwarfed the lawyer's stature. Outside his book-lined office, he was an insignificant smear of color—yellows, reds, and browns on the grey steps to a grey building. The woman in black was part of the darkening sky, her strength of purpose as palpable as the smell of rain in the air.

After a moment, he said, "All right, you're going to take the box to him, as the will asked. But remember he's a black sheep, if ever there was one. Don't be misled by a glossy exterior."

"Ah." She lifted her head and gave an ironic little smile. "He is handsome."

Tate made a gust of objection through his lips, the sound of a middle-aged, slightly paunched man trying to minimize such an attribute. "Just don't be misled by that."

"I won't be. Nor put off by it."

"Handsome men don't have to account for themselves as often as they should."

She thought about this. "You're probably right."

"And he's worse than just handsome. He's selfish. Unruly. A breaker of rules, a builder of nothing."

"You don't like him I take it."

"I didn't say that." Tate paused, frowning. "He's rather likable," he corrected. "But he's also one of the most frustrating young men I have ever met. Not your sort at all."

"Ah, young too." She smiled and looked down. "Young and handsome. No, definitely not my sort."

Tate pulled a glum mouth, then contradicted himself. "Actually, he's not so young anymore. He must be approaching forty." After a pause, he added, "He's one of those men one doesn't expect to age very well: perpetually eight years old. He has no vocation, no avocation, no occupation—except drinking and gambling and women. He lives with a married woman, an American."

She laughed, gently shaking her head. "Arnold, having impugned the man's character, you are now trying to slander his taste as well. Stop being so smug." She continued to smile, not meanly but with a kind of teasing forbearance. "If the man is shallow or dissolute or immature or whatever you're trying to say, I'm sure I'm not so stupid as to miss it. And in any event, I'm only delivering a harmless little box Henry wanted him to have."

The lawyer clamped his mouth shut.

They stood in what would seem to be the silence of opposition, Tate frowning with a slight mouth, she looking down, trying to minimize her faint, intransigent smile.

Five minutes later, Graham sat in the vacant chair between his solicitor and barrister. He wedged himself into it, folding and bending a body never meant for the narrow, curved design. In uncomfortable situations, Graham became particularly conscious of his own height and double conscious of it when he saw others fidgeting and standing up straighter.

Tate rose and pushed his chair in, as if he would stand for the whole proceeding. Then he stretched, got books out from a case behind the desk, and laid them out on the desktop, three, four, eight, more; fortification.

Tate was balding man of perhaps fifty-five, of medium height, with a tendency to carry slightly more than medium weight. He was squarely built and bluntly shaped with small feet and short, spatulate hands. He had to strain at the high shelves, the heavy law. Graham could have spanned several volumes at once with his long fingers.

"Shall we begin?" The Q.C., in a valley of books, aligned papers on the desk.

Graham had a sense of the past repeating itself. The barrister still seemed the adversary. The sound of his voice—mellifluous, Olympian, full of sincerity—worked undoubtedly to his professional advantage, but it was not reassuring. It implied that truth could afford to be questioned.

Graham claimed one last trivial digression, a curiosity he couldn't quite dismiss. "Her complete name," he said "I should know—" He could vaguely recall old letters, bits of remembered conversation, and these memories made him want to smile for some reason. "You didn't tell me her first name. I'm sure Henry told me once, yet I can't recall—"

Tate looked up, his cheeks puffed as if he might blow Graham away.

"It is a sound, virtuous, old name," he said. Then his cheeks sagged, as did his head. "Her first name is Submit."